A
DESPERATE
PLACE

A DESPERATE PLACE

A McKENNA AND RIGGS NOVEL

JENNIFER GREER

CROOKED
LANE

NEW YORK

Copyright © 2020 by Jennifer Greer

Published in the United States by Crooked Lane Books, an imprint of The Quick Brown Fox & Company LLC.

Crooked Lane Books and its logo are trademarks of The Quick Brown Fox & Company LLC.

Library of Congress Catalog-in-Publication data available upon request.

ISBN (hardcover): 978-1-64385-384-0
ISBN (ebook): 978-1-64385-385-7

Cover design by Melanie Sun

Printed in the United States.

www.crookedlanebooks.com

Crooked Lane Books
34 West 27th St., 10th Floor
New York, NY 10001

First Edition: July 2020

10 9 8 7 6 5 4 3 2 1

For my mother
Lillian Olivia Whiteley

1

"THIS IS HELL," Whit McKenna grumbled.

The sun's blazing heat rose from the asphalt in a haze and merged with billowing black smoke from the roof of a pale-yellow turn-of-the-century Victorian. The mansion was nestled on a quiet tree-lined street amid other carefully restored homes of a bygone era. Flames engulfed the turret on the south side and the siding wasn't putting up much of a fight; the crisp old wood succumbed to the fire with little resistance. A gust of hot wind pushed the smoke across the well-manicured lawn and up into the branches of an old oak tree, emerging like a dark ghost into the pale-blue August sky.

Standing on the blacktop in the middle of the street, Whit felt as if she'd stepped into an oven. Temperatures had soared over a hundred the past three days, and forecasters for Southern Oregon projected at least another week of sustained triple-digit numbers. She could only imagine how the scurrying fire crews must feel in their heavy protective clothing. Four massive fire trucks and other emergency personnel flanked the corner house.

Always alert to potential stories for the crime–and–emergency services beat, she'd followed the sirens. Although a fire was not prime news, she was a forty-two-year-old journalist returning to work after a much-publicized fall from grace as a prized reporter with the *L.A. Times*. After eight months of post-traumatic stress, she considered herself a survivor dredging the bottom of the news media swamp at a small-town newspaper. Still, she could at least do the historic home proud and turn the house fire into a feature and make it read like Hemingway.

As she tried to gauge her best vantage point, a trickle of perspiration trailed from her forehead, and she flicked it away irritably.

Upon seeing the fire chief emerge from around the back-yard through a haze of smoke, Whit eagerly crossed the street in pursuit. She was halfway onto the well-manicured lawn, her arm raised to flag him down, when a sudden explosion from the center of the house sent flames bursting through the down-stairs windows, tossing shattered glass and flaming debris into the air like projectiles.

Whit and the fire chief hit the ground hard. Her right knee slammed into an exposed tree trunk and her chin slid across the grass. Bits of burning debris sailed in the air around her. For an anxious second she pictured her long red hair sparking into a mini inferno, so she held up her steno pad, which was obviously not enough shelter. Her knuckles felt the heat from the fire as she choked on acrid smoke.

The blast tore a large hole in the side of the house, expos-ing the interior living room and what looked like a gas fire-place, which would explain the explosion.

"Lady, get back. *Get back!*" The chief hauled her up by the arm just as she caught sight of a man in a semi-sitting position, wedged between the partial wall and a smoldering upended living room chair. A thin man, shirtless, his naked chest badly scorched and blue plaid pajamas singed into the flesh on his legs. One side of his face was blackened bone, teeth exposed by lips drawn back in an eternal scream, as if the heat had shrink-wrapped his skin to his skull.

Though she'd seen every kind of war-torn body and accidental disfigurement, this was shocking even for her. She sucked in her breath.

The fire chief tried to pull her along, but she pushed back. "Look!"

He caught sight of the dead guy and shouted at two other firemen, who hauled one of the hoses closer and aimed water at the flames around the body, but she was certain the guy had no possibility of being alive.

Tugging on her, the chief half carried, half dragged her across the street. She stumbled over fire hoses, but his grip forced her upright. He deposited her in a small group of neighborhood gawkers, paused just long enough to ask if she was all right, and rushed away, yelling commands to fellow firefighters.

Heart still thumping wildly in her chest, Whit hurriedly snapped some pictures, zooming in to get a better look at the corpse with her iPhone just before a tarp was thrown over the body. Not that the *Medford Daily Chronicle* would publish any pictures of the victim, but it might help her identify him later. She was lucky she hadn't been any closer.

A woman standing next to her pointed out, "You're bleeding."

A trickle of blood trailed down her shin. After further inventory she decided she hadn't fared too badly, with only a minor scrape and a couple of singed spots on the shoulder of her white blouse. She tore off a piece of paper from her steno pad and dabbed the blood from her knee, then flexed her chin a few times. Everything seemed to be working.

Her phone rang. She grimaced at the tune for her editor— a song by Taylor Swift, "You Need to Calm Down." Emma, her fifteen-year-old daughter, thought it was amusing, so she'd downloaded it. Whit had to agree. Stu was a wiry little guy who seemed to always be on the verge of hysterics.

"Hey, Stu."

"Where are you?"

"I'm at a burning house that just exploded."

"Yeah. Heard it on the scanner. A photog's on the way. Anyone in the house?"

"Yes. At least one victim." She glanced across the street. The vic was being transported to an ambulance for either "dead on arrival" at the hospital or a trip straight to the morgue. All the activity had shifted back to the house. Two firefighters hosed the roof and four others tugged a hose around back. "No luck in saving the house or the vic, I'm afraid."

"A shame. Find out who lives there. Talk to the neighbors. Talk to the fire crew. Find out if there are any more victims. Kids, pets."

She closed her eyes briefly, trying not to react to Stu's penchant for telling her what to do at every turn as if she were a novice reporter. With twenty years of reporting under her belt, it was all she could do to bite her tongue, but this was her life now.

Hopefully there were no more victims, especially children. There was nothing worse than covering the death of a child. She'd written her fair share—homicides, drownings, fires, car accidents, war zones—and it never got any easier.

"I'll check it out. Anything else?"

"Yeah, as a matter of fact. Listen, McKenna. Got another story. Here's the deal. It came across the radio as a bear mauling, out in the Applegate, up by Gin Lin Trail."

"A bear mauling out in the Applegate?" *The woods . . .* "Don't you think this fire takes precedence?"

"Not when this story is a homicide."

Whit frowned. Sometimes Stu got ahead of himself and dished out critical information in spurts that made no sense, usually with agitated little hand movements. Especially if the story was hot. When he started stammering, it was a surefire sign that she was about to be gifted a front-page lead.

"Did ya hear me? A homicide!"

She couldn't resist a little goading. "A homicidal *bear*?"

"Ha-ha!" Stu slurped maddeningly on a straw, reminding Whit of her parched throat. "I said it came across as a bear mauling. But I don't know. Fifteen minutes later it sounded like dispatch had upgraded the call to a possible homicide."

"That's odd."

"Yeah. Anyway, after I heard 'homicide' on the radio, the cops got sneaky and switched to cell phones."

"How conniving."

"Yeah. Classic, huh? But as usual I outsmarted them. I called my forest ranger buddy. He confirmed. Now we have a possible homicide. I need somebody to go check it out. That's you. If it pans out and we have a homicide, I'll toss the fire story over to the new intern, George."

"Any stats?" She turned and noted the crowd that lined the road, kids on bikes mostly, a few neighbors and a young woman wrapped in a beach towel, hair dripping. An ice cream truck, its carnival music playing from a loudspeaker, cruised to a stop not far away. Drive-by rubberneckers paused for a better view. They were all potential quotes. And ones she'd need to move on before the wolves descended.

Too late. Two news crews arrived just then, parking half a block away. A blazing house fire was always great footage for television news.

Stu was shouting into the phone. "What's that annoying racket?"

"An ice cream truck. Hold on, I'll move." She sprinted away from all the noise, pausing under a shade tree near a lawn gnome. The gnome was sitting on a toilet reading a book, half hidden in the ivy. *Tacky.* "Go ahead, Stu."

"The woman's body was found up by Gin Lin Trail. I already sent Bryan out for photos. So far all I have is . . . Caucasian, female, no age yet."

With more than a little trepidation, she asked, "How far into the woods?"

"The trail starts right off the road there. Don't worry, you'll find it easy enough. The place is probably crawling with cops by now."

Her stomach shrank into a hard knot at the thought. "Ah . . ."

"What?"

If she didn't jump on this lead, he'd just toss the treasured front-page homicide to another reporter. She was hardly in a position to pick and choose her stories. Damaged goods.

"Give me another thirty minutes here, and I'll finish by phone later." She glanced at her watch; it was nearly four thirty PM on a Friday. With any luck, Stu would be the first to figure out the body in the woods was a homicide. Getting a jump on the other reporters was half the battle, but she'd be faced with five o'clock traffic.

As if reading her mind, Stu said, "Take the Upper Apple-Gate road. And McKenna? Don't hog the info. Let me know as soon as you have some firm details."

She hung up with a sense of urgency, her nerves buzzing. And something else . . . just the tiniest bit of terror.

Did it have to be in the woods?

She realized she was white-knuckling her phone and relaxed her grip.

"Hey," a guy in his early thirties called to her from the driveway of the vulgar-gnome house. He wore khaki shorts and a purple Hawaiian-print shirt and held a Samuel Adams beer in his beefy hand as if he were at a barbecue. His gaze traveled over Whit's slender figure, lingering on her long tan legs, exposed by her above-the-knee skirt. His heavy-lidded smirk raised her hackles.

Don't go there, barbecue boy . . .

When his inspection finally traveled back up to her face and he caught the drop-dead look in her cool blue eyes, he changed course, scratched behind his ear, and nodded toward her pad.

"You a reporter?"

He was a lush, and possibly a perv if the gnome was any indication of his character, but he was an eyewitness nonetheless, and she was running out of time.

She forced a smile. "Whitney McKenna, *Medford Daily Chronicle*. You know who lives there?" she asked, nodding to the burning house.

"Yeah, man. He's an attorney. DUIs." He took a step toward her and gave a conspiratorial laugh. "He's good too. Got me off."

The fact that this guy bragged about driving drunk came as no surprise. "You have a minute for an interview?"

He beamed, his ruddy face glistening. "Sure."

Down to business now, Whit stuffed her unease about the woods to the back of her mind. She swapped the pad for a digital recorder from her shoulder bag and fired off questions in rapid succession.

The guy was a treasure trove of quasi-personal information on his neighbors. Borderline peeping tom, he probably used binoculars; but if the details were accurate, then she had hit pay dirt.

2

THE APPLEGATE ROAD ambled through green vineyards and acres of farmland partitioned with white picket fences. During the drive, Whit chugged down a diet Pepsi and munched a McDonald's burger from a drive-through on the outskirts of town. She hadn't eaten today, so she hoped the food would tamp down the fluttering wings in her stomach.

She turned right onto South Stage Road and cranked up the air conditioning in her Chevy Tahoe, aiming the vents at her hair. She reeked of smoke. She'd interviewed the fire chief standing near the smoldering ruins of the house. Information that she needed to share with Stu. She reached across and tapped her car speakerphone. Stu picked up almost immediately.

"What's the scoop?"

"The fire chief is listing the fire as suspicious. The explosion was caused by a gas leak that blew out the wall and exposed the body. I saw it up close and personal. The guy was pretty badly burned. The fire chief said they were investigating the actual cause of the fire; ID to be announced by the medical examiner."

"Stories heatin' up! No pun intended." He laughed at himself.

Ignoring his attempt at journalistic humor, considering she still had the mental picture of the ghastly fire victim in her mind's eye, she continued. "I interviewed a neighbor who shared some interesting tidbits. The fifty-something attorney, Bobby 'Bo' Delano, the married homeowner and probably the fire victim, was having an online affair with a twenty-one-year-old Czechoslovakian woman."

"No shit?"

"Yes. Last month Delano's wife discovered his indiscretion and fled their home amid a flurry of moving vans, according to the neighbor."

"That's interesting, but I still don't see the point. Oh, wait. Don't tell me. The Czech chick moved in?"

"Good guess."

"No guess, superstar. That move is right out of the divorcée handbook. All the best midlife-crisis guys know that one."

"Well, I'm glad life has not made you jaded."

"Naw . . . just realistic."

"Anyway, a few days after the wife left, the Czechoslovakian woman—or as the neighbor described, 'lanky blonde'—took up residence with Delano, along with her Chihuahua and Siamese cat. Yesterday, during a screaming match with the attorney in his front yard in which the woman called him a 'madman and lunatic,' the blonde packed up her belongings into a taxi and vacated the property, taking her pets with her. One would assume the affair is over."

"Titillating info, for sure."

"You have to wonder if the wife or the girlfriend doubled back for revenge."

Stu chuckled. "Hell hath no fury like a woman scorned."

"My bet is the victim is the cheating attorney."

"You'd make bank on that one. Are you almost to the Applegate?"

"Yes, I'll call you when I head back."

Whit hung up, her thoughts turning to the Applegate victim. She had no illusions. She'd been in the business too long.

This assignment might pan out as a lost hiker who perished in the woods and was later eaten by a bear, or maybe a bear attacked some hapless camper who stupidly left food inside his tent. She still held out hope for a delicious crime story, but she had to be realistic. Nine times out of ten, initial reports were bogus. The victim could be the result of a car accident or any number of things. She'd learned a long time ago not to jump to conclusions.

Eager to get to the site and find out the real story, she pressed on the accelerator, slowing briefly as she drove through Jacksonville, an old mining town–turned–tourist destination with a one-street storefront, then accelerated once again, zigzagging through lush wooded hillsides flanking Highway 238.

When she turned right onto Upper Applegate Road, she could feel the tension building with each passing mile. A nameless dread.

Just breathe, girl.

Ten minutes later she pulled up behind a circus of law enforcement vehicles parked along the single paved road. Whit spotted a blue F-150 belonging to Katie Riggs, medical examiner detective and new best friend. She had Katie to thank for encouraging her to reenter the gritty world of journalism. They'd bonded at a book club over their life crises when Whit first moved to Medford and frequently met for coffee or a glass of wine. The relationship had a rocky start, but they were able to overlook the obvious: police viewed reporters as vultures and journalists suspected every government entity of corruption. The new friendship had certainly helped Whit keep her sanity the past six months. Katie was a rock.

Whit popped a piece of mint gum into her mouth to cover the onion breath from the burger. She angled the rearview mirror and studied the scrape on her chin. It was only skin-deep, but pink- and red-streaked from a grass burn. A dab of face powder from her compact and she was good to go.

Resigned to walking a long way to the crime scene, she was glad of her flat sandals. She grabbed her tote bag and stepped out into the searing heat. The paved road hugged the Applegate River to the left and the entrance to Flumet Flat Campground to the right. The sweet, pungent scent of pine and the musty smell of dank earth and bramble along the river rekindled the spirit of anxiety that had haunted her for eight months. She sensed it now, creeping like poison from her adrenal glands, forcing her heart to pump faster.

Ignoring her body's traitorous response to the woods, she increased her pace. In minutes the steep road had her catching her breath. With a derisive smirk, she was grudgingly thankful for her early morning boot camp. The one-hour kick-your-butt six AM exercise had not only toned her muscles but, more importantly, relieved some of her anxiety. Katie had challenged her to try the class. Now she was in the best shape of her life—physically, anyway. Whit neared the police barricade, about a football field past the campgrounds. It seemed everyone from the camp had gathered as close to the scene as possible.

"Excuse me." She nudged her way past kids on bikes, bikini-clad teenage girls flaunting their newly developed bodies, curious moms and dads, and barking dogs. Finally she came upon some old-timers who'd parked their lawn chairs in the front row just outside the yellow crime scene tape. The barricade stretched across the narrow road, framed by a campground on one side and the Applegate River on the other. Sticky with perspiration, she peeled her blouse from her back.

A sheriff's deputy stood stiffly behind the tape. His name tag read *Parker*.

She flashed her credentials with as much authority as possible. "Whit McKenna with the *Medford Daily Chronicle*. Can you confirm that a body was found in the woods?"

"You need to direct your questions to the detective assigned to the case."

"And who might that be?"

"I can't say."

She prodded him for information, but he was a stone wall. Frustrated, she turned away and caught sight of Bryan, a summer intern and photographer, on the other side of the river. He crouched in the underbrush on the steep embankment. His camera was aimed across the river at an ambulance and a group of law enforcement personnel. What Bryan lacked in experience, he made up for with enthusiasm. He caught her eye and gave her the thumbs-up. She waved.

Turning around, Whit scanned the area. With all these people, *someone* must have seen *something*. Her roaming gaze settled on a weathered old guy with bronzed skin, wearing a T-shirt and jeans, who paced alongside his Dodge Ram truck parked near the river under the shade of a Douglas fir. A golden retriever sat in the bed of the vehicle, tongue lolling in the heat.

The guy paused to ruffle the dog's ears. The back of his white T-shirt read: *Here . . . fishy, fishy.*

Instinct told her this was more than a curious onlooker, as he was the only one not peering beyond the crime scene tape, anxious to find out what all the fuss was about.

"Not catching any fish today, huh?" Whit approached the old man, her voice raised over the gushing river only a few yards from his truck. He turned, his expression edgy, blue eyes sharp.

"Nah. I only drove up here 'cause of old Doc Masterson; you know, the vet over by the McKee Bridge store?"

Whit nodded. She had no idea who he was talking about.

"Well, he told me about a place called Big Flat Rock." He nodded his head to the left. "Right there in the middle of that river. Said he caught *four* steelhead just during his lunch hour! Heck, I didn't even get a chance to unload my fishing gear before Red here took off after that bear."

Jackpot.

Her heart skipped a beat, then plunged into overdrive. The thrill of the hunt coursed through her veins as if she'd never left her career in the dust.

"So . . . you were the one to find the body?"

"Eureka, huh?" She felt a twinge of compassion. The old guy possessed the same glassy-eyed look she'd witnessed on the faces of war-ravaged villagers in Afghanistan.

"That's quite a discovery," she said, hoping he'd elaborate.

"That's for sure. And now I'm stuck here. The detective told me not to leave until he had time to get a full statement from me, so I been hangin' out here for darn near an hour. I finally crossed that yella tape to come check on my dog. That fella over there"— he pointed to the deputy on guard—"told me I had to stay put. It's Friday. During the summer our church has a barbecue every Friday. Tonight it's at our place." He grinned sheepishly. "I was planning on grillin' my catch and showing off for the boys, you know?"

"Uh-huh." Whit smiled, warming up to him. "A man with a fish story and proof to match is a holy thing."

He laughed gruffly, "Hey, you're all right."

For a woman, she interpreted, without taking offense. "Listen, would you mind if *I* asked you a few questions. I'm with the *Medford Daily Chronicle*."

"Well." He paused a moment, glanced over at the deputy, then shrugged. "I guess that would be all right. It's a heck of a story, ain't it?"

"Yes, it is."

"Don't find buried bodies every day."

"Quite a shock wasn't it?" Whit pulled her micro-recorder out of her tote bag, but kept her pad and pen handy for backup.

"Damn right! Oh, pardon me, ma'am. It *was* a shock, all right. If I had a smoke, I'd light up right now. I quit years ago, but that business had me thinkin' about those Luckys. Haven't felt like that since Korea."

"I understand. Maybe it would help if you talked about it. Would you tell me your name?"

"Jerry Wolcott. I'm a retired grocery store owner. I used to own JW's Grocery out off Old Stage Road. I was famous for my home-ground sausage. You probably heard about it. Folks used to come from all over the Rogue Valley. Still do. I sold the recipe with the store." He shook his head sadly. "Now the guy that bought the place is selling my brand all over the internet. It's the darnedest thing. I kinda wish I'd-a kept that recipe to myself."

"I bet." Whit positioned her back to the deputy to hide her recorder. Better if he didn't know the press was questioning their witness. They'd kick themselves later for not taking better care of shell-shocked Mr. Wolcott. "You say Red found the bear and the body?"

"Yeah. He took off running the minute his feet hit the ground. I thought he was after a squirrel. He likes to tree those suckers."

"Some squirrel this time!"

He ruffled the dog's ears lovingly. "I guess I better thank the good Lord that Red wasn't chewed up by that bear."

"He ran it off?"

"No, ma'am." His gaze wandered away, remembering, and he gave a shudder. "That bear was already chewing on that lady's leg, and he wasn't goin' nowhere. Uh-uh. Red was quick enough to stay out of the reach of the bear at first, but it wouldn't have been long before that bear tore into him. No." He turned and pointed at the gun rack in the back window of his truck. "I grabbed my gun and shot over the bear's head. The bullet ricocheted off a tree and sent splinters into the bear's face. He roared in pain and off he ran, right up that road there about half a mile."

"Can you describe the body?"

He frowned, scratching the back of his gray head. "All I saw was a leg. I think the bear didn't have enough time to dig up the rest of her."

"Then how do you know it was a woman?"

"Cause the foot was wearing a red sandal. The kind with a long skinny heel. And the bear had already chewed off the foot, or most of it anyways. I'll sure never forget something like that."

"So, your shot put the bear on the run. What happened next?"

"Yeah, but that didn't stop old Red." He paused to affectionately rub the dog's head again. "He tore up the road, chasin' that bear. Treed it too," he said proudly. "I wasn't taken no chances, though. I put a leash on Red and ran him back to the truck so I could call nine-one-one. I was distracted by that poor woman's body. I don't know what happened to the bear after that. The Department of Fish and Wildlife are out there searching for it now."

"About what time did you call nine-one-one?"

"I'd say about three this afternoon."

Whit glanced at the gun rack. "Where's your gun now?"

"The cops took it. Said it was evidence."

"What kind of gun was it?"

"I just had my small one on me today. It's a twenty-two-caliber Ruger rifle. Did the job, though."

"Mr. Wolcott, did you see anyone else near the body or in the woods?"

"Just call me Jerry. And nope. Not until I fired that shot; then a couple of kids came runnin' down the trail that way." He pointed across the road and up the mountain toward Gin Lin Trail.

"Kids?"

"Yeah. Boys. I'd say about eleven or twelve. Two of them. I think Red's crazy barking got their attention; then when I shot the gun, they came over to see what happened. I went tearing up the road after Red and the bear. Haven't moved like that in years. When I got back, the boys were standing there staring at the woman's body. I yelled at them to stay back and told 'em I was calling nine-one-one."

"Are the boys still here?" She scanned the crowd along the road.

"Maybe, in the campground somewheres." He glanced over her shoulder. "Uh-oh. Here comes the law."

Whit stiffened and quickly requested his phone number for future reference. She thanked Mr. Wolcott and gave him her card. After dropping the recorder into her bag, she turned, ready to escape, but instead faced a tall man in a teal-blue dress shirt and tie, loosened at the neck.

Mr. Wolcott said, "This here is the detective who asked me to wait and give a statement."

"It looks like you've already given one." The detective's gaze traveled swiftly, taking in her scuffed chin, burn holes in her blouse, grass stains on her skirt, and the still-bloody scrape on her knee. She could read the curiosity on his face, but he refrained from asking what happened to her.

With a polite smile, she offered her hand, taking note of a bruise under his eye. "Whit McKenna, *Medford Daily Chronicle*."

He hesitated for just a second. "I've . . . read some of your bylines." He gripped her hand in a firm shake. "Today, though, I would have preferred to debrief *my* witness *myself*."

"Oh, well . . ." She pulled her hand free. "Maybe you should have had your witness wait *behind* the crime scene tape."

"Point taken. Did I see you with a recorder?"

She met the challenge in his tone. "Did you?"

"I have the right to confiscate evidence if I deem it pertinent to the investigation."

"I'm sorry, I missed your name. Detective . . . ?"

"Jacob Panetta, Medford Police Department."

"Panetta?" Suddenly aware of who he was, her gaze fell to his bruised cheek. "Aren't you on suspension until next month?"

His lips thinned. "Nice article."

Last week she'd written a story about the battery and assault charges leveled against Panetta by one Detective Tucker, so his sarcasm was not lost on her. Her source at the police station, a busybody waiting to pay a parking fine, had said Tucker made a derogatory comment about Panetta's family and that started the fistfight. Whit was sure her very public coverage of the incident had not helped to reduce disciplinary action against Panetta. Fat chance he would dole out any information.

Mr. Wolcott felt the need to intervene. "I'll be tellin' you the same story I done told her, Detective. Ain't no harm done. Now, for cryin' out loud, I have got to get home to my wife, because we're puttin' on a barbecue at our house tonight."

Whit thanked Mr. Wolcott for his time and seized the opportunity to escape. She felt Panetta's penetrating gaze on her departing back. Dismissing the encounter as unfortunate, she marched down the road and into the campground in search of the witnesses.

After asking around, she finally found the mother of one of the boys who had seen the dead woman's grave: a heavyset woman in a red T-shirt and jean shorts, her mouse-brown hair in a sloppy ponytail. She was busy hanging wet towels over a clothesline suspended between an aged motor home and a tree.

"They took off up that trail again," the mother said, exuding beer breath in a raspy two-packs-a-day voice. "I think they've got a fort built up there."

"The trail?" Whit pointed to a winding swath of ground dirt and gravel that disappeared into the woods and tried to swallow the lump of sawdust that had suddenly swelled in her throat. "Okay. Sure. How far in, do you think?"

"Oh, I don't know. We've been using walkie-talkies to call them to dinner, but the batteries finally wore out."

"I see. So you have no way of communicating with them?"

"Not right now."

"What about a cell phone?"

The woman shrugged weary-sloped shoulders, as if camping with preteen boys was more than she'd bargained for—hence the empty beer bottle on the picnic table next to an overflowing ashtray. "No. No cell phone. I wouldn't let him bring it, 'cause he'd just lose it, and reception up here ain't very good anyway." She frowned, her gaze on the trail. "I don't like them out there without the walkie-talkies, especially with a bear running about. I sent my husband into town to pick up some batteries; he should've been back an hour ago. I was gonna send him after the boys. Since you're headed that way, would you mind telling them I said to come on back? Besides, I think we have a storm comin' in."

"Sure, if I see them."

Whit glanced at the sky; darkening clouds cast shadows over the mountains to the south. She'd been too preoccupied to notice. All the more reason not to go wandering into the woods.

She turned away and cautiously approached the trailhead. It slithered its way into the woods like a flat, gray snake weaving back and forth up the incline until it disappeared amid peeling branches of madrone and birch trees.

It would be like walking a gauntlet, she thought, as haunting impressions slipped through cracks and crevices in her psyche. As if to say whatever lay ahead on the trail would be her undoing.

Over the years she'd endured every kind of hardship while chasing stories and been witness to atrocities that no one should ever have to see. She'd known the risks. Perhaps she'd led a reckless life. *Obsessive*, John, her husband, would have said, while comforting her after a particularly ugly nightmare and urging her to consider another career. *Let it go*, he would say. Someone else would cover it. *But who?* she would ask. What if no one did? His response was always the same. *You can't put out every fire in the world, Whit. Let it go.*

Of course she hadn't let it go, even now, after fate had inevitably slaughtered the very life she'd held most dear. And that . . . the fear of seeing that, reliving it, terrified her like nothing else ever had.

Still, she'd never abandoned a story in her life, and she wasn't going to start now.

Resolute, jaw determinably set, Whit began the ascent.

3

STIFLING HEAT AND threatening storm clouds cast a pall over the forest. Medical examiner detective Katie Riggs could see it through her camera lens as she shot pictures of the partially buried body. The air in her lungs weighed thick and heavy. Her navy slacks and cotton polo shirt were sticky against her skin. Slender and petite, she wore her blonde hair cropped short, a convenience she'd adopted after her last chemo treatment a year ago. She still craved heat to alleviate the almost constant chill in her bones, but this sweltering weather was too much even for her.

She pulled a tissue from her back pocket and wiped perspiration from her forehead and lip. Thankfully, she didn't need to worry about makeup. She'd never used it, and raised with three brothers and no mother, she never missed it.

With a sigh, she knelt to study the only part of the corpse visible above the haphazard grave, wincing at the stench of decaying flesh. If she waited a few minutes, her senses would numb to the putrefaction. Camera lens focused, she shot several photos as a ray of sunlight cut through the trees with the precision of a spotlight on the partially severed leg. Teeth marks were clearly visible on the calf and the instep of the foot, along with some nasty claw marks. The lack of blood indicated the wounds were definitely postmortem. Splintered bone protruded from a compound fracture where the bear's jaws had snapped the tibia, and below that carnage dangled a red-sandaled foot.

She angled the camera lower, her lens capturing the broken ankle, the delicate, dusty, patent-leather sandal straps that encased matching red-painted toenails, the slender toes crusted with dirt. That single shot signified the brutal end of this woman's life. A tragic picture that needed no words.

The transition from homicide detective to medical examiner detective had been a diversion following Riggs's recovery from surgery that left a paper-thin scar along her hairline and around the front of her ear. The right side of her face was slightly thinner than the left. Something the average eye would miss, but a reminder for her every morning when she looked in the mirror that life was indeed short. And turning thirty-seven next December was not a given.

She lowered the camera, listening to the rushing of the nearby river that filled the silence of the forest amid the buzz of flying insects. She shifted her position and focused on the wooded hillside, where a sandy trail snaked away in the distance. Frowning, she brushed a hand through her blonde pixie cut, her gaze searching the forest for any clues. Shadowed by tall alder and pine, high on a ridge, Gin Lin Trail twisted its way to a campground about a quarter mile away.

It was possible that a hiker on the trail had scared off the perp before he'd had time to stack enough rocks on the grave. River rocks were embedded in the ground all around. It would have been a tough dig and probably took longer than expected. Even so, the body could have remained undetected for a long time. The killer certainly had not bargained on a hungry bear digging up his kill.

Standing, she slipped on a pair of latex gloves from her kit and paused to examine her new tattoo on the inside of her wrist, the skin around the cross and praying hands still raw and raised. She'd discovered the power of prayer during her battle with cancer. Now that she was cancer-free, she worried that she'd forget. Focus on mundane things, like what to wear, what to eat, and before she knew it, the grim reaper would come calling again, and this time he'd be pissed because she'd already escaped him once.

"Nice tat."

Riggs glanced up, surprised to see Detective Jacob Panetta. Light on his feet, he had an annoying way of approaching unnoticed, like a ghost appearing out of thin air.

"Hey, Panetta!" She smiled, glad to see him. "I knew they couldn't keep you down for long."

He cocked his head to the side with a self-effacing grin. "It's my natural magnetism and charm. The brass reinstated me yesterday." He reached into his pocket, pulled out a bottle of Tylenol, and popped two in his mouth, swallowing them dry.

Nearly fifty and lean, with a youthful countenance despite the gray in his dark hair, he was a handsome man. Today he had dark circles beneath those mischievous brown eyes. In the week since she'd seen him, he'd lost some weight, and was sporting a cut under his left eye that still shadowed a greenish-yellow bruise.

She said, "You're not your usual Mr. GQ today. More like a *Survivor* contestant."

"Ha-ha. Very funny."

"You okay?"

"I spent the last three nights with my punching bag in the garage instead of sleeping." He grinned wolfishly. "I've given it a name and drawn two beady eyes on it."

"What's the name?"

"Do you need to ask?"

She shook her head. "You're still angry at Tucker?"

"He said things about Ellen." His lips thinned. "He's lucky I didn't kill him."

She had no doubt that he could have delivered a mortal injury. He had served full-term in Army Special Ops and transferred to the FBI, where he'd worked for twenty years in Hostage Rescue. Because of family issues, he'd retired and moved to Medford. But, unwilling to adapt to retirement, he'd acquired a position with the Medford Homicide Detective Unit a little over a year ago. Just a few months before Riggs was diagnosed with stage-two melanoma. "I don't blame you for decking him. I don't think anyone does." She cast a glance at the tan line that remained where a wedding ring had once been. Everyone knew Panetta's wife had a drinking problem and had left him six months ago for a barfly who "had time for her." Tucker, one of four homicide investigators, wasn't known for his tact. "Tucker's an ass. You did everyone a favor."

"Tell that to the brass." He shrugged. "They don't appreciate me the way you do."

She shook her head. "All things considered, you got off easy."

"Yeah, well, your friendly journalist didn't help matters. Did she say who fed her that story?"

"Oh, you met her today? She's here?"

"Yes to both. Her pictures don't do her justice."

Riggs smiled. "She's a beautiful woman, even when she's in the trenches. I thought you might notice."

"Who wouldn't? So, I've been meaning to ask. You weren't her source, then? For the story she wrote about me?"

"No, of course not! I don't rat out fellow cops."

He nodded. "I didn't think so. Kind of odd, you two being friends. How does that work? With your jobs, I mean?"

"Very carefully. As to her writing about you, that's your own fault. You and Tucker didn't pick a very private place to go at each other . . . right there in front of the ticket window."

He shrugged.

Then, changing the topic, Panetta pointed to the nearly severed foot. "Cinderella didn't make out so well this time."

"No kidding. Speaking of Cinderella, the vic's shoe is a Sergio Rossi, Italian and expensive. I looked it up on my cell. This woman was either wealthy or she had a sugar daddy."

He eyed the shoe, a dark frown suddenly appearing.

"Something wrong?"

"Could be." He walked around to the head of the grave. "If I were a betting man, I think I'd win on this hunch. It's not gonna be good. But we won't know until we dig her out."

"What hunch?"

"Naw . . . I like to hedge my bets. Let's just say my being here is not a coincidence."

Riggs knew him well enough not to expect an answer. It had to be something big if he was back to work already. Decisions from on high were not revoked easily. "Okay. Any details from the witness yet?"

"Mr. Wolcott took a shot at the bear and wounded him, which is why we still have a body." He turned and pointed to the tree next to him. "Looks like the bullet splintered the tree here." His gaze traveled to another pine six feet away. "Probably ended up over there."

At the sound of footsteps crunching the leaves underneath, they turned and saw Sergeant Detective Blackwell of the sheriff's department lumbering their way. He ignored the crime tech crew setting up equipment for a grid search and walked directly toward her.

In his late fifties, potbellied with a pockmarked jaw and gravelly voice, Blackwell was a transplant from Texas. The drawl made people underestimate the man. He had a law degree and was often asked to help with chain-of-evidence procedures. The guy could be teaching or practicing law, but he preferred the grit and grime of detective duties. And his ailing mother lived nearby in Jacksonville.

Riggs had worked with Blackwell the past year at the sheriff's department, where the ME's offices were located. She respected his intelligence, and he had a decent sense of humor. He'd supported her during chemo by shaving his head.

He tipped his hat, revealing a full head of silver hair. "Riggs . . . Panetta." He pulled a cigar from his pocket and clenched it in his moustached mouth. At her frown, he said, "I'm not smokin', just chewin'. Don't want to pollute the crime scene, and I know how you feel about secondhand smoke."

Blackwell turned his penetrating stare on Panetta. "I coulda sworn you were off duty. Been reinstated?"

Panetta sighed. "Apparently."

Puzzled, Blackwell said, "I heard you weren't comin' back until next month."

"My leave of absence was cut short."

"Hmmm." Blackwell motioned toward the body. "That's an ugly business. You got an ETD yet?"

"I'm not sure." She glanced at the grave. "Time of death is difficult to determine on this one. If the grave were deep enough, the chill in the ground would have preserved her like a refrigerator. But, from the smell, I don't think that happened. It's close enough to the road. It probably got full sun during most of the day. Could have worked like a fire pit and helped decomp the body. We'll need to move her and get a temperature reading of the ambient air in the hole." She reached down to the black kit bag resting at her feet. "Help me spread out the tarp, and you two can move the body."

Riggs pulled two pairs of latex gloves from her bag and handed them to the guys.

Blackwell busted one of his gloves open. "Ah . . . damn."

With a grin, she supplied another. "You're a bull in a china shop."

He accepted the glove with a smirk. "There's lots of things I could say to that, but I'm not gonna."

Too late, she realized her reference to a bull could be utilized as fodder for the male ego. "You're a gentleman, Blackwell."

While Riggs kept busy with her camera photographing their progress, the guys relocated the heavy stones to a nearby tarp. The crime lab unit would painstakingly sift through the pile later.

Pausing for a breather, Panetta asked Blackwell, "Are you point man on this one?"

"Yep. It's county jurisdiction. We've already established that MADIU is takin' the case. Detectives are canvassin' the campgrounds now. We got a temporary command center set up at the ranger station. We're gonna hitch up there in an hour." He chewed the tip of his cigar, dark eyes questioning. "You up for it?"

The inference that Panetta might not be at peak performance probably hit home hard. The sting was barely perceptible—only a clenched jaw.

MADIU was Jackson County's Major Assault and Death Investigation Unit. The interagency group was county-wide and worked diligently with the DA's office to bring cases to trial. Because the agencies all cooperated—most of the time—they had a high clearance rate.

Panetta challenged Blackwell's penetrating gaze. "Why wouldn't I be?"

After a long moment, Blackwell shrugged. At least he had the decency not to bring up the fight. Turning to Riggs, he asked, "Has the ME been notified?"

She nodded. "I called Dr. Weldon an hour ago. The autopsy is scheduled for tomorrow morning. I'll x-ray the vic late tonight at Rogue Community Hospital. The x-ray staff complained about the offensive smell of decomposing bodies during prime hours."

Blackwell scowled. "Can you get the results to me by tomorrow noon? You'd think an x-ray machine would be priority for the ME's office. Stinkin' budget cuts. Well, Panetta, you can buddy with Riggs during the autopsy."

Panetta flinched.

For a trained special ops guy, he was awfully squeamish, Riggs thought, not for the first time. When she had asked him about it months ago, he'd simply said the whole autopsy process was distasteful to him, like watching someone getting scalped. He preferred hand-to-hand combat any day.

He made no mention of that now. "Sure. I could use a good diversion. Sign me up."

That settled, Blackwell shoved the cigar to the corner of his mouth and bent to the job at hand.

After a few minutes of rock removal, Blackwell heaved a large stone, then straightened and stretched his lower back. "It's hotter'n hell out here." Face flushed, he leaned over, resting his hands on his knees.

Another few minutes and Riggs feared he'd pass out in the heat.

Unable to just stand by and watch, she helped with the smaller rocks.

They worked in silence, each preparing with weary anticipation for whatever lay beneath Mother Nature's carpet. Riggs shared their natural reluctance to view the dead woman's cast-off remains, abandoned for insects and wild animals to consume. Over the past year she had analyzed that aspect of death as well. What to do with her body. Cremate it or bury it or place it in a mausoleum above ground. She'd chosen a dignified sienna bronze casket with a velvet rose interior. The thought of burning her body to ashes horrified her, and any hack could break into a mausoleum. No, eight feet under in a respectable, nonrusting bronze casket was the ticket. Now, seeing this poor woman, tossed into the dirt like garbage in a landfill, she imagined herself slung into that hole, beneath the dirt and rocks, with slimy creatures dining out on her flesh.

With renewed energy, Riggs heaved rocks. "Let's get her out of there."

Sweaty and miserable, they removed the last of the rocks and debris. The corpse, shrouded in dirt and leaves, lay face-down wearing what had once been white capri pants and a red halter top, her long dark hair a tangled mass. With a collective sigh, they shared an unspoken relief that the victim had not been hacked to pieces by some freak, and there were no obvious signs of torture.

Riggs knelt by her black bag and retrieved the thermometer. "The grave is relatively shallow. Makes me think the perp wasn't familiar with the area. There're a lot of mountains and hills around here that aren't embedded with river rock he could have used."

With a swipe from the back of his arm, Blackwell cleared the sweat from his brow. "I'm bettin' he saw the dead-end sign and figured this was about as deserted as he was gonna find."

"What about the campground?" Panetta asked. "It's not that far away."

"In the dead of night," Blackwell said, "I'm thinkin' the joker assumed this was remote enough, 'cause he didn't know it's a popular fishin' spot. Means he's no outdoorsman." He studied the body. "She clear enough to hoist her to that tarp?"

"Yes." Riggs leaned forward, ready to get the ambient temperature of the grave as soon as the body was lifted out.

"Shoo." Blackwell knelt at the head of the grave as a warm gust of wind from the approaching storm stirred up dust and whistled through the tree branches. The stench of decomposing flesh whirled around them. "This one is ripe! Let's get on with it."

Stone-faced, Panetta positioned himself at the vic's feet and grabbed hold just above the broken ankle. "Ready."

"On the count of three," Blackwell said. "One, two, three . . ."

In unison, they easily moved the vic, who couldn't have weighed more than 115 pounds. They rolled her onto her back. She was slender, though her abdomen was swollen with decomposing gases. Riggs estimated about five foot seven, approximately forty years old. She wore large gold hoop earrings, and several expensive diamonds still graced her hands. Robbery was definitely not the motive. Riggs thought she might have been quite beautiful when she was alive. As she had suspected, bugs had found a way to start feeding on the cadaver's flesh.

"This is *not* good," Panetta said. He bent forward, peering down at the vic.

Waiting for a reading on the thermometer, Riggs glanced up at his tone. "What?"

"Do you know somethin' we don't?" Blackwell asked, uneasy.

"I hope I'm wrong." Panetta pointed to the vic. "But I think this is Niki Francis."

"The actress?" Riggs asked, incredulous. Her gaze darted back to the bloated face, the lavender flesh. It held little resemblance to the famous actress who had quietly moved into the Southern Oregon foothills five years ago.

He nodded. "*That's* why I was reinstated early. The captain contacted me yesterday with orders to investigate a high-priority missing persons report."

Blackwell shifted his cigar to the other side of his mouth and moved in closer to the vic, peering at her face. "What makes you think this is Niki Francis?"

"Her housekeeper said she'd been gone for a few days, but hadn't reported it because Niki sometimes disappeared without telling anyone. But when she didn't return her manager's calls from LA and didn't show up for a new movie she was filming in New York, the manager called the police station to voice her concerns."

"And the brass called you?" Blackwell asked.

Panetta nodded. "The possibility of an abduction for ransom crossed their minds, or some wacked-out fan. My history with the FBI came into play."

"That explains your bein' here," Blackwell said. "So what'd you find out?"

"I checked her phone records. There's been no activity for four days. No banking action either. The last ping on her phone and her car's OnStar alarm was about ten miles up the road, at Applegate Lake. At first I thought she might be staying in a cabin nearby. I did some investigating and came up empty. Now I'm thinking the car and the phone are both probably underwater."

Blackwell asked, "How come I didn't hear about this sooner?"

"The brass insisted on containment until I had more information. I was putting together a team with the canine unit to search the area when the possible homicide was reported."

"Holy shit." Blackwell glared down at Riggs. "I've changed my mind. The media is gonna be all over us. Get that housekeeper or somebody to ID the body. Dental records. Whatever. And to hell with the hospital staff; I need that autopsy ASAP."

4

Five minutes up the trail, and the hair on the back of Whit's neck stood on end. Even the suffocating heat didn't relieve the icy chill of her skin.

Sounds of the river reverberated off the mountain in whispered echoes, amplified by the vast forest. A shadow passed across her face and she flinched, glancing up. Flying low over the trees, an osprey glided past, its six-foot wingspan cast dark shadows across the green foliage like something prehistoric. The bird of prey had a fish in its talons, still dripping water from the river. It circled wide, emitting loud, panting screeches like a monkey, then landed in a nest at the top of a tall pine.

She shivered and moved on. With all the excitement down on the road and the threat of a bear, she'd not passed a single soul on the trail. No diversion to dispel the rising terror. It was like an emotional assault from all sides.

Faced with yet another bend in the trail that led higher up the mountain, she stopped short, paralyzed with overwhelming dread.

Her breath came fast and shallow, ears drumming with the pulse of her pounding heart.

The sky crystallized into shards of sparkling blue through the canopy of trees. The bird's caw transformed into an eerie cry for help. Pine and spruce trees pressed in on her. The air seeped, damp and cloying, into her lungs.

With eyes squeezed shut, she began to count.

Deep breath in . . . one . . . two . . . three . . . four . . . five, breath out slowly. Deep breath in . . .

Oh God . . .

"Run, Whit!" John whispered in her ear, pushing her ahead of him.

She leaped forward, but after only a dozen racing steps, she heard the single shot, and turned to see the spray of blood erupt from John's head. She watched his body fall limply to the forest floor, still gasping for air.

Rushing to his side, she huddled over him, frantically trying to stem the pulsing blood.

A kick in the ribs sent her rolling into the underbrush, the air knocked from her lungs. Viciously hauled by her hair back to the trail, she fought, arms flailing against her attackers.

A fist like a sledgehammer split her lip.

Her face crushed into the grainy trail. Spitting blood and dirt, she tried to crawl back to John.

Another kick flipped her onto her back, her head cracking against a rock . . .

Sensing sunlight on her face, Whit opened her eyes and found herself crouching on the trail. With each breath, the scent of pine nauseated her.

Just like Korangal Valley . . . the Valley of Death.

Lurching to her feet, she leaned over a fallen log and vomited the burger she'd eaten an hour before. She heaved until her stomach was completely empty.

Wiping her mouth with a trembling hand, she turned and sat on the log.

Eight months ago, her assignment with the *Los Angeles Times* had been to report on the liberation, or lack thereof, for women in Kabul and northern Afghanistan. Her husband, a freelance photographer, agreed to go on the assignment with her while their daughters were vacationing in Oregon with her parents. The risks were minimal. But on their third day they were kidnapped in Kabul by al-Qaeda extremists who had bribed their interpreter. They were whisked away in a taxi to Korangal Valley in northeastern Afghanistan.

In 2010, the U.S. military closed Korangal Outpost, and the valley was quickly dominated by the Taliban. American forces dubbed it the Valley of Death because of the large number of American lives lost between 2006 and 2009. Current rumors of Russia and Pakistan working with the Taliban against Afghan forces and the resulting suppression of life in the northern regions had been the drive behind her story. Although the Taliban had been behind a recent car bombing in Kabul that killed twelve people, including a U.S. service member, they had been assured of their safety by the American Embassy.

Whit and John had been well aware of the history in that region and after being kidnapped knew they were facing an almost impossible situation. They would surely be used as collateral damage for whatever message the terrorists intended. Only a spattering of American soldiers remained in the area and only off the grid, and renegade Taliban lived by their own set of rules. Some were no more than mercenaries, in the game for the thrill and the money; others were radicals who simply hated Americans.

After being dumped in a wooded area and forced to march along a trail into the mountains for several hours at gunpoint, they had all stopped to rest.

The fatal moment.

Damn it!

Breathe in . . . hold it . . . one . . . two . . . three . . . four . . . five . . . slowly release.

How was she supposed to get through this story?

Shit!

Just breathe, girl.

The natural sounds of the forests gradually penetrated her chaotic thoughts as her heart rate slowed. She focused on a stream of ants trekking across the ground at her feet. She wished she hadn't remembered. She didn't want the ugly details. But there was no going back now. The nasty images were planted front and center in her mind, like waking from a nightmare. One that instilled a sense of terror long after waking.

The worst of the memory . . . during their march through the woods, she'd kept prompting John to make a run for it, fearing they were on a death march anyway. She'd understood enough of their kidnappers' bickering among themselves to fear the worst. They'd be used as pawns to shock the world in a public beheading, no doubt, like other victims. It was her insistence to run, even though John argued against it, that had gotten him killed. She saw the opportunity to escape when the kidnappers stopped to take a leak, and John had reluctantly agreed.

The American recon team who rescued her just happened to be in the area on an unrelated mission when they heard the gun fire. Would John still be alive if she'd just listened to him?

The sick reality of that question haunted her. Guilt wrapped its cloying arms around her heart and squeezed until she felt she couldn't breathe.

Unaware of being watched until she heard a distinctive snicker, she stood on shaky legs and scanned the hillside.

"Hey, lady," a voice called out.

Whit swung around but didn't see anyone. "Hello?"

"Up here."

High above her, on a moss-covered boulder, peered two heads barely visible through tree branches that hung over the rock.

"Are you okay?" one of the boys called down. "We thought you might be having a heart attack."

"Yeah." She forced a pathetic laugh. "So did I."

"Well, are you?"

She shook her head. "No. Just . . ." *Mortified that anyone witnessed my breakdown.* "I ate something that made me sick," she lied smoothly.

"Oh, as long as you're not contagious."

She approached the rock, craning her neck. "Are you Jimmy and Connor?"

"Yeah. How'd you know that?"

"I spoke with your mother. She said you wouldn't mind answering a few questions. I'm with the *Medford Daily Chronicle.*"

Their faces disappeared as they conferred with each other. She wiped the perspiration from her face with the back of her hand.

Fortunately, a sense of numbness had settled in. The suppressed memory, now so vivid, seemed as if it belonged to someone else or something she'd seen in a movie. She would do what she'd always done after seeing some kind of horror: tuck it away for some other day, when she could handle it. Shove it down deep and keep moving. She sure as hell couldn't handle it right now.

Groping in her bag, she found some mint gum, and popped a piece into her mouth.

Nothing like the taste of vomit.

In a moment they poked through the brush again.

"Cool! Come on up."

Scaling a massive rock was not on her agenda right now. "Ahhh. Would you guys mind coming down here?"

The blond called back, "It's not hard. Just go back down the trail about fifteen feet, and you'll see a clearing that leads right to us."

She glanced at the trail, contemplating an escape back to her car as the heavy air weighed on her like a steaming blanket.

Then the blond yelled out, "It's okay, you can do it." Those simple words of encouragement, however innocent of the truth, brought tears to her eyes. She nodded. "Yes. I can."

The trail opened up to a narrow clearing of brush that a casual eye would never notice. No wonder they were able to hide out up there.

One of the boys called through cupped hands, "Stay in the center so you don't get poison oak!"

That would be the coup de grace for the day.

Whit made her way to the foot of the rock. Little rivulets of perspiration trailed down her sides, as much from stress as the heat.

The mammoth rock thankfully had a gradual incline on this side. Relieved that she didn't have to climb, she stepped over two pairs of dusty flip-flops and ascended the rock, taking a seat on the blanket spread out at the top.

The blond said, "I'm Jimmy, and this is Connor." He had a mouthful of braces, and proud of it.

Both boys were thin, with narrow shoulders exposed by tank tops and spindly legs in cutoff jean shorts. Neither had yet developed masculine features, although Connor, with sandy-brown hair shagging over his ears and bright blue eyes, had a spattering of acne across his jaw. He was also sporting a healthy-looking scab on one knee. Connor tucked his chin against his chest, perhaps a bit shy, allowing his shaggy hair to fall across his brow. "You're our first guest. How do you like the place? Pretty cool, huh?"

"Yeah, we wouldn't have called out," Jimmy explained, "but, like, we thought you might be in trouble. You're the only person—well, besides us—who knows where our hideout is at."

"Thanks. I'm fine now." She was grateful for the distraction, so she was going to hang on like a pit bull to this story. She surveyed their camp. "You guys have a great fort."

The top of the rock lay relatively flat. Above, a tarp had been spread out up in the low-hanging branches of a tree, and beneath lay sleeping bags, pillows, flashlights, mosquito repellent, and a large basket of chips, crackers, peanut butter, and other snack foods. On the other half of the rock, where Whit sat under open sky, was an assortment of blankets to cushion the hard surface. A small ice chest rested in the corner alongside a stack of board games and a couple of pairs of binoculars. Most of the rock was shaded by a nearby tree.

Towheaded Jimmy grinned, his sunburned face alight with pride. "Yeah, man. It's sick!"

"Looks like you boys have been camping out here at night as well."

"Sure." Jimmy pointed to the tarp. "We have a roof in case it rains. But we can't stay out here all night. My mom wouldn't let us."

"Smart mom. She said to tell you boys to come back to camp for new batteries for the walkie-talkies. She's also nervous about a bear in the area, so she wants you closer to home."

"No way!" Jimmy protested.

"We should head back."

"No way, man!" Jimmy insisted. "I'm not leavin'."

They weren't her kids. There was nothing she could do about it. With a sigh, Whit agreed. "All right, we'll do the interview here." She grabbed her digital recorder from her bag and held it out between them. "The fisherman who found the body said you guys witnessed him shooting at the bear?"

Both boys immediately cheered up, their faces beaming with secrets begging to be shared. They burst out chattering at once, elbowing each other out of the way.

"Wait a minute." Whit raised her hands. "One at a time."

Jimmy clamped a hand over Connor's mouth. "Sure, we saw it; then we ran down there to see what was goin' on."

Connor finally freed himself. "That's when we saw the *body*. The bear had, like, *mangled* that lady's foot. And, like, *tore* half the leg off."

"And now we think maybe we seen the killer!" Jimmy jumped up, grabbed a pair of binoculars, and handed them to Whit. "We've been watching the cops dig up the body. Come on up."

She stepped tentatively toward the edge of the highest peak, holding on to a tree branch for support. Jimmy picked up the other pair of binoculars and pulled back a couple of leafy branches, creating a small window.

"Look there." He pointed down a steep slope on the other side of the trail.

Whit sat on her knees and steadied herself.

She gazed through the binoculars. At first she saw nothing but a blur, but as she adjusted the lens, she gasped at the clarity. With all the switchbacks on the trail, she had lost her sense of direction. Trees and brush prevented her from seeing every detail of the crime scene, but she smiled when she recognized Katie Riggs. A group of detectives gathered around what was presumably the victim, concealed now in a body bag.

"Good God!" She fished her cell phone out of her pocket, zoomed in, and took several shots.

"Yeah," Connor laughed. "Front-row seats, man! We were like . . . insane!"

Slowly, Whit lowered the phone and turned to the boys. "No wonder you two came back up here."

Impatient to get to the facts, Whit settled the boys back down on the blanket where they could talk. Nothing like a hot lead to pull her back on track. She set the recorder between them and, taking no chances, jotted notes on her steno pad as well.

After collecting names and phone numbers, she asked, "So you saw the killer?"

"Sure!" Jimmy said, nodding happily.

Connor shook his head, the shaggy brown hair flopping. "Not really, man. Well, we *did*, but like . . . it was super dark."

"I think it was Tuesday morning, but I'm not real sure," Jimmy said. "About four or five days ago."

"Yeah," Connor explained, "it was our second day here and we wanted to sleep on the rock, but Jimmy's mom wouldn't let us."

"Yeah, so we snuck out of our tent down by the camper early, like three or four in the morning, and hustled up here while it was still dark."

Connor's bright blue eyes widened. "It was sooo creepy at night!"

"That's the whole point, Connor!" Jimmy shook his head in disgust. He turned and spit into the brush, wiping his mouth with the back of his hand. "Anyway, it was super quiet up here that early in the morning, but we kept hearing these weird scraping noises. But we couldn't see anything 'cause it was so dark."

Whit nodded. The noise would likely travel over all the foliage to their perch at the top of the hill. Even now, she could hear an occasional voice or car door slamming from somewhere down below.

"Yeah, so we ate some Hershey bars and waited until dawn. That's when we saw the guy. The morning mist was out, so we couldn't get a very good look at him. And he wore a blue or gray baseball cap."

"Uh-huh," Jimmy broke in. "And the guy was diggin' with a frickin' shovel! How creepy is that?"

Connor shrugged. "At first we figured it was just a fisherman out digging for worms or something. But, like, it could be something sinister too. So we went down for a better look."

Whit frowned. "You went down to the road?"

"No way, man," Connor laughed. "We're not that *stupid*!"

Jimmy leaned forward and pulled the tree branches back. "See how the trail leads up around that bend to the other side of the hill? We got closer to the action, but by the time we got there, the guy was piling rocks and dirt over the hole he'd been diggin'."

"Yeah, and the mist from the river moved in real thick, so it was tough to see," Connor said.

Jimmy slapped him on the back. "So George of the Jungle here grabs a branch and tries to lean out over the hill." He laughed, the high-pitched glee of youth in puberty. "The branch broke and just about tossed his butt down the hill."

"Holy crap, that was a close call."

"So, what happened?" Whit asked.

"I saved his sorry a . . ." Jimmy laughed again, and sat back down. "He took a tumble, but I grabbed the belt loop on his shorts. He made a hell of a lot of noise. Especially when he screamed like a girl! Then the killer stopped moving rocks and hurried away. Like he was busted, man. Then we heard an engine start."

"So you never really saw his face?"

"I didn't scream like a girl!" Connor protested.

"Dude . . . you know you did!"

"Suck the big one, man!"

Whit interrupted. "Guys!"

Jimmy slapped Connor on the back. "Come on, man. It's cool."

Connor shrugged and gave up the fight, running the back of a dusty hand across his nose.

"Okay," Whit asked again, "so did you see his face?"

"Naw." Jimmy shook his head. "It was too dark and foggy. He was dressed in black, except I could see his arms. He was a white dude. Couldn't see his face 'cause of the cap." He leaned back thoughtfully, chewing his lip between the bright metal braces. "But, ya know, later we were talking about it, and I'm not sure, but we mighta heard a second car door."

"You mean the killer had someone with him?"

"Maybe. I don't know. Sounds echo up here."

"But you didn't see anyone else?"

"No. Just the one guy."

"What about later? Did you find his digging spot?"

"We tried." Connor scratched his head. "It's hard to tell from down there. The rocks and dirt all look the same."

"Until the bear dug her up," Jimmy added. "Now we know what that guy was up to. Burying a frickin' *body*!"

"Got a look at the truck, though." Connor held up his hand, and Jimmy high-fived him. "It was black with a king cab."

An eyewitness account. It doesn't get any better than that. Whit smiled. "Nice work, boys."

5

RIGGS CRUISED THROUGH the security gate at Judge Cordero's Tuscan-style home on Cherry Lane. On the crest of the long driveway, above the heavy-leafed shade trees, basked a terra-cotta–tile roof in the fading sunset. Near the gated entrance was a sign, one of many planted throughout Medford, asking its citizens to vote for Cordero as "Our Next State Representative." The judge had managed to keep his nose out of controversial rulings and was well respected. Riggs thought he'd probably win the seat without a problem.

She parked her company-issued Ford F-150, which sometimes served as the coroner's van, under a tall portico at the front entrance. Blackwell's demand for an expedited autopsy sent her scurrying to make all the arrangements with the medical examiner. As the ME detective, she acted as the eyes and the ears on the ground, helping Dr. Weldon piece together the evidence. The judge was expecting her. Reluctantly, she leaned across the seat and moved a pile of books she'd picked up from the library onto the floor: anatomy, forensic psychology, and three suspense novels. The Niki Francis case would dominate her life for the next few weeks. Personal reading was out of the question. She grabbed her iPad for the DocuSign on dental and medical records. She could have sent the documents via email, but she had a good rapport with the judge and wanted to ask some questions.

It was dusk, just after eight thirty, and the setting sun cast a pale-pink hue from the west in a darkening indigo sky. She stepped onto the cobblestone circular driveway. On the quiet hillside she heard the low rumble of thunder off in the distance. A warm breeze ruffled her short blonde hair but was little relief from the day's heat.

She crossed the courtyard, past a three-tiered fountain, and approached a heavy wooden entrance. Before she could knock, Judge Cordero opened the door.

"Detective Riggs." He was tanned, of medium height with a barrel chest, and usually cheerful, but tonight he appeared somber.

"Judge, nice to see you." It wasn't the first time she'd dropped in at Cordero's home on business or the occasional summer party.

She followed him through a vaulted great room and stepped out French doors to a pool patio. Riggs recognized the soft strains of a Hawaiian ukulele playing over hidden speakers, which didn't surprise her, since the judge and his wife owned a home in Hawaii.

The infinity swimming pool reflected pale-blue lights from beneath the water and appeared to flow endlessly off the edge of the hillside, where below spread a panoramic view of city lights. Beneath a vine-covered trellis sat Cordero's wife, Celeste, at a glass-top table, the remains of their evening meal, what looked like a Cobb salad, still in front of her. Both were dressed casually in shorts and cotton shirts with flip-flops.

Celeste, a slender woman in her late sixties, was incredibly well preserved. Riggs suspected a pinch and a tuck here or there. She wore bleach-blonde hair cut in full layers around her shoulders, a stark contrast with her dark tan. A social butterfly with a network that spanned the entire valley, she owned a flourishing real estate business. Her name recognition was better than her husband's.

Usually chatty and vivacious, Celeste seemed edgy. Riggs wondered if she'd interrupted a family dispute.

The judge offered Riggs a chair and some water, which he poured from an iced pitcher garnished with lemon slices. The air beneath the canopy of trumpet vines smelled of sweet honeysuckle, stirred by an almost pleasant breeze, as if the expansive pool had managed to cool the air around it. Riggs sat with a deep sigh.

Judge Cordero said, "I'll just go get my reading glasses from the study."

Celeste sat petting a black-and-white Pekinese dog with a pink ribbon in its hair. With each stroke, diamond rings glittered on four of her fingers, and a diamond-and-ruby tennis bracelet dangled from her tawny wrist. "Drink up, Detective; you'll die of dehydration in this heat. I had the devil of a time trying to convince a young couple from Washington that this is unusually hot weather for us. I thought Ed, the poor husband, might collapse from heatstroke."

Riggs sipped her ice water, enjoying the tart lemon aftertaste, and wished she could stay and relax for a while. Dread for the upcoming autopsy simmered beneath the surface. Performing an autopsy on someone she'd come to know in film and television was almost like slicing into a family member. Shifting from the macabre thought, she asked, "You showed houses today in this heat?"

"Oh, I never take a day off. Not really."

"Did you find a house for your clients?"

Celeste drained a martini glass with a graceful twist of her hand. "Made an offer an hour ago on a lovely little Tudor on the east side."

"Congratulations."

"Thank you. But I don't like to count my chickens. It's never a close until it's closed." She sighed heavily. "Still . . . we had good numbers this week, so I was ready to celebrate, at least until I heard about poor Niki."

The judge returned and stood at his wife's shoulder. "Detective Panetta came by earlier with a warrant to search Niki's property and told us the terrible news. It's tragic. We're heartbroken."

"Then you knew her well?"

"We had all become quite good friends." Celeste poured another martini from a metal tumbler. "I'd offer you a cosmo, Detective, but of course you're on duty."

"Thanks anyway." Riggs handed the iPad to the judge. "This is a warrant for dental and medical records."

Celeste shuddered. "To think you're talking about our dear Niki." Tears gathered, spilling over. She reached for her red linen napkin, dabbing at her eyes, black mascara running. "I'm sorry. This is just overwhelming. Niki murdered and buried . . . only to be eaten by a *bear*."

She'd obviously been hitting the juice, Riggs thought.

"I'm sorry you had to hear that." Riggs noticed for the first time an ashen tinge under her tan. She really was in shock.

The judge patted his wife's arm. "We were close friends of hers," he explained. "Her property, Casa Blanca, is just up the road, and when she was in town, we often dined together, either here or at her place."

Celeste leaned back in her chair. "I sold Niki her house five years ago. She bought the property hoping to get away from the prying eyes of Hollywood. She loved the ranch. She loved the privacy."

"So, no big parties at her home?" Riggs asked. "Celebrities over for the weekend?"

"She was not into the whole party scene. The most important thing in the world to her was her craft. Maximizing her acting ability. She hired acting coaches to stay at the ranch for a week at a time. Very studious. Not many people knew that about her."

"Any recent acting coaches staying with her?"

"No. Well, I'm not sure. I was in Hawaii for a week and very busy when I got back."

"Does she have family or friends who visit her?"

"She has a son who visits from time to time. Mark is a stockbroker in New York. I passed along his information to Detective Panetta."

"I assumed you knew her, but didn't realize you two were such close friends. I guess I shouldn't be surprised. You know everyone in town."

"Yes. I do know a lot of people. It's my business. But Niki was different. We really hit it off. We played tennis on the court behind her house twice a week. She often came over and lounged with me by the pool. She was a hoot. Always sharing some scandalous story she'd heard or seen while on set some-where." As if remembering those poolside chats, Celeste peered over the top of her martini with unseeing eyes. "You notice *she* managed to stay away from scandals. A very private person. Not many people knew she lived here. She was reclusive. Hardly left the ranch. When she did go into town, she usually had her bodyguard with her. With the surveillance at the house and her bodyguard, I don't see how anyone could have murdered her."

"Was she in conflict with anyone recently?"

She blinked suddenly; her gaze intensified, and Riggs thought she saw fear. "No. Unless . . . there's a great deal of competition to get the big movie roles. Sometimes the fur flies, if you know what I mean."

"So you think it's possible a competing actress could be capable of eliminating the competition?"

Celeste shrugged. "We are talking about millions and mil-lions of dollars, after all."

Riggs nodded. She found that theory a little difficult to believe, but people had been killed for much less. "Yes, we can certainly keep that in mind. Anything else?"

"Not that I recall." Celeste pursed her lips and looked away.

Riggs noted the evasiveness, the lack of eye contact, and wondered why. She pressed for more. "So, that's it, then? Nothing else comes to mind?"

"No," Celeste said swiftly. "I'm just trying to consider all the possibilities."

"When was the last time you spoke to her?"

"A week ago when I got back from Hawaii. She came over for a swim. We talked about going back to Eden Retreat for a spa day and shopping at Assez Boutique in Ashland." She twisted the stem of her martini glass between French-manicured fingers. "What a tragedy. I will miss her *terribly*. As will her fans."

"Did she appear nervous about anything lately?"

Celeste shook her head. "No. Everything seemed fine. She was looking forward to going to New York to film her next movie. She had plans to spend time with her son there."

"She was on good terms with her son?"

"Yes. Very much so."

"When was the last time you heard from her?"

She frowned. "She tried to contact me four days ago while I was having lunch with a client. I always turn off my phone at mealtimes. I think it's so rude that people talk on the phone right in front of you as if you're not there." She turned to the judge. "Don't you think so, darling?"

The judge nodded, his expression one of long-suffering. As if Celeste might frequently drink to excess. Perhaps his wife could be something of a prima donna.

She continued. "Anyway, my phone was off for about an hour. She left three messages asking me to call her right away." She shook her head sadly. "I wish she'd said what was so urgent, but by the time I called her back, there was no answer. I tried again that evening. A couple of days later I went over to her house, and Annie said they had just reported her missing. I've been worried sick ever since."

Riggs pressed. "Are you *sure* you don't have any idea why she called? She left no message at all?"

"No. Since Detective Panetta broke the news a few hours ago, I've been racking my brain, but I just don't know. I keep having this wave of regret. It splashes over me, leaving me chilled to the bone." She shuddered, spilling her martini; a bright-red stain seeped into the white linen tablecloth. "It's so disturbing. I feel like I failed her. Maybe, just maybe, I could have saved her if I'd *only* answered the phone."

With a pat on his wife's shoulder, the judge tried to comfort her. "Don't work yourself up, Celeste. You'll only make yourself sick. It's bad enough that Niki was murdered. *You* are certainly not responsible."

In answer, she polished off the rest of her martini.

The judge signed the warrant and handed it back to Riggs. "We hope you find Niki's murderer. Celeste and I will do whatever we can to help."

Riggs collected her iPad. "I just came from the initial briefing. Detectives canvassed the campground and the few businesses in the Applegate. So far we have nothing, but I'll keep you informed."

The judge nodded. "This comes at such a difficult time. Here I'm running for office, and now the media will descend on this town like locusts. Everything all of us do will be under a microscope. I'm not looking forward to that. Frankly, I find no joy in my bid for office now. Her death is a real blow."

Celeste rose to walk Riggs to the door and suddenly winced, rubbing her neck.

Riggs asked, "You okay?"

"Yes. Just a pinched nerve, I think. It's kept me from playing tennis this week, unfortunately. Well, anyway . . ." The Pekinese jumped down and trotted to the house, disappearing through a dog door. "I offered to help Niki's son coordinate the funeral. He's not handling it well. He refuses to accept it."

Riggs dug a business card out of her back pocket and handed it to her. "If you think of anything at all that might help the investigation, please call me. Sometimes it's the smallest details that solve a case."

Celeste collected the card, tears welling once again. "If I'd only answered my phone when Niki called."

"You couldn't know," Riggs reassured her. She walked away, the heat of the night heavy and miserable.

6

Floodlights illuminated the perimeter of the brick drive-way, momentarily blinding Riggs. She slowed past two white vans and five cruisers. Panetta's department-issued Ford Taurus sat behind the vans. Near the front steps, blocking the turn-around, sat a dark-blue Mercedes, probably belonging to the vic.

Casa Blanca Ranch spread across sixty-seven acres, with horse pastures, stables, guesthouse, pool, and tennis courts—all the amenities of the rich and famous. A wide-sweeping porch graced the two-story country estate. Every window was aglow, casting pale-yellow shadows into the night as detectives searched the most intimate places of Niki's home.

The famous recluse had moved to this quiet town in the Rogue Valley to lead a very private life. Now, every dark secret would be exposed to the eyes of strangers. Her privacy, prob-ably every famous person's most prized possession, now onstage, spotlights glaring into every crack and crevice.

A police officer stood at the front door, watching Riggs park her car. As she approached the steps, he greeted her. "Good evening, Detective Riggs."

"Hey, Gunter. How's it going?" She waited while he logged her in. Gunter was in his midtwenties, first year on the job.

"Not a lot of progress in there, from what I hear. Detective Panetta is in the study. Just make a right down the hall and through the kitchen. Fancy place. There's even a home theater that seats twelve people! Must be nice."

A light breeze smelling of damp earth stirred the night air.

Riggs glanced up at the house. "Yes, except it didn't end well."

She climbed the porch steps and paused on the veranda, taking note of the white wicker furniture and an impressive display of colorful flowers in hanging pots. No Hollywood glitz here. She imagined Niki sitting on the patio in the morning with a cup of tea, relaxed, away from prying eyes. What a shame. Now the beautiful actress lay in a body bag, her life over without warning.

At the door, she slipped a pair of paper booties over her shoes and stepped inside.

The dark, cherry-stained hardwood floor glistened under a glowing chandelier showcasing a sweeping staircase. Across the room, a row of glass doors led to what she presumed was the back porch. A uniformed officer stood guard. She waved and proceeded down the hall.

"I don't care! Just bag it!" Panetta stormed from another part of the house.

Riggs followed his irate voice through an enormous kitchen with a stone fireplace, where a huge Great Dane was resting in the doorway. The dog hardly lifted his horselike head as she stepped over his legs, the brown eyes disinterested, as if somehow a dark depression had settled into his soul. Poor guy would never see his owner again. Maybe he knew.

She moved down a curving hall and passed two disgruntled uniformed officers carrying brown paper bags wrapped in plastic. She nodded as they passed. Eventually she found a book-lined study. Here the air smelled richly of firewood. No gas fireplace for Niki. Stacks of wood and kindling sat on the grand hearth. She'd had no need of a fire the past few months, but the books had picked up the smoky scent from previous winters.

The room had an open-beamed ceiling, a red leather sectional, a flat-screen television on the opposite wall, and several tables stacked with reading materials. The two-story walls were lined with books from floor to ceiling. A tech guy hunched over a computer desk in the corner, loading a laptop into a box.

"Hey, Panetta. Anything new?" she asked, pretty sure of his response.

His dark frown said it all. "Blackwell's hell on wheels. The DA is breathing down his neck on this one. So far, the mayor, the chief, and the governor have put their two cents in, so Blackwell was forced to welcome in the FBI. He's briefing them now. Which is smart anyway. We'll have access to so much more with their help." He cursed under his breath. "After two hours of combing through everything here, we've found nothing of overt usefulness."

The tech guy hurried away down the hall with the computer, as if he'd rather be anywhere else.

"I've never seen you so intense." She studied his scowling face. "You're stressed about your divorce. When's it final?"

"Yesterday." He rubbed tired eyes. "Twenty-seven years of marriage . . . *gone.*"

Riggs tried to encourage him. "You did everything you could to save it. After your wife went through two rounds of failed addiction recovery, you retired earlier than you wanted to and moved here so Ellen could be with her family. I don't know anything else you could have done. She has a disease, and there's nothing you can do about that." This high-profile case would put all of them under a lot of stress. He needed to stay focused. "It will get better in time. For now, just try to put your mind on your work so you're not dwelling on your divorce."

He sighed. "You're right. You're right. It's just that . . . not to sound arrogant, but I've always achieved whatever I put my mind to. But I can't beat this, no matter how hard I try. For the first time in my life, I feel like a failure. I can hardly say the word out loud. It doesn't sit well."

"You can't win against your wife's addiction. That's something she has to face on her own."

"Yeah. But I feel responsible, because I was gone so often on missions. She was lonely, always afraid I would come back in a body bag. Between the military and my service with the Bureau . . . let's just say I wasn't home much. She practically raised our son on her own. In the end, she attempted suicide." He shuddered at the memory. "That's when we moved here, to be near her family. I was so sure we could fix it, but now that I look back, I think my marriage was the one thing in my life that I didn't give a hundred and ten percent. My most intimate mission, failed."

Those brown eyes, which reflected the wars he'd battled, focused on her, and for a moment she glimpsed the hard edge of a warrior's heart, his steel determination, and realized just how far he had fallen from his own personal grace. He was no longer an admired and envied member of the elite Delta Force or the FBI's Hostage Rescue Team. Now he was a mere detective in a small town, recently suspended from active duty and with a wife who'd left him for a drunk. She could see it on his face. Shame cast its humiliating shadow over his impeccable accomplishments.

Riggs would not stand for it. "You did what you were put on this earth to do, Panetta. You served in two of the most respected military units in the world. Few people are cut out for that kind of life. And instead of retiring, you were in a position to move up the chain to a top political post, and you know it. But you've *chosen* to support your family. Granted, a little too late, but you have nothing to be ashamed of. There are lots of wives who cope with men in action and don't turn to alcohol. She knew who she was marrying when she married you. You both just misjudged *her* strength. Like I said, it will get better. Just give it time."

He half smiled, his dark-brown eyes crinkling at the corners, his voice calm and controlled. "I bet you mothered your older brothers too."

She nodded, relaxing a little. "You might say I was the peace-keeper. Someone had to be."

"That fits." He cocked his head to the side, thinking. "What about your mother?"

"She died of cancer when I was eight." The thought never failed to tighten her throat, faded grief skimming just under the surface. "Dad did his best; he was a cop too, you know, but working two jobs, he wasn't around much."

"Sounds like cancer runs in the family?"

"Yeah." She glanced down at the tattoo on the inside of her wrist, inexplicably reassured at the sight of the cross and rosary beads. Not that her family had attended church much when she was growing up, except maybe on holidays. She had distinct memories of her mother praying for her father, and the Bible tucked into her mother's nightstand. A Bible she still held dear and kept in her own nightstand drawer. It wasn't much of a legacy, but she felt it was an important one.

A strident voice raised in anger carried down the hall.

"That's the vic's son." Panetta grimaced as if in pain. "He showed up an hour ago. He jumped on a plane from New York as soon as he heard his mother was officially missing late last night. He's decided to challenge my search warrant, because he doesn't believe his mother is dead. In denial or something. He's somewhere in the house 'making a few calls.' Probably to an attorney. I'm having one of the patrol officers escort him to the morgue for viewing. I advised him against it since the housekeeper already ID'd her, but he's insisting."

"I guess you can't blame him. Once the guy sees his mom, he'll probably calm down and let us do our job."

"That's what I thought."

"Did you get a chance to question the housekeeper again?"

"Yeah. Pretty much the same info from the missing persons report."

"What about the bodyguard?"

"He was helping the horse trainer with a couple of the horses that afternoon." He sighed, working his shoulders in a rotation, as if alleviating the stress in his muscles. "One thing I know, this is not the murder scene. We've reviewed the video cameras from the front and back entrances, and no one came in or out before or after we saw Niki get into her car and drive away at one forty-eight on Monday afternoon, except the housekeeper. When the vic left the house on the video, she was wearing the same clothes we found her buried in."

"That coincides with approximate time of death."

He nodded. "At least that's something."

As an avid reader, Riggs admired the selection of books. "Looks like she enjoyed reading. Perhaps something of a student? According to Celeste Cordero, she studied her craft and took acting very seriously."

"Seems like it. The housekeeper said she pretty much lived in this room when she was home in the winter."

"Mind if I browse?"

"Help yourself." Panetta stepped over to the desk in the corner, sifting through drawers.

With a thoughtful eye, she shot pictures of the room, then pulled latex gloves from her pants pocket and put them on. Her gloved fingers traced the titles of several hardbound books in the bookcase—some popular fiction, a complete collection of classic literature, art and theater and history books. Fitness magazines and several medical journals lay fanned out on the coffee table along with two movie scripts Niki had probably been considering. Riggs picked up a *New England Journal of Medicine*; the page was folded back to a story on cancer research. Another journal had been paper-clipped on a lengthy article about spinal injuries.

Riggs asked Panetta, "Do you know if Niki had ever been diagnosed with cancer?"

"Not that I know of. Why?"

"That's what she was reading about." It was like déjà vu. The first weeks after being diagnosed with melanoma, Riggs had inundated herself with information on current cancer treatments, health foods, natural remedies, and so on, taken from books, journals, and the internet. Her interest in medical issues perked up, so when a position opened with the medical examiner's office, she applied. Once accepted, she immediately transferred from homicide. She eagerly attended every training course available. All things that led to death fascinated her. Not that she was obsessed or anything—even though Richard, her husband and a solid, no-nonsense, down-to-earth prosecuting attorney for the state, had accused her of just that. He wasn't too keen on her transfer to the ME's office and insisted she'd developed a morbid curiosity about death. In her defense, she'd contemplated a nursing degree in college, but after one of the girls in her dorm went missing and was never found, her curiosity turned to criminology instead.

It just seemed odd for Niki to have all this focus on medical issues unless she was sick. "What about a spinal injury? Did the housekeeper say anything about her health?"

"No. Except that she had complained of a headache and nausea last week and refused lunch on Monday. That was the last time she was seen alive." He rubbed his chin thoughtfully. "Her kitchen is stocked with thousands of dollars of health foods, supplements, that kind of thing. She also has a pretty extensive gym, but don't all actors? They have to stay in shape to make the big bucks. Especially cougars."

"True." Riggs rummaged through the other medical journals and fitness magazines. The lady had obviously been interested in staying healthy. Panetta was right. Actresses were in fierce competition for prime roles. And Niki was definitely in the cougar category, competing against much younger women.

Riggs wandered down the hall and up the sweeping stair-case to the master bedroom. This would be the most intimate room in the house and should hold clues to Niki's personal life.

Unprepared for the grandeur, she felt her jaw drop when she entered the massive room. Unlike the study with its functional, cozy furniture, the bedroom screamed self-indulgent luxury, bathed in gold and cream colors fit for royalty. Rich perfume permeated the air, so strong it was as if Niki had just slipped from the room. This was hardly Riggs's first residence search, but in the hushed quiet she suddenly felt like an intruder, like Niki would walk in at any moment. Of course she knew better, but the sensation persisted. Maybe because she had a guilty curiosity about how the famous actress had actually lived that had nothing to do with police procedure. A natural curiosity, she supposed.

She shot photos of the huge canopy-draped bed with its gold silk–padded headboard and cascading gold-embroidered white drapes. The lounge area in the center of the room had a cream couch and chairs with a few gold accents. The gold chandelier in the arched ceiling dangled crystals and cream shades. It reminded her of a tour she'd once taken of the Biltmore Estate in North Carolina.

She crossed to the nightstand, which was covered in fine powder. The room had already been tested for prints. Riggs opened the drawer, oddly surprised to find a Bible. She flipped through it, reading some of the underlined passages.

Also in the drawer was a book on bipolar disorder, and a well-frayed script. Apparently in Niki's upcoming shoot in New York, she'd been scheduled to portray a teacher suffering from bipolar disorder who eventually became teacher of the year. Riggs wondered who else might have wanted that role and if they might have been willing to kill for it.

Another nutritional book at the bottom of the drawer held a couple of local restaurant menus offering organic ingredients and a brochure for Eden Retreat. She opened the brochure. At the top of the page, Niki had written *REST*. There was no date. Maybe she'd gone there to rest after filming a movie. The only other items were a bottle of melatonin and some Tylenol. So the actress probably had trouble sleeping and suffered from headaches or joint pain. Fanning all the drawer's contents out on the bed, Riggs shot a picture.

Someone connected to any of these fragments of Niki's life might be the killer. A jealous actor competing for the next Oscar role, a jilted lover, even a crazed fan.

"Anything?" Panetta asked from directly behind her shoulder.

She jumped nearly out of her skin. "I hate it when you do that! Sneak up on me."

"Must be my pantherlike stride," he said with his quirky smile.

Riggs inhaled slowly to steady her pulse. At least Panetta appeared to be in a better mood. He reminded her of her oldest brother, Ben. He had that same gift of banter, but when it came to serious matters of the heart, he stuffed his emotions until he was ready to explode. "Any luck with her planner?"

"No. I'm getting her cell phone records. I've collected all the data from her email account. She deleted everything up to the day she disappeared, so we're taking the computer to the lab. I think we're going to have a very wide net for this one. A lot of ground to cover."

"Yes, I suppose so, but I'd like to start with her medical records. Where can I find the housekeeper?" With her help, she might be able to reach Niki's doctor tonight. It would facilitate the morning's report.

"She's in her suite on the other side of the kitchen. She went straight to bed after viewing the body. Autopsy still on for ten?"

"That's the plan."

With wry humor, he said, "Can't wait. You can't get that kind of blood and guts at the movies. I'm gonna go hunt down a cup of coffee." With a salute, he disappeared through the door, his retreating footsteps soundless.

Riggs found the housekeeper heavily sedated in her room but managed to get Niki's physician's data, and asked if the actress had ever had any serious health issues.

"Actually, she looked pretty good." Annie said, shaking her head. In her midthirties and stout, she had the faintest of British accents. A swath of dark hair dislodged from a high ponytail and fell across her brow, half shielding a red-rimmed nose. She'd clearly been crying. She sniffed as if to prove the point, and clutched the lapels of her white terry cloth robe. "In fact, I kinda thought she'd had a few nips and tucks. Secret, of course, but I never saw. She even stopped using reading glasses. Said she didn't need them. Kinda odd. But she might have had that Lasik surgery. I don't know. Seein' her tonight was . . ." She brought a tissue up to her nose, eyes squeezed shut.

"I'm sorry you had to go through that."

"I've worked for her going on six years. Moved up from LA with her. She wasn't snobby like some of those actresses that come by. She made me family."

"She seemed like a nice person. Anything else happen the past week or two? New friends? Old friends? Anyone come into the picture?"

Annie shook her head sadly. "It was pretty quiet the past month. When she's studying for a new movie, she doesn't socialize all that much. Always studying for the new role. She visited some with Celeste Cordero, up the road. And of course her weekly visits to her psychiatrist."

"Who was that?"

"Dr. Heinemann at Eden Retreat. She's been seein' him for several years now. Swears he does magic. 'Course Niki and Celeste go to the retreat for massage therapies as well. She even bought me the full spa package last Christmas." Her face crumpled at the memory.

Riggs reached out and squeezed her hand. "Did you notice anything else?"

"No." She kept her head down. "Just that she looked especially happy and healthy the past few months; well . . . until that last few days." Her head suddenly snapped up, face tearstained. "Oh, I'd nearly forgotten. Maybe I was imaginin' stuff, but I thought I saw fear in her eyes that last morning. I was passing through the kitchen just as she got off the phone and could have sworn she was frightened. For a moment I thought she'd gotten bad news about her son or something."

"Who was she talking to?"

"Don't know. I asked if everything was all right, and she nodded but didn't say anything." Annie shrugged her shoulders. "I didn't want to pry, so I just gathered my purse and shopping list, and that was the last time I saw her."

"Did you hear any of her conversation?"

"No. Wish I had."

Panetta would pay close attention to all the calls that last day from her cell phone records, but Riggs would remind him of that call anyway.

For the next thirty minutes Riggs poked around in Niki's kitchen, photographing all the health products and vitamins. She turned all the items to face label out and shot another picture. Many had labels from Eden Retreat. She'd pay a follow-up visit to the spa tomorrow. Stepping back, she eyed the pantry. A virtual health food store was lined up shelf after shelf. By the time she left the kitchen, Riggs felt she understood Niki's drive for perfection, because that's what it really was. More like an obsession.

Unfortunately for Niki, all that effort and energy hadn't prolonged her life after all.

7

Located downtown in an old brick building, the *Medford Daily Chronicle* was sandwiched between Engelhard's Linen Supply and the Gospel Mission's soup kitchen. The interior of the building had been renovated many times over the years, and as newspaper budgets had fallen fast with the advent of twenty-four-hour television news and the internet, which siphoned off advertising dollars, the carpets and lighting could have used a good influx of hard cash. The place smelled like an old leather shoe. The paper had transitioned to online news a few years before Whit arrived, thanks to a team of young media geeks.

The newsroom, located on the second floor, housed fourteen desks arranged in huddled cubicles, which were mostly vacant now—except for the sports reporter in the opposite corner, as everyone had filed their stories and gone home for the day. It was well past nine and the night crew had settled into their jobs. Travis, one of the copy editors, cruised down the hall to the lunchroom for some leftover cake. Forsythe and Clayburn were working on page layout. Their familiar voices drifted to Whit where she sat at her desk, observing the summer storm through dark glass. The scanner chatter buzzed in the background, mingling with television news, which was monitored by a couple of sleepy interns.

Whit could practically feel the deadline chewing away at her frayed nerves. Normally she fed off the adrenaline of an approaching deadline. Journalists were generally adrenaline junkies. She was no different than most, but that was before . . .

She cracked her knuckles one at a time, and with a deep breath she turned and faced her computer. Precious minutes ticked by as her hands hovered over the keyboard. Nothing.

Damn!

She pictured Stu's face turning purple at the thought of a missed deadline that would leave a big hole in the paper. No, better still, he'd pace behind her and use little frantic gestures with his hands and rattle off pithy little machine gun–style sentences: "Make it snappy. Put the story to bed. Bust it out. Deadlines don't wait." And so on.

Cursing under her breath, she sat drumming her fingers on the desk and watched flashes of lightning. Rivulets of rain, reflecting the city lights, trailed like glitter down the windows. Nothing set the mood to write like a good storm. Unfortunately, the nightmare of today's flashback repeated like a reel playing in a loop, tormenting her with horrible clarity of that dreadful day in Afghanistan. Try as she might, this time she couldn't push the images into the recesses of her mind.

The profound pain of knowing she had failed him, urged him to his death even, was like nothing she'd ever experienced. Every ounce of energy in her begged to hit rewind. If only she could relive it. She'd do it all differently. At the very least, she might have tried to bargain with their captors. Tried to buy some time. The finality of John's death left a well of almost unbearable pain. A deep ache she feared would never leave her.

If John were here, he'd say, "Eyes on the story." Because that's how he saw the world: through the lens of his camera. He was a conduit that brought to light the best and the worst of humanity. So was she. This was not a job she could walk away from. It was *who* she was. The more she focused on her job, the less she had to think about Afghanistan.

Eyes on the story.

Yes. She could lean on John's strength until hers returned. He might not be there physically, but he was there in every other way. She could imagine him with her now. By her side, at least in spirit.

Feeling calmer now, she flipped through her steno pad; the interview notes slowly drew her back into the story. Facts for the fire were scarce. She had to fill in with backstory. The fire chief had confirmed a fatality. The victim's wife had identified the body and confirmed Bobby Delano as the deceased. Cause of death "undetermined" pending the autopsy report. The fire was listed as suspicious and still under investigation.

Barbecue boy, Jim Jorgensen, had suggested that Bo Delano was probably drunk and lit the house on fire by mistake. After witnessing Delano wandering around his front yard in a pair of pajama bottoms mumbling to himself the day of the fire, Jorgensen had ventured across the street to ask Delano if he was all right, and the attorney had flipped him off.

Several phone calls to Delano's wife proved futile, so Whit gathered details from the fire chief, neighbors, and work associates. According to all of them, Delano did *not* have a drinking problem. He was health conscious and belonged to a running club from which he had won numerous first-, second- , and third place awards. But clearly he had *some* kind of a problem. Most people did not like to speak ill of the dead, so her initial interviews were not as productive as she would have liked. She needed to reinterview Delano's work associates, put a little pressure on them. Maybe they would open up. Instinct told her to dig deeper, and she would, tomorrow.

Gradually the story took shape in her mind. A troubled man who'd lived a respectable life as a highly regarded attorney with a caring wife and family, whose life suddenly slid out of control and ended with bizarre behavior that led to a separated marriage, an untimely death, and the charred ruins of his million-dollar home.

Not to be jaded, but it sounded like Mr. Delano had been on drugs. She would never insinuate that in her story, but that's probably where her investigation would lead.

Back in the saddle, Whit's fingers flew over the keyboard. The tapping keys and pelting rain were music to her ears. She wrapped up her thirteen-inch story, ran the spell check, and emailed her work to Travis in layout. Today's story would run with just the facts. She no longer had a leisurely week of collecting facts to weave together for an in-depth report as she had at the *L.A. Times*. A small newspaper ran with a skeleton crew, and each reporter pumped out multiple stories at once. She had adjusted to the pace. Hit it and quit it. She would write a follow-up feature, and it would take a few more days to gather the facts and collaborate witnesses and get the coroner's report.

She clicked on a new screen and began the lead for her Applegate story.

Her cell phone buzzed. Whit smiled. The text was from her fifteen-year-old daughter, Emma.

Mother . . . when are you coming home?

Emma had yet to adjust to *not* having a full-time mom at her disposal. Since John's death, Emma seemed more clingy, while Jordan, a year older and driving on her own, kept pushing her away. The truth was that both girls were more emotional and needy in their own way. Working outside the house was like a guilty pleasure.

You know I have to work late tonight. Are you all right?

Yes. Jordan and I made mac'n cheese for dinner. Im bored.

Enjoy it while you can. School starts next week.

Ugh!

Get some sleep its after 10

Reggie misses you!!!

Whit's thirty-two-pound fawn pug was a spoiled beast who slept in her bed and snored like a drunken fat man. He had been a gift from her dad six months ago, so "she wouldn't be lonely." Within a few days he had captured her heart.

Give him a kiss for me. And Jordan too. Is she all right?

Yes. She's watching the history channel. Boring! I went downstairs. Watched the Kardashians.

Lovely choice. Are the doors locked?

Yes.

Okay. Double check. I really have to go. Good nite. Love you.

Love you too!

At the sound of whistling, Whit glanced up.

Bryan, the lanky photographer, his shaggy brown hair flopping over his eyes, grinned over the top of her cubby. "Greetings, McKenna. I come bearing gifts."

She perked up. "What have you got?"

"Only the crime-photo equivalent to the *Mona Lisa*." His white T-shirt was smeared with mud, and an angry-looking red scratch puckered the skin along his forearm.

"What happened?"

"Mayhem in the line of duty. I slipped down the embankment!" He held up his arm to reveal a shallow gash from his wrist to his elbow. "Ripped my arm on a tree branch. I had to crawl back up through clusters of poison oak. I'm doomed tomorrow."

"So we both took a header today." She stuck her leg out from under the desk so he could see her scraped knee, now swollen and bruised. "I was standing too close to the house fire when it blew."

"Cool." He nodded slowly, brows raised with new respect. "Took one for the team. Excellent."

Whit smiled. "Where're the pics?"

He nudged his chin toward her computer. "Already uploaded them."

She clicked into the *Chronicle*'s photo gallery, and a group of pictures of the crime scene near Gin Lin Trail appeared on the screen. One image, a close-up of the body bag being lifted to the gurney while emergency personnel stood in the background, would definitely make the front page. "Great shot!"

"Pulitzer, baby. Pulitzer."

"You'd have my vote. Wish we knew who was in that bag." The second photo showed a bear lying on its back. "Is this the bear that dug up the body?"

Bryan nodded. "Yeah. The flesh-eating bear crossed the river, and before it decided I was good eatin', the Department of Fish and Wildlife took him down with a tranquilizer gun."

"What did they do with him?"

He shrugged skinny shoulders. "Don't know."

"I'll find out." After reviewing the photos again, Whit pointed to two of them. "Let's run these."

"Great minds think alike. My fave, too. I'll pass them over to page layout. I caught some video for the online rag as well."

"Well, hold on, hotshot. I also got a few pics today. Mine aren't as good because they were taken with my iPhone, but they'll do for second page." She showed him her crime scene shots, and he grudgingly gave her credit for scoping out an aerial scene.

"I'll sharpen those up a bit for you."

"Thanks."

He turned abruptly, scratching his left arm. "I'm off to shower, then grab a pizza and beer with some buddies. Ciao!"

"See ya."

After rereading her notes for the Applegate story, she decided that the fisherman, Mr. Wolcott, provided a nice descriptive scene. However, a key element was missing—the *who*. The police had not ID'd the body yet, or so they'd said. But it was officially a murder investigation, so she could run with that.

Thank God her sleuthing had uncovered the kids who'd witnessed the killer burying the body. She couldn't use their names because they were under eighteen, and she wanted to protect their identities anyway, but she could certainly use their eyewitness account, and with any luck trade the information with Detective Riggs. Unless the cops had found the kids too, but that wasn't likely. She'd been unable to persuade them to come back to camp. They refused to leave their eagle-eye vantage point on the rock.

Whit popped a piece of spearmint gum into her mouth and read local missing persons reports for the past month. Only one other adult had been reported as such, and that was a male in his seventies. She didn't have enough information to search NamUs—National Missing and Unidentified Persons—which collected data from across the nation.

She wrote diligently for the next hour, the police scanner a muted static in the background. She paused to gather murder statistics for Jackson County and fleshed out the story with some history of the last murder victim found buried in the Applegate. A fifteen-year-old girl who'd disappeared walking to church, her bones discovered twelve years later. Whit had recently covered the murder trial, all the while thinking of her own daughters. Both were fiercely independent but still vulnerable and naïve, the very attitude that made young women easy pickings for creeps.

The Gin Lin Trail victim was a fresh homicide with fresh leads. She needed more information.

Whit reached for her phone and sent a text to Riggs.

Quid pro quo.

8

A BRIEF THUNDERSTORM HAD passed, and now a humid quiet settled over the valley. The night air glowed yellow beneath the parking lights as Riggs watched the transport van back into the delivery bay of the Oregon State Police Crime Lab in Central Point, where the medical examiner's facilities were located. She noted the time of arrival on her notepad: 10:01 p.m. She'd tailed the van from the hospital where Niki's body had undergone x-ray procedures. Because this was a criminal case, she kept a visual on the body during transport to maintain chain of custody at all times.

A couple of local TV vans had also followed, probably wrapping up last-minute video for the early morning shows. So far they had not intruded, so she had no problem. If the news crews had any idea who they were trailing, they'd storm the gates for close-ups and questions. No one, not even the transport crew or the x-ray technician, knew the identity of the victim found in the Applegate. X-rays were usually taken with the body bag in place, so this case seemed no different to the hospital tech. He had asked a few questions, but Riggs gave vague answers. So far, so good.

She sipped the remains of a green smoothie that Richard had dropped off at the hospital. Bolstering her immune system had been a priority after chemo. He had purchased an industrial-strength Vitamix and made it a personal mission to feed her a smoothie three or four times a week. He was not happy with her long hours and insisted on making his "quick kick" tonight. This one had spinach, kale, arugula lettuce, coconut milk, avocado, apple, strawberries, blueberries, flax seeds, and ice made with purified water. The fruit made the whole thing bearable, though it still tasted slightly bitter. Her empty stomach was less discerning and zealously absorbed the chilled liquid.

She drove into the loading bay and parked next to the van. She stepped out of the truck as the heavy metal door rolled to a close behind her with a tomblike thud.

The attendants efficiently unloaded the body and wheeled the gurney through the receiving doors straight into the windowless autopsy room, which housed only one autopsy bay and a refrigerated wall unit large enough for six cadavers.

Her phone buzzed with an incoming text. Riggs unclipped her phone from her belt, saw the message from Whit, and smiled. She was so proud of Whit for getting back on track with her career. However, their relationship had certainly been put through a ring of fire because of their opposing jobs. The first month back on the job, Whit traded information on an apparent suicide, having discovered evidence that exposed the victim's relative as a potential murderer, but Riggs already had the information and refused to provide a lead in return. A level of trust had to be established. Whit was a professional and understood the nature of informant trades, so the situation resolved itself, but not without a few days of tension. They also had a mutual agreement that their friendship was not a card on the table to be played in place of a real lead.

She returned the text to Whit. They would meet at Porter's later and negotiate a trade.

The attendants parked the gurney in the autopsy bay.

Dr. Bruce Weldon, the medical examiner for Jackson County, thanked the attendants and sent them on their way. He waited until the door closed behind them, then addressed the corpse in his usual dramatic fashion.

"What a privilege, and what a sad occasion, dear Ms. Francis. If only I could have met you under better circumstances."

He was a beefy sixty-two-year-old with thick, dark, often-disheveled hair crowning a hulking six-foot-five frame and hands like padded gloves. He was a wine connoisseur and lover of literary classics who frequented the Ashland Shakespeare Festival and nursed a small winery he'd inherited from his brother. It was no secret he liked his vino in his off hours.

Riggs suspected every autopsy was a stage performance for Weldon. Each case was a dark mystery to be solved. Horrible twists of fate and the macabre fascinated him. He was unusual, to say the least, but seemingly harmless. She humored his propensity for drama, convinced that he had missed his true calling: acting. Ironically, Niki Francis could not have chosen a more perfect medical examiner to be her costar for her final scene on earth.

In the locker room, Riggs quickly changed into scrubs. Running water into the sink, she used a bar of soap and scrubbed the day's grime from her face, then applied a light moisturizer. After a quick glance in the mirror, she noted the shadows beneath her gray eyes, a lingering effect of chemo. Her gaze fell on the paper-thin scar that trailed alongside her hairline and puckered just slightly under her ear. She didn't mind the scar. Like so many other cancer survivors, she accepted it as a badge of courage.

Refreshed and confident, she stepped into the autopsy bay, slid a plastic bib over her scrubs, gloved up, and joined Dr. Weldon in examining the x-rays.

Under the whir of ceiling fans, neither talked as they prepped for the coming procedures. They were fully aware of the magnitude of their work this night. They would document everything diligently. The recorder, with suspended mic, was already turned on. The murder of Niki Francis, like the deaths of Whitney Houston and other mega-celebrities, would no doubt generate a media frenzy, especially given the nature of her demise.

Detective Panetta quietly stepped through the door and reached into the linen basket for a surgical gown. Though his expression was grim, he teased, "Looks like I got the lucky straw tonight."

Weldon took him seriously. "That's true enough. We don't often get celebrities in this neck of the woods. I would've preferred to conduct the autopsy in the morning, though." He shook his head. "Lots of people around here are feeling threatened. Afraid this case will be confiscated right out of our hands. Then, if something goes wrong, all we're left with is the blame and none of the credit."

Panetta nodded. "I have it on good authority that the DA and others want some answers *before* they face the national media." He slipped the gown over his street clothes and bent to cover his shoes with booties.

Weldon addressed the corpse. "Ms. Niki Francis, it's show time."

Riggs and Weldon put on clear plastic face shields. Panetta arranged his paper mask over his mouth and nose and nodded.

Weldon snipped the tag from the body bag. "Note the time: ten oh eight PM."

They studied the cadaver for any obvious clues. The fingernails and toenails were scraped and cut to the quick and put in marked plastic bags; the clothes were carefully cut off and set aside for Riggs to tag and photograph later. They examined the external body, which was bloated now from internal gases, the skin on the victim's back a marbled blue.

Weldon commented, "She was lying on her back for the few hours after she died, according to the livor mortis. There are no signs of defense wounds or bruising."

"No broken bones, except for the bear attack, of course," Riggs said, stepping around the table as she photographed the body. She leaned over the vic's face. "There is the suggestion of a handprint on her cheekbone. A slight bruising? Do you see it?"

"Hmmm. You're right. That might suggest suffocation. A hand over the mouth and nose." Dr. Weldon shifted his focus to the x-rays glowing from the wall screen. "This one is a bit curious. X-ray number four."

Riggs approached the screen with a sense of foreboding. She pointed to a gray area near the spine at the base of the skull. "Looks like the cervical vertebra has a tumor, which I find very interesting, considering some reading material we found at the vic's house this evening. This *is* a tumor, right, Dr. Weldon?"

"Very possibly." He pushed his bifocals higher up on his bulbous nose. "There's calcification as well. Hmmm. Could be a bone spur from an old injury. Let's see when we get in there."

Riggs made eye contact with Panetta, who inclined his head. They silently agreed that the actress might have known about the tumor because of the medical journals found in her study. If Niki knew, then she must have sought treatment from her doctor, but as of yet Riggs had not heard back from her primary care physician to confirm. Not that it had any bearing on the case, but every piece of the puzzle had to be gathered and assembled. The people closest were interrogated first, then the net spread out from there. In this case, all possible contacts had to be investigated nearly all at once. Tonight the team was assisted by every available patrolman. The entire network of city, county, state, and federal law enforcement were scouring every possible lead. And all of them were waiting for the autopsy report.

Weldon used a scalpel to make the Y-incision from each shoulder, down the middle of the stomach, making a short jog around the belly button and down to the pubic bone, exposing the stomach and chest. It always amazed Riggs how quickly the ME worked, slashing away at the layers of skin, cartilage, and muscle like a butcher at your local grocery store. The dead had no need of meticulous lifesaving surgery, though she found Dr. Weldon's skills surprisingly precise.

The smell of rotten flesh and bacteria that had grown in the vic's intestines amplified, wafting into the small confines of the room, settling in Riggs's nose and the back of her throat, even into the pores of her skin.

Panetta blinked a few times but said nothing.

In minutes, they became accustomed to the smell, their bodies adapting. The natural urge to abandon the task passed with a sense of relief. Riggs felt her shoulders relax, and she focused entirely on the possibility of finding the cause of death.

"You could pass for a much younger woman, my dear." Weldon sliced the flesh to the pubic bone. "You're lean and obviously took good care of yourself. No self-indulgence here."

Riggs met Panetta's gaze over the victim's body. They both flicked a glance at Weldon's wide girth bulging under the surgical gown. She'd wondered how he could continue his path to obesity after viewing, up close and personal, the effects on the human body that an unhealthy lifestyle could produce. More aware than ever of her own body after surviving cancer—and after months of watching Weldon slice through mounds of yellow fat—Riggs was very particular about her diet.

Weldon picked up a pair of garden shears and cracked through the ribs, opening the chest cavity.

Panetta grimaced, cringing with each hard snap of bone.

Riggs had gotten used to the smells and noises of the autopsy room to a certain extent over the past eight months. However, bone cracking still had the power to make her cringe. She asked Panetta, "Are you all right?"

"I have to admit," Panetta said from behind his surgical mask, "my trips down the gardening aisle at Home Depot are not as pleasant as they once were."

Weldon paused, gardening shears in hand, then addressed the corpse again. "You don't mind the bone snappin', do ya, Ms. Niki Francis? You just want justice. I hear ya. You've come to the right place. I'm not gonna' let ya down." He proceeded to chop the ribs loose.

Riggs lifted the chest plate and ribs, setting them on a nearby table. They began scooping blood and decomposing fluids from the chest cavity into a plastic flask for measuring.

She photographed and weighed each organ, taking careful notes; then Weldon sliced them open, searching for any abnormalities. Riggs selected a portion from each cut and placed them into containers filled with formalin for further testing. It was hard not to think of Niki Francis as she remembered her in the movies. She'd never helped with an autopsy where she knew the corpse, because it definitely made the process personal. It was unnerving.

Weldon slid his hand under the victim's neck. "I can feel the tumor. That was causing you some grief, wasn't it, Ms. Francis? Well, we'll just see about that." He turned to Riggs. "Stitch her back together so we can turn her over. I'd like to incise the tumor now."

The organ remains were transferred to a plastic bag, which Riggs pressed into the body cavity, and returned the chest plate to its original position. She stitched the Y-incision closed with large, zigzag stitches.

With little effort they rolled the body over. Riggs tucked the chin and handed Dr. Weldon the scalpel again.

He worked his way down, slicing quickly through muscles and finally exposing the vertebrae. "Oh my." He paused, silent for so long Riggs wondered if he was all right.

"Dr. Weldon?"

He finally nodded confirmation to himself. "Looks like an osteochondroma."

"What's that?" Panetta asked.

Weldon explained, "This type of tumor is generally benign. This is not what killed Ms. Francis."

"When we were at the vic's house earlier today," Riggs explained, "we found a lot of reading material on rejuvenation medicine. Spinal cord injuries. Maybe she had already been diagnosed. What side effects would she have at this stage?"

"Guessing from its position on the vertebrae, numbness, tingling in her arms. Maybe nausea, headaches."

"So aside from feeling the lump, she would have had symptoms?"

"Oh yes." He peered intently into the incision, tilting his chin up to view the tumor through the lower half of his bifocals. "Now that *is* a coincidence."

"What?" Riggs asked.

Weldon quickly cut away the last of the tendons attached to the tumor and scraped it loose from the bone. He positioned it under the surgical light.

Panetta stepped closer, his nose wrinkled at the bloody glob, which was about the size of a tangerine.

Weldon held out his hand. "Riggs, hand me the magnifying glass." With infuriating slowness, Weldon examined the tumor under the magnifier. He tapped a white spot with the scalpel. "Not really a calcification." He shook his head. "No. More like a . . . *tooth*."

"A tooth?" Panetta frowned.

"If my deduction is correct, and I believe it is"—Weldon stared hard at Panetta, enjoying the suspenseful moment— "another teratoma."

"Teratoma?" Panetta eyed the tumor as if it might be contagious.

"This one is rather grotesque, I must say."

Riggs leaned in and visually examined the tumor through the magnifying glass. What she saw literally raised the hair on the back of her neck. She pulled back, a hand involuntarily going to her throat.

Panetta glanced at Riggs, clearly even more unnerved by her reaction, and took a step back.

"What exactly," he asked, "is a *teratoma*?"

"Teratoma is Greek for 'monstrous tumor.'" Weldon held it aloft. Riggs took the opportunity to shoot several pictures of it, carefully including the doctor for good measure. He would appreciate that later. Holding up a ruler for measurements and special context, she shot four more pictures as Weldon rotated the tumor.

Growing frustrated, Panetta demanded, "What . . . is a *monster* tumor?"

With a hint of a smile between his well-cushioned cheeks, Weldon explained, "This, detective, is a germ cell tumor. Basically, an abnormal development of pluripotent cells. They're usually congenital by origin, and found in the reproductive organs."

"In layman terms," Panetta prompted.

"They're relatively rare tumors, made up of all three germ cell layers. For instance, in this particular mass"—he paused for effect, making sure Panetta made eye contact— "I can see a tooth, some bits of hair, and what looks to be an . . . *arm*."

Panetta looked horrified and crossed his arms as if to ward off a chill. "Are you serious?"

"Oh, quite." Weldon smiled broadly, beneath his clear plastic splash shield. "It's not uncommon in these types of tumors to see organs and body parts; sometimes we even get an eyeball."

"Monster tumor. I get it, but I've never heard of it."

"I assure you, they're quite real, as you can see. Pull the tray over, Riggs."

She rolled the surgical tray up under the light. To think such an anomaly could grow inside a person was truly repugnant, like an alien fetus.

Weldon set the tumor in a shallow pan and angled the magnifying glass so he could apply the scalpel. He cut around a circular ridge and split the tumor, pulling it apart to reveal a cyst within the tumor, which he sliced open. "Morbid!"

Almost reluctant, yet captivated, Riggs examined the exposed nucleus of the cyst. "Oh . . . my God."

Panetta swallowed hard. "Can it get any worse?"

"Look for yourself," she said, and snapped more pictures.

He leaned in over the magnifying glass. Perplexed, he frowned, then paled noticeably.

Riggs said, "It looks like a lower torso with a leg and hair."

Panetta excused himself to get fresh air, the door hydraulics hissing closed behind him.

Riggs returned her attention to the tumor, fascinated and repulsed at the same time. Something Weldon had said earlier surfaced. "You said *another* teratoma. What did you mean by that?"

"Oddly enough, I did an autopsy this afternoon on a fire victim, and he also had a teratoma. Only his had developed in the temporal lobe of the brain. I've sent it over to Dr. Kessler's lab. It wasn't as defined as this one. Again, not the cause of death, although it certainly could have caused some nasty headaches. Maybe a bout or two of hysterics."

"Hysterics?"

"Oh yes. The dastardly thing was partially brain cells. So his immune system would have attacked it *and* his own brain."

Riggs shuddered. "What was the guy's name?"

"Delano. Robert Delano. I happen to know his wife. She's on the Shakespeare Festival board with me."

"And cause of death?" Riggs felt her heart quicken. "Was it fire related?"

Weldon shook his head. "No. I don't think so. His lungs were clear. I believe he died before the fire started, probably of a heart attack. His CK, creatine kinase, was elevated. Which wouldn't surprise me in the least. No doubt he was quite tormented. Poor bastard."

Panetta returned to the room, pale but composed. Riggs made a point of ignoring his departure. It was the first time he'd ever left an autopsy.

Even so, he must have felt the need to defend himself. "I'm trained for warfare, not science. And that thing is sickening."

She agreed with him and quickly filled him in regarding Delano's teratoma.

He frowned. "That's a very big coincidence."

"That's what I thought."

"Yeah." Panetta rubbed his chin. "Two vics on the same day infested with *that* thing. What are the odds?"

Riggs eyed the tumor, intrigued from a medical perspective. But after twelve years as a police officer, six of those spent in homicide, she had no illusions. She didn't believe in coincidences.

9

PORTER'S, A RENOVATED 1910 railway station that had been converted to an upscale restaurant, had few patrons after midnight. The cozy bar boasted its use of the original passenger ticket counter with its glossy, dark wood, imbuing the room with ambience from another, far more elegant era. Shadows of amber and gold warmed the brick walls, creating an overall pleasant experience, with subdued lighting from replica craftsman-style chandeliers. The rich atmosphere attracted mostly professionals and the local elite. And fortunately for Whit's tight budget, Porter's also served inexpensive appetizers from nine PM until closing.

The place smelled of sweet potato fries and grilled steak. Her stomach growled.

After scanning the four groups seated around bistro tables and a few loners occupying the bar, automatically evaluating their level of threat or usefulness and finding none of either, Whit zoned in on Katie Riggs sitting on a cozy corner couch. She made a beeline for the high-backed chair next to her best friend, more eager than she cared to admit for a drink. Like any good journalist with a healthy sense of rebellion in their soul, she considered alcohol mandatory recreation. Not the wrinkled, sodden, old-school version; more like the wine and martini crowd . . . unless you were overseas, and then anything goes.

On the way over, in the car, she'd called Stu and persuaded him to hold additional space above the fold for her story. After much *needless* bickering, he'd reluctantly agreed to wait until one AM. Her argument for more inches had been solid. She figured the dead woman was a local dignitary, because the district attorney's office had announced a press conference to be held at nine AM with Mayor Ostrander. The fact that the mayor was involved suggested the body was a notable person. The DA, Edward Littrell, was a media hound who sucked up the spotlight at every opportunity, especially around election time. But if the mayor put his mug on camera during a murder investigation, there had to be a good reason.

However, her inquires had been unable to dig up any buzz on the street. Even Stu couldn't strong-arm it out of his stash of cronies. Riggs was her last hope.

"Hey, McKenna!" They exchanged a fond hug. Riggs wore jeans and a black tank top, slender and beautiful as always in a natural way. "I ordered your favorite, Pinot Gris."

"Thank God!" Whit hadn't found time to change from her stained skirt and white blouse. She needed to get back into the habit of stashing a change of clothes in her car and at her desk. Eight months off the job and she'd relapsed into a rookie. She had, however, slipped her long, red hair into a ponytail.

"You look a little worse for wear," Riggs noted, her hand plucking at the singed fabric on Whit's blouse. "What happened?"

"All hell broke loose. That's what happened."

Riggs's gray eyes widened in alarm.

Whit settled into a leather armchair next to the couch. The private nook beneath the stairs set them apart from prying eyes. The waitress stopped by, and they placed their food orders, although Whit wasn't hungry. She emptied half the glass in two long sips. She suppressed an "Ahhhh." The chilled wine was crisp and blessedly cool on the back of her throat.

"Hey girl," Riggs said, with raised brows. "Thirsty?"

"I had an episode today."

"What kind of episode?"

"A flashback."

"Afghanistan?"

"Yeah."

Riggs set her cappuccino, on the table and leaned forward, elbows on her knees. "Tell me what happened."

"I was up on Gin Lin Trail."

"Panetta said you were there, but I'm surprised you would venture up the trail." She asked, "What in the world possessed you to go into the woods?"

"My witnesses. It was do or die; otherwise I wouldn't have done it. I was halfway up the trail when it hit."

"Are you all right now?"

"I don't know." She bottomed the rest of the wine, eager to douse the fire burning in the pit of her stomach, embers of unease. "I've been a wreck all day. Holding it together like a junkie."

"I'm sorry."

"Honestly, Katie. I don't *want* to remember. I never told you this because I felt . . . I don't know . . . weak, but I still have John's last text message on my phone. Do you know what it says?"

Riggs shook her head.

"It says: *Meet you in the lobby.*" She felt tears prick her eyes and quickly blinked. She took a deep breath and blew it out. "I've read it every day since his death. Until today I was waiting safely in the lobby. I liked it there."

"You told me that's all you could remember. I assumed it was because you cracked your head on that rock. So you purposely suppressed the memory?"

Whit nodded. "Probably. Cowardly, huh?"

"No. Just human. I'm sorry, Whit."

"Every time I think about the memory, I just feel sick."

"Grief is a battle you can't run from." Riggs sipped her coffee thoughtfully. "You're not the only one with secrets. I never told anyone, but my near-death experience with cancer sent me into a tailspin. My fear of death was starting to get the better of me. I was obsessing. Losing my edge out there in the field. So I figured the best way to tackle it was head on. That's why I transferred from the violent crime division to the ME's office. Don't let fear keep you from processing your grief."

Noting the firearm and badge attached to her belt, she was reminded that Katie could relate to her better than most. They'd both lived their lives on the front lines. She looked into Riggs's eyes and knew she understood, and returned a grateful smile. "You're a wise old soul."

Riggs smiled back. "That's what they call me. Can you talk about the flashback?"

With a deep breath, Whit found the courage to relive the disturbing scene and share it with Riggs.

All the while, the visual clarity, so perfectly real.

No time to think, just a mindless dash into the woods. Stark sunlight piercing the trees broke through the shadows to the forest floor, illuminating the leaves, pale lime and speckled with dark green. Seconds before the air-shattering crack of the gun, the summer sound of a honeybee. She swirled around, coming to a halting stop by grabbing a tree branch. John's blue eyes, wide with fear, seemed to stare into her soul. The spray, dark droplets exploding into the sunlight like rubies tossed into the air. His whole body jerked upward and collapsed with a cloud of dust.

Dry mouthed, Whit swallowed. "Before now, I only had the information that the medic told me on the chopper, and the doctor's brief summary of my injuries. All the personal, Technicolor images were apparently buried somewhere in my mind."

"I can understand why. It sounds brutal. I don't know what I'd do if I witnessed Richard being shot. Denial is a natural part of healing, but you can't stay there."

Whit polished off the wine in her glass, trying to hide the tremor in her hand. "I know that's true, but today, seeing John's face after the bullet tore through his head—it left me numb at first. He didn't die immediately, as I had thought. He called my name. Made eye contact with me when I turned around. His face full of shock, his mouth dropped open, eyes wide with fear. I can't get that image out of my mind."

Katie nodded. "Murder is life smothered midsentence. John's life was not fully lived out, and neither was yours. I'm sorry. The reality is you have to make a new life without him for your sake and the girls."

"I don't know how I can learn to live with the guilt. That I pressured him into risking his life."

"To be honest, from what you described, it doesn't sound like John ever intended to make it out alive. By shoving you in front of him, he was basically acknowledging what you had already said. There was no hope of surviving if you stayed with your captors. The odds of making a run for it weren't great either, so he chose to sacrifice himself to give you a head start. Otherwise he would have pulled you along behind him, but he didn't."

"I hadn't thought of that." Whit tried to remember every detail of their twenty-second sprint into the woods. Tears suddenly filled her eyes. "For me to be so far ahead of him, he must have stopped."

Riggs nodded and handed her a tissue. "I think he meant to save your life. Perhaps he hoped they wouldn't shoot him if he stopped and bargained for your life."

She wiped the tears away. "I'm not sure what to think."

Taking a moment to absorb the conversation, Whit leaned back into the curve of the chair, her pulse slowing as the wine soothed frayed nerves. But the bloody images kept sifting through her thoughts. Overwhelmed with the day's events and understanding that she might never find the answers, she searched for a diversion, and focused on Riggs's new tattoo. "What's this?"

Riggs extended her slender wrist. "A reminder that I'm not alone."

Whit examined the cross. "If I thought a tattoo of a cross would banish my demons to hell, I'd do a full-body tattoo, like the Koita women in Papua New Guinea."

Riggs laughed, but her gaze was sympathetic.

"Although, I have to admit," Whit continued. "I've said more than a few prayers since John's death. Especially for Emma and Jordan. I didn't mean to make light of your tattoo."

"Don't worry about it. A little humor is the best medicine."

For the first time Whit noticed soft jazz playing in the background. Alcohol buzzed through her brain, lulling her into a fog. She blinked, recalling too late how empty her stomach had been.

Riggs smirked knowingly. "The wine knocked you for a wallop, didn't it?"

"Am I lisping? *Drooling?*"

She laughed. "No. I just know you."

"Well . . . no worries, Detective Riggs. I might be two steps away from a straitjacket, but my journalism skills are still golden."

With a shake of her head, she asked, "Okay Lois Lane, what's the scoop?"

Whit sat forward, more than ready to push the afternoon from her mind and get back to work. The story had always been her hiding place. As long as she was working the news, gathering the facts, telling the story, she had purpose and meaning, and sometimes she could escape the realities of her own life.

"You're gonna love this. It's a description of the killer's car."

"Are you serious?"

"Absolutely."

"Credible witness?"

Affronted, Whit said, "Of course. For their age. Now, you tell me. Who is the Applegate victim? A local hotshot?"

"Yes and no." Riggs frowned, the fringes of her blonde bangs hitting her eyelashes. "What do you mean . . . for their age?"

"They're minors, but very astute minors. So, was she a local celebrity?"

"Local *and* famous. But I'm not so sure about the minors. How old?"

"Almost teenagers. Old enough."

Riggs tilted her chin up as she wrestled with her thoughts. Nodding, she came to a decision. "Every minute counts during the first twenty-four hours of the investigation. We *need* that lead. Especially in this high-profile case. And you'll release the information only a few hours before the press conference anyway. I'll trade, though I still have reservations."

Relieved, Whit said, "I think it's a solid lead. The kids showed me where they witnessed the guy digging the grave. We were on a rock above the trail. I had a bird's-eye view of you and the other investigators today. Here." She leaned forward and showed the pictures on her iPhone taken from the hideout earlier today. "I wouldn't do anything that might jeopardize your job, you must know that."

"I don't think you would. But as you and I know, life sometimes takes curves not of our choosing."

"I'm betting Stu will want to post it on our online edition almost immediately, before the hard copy hits the streets," Whit warned.

"We need that lead. Hours count, and I don't expect you to just hand it to me. No self-respecting journalist would."

"Thanks, Katie."

"All right, McKenna. God is smiling down on you with this one. Are you ready?"

Whit gathered her pen and pad. "Who is it?"

"We confirmed the vic as Niki Francis . . . the actress."

"Niki Francis? I can't believe it." Never in a million years had she envisioned a person of such media magnitude. "You mean *the* Niki Francis? Good God!"

"Unfortunately, it's true. Her housekeeper filed a formal missing persons report yesterday. We've confirmed her ID through dental records."

"I'm . . . I'm shocked!" Images of the actress flashed in Whit's mind: vibrant and beautiful, sometimes gutsy and strong, at other times playful or deeply dramatic. Her flirtatious smile while accepting the Oscar last year, and the huge donation she'd recently made to the Feed the Hunger Foundation. The magnitude of this story was not lost on her. "There hasn't been a death with that kind of star power since Whitney Houston."

"I know. It's hard to believe. She was larger than life. I've been trying to wrap my brain around it all day."

"Cause of death?"

"Preliminary reports are inconclusive. We'll know more when we get the tox report in a couple of weeks. But whatever the cause of death, someone dumped her there in that hot, dank hole with crusty river rocks and bugs." She shuddered. "The kind of death I have nightmares about."

Whit asked for descriptive details about the body at the scene to verify her information from the fisherman, Mr. Wolcott. "Not much to go on."

"No, but we're following up on some leads that I'm not privileged to share just yet. I'm not sure of their relevance anyway."

"Leads from the autopsy? Needle marks? Do you think drugs were involved?"

"Nothing like that. Though I can't say for sure that drugs were not a factor. But I will tell you the approximate time of death was Monday, early evening. The MADIU team is investigating the case. Tonight the state police and the FBI have joined the team."

Already the lead for Whit's story was beginning to formulate. The small-town murder of a highly publicized celebrity was definitely hot news. National and even international media would descend like cats on cream, lapping up every tiny scrap of information. And she, PTSD washup, would get the first lick. Maybe God *was* smiling down on her.

"Okay. Your turn," Riggs prompted.

Fired up now, she eagerly shared details of the witnesses and their story. "According to those kids, the killer drove a black or dark-navy king-cab truck."

"Make and model?"

"Don't know. But after an hour of questions, the kids remembered seeing a University of Oregon *O* sticker on the back window of the truck. Must be a Ducks fan. That's as descriptive as they could be. It was very foggy the morning they saw him burying the body. But I don't think there's that many dark king-cab trucks around."

"You forget." Riggs pulled a pad and pen from her back pocket. "This is Oregon, not LA. They ride trucks here like cowboys rode horses in the Wild West, and nearly all of them are Ducks fans. They won the Rose Bowl. It's serious football here. So a Ducks sticker doesn't really narrow our search, but it helps some. Maybe we'll get lucky. It's a lead and a good one; thanks. I'll call it in right now. If we question the kids right away, maybe they'll remember more."

"They also believe the guy was white because he was wearing a short-sleeved shirt and shorts, and there was enough light to see his arms. They couldn't see his face because he was wearing a baseball cap."

"Any description of height, weight?"

"No."

"I better call this in now." She stared at the information thoughtfully. "I wonder how the MADIU team missed these witnesses. I know they canvassed the area thoroughly."

"In all honesty, their hideout was nearly impossible to find. And they were determined to stay and watch all the drama. Even their parents didn't know where they were."

"That might explain it, but I don't think the chief is going to be too happy that we missed this. Somebody's head is going to roll."

"I hadn't thought about that." Whit frowned. "I hope not yours."

"Most likely Blackwell, since he's the lead on this one. All that aside, I'm grateful we have something solid to go on." Riggs slid her phone from her belt and dialed. "Blackwell will want this information immediately. The team will be up all night anyway."

"Good luck." Whit pulled her laptop out of her bag and set it in front of her on the table. Logging on to Wi-Fi, she researched details about Niki's career. She retrieved the Applegate story from her email, where she had sent it before leaving the office. Years of writing on deadline in elevators, taxis, planes, and just about every mode of transportation, including a military Humvee, had prepared her well to write under pressure.

She could taste victory. A story of this magnitude would propel her back to the top of her game. Give her credibility among her peers again. Not that she didn't still have supporters, longtime friends at the *Los Angeles Times*, but in that arena of writing it was a small world, and journalists were born gossips. Her fall from grace had been well reported. Wouldn't it be great karma if she bagged a story that landed her back on top of the heap? A nagging doubt surfaced, but she refused to consider whether she was emotionally ready to reclaim her place in the big leagues.

The restaurant server brought their food. Riggs ate her shrimp salad quickly and left. The new lead generated multiple trails to follow and would require every available cop. Whit returned her second glass of wine to the bar, then ordered a Diet Pepsi. Brain cells had to be firing at optimum levels to fine-tune the first six inches of her story. She munched warm, salty fries, thinking through her lead.

Blocking out every sound until she was alone with her thoughts, Whit faced her computer. She teased the lead, writing and deleting repeatedly until she was satisfied.

From beneath piles of river rock and gritty dirt, homicide investigators uncovered the body of Niki Francis buried in a shallow grave near Applegate Lake. The mega star's corpse was discovered by a local fisherman, Jerry Wolcott, and his dog, when a hungry black bear dug up a portion of the actress's remains.

She would quote Mr. Wolcott for a description of the body. After weaving in a bio on Niki Francis, she forwarded the entire story to Stu via email, and sent him a text requesting the lead above the fold, with the bombshell headline NIKI FRANCIS MURDERED, BODY FOUND BURIED IN THE APPLEGATE.

True to form, Stu called ranting at her to verify, verify, verify her facts, and demanding to know her source, which she refused to give him.

"Look, McKenna. I'm not running a story like that without a source."

"You know I can't do that, Stu. You'll just have to trust me. I am absolutely certain my information is correct. My source is solid. A member of the police department. Trust me."

"Why? I don't have to trust anyone. In fact, I don't *ever* trust anyone."

"Fine. Don't print it. You'll miss out on the most sensational scoop this newspaper has ever had."

Silence greeted her for several seconds. For three months now she'd swallowed her pride and worked relentlessly to write well-crafted stories, no matter the subject. She'd fought hard to earn her self-respect back, and the respect of her peers, who couldn't quite mask the looks of pity cast her way. As degrading as it had all been, she hadn't quit, fully aware that her daughters were watching.

Opportunities like this headliner came along once in a lifetime. Normally she would give Stu the name of her sources if they were on the record, but Katie had agreed to the quid pro quo only under promise of anonymity.

In the silence, Stu breathed into the phone. Her heart pulsed in her ears.

Finally Stu said, "I'll head back to the paper and make sure the copy people don't screw it up."

"Excellent!" Enjoying a little jab, Whit said, "Just make sure my byline isn't misspelled."

Stu grunted. "Egomaniac."

Laughing, Whit hung up, but another part of her braced for what was sure to be a media war zone beginning bright and early tomorrow morning.

10

THE EXHILARATION OF writing a front-page international story left Whit deflated and feeling strangely lonely. John wasn't waiting to share her victory. No chilled wineglasses ready to raise in a victory toast. No strong arms eagerly wrapping around her while he listened to the myriad details of her journalistic coup. With a regretful sigh, she turned the key in the front door of her townhome.

It was after one in the morning and she wanted nothing more than to pour a glass of wine, fall into bed, and wipe everything out of her mind. In the shadows of the living room, she hung the keys on a rack by the door. The muted sound of the girls' television carried from upstairs, so presumably at least one of them was still awake. She kicked off her shoes just as Reggie came barreling around the corner from the kitchen. The mass of panting, quivering, fawn-colored pug practically knocked her over.

"I missed you too!" She plopped into a chair and gathered him up in her arms and tried to dodge his slurping tongue. His fur was soft. He cried and whined in a high pitch, as if admonishing her for leaving the house without him. She laughed in spite of herself. "You beast!"

"Hey, Mom." Jordan emerged from the hall with a half-eaten sandwich in hand. "He sure misses you."

"He's telling me all about it." Whit lavished Reggie with hugs and kisses; then, sufficiently loved, he jumped down and pranced toward Jordan. "How are *you* doing?"

Jordan shrugged. "I'm fine. Bored."

"What are you doing up so late?"

"Got the munchies."

"Munchies?" Whit suspected Jordan had been smoking pot lately. Surely she wouldn't be so blatant. On closer inspection, her eyes were awfully red.

Deciding to fortify herself with a glass of wine before any confrontations, Whit brushed the blond fur off her skirt and headed toward the kitchen. She paused and embraced Jordan, holding tight, knowing it was their last year together before college.

Marijuana had a distinctive smell, and it clung to Jordan.

Whit reached up and cupped Jordan's chin. "I love you. You know that?"

A soft smile touched Jordan's mouth before she rolled her eyes, as if it was all too embarrassing. "I know, Mom."

Awash in disappointment about the pot, Whit released her and padded barefoot to the kitchen. She rummaged in the cabinet and tossed Reggie a jerky stick, then poured a glass of wine. A weak substitute for the strength needed to confront an authority-defiant teenager, but she was all tapped out.

Jordan had followed them into the kitchen. "So, I was thinking of driving to the coast tomorrow to take some shots of the ocean. The cliffs are beautiful, and I want to enter a few contests. Can I use Dad's equipment?" She leaned against the counter, her curly brown hair, with an unfortunate swath of bang recently dyed fuchsia, hanging over the shoulders of her Led Zeppelin T-shirt nearly to her hips, which were encased in baggy black sweat pants.

Whit sipped her wine.

Jordan had been close to John, often going out on assignments with him. She'd reveled in the mud-soaked shoes required to capture the perfect shot of the New Year's Day flood; the hours trapped on the roof of the Holiday Inn hotel, sitting in blazing heat for an aerial shot of the president's motorcade; even climbing steep terrain in the dark to capture a perfect sunrise photo. They had the same spirit of adventure. Every time Whit looked at Jordan, she saw John's inquisitive blue eyes.

All of John's camera equipment had been carefully packed before moving from Los Angeles. Whit hadn't had the heart to unpack most of his things yet. "You know it's very expensive equipment. And you're hard on things."

"I'd be careful." She popped the last bite of sandwich into her mouth, a defiant tilt to her strong chin. Even her mannerisms were like John's. If he faced an argument with no intention of changing his mind, his chin lifted just like that, and he never said much, but she knew the conversation was over. But Jordan was her daughter and the last word had to be her own.

"Careful? Let's review the past six months. You've lost your phone three times. You've blown a tire on your car playing wheelies in a parking lot at midnight. You ran the battery down in the car on a two-lane road in the middle of mountains in the dark of night. You drove the car into an orchard and got stuck in the mud and had to call a tow truck. These are not the things a 'careful' person does."

"So I'm clumsy."

"Come on, Jordan. Then there's your appearance. You stopped wearing makeup, and half the time you don't even brush your hair. You dress in these sloppy sweats no matter where you're going. Personal hygiene seems to be a thing of the past. I'm concerned."

"Hey, I'm a hippie." Jordan shrugged. "A free spirit. What can I say?"

Whit could feel her temper rising. "First of all, you can take responsibility for your actions."

"I'm a teenager, Mom. That's what teenagers do."

"Only the ones headed for trouble." Whit swigged her wine in frustration. "Listen, I know your dad's death left a big hole in your life. And probably a lot of feelings you don't know how to handle. Hell, I don't know how to handle it either. But we have to do our best. Under the circumstances, I haven't said much. I've been trying to be compassionate, but now I think I've just been foolish."

"Foolish?" Jordan flipped a cascade of curls over her shoulder. "It's *my* life. If I want to screw it up, that's *my* business."

Whit swallowed hard, her pulse pounding in her ears. "Are you smoking pot?"

"What if I am?" Her eyes flashed defiance. "I'm almost eighteen. I can do what I want!"

"You do what I say in *my* house. Are you or are you not smoking pot?"

"Dad said he smoked pot in high school."

"So that gives you a reason to make the same mistake? You're smarter than that, and I won't have it."

Flushed with anger, Jordan raised her voice. "Yeah? I don't think you need to be talking to me about *pot* when you're drinking *wine. Again* . . ." She jabbed a finger at Whit's glass, slapping the stem.

Whit gasped as chilled wine splashed across her blouse, soaking through to her skin and sloshing onto her bare feet. Dark, seething fury surged through her, an instant wrath that she never saw coming. "What . . . is . . . the . . . *matter* . . . with . . . you!" she shouted, every instinct urging her to attack. Frightened of her own emotions, she spun away, eyes squeezed shut. "Get out!"

She caught hold of the counter as the room spun. The glass dropped from her fingers and crashed to the floor, shattering. The images of John's death in her mind's eye were so very vivid that it seemed her wine-drenched blouse became the blood-soaked shirt she'd worn that dreadful day.

Whit sucked in raw air, gulping as if she'd been drowning underwater.

"Mom?"

Jordan's arm was wrapped around her waist as they leaned against the counter.

Whit cried into her hands. Grief enveloped her so completely, with gut-wrenching sobs, that she had no resistance to fight it, nothing to dull the avalanche. All the willpower in the world could not suppress it anymore. The horror of John's last minutes on earth tore at her heart.

Lost in her tears, Whit moved willingly as Jordan guided her down the hall to her room and stuffed tissues into her hand. Exhausted, she fell across the bed, allowing the racking sobs to vent her pain.

After a while, she became aware of Jordan kneeling on the floor next to the bed, her hand on Whit's shoulder. Gazing into those concerned blue eyes so like John's, she apologized. "I'm . . . I'm sorry, Jordan. It's been a long, difficult day."

"It's okay." Her voice quivered with tears. "I didn't mean to spill your wine. I didn't mean . . . to make it worse."

Whit squeezed Jordan's hand. "You didn't make it worse, honey. This was a long time coming, months of grief, and it's been building all day. You did nothing to cause it. I'm just processing a lot right now, just like you are."

She nodded thoughtfully. "It's been hard, Mom."

"I know."

Jordan frowned, "You scared me just now. I thought you were going to pass out. Do you need to see a doctor?"

Blowing her nose, Whit shook her head. "I'll be all right in a minute."

"Are you sure? I can call Grandma and Grandpa, or I can stay here with you for a while."

"No. Go on up to bed and get some sleep. I needed a good cry. I'll be fine." This would not be their last confrontation, Whit was sure. But at least Jordan seemed more receptive.

Now was probably a good time to press her point. "And Jordan?"

"Yeah?"

"I'll think about your trip to the coast. Borrowing your dad's cameras. Promise me you'll make a real effort. Clean your room. Take a shower. Stop the drugs."

"I will, Mom." Jordan hugged her and left the room, her footsteps creaking on the stairs.

Reggie nudged her leg and got in a few slobbery licks before she bent down to pet his head. She slid off the bed and walked to the utility closet in the hallway and grabbed a broom and dustbin.

After the cleanup, she poured a new glass of wine and carried it to her nightstand. Maybe it would help her calm down. What bad timing for the dam to break, in front of Jordan, and while she was knee-deep in the Niki Francis story.

Whit washed her face, changed into a comfortable nightgown, and propped against bed pillows as she opened the nightstand drawer and pulled out an old Flor de las Antillas Belicoso wooden cigar box. She flipped the lid, exposing an array of John's personal items. Gold cuff links he'd worn to a photojournalism award ceremony at the Waldorf Hotel in New York. He'd rented a tux with a red cummerbund and been sexy as hell. They had celebrated with friends late into the night, then returned to their hotel room and made languid, passionate love. She fingered a few favorite coins he'd collected from various countries they'd visited. Each symbolized a special date. His thirty-sixth birthday in Baghdad, where they'd met, a war zone, which in a way defined their lives together. She picked up and sniffed two half-smoked cigars from the days that Jordan and Emma were born, with the words *It's a Girl!* stamped on them. She smiled at those, recalling how he'd been kicked out of the hospital for lighting up in her room, always a lark and a rebel.

She slipped on his gold wedding band over hers. There was no hurry to remove her ring. In her heart, she was still a married woman. She absently rubbed the smooth metal around her finger as tears wet her cheeks. Even though his camera had captured some of life's cruelest moments in some of the most violent places on earth, John never lost his amiable smile or his generous heart. Unlike her, impulsive and headstrong, he was thoughtful and reasonable. Comforting . . . so comforting . . .

She had half nodded off to sleep when Reggie's boisterous snores brought her awake with a jerk. He snorted and hacked on something, then fell back into his doggy dream world.

Dropping the coins and John's ring back in the box, she caught sight of the silver lighter. The last time she'd seen him use it was the morning they were kidnapped from the Serena Hotel in Kabul. After breakfast at Café Zarnegar, John had walked outside and sat near the fountain to smoke his cigar, while she gathered their equipment for an interview she'd scheduled with the Ministry of Women's Affairs. She had no idea how she had ended up with the lighter. She flicked the lid open, remembering his hands using it many times. With a sigh, she slipped it back into the box.

Closing the box lid, she replaced it in the drawer, then polished off the wine and switched off the light by the bed. Curling up next to Reggie, she immediately fell asleep. Her dreams were a riotous mix of the day's events, with raging fires and buried bodies.

Whit awakened drenched in a nightmarish sweat that soaked her hair and nightgown. Fumbling in the dark, she sat up and turned on the bedside lamp, utterly grateful to be in her bedroom, Reggie's sleepy face a mask of confusion beside her. Grabbing her cell phone from the nightstand, she checked the time. She'd slept for only three hours. It was five AM.

Groaning, she slipped out of bed and went to the kitchen for a glass of water. Her class at the gym started in an hour, so she saw no point in going back to bed. She put on a pot of coffee and changed into gym clothes. No better way to start the day than caffeine and adrenaline.

11

Mostly moderate- to lower-income single-family homes bordered the City Gym, where Whit stood with hands on hips, trying to cool down, eyeing the horizon. A hazy pink sunrise was just emerging over neighborhood rooftops. Even at seven AM the temperature was already eighty-six degrees. The stagnant air failed to cool her sweating skin. Diesel fumes from the four-way stop at the corner lodged in her nose and throat, clinging to the humidity like a damp, musty towel. The day promised to be another scorcher.

The boot camp coach had singled her out this morning and paced the whole boot camp class on Whit's tired efforts to keep up. The strenuous workout scoured away every last bit of yesterday's stress marathon, but she still had a full day ahead of her. Running on three hours of sleep would be a trial.

She had missed Katie this morning. No doubt she had spent the night chasing down leads and was catching up on much-needed sleep. Whit glanced at her phone lying on the bench next to her car keys. She'd had seventeen calls in an hour. The front-page article on Niki Francis had hit the streets and the internet with a loud, reverberating boom. True to form, Stu had posted the story on the internet almost immediately, forwarding it to the media networks around the world. Several of the ladies at the gym had carried newspapers from home with the front-page story, congratulating her. In a way it was validation for clinging to threads of courage and returning to journalism instead of cowering at home.

Quickly gathering her things, Whit crossed the parking lot scrolling through her emails. She started the car and turned on the air conditioning, then collected pen and pad and called her voice mail, which had automatically attached to her car's speaker system from her iPhone. A couple of messages were from other reporters at the *Chronicle*, praising her article. The rest of the messages were from a slew of major media outlets: a couple of old friends from the *L.A. Times*, colleagues from the *New York Times*, and broadcast journalists from CNN, FOX, NBC, et cetera, all wanting to interview her about Niki Francis.

Her phone rang. The number was local and vaguely familiar. "Whit McKenna, *Medford Chronicle*."

"Miss McKenna?" a woman's voice responded. "I'm Gale Delano. Bo Delano's wife. You called last night and left a message."

The fire victim's wife. Whit sat up straighter. "Yes, Mrs. Delano. I'm very sorry to have bothered you at a time like this."

"Thank you. I'm calling because I gave a statement to the police, but they appear to be obtuse. One would think our police force could hire officers with an IQ above seventy."

Whit's brows rose at that. "What statement did you give them?"

"I told them my husband was murdered."

"Murdered?" Her heart skipped a beat.

"Yes. By the way, I read your article about my Bo in the paper this morning. I hate what people are saying about him. People need to know the truth, not just hearsay."

Whit bristled at that. "I had multiple sources confirm my information. And if you recall, I did give you an opportunity to contribute to the article."

"That's what I intend to do now. Do you have time to meet with me this morning?"

She thought of the nine AM news briefing with the mayor. If she hurried . . . "I have an hour; that's about it. Starting right now."

"I usually walk in the mornings. Can you meet me at the Bear Creek Path?"

"Yes. In ten minutes?"

"Very good."

Whit hung up and sat staring at her phone. Mrs. Delano did not give her warm fuzzies. However, if she was right and her husband was murdered, maybe Riggs would confirm it from the coroner's report. Whit sent a text asking her for cause of death.

Opening the glove box, she grabbed a box of towelette wipes and vigorously cleaned under her arms; grabbed another wipe and scrubbed her face. Fumbling through her bag, she pulled out a makeup case. She applied mascara and lipstick and ran a brush through her hair, pulling it back into a pony-tail. Good enough.

She arrived at the Bear Creek walking path a few minutes early, so she sat and waited in her car. The path, banked by tall trees on either side of the creek, ran the length of the city and meandered through neighborhoods, along the freeway, and behind the park. Joggers, seniors, and young mothers pushing strollers were already enjoying the sun-soaked path. At the base of a sloping hill was an amphitheater; to her right, a twenty-five-thousand-square-foot skate park and four tennis courts.

Katie replied to her text.

Sorry I missed the workout this morning. I'm on my way to collect an accident vic. Read both your articles. Nice. Delano? Haven't released autopsy report.

Anything suspicious?

Why?

Talking with Mrs. Delano. She thinks he was murdered.
Inconclusive. Let me know if you come up with a trade.
Will do.

Inconclusive meant Riggs didn't know yet. Talk of a trade meant it was possible. Maybe probable. Very, very interesting.

Whit heard a car door slam. A sleek red BMW had pulled into the space beside her. It shone like glass in the sun. The woman who uncurled from behind the wheel was tall and slender, early sixties. She wore pale-yellow walking shorts, a yellow-striped tank, and spotless white tennis shoes. Her light-brown hair was cut in a neat bob at her shoulders. The perfect picture of a well-to-do lawyer's wife.

Whit grabbed her mini recorder and joined the woman on the sidewalk. They shook hands, the grip firm. After introductions, they fell into step together on the path.

"Your picture doesn't do you justice," Mrs. Delano said. She carried a small packet of tissues. "The one in the *Chronicle*, beside your byline. I always wanted red hair, but not everyone can carry that off. Yours is very pretty."

"Thanks." Whit had not expected compliments after the surly phone call. They walked facing the sun.

It was a beautiful morning. The birds flitted through the trees, chirping gaily; the stream gurgled gently beside them as if the tragic events of yesterday had not happened. But the sordid scenario of Mr. Delano and his last days, in which he abandoned his wife, abused his girlfriend, appeared drunk and disorderly in his front yard, and blew up his house, had already been clearly documented in the *Medford Chronicle*. Whit hated to be a cynic, but she suspected the public account of Mr. Delano's moral decline was the *real* tragedy for Mrs. Delano.

She asked, "Do you mind if I record our conversation? It's easier to walk and talk that way."

"Yes. Of course." They veered to the right as a pair of skateboarders rattled past.

Mrs. Delano, even in flat shoes, had to be close to six feet tall. Add the stiff, bridled way she carried her shoulders and the measured softness in her tone—intimidating right out of the gate.

"So, why do you think your husband was murdered?"

Mrs. Delano hesitated, turning her head to watch the stream. "Sorry. This is more difficult than I thought. If I think about Bo—the finality—if I think about the *finality* of it, I can't breathe."

Whit's throat tightened as she remembered last night's forage through John's memento box. Only someone who had lost a loved one could truly comprehend how hard it was to face that brutal moment of acceptance. Irrevocable. Absolute. Never to be heard or seen or touched again.

Stopping beneath the shade of an elm tree, Whit said, "If you're not up to talking right now, we can reschedule."

Stu would call her a sap and shoot her if he ever found out she'd had a source on the hook and offered to let her go. Journalism aside, Whit refused to breach her own personal moral code on this one. She'd learned a few lessons about invasion of privacy since John's death, when she'd faced a barrage of reporters on her return to the States. Intimate questions at vulnerable times.

"Oh, no," Mrs. Delano replied firmly. "I insist we talk now. I have to do this for my husband and my sons."

They resumed walking.

"Yesterday the police were insinuating that Bo was drunk and set the house on fire for insurance money. We didn't need the insurance money. I think the house was set on fire to cover up his murder."

"Why do you think that?"

"You'd have to know something about my husband to understand. We were married thirty years. We had a very compatible marriage. Two children, both boys." Her chin lifted with pride. "Bobby Junior is an English professor at

Berkeley, and Joseph is in law school at UCLA. My boys have always admired their father."

"So what changed?"

"He became obsessed with his health. Last year he joined a running club. Sometimes he ran ten miles *before* work. Then he began ordering very expensive water called Kona Nigari."

"Kona Nigari?"

"Yes. It's desalinated water from two thousand feet below the ocean surface near the big island of Hawaii. It cost over five hundred dollars a liter."

"Five hundred dollars? Does it have gold flecks?"

"Outrageous. I know." She shrugged. "I thought he was just in a midlife crisis."

"Expensive crisis."

They walked off the path toward a bench on the banks of the creek next to a large willow tree with branches that draped nearly to the ground, like emerald streamers. Tiny yellow birds darted about beneath the canopy. With a sigh of relief, Mrs. Delano sat on the bench, and Whit joined her.

Her tone hardened. "Three months ago, without speaking to me about it, he withdrew fifty thousand dollars from our savings account. When I asked what he did with it, he refused to tell me."

"Fifty?"

"Yes. Said it was personal and none of my business. *None . . . of . . . my . . . business!*" Her cheeks flushed with renewed anger. "That was the end of my trust. A few days later I cashed out some of our stocks and bonds. He was behaving so irrationally. I was scared."

Self-preservation, Whit thought. She might have done the same thing.

"Suddenly Bo said he needed a rest and left for our cabin on the coast for two weeks. When he returned, he seemed different. After a few weeks I began to study him. I think Bo had a facelift. It would explain the missing money and his youthful appearance."

Having seen him only once, as a burned corpse with that frozen scream, Whit suppressed a shudder and simply said, "That makes sense."

"One morning he left his computer on and his Facebook page open. I took the liberty of reading it. He'd been having a conversation for weeks with a young woman from Czechoslovakia. There were several photos of her clad in only a bikini. A ten, if you know what I mean."

Whit nodded, although she'd gathered as much from barbecue boy.

"Perhaps," she said, "I'm jaded from hearing so many stories of a similar fashion from my friends, but I wondered if he had begun to view me as some men in midlife crisis view their wives of thirty years, with laugh lines, a little sagging around the chin area—a body no longer hard and tight in all the right places. Not that there was any excuse, but he was so exacting with his own body. Maybe he decided he needed a newer, brighter model."

"The typical cliché, but I hope that is more rare than it seems."

"Maybe. I would like to think so, but now I'm not so sure. Then a few weeks ago he became distant, unapproachable. More and more defensive. Volatile at times. Throwing things in fits of anger. Shouting. He was always such a controlled person; it was as if I was suddenly living with a stranger." She shook her head as if she couldn't bring herself to say the next words.

Whit offered encouragement. "Go on."

"He . . . he asked me to move out. *Evana* was moving in. I . . . I was literally speechless." She cleared her throat. "Of course I moved out."

Whit thought Mr. Delano sounded like a first-class jerk. Maybe he deserved whatever fate had dealt him.

"He deteriorated quickly after that." She frowned. "I tried to tell the police, but they kept insinuating that Bo had a drinking problem. He didn't."

"Drugs?"

"No." She shook her head emphatically. "The day before he died, he called me from work. He complained of a migraine. He said, 'It's eating me alive.' He started to cry, then got very angry, spewing obscenities, which was not at all like him. Then he said, 'Stabbing. Stabbing at me. The pain is terrible.' He sobbed into the phone and said, 'He's killing me.'"

"Who was he referring to?"

"I don't know. He hung up on me. I tried to call him back, but he wouldn't answer. Lizzy, his secretary, said he'd stormed out of the office. I thought he'd call back."

"Did he?"

"No. I wanted to go see him at the house, but *she* was there. I shouldn't have waited, because he died the next day." Mrs. Delano choked back a sob, smothering it with a tissue. "What a terrible, terrible way to end a thirty-year marriage."

Whit tried to think of something consoling. "In all fairness to you, even if you did persist in reaching him in person, I don't think Mr. Delano was in his right mind. From all accounts, he was hostile and abusive to his girlfriend and the neighbors. It doesn't sound like the situation would have improved. It might have even been worse."

She nodded, tears on her cheeks. "In the space of two months he became a monster I hardly recognized. Oh, not physically. Physically he looked almost young and strangely vibrant. It was odd." She reached across and clutched Whit's hand. "You're an investigative reporter. *Please.* I *need* to know what happened to my husband."

"Why not just hire a private eye?"

"No. I need his reputation cleared by the press. Not a hired hand."

Whit stared into watery blue eyes pleading for help and almost lost her objectivity. What it must have cost this aloof woman to ask for help, a woman who seemed to have lived her life within the upper crust of society, above the fray, until the past few months, was hard to imagine. It was tempting to help her, but she'd be bound as a reporter to write the truth even if what she found demonized Bobby Delano, possibly implicating him in criminal activities.

"I'll seek and print the truth," Whit warned. "If you're comfortable with that, then I'll need your full support."

"I expect nothing less."

Whit considered her obligation to the Niki Francis story and almost referred her to another reporter. She didn't need any additional stress. Yet she felt an obligation, from one widow to another, to at least try.

As if on cue, her phone buzzed with a text from Stu.

All hell is breaking loose. Come in early.

Great. The tempo for the day. Maybe that was an omen to pass Delano to another reporter, but she couldn't let go. Not yet.

"All right. I'll pursue the story."

They stood and walked the path in silence, the sun's penetrating heat on their backs, the soft tread of their shoes and buzzing insects accompanying their thoughts.

Something dark and unsavory had happened to Bo Delano, of that Whit was sure. People didn't drastically and suddenly change after thirty years of marriage. The catalyst might have been drugs, or maybe he'd gotten involved with the wrong kind of people. She was going to find out. However, she wasn't the only one investigating this story.

Whit said, "We'll have to work fast if we want to get ahead of the police. I want you to write down everything you've told me on a timeline for the past three months. Dates, places, names. All his personal contacts, like his accountant, broker, physician, counselor, et cetera, and give me all your financial records for the past three months. I'll also need access to his Facebook if you have it. Don't assume I know anything. Also, think long and hard on his client list. Anyone who might be out to get him. Even coworkers, past employees, opposing attorneys."

Mrs. Delano nodded. "I'll get started right away."

"I'll need the information tomorrow."

She stopped short and smiled. "You don't mess around, do you?"

Whit smiled back. "I'm kind of all or nothing."

"Good. Let's meet around eight o'clock tomorrow night at my place. I'll try to have everything ready by then."

When they reached the parking lot, Mrs. Delano added, "I knew you were the right one. It's the red hair."

12

Detective Tucker yanked back the tarp.

The nude body sprawled across the textured concrete like a twisted and broken shadow in the predawn light. In contrast, her pasty white face, turned toward the underwater lights, appeared ghoulish with her mouth hanging open, long dark hair trailing eerily in the water. But this was no shadowy specter—it was the cold dead body of someone Riggs knew.

"The neighbor she jogs with found her this morning at five AM," Tucker said. "Standing appointment, twice a week, unless one of them cancels. Ungodly hour for jogging, but hey, whatever floats your boat." He snickered at his own off-color joke. "The woman said she found her floating at the shallow end against the suction intake. This is as far as she could pull her out. The vic was long dead and past any CPR, so the neighbor left her here and called nine-one-one. Drug OD maybe. Boozer for sure."

Riggs sighed. Tucker had his good qualities, surely? His buzzed hair, square jaw, and muscular frame were probably attributes of steroids, but who was she to judge? He somehow always seemed to rub people the wrong way. She was no exception to his lack of charm. Right now she had to suppress the urge to snap at him.

Ignoring Tucker, Riggs squatted down beside the vic, Isabel Rodriguez, a defense attorney with a popular local television show called *Legal Matters* that aired once a week. Jackson County residents called in to ask legal questions, often with both parties in the dispute on the line. Like Judge Judy, Rodriguez indiscriminately criticized and corrected, often chastising those gutsy enough to call in to the thirty-minute show. An instant success, even garnering national attention over the past two years, she had become famous, at least locally.

Of course, Riggs's husband, a prosecuting attorney, had gone toe-to-toe with Isabel in court numerous times, but they were friendly socially. Richard had a great deal of respect for the opposing attorney and liked her as a person.

Now, to see her like this. Riggs shook her head. She let out a deep breath and leaned in, studying the body. Isabel appeared to have a few cuts and bruises on her right hand. Possibly defense wounds? Natural causes from something else? Riggs gently lifted her hands, examining the nails, which were clean and well groomed, but she'd been soaking in chlorinated pool water. Her skin was wrinkled, naturally, from about eight hours in the pool. Fat chance of finding anything under her nails now.

A quick examination of her body revealed faint scars from breast implants. Another scar on her stomach; possibly liposuction? The full lips suggested lip augmentation. Rodriguez the TV personality had played up her sultry good looks on the show. Although she was in her early fifties, no one would have guessed that. The tight dresses, long dark hair, red-painted lips. A sexy attorney whose wit and savvy legal knowledge smacked down callers with little regard for genteel etiquette. Perhaps she'd made an enemy or two?

With a sigh, Riggs reached out and touched her face, bloated and white, then noticed that one of her pearl earrings was missing. There was no clothing nearby, not even a robe, so apparently she had gone swimming in the nude and somehow drowned. A folded towel lay on a nearby lounger. The pool was clean, no floaties, no empty wineglasses, nothing suspicious, but until the autopsy and drug screening came back, Riggs would treat it as a suspicious death.

"A real looker." Tucker leaned annoyingly over the vic. "She's that TV personality. You know, *Legal Matters*. Probably had one drink too many or maybe a few more than too many, from the looks of it."

These were assumptions that Riggs refused to participate in. "Tucker, my husband and I have known Isabel for about five years. I've seen her at all kinds of events around here, and she's never been one to overindulge, at least not like this. She's an active member of the community, she ran a successful law firm, her own television show. All that work certainly didn't happen in a drunken state. Something isn't right here."

One bad day turned into a terrible tragedy? She hoped not.

The early morning sun rose beyond a row of elm trees at the edge of the property. Crimson clouds cast a glittering sparkle on the pool water like pink diamonds. A sunrise that poor Isabel would never see.

With real regret, Riggs stood and nodded to the ambulance crew to load the vic onto the stretcher.

She asked Tucker, "Where's the friend who found her?"

"I interviewed her and sent her home. Told her to keep herself available for further questions. She was a real mess. Pretty useless."

Riggs would have liked to speak to the witness, but perhaps it was better to wait until after the autopsy.

Tucker added, "I get that the vic was a friend of yours, but I'm tellin' ya, Riggs. That girl put on some kind of a personal party last night, from the look of things."

Riggs spread her hands wide. "I don't see anything out here that would lead me to believe that. No glasses, no bottles. Usually there's some evidence of a party. Nothing."

"Go look in the house. Booze central."

She followed the stone pathway toward the house, a one-level sprawling ranch house in the foothills south of Medford. It was positioned on a hill with valley views and no nearby neighbors. With the shrubs and trees bordering the yard, there was little chance of any witness. Considering the level of privacy, it was no wonder Isabel had felt comfortable enough to walk around outside in the nude, especially at night.

Riggs slipped booties over her shoes. Entering through the French doors into the great room, she saw a lamp leaning off the edge of a table at the end of the couch. She walked over and righted it. Signs of a struggle? Everything else in the room was in its place. Rodriguez had been a minimalist, it would appear. No children or spouse, and the decor shouted cold leather and metal, except for the abstract paintings done in primary colors on the walls. The leather furnishings, all black, were top of the line—Italian, she guessed. A pair of red fur slippers were tucked under the glass-top coffee table. On intuition, she crouched on one knee and looked under the couch and the table. Nothing there, but to her left, something shinny caught her eye. A tip of a needle. A sewing needle? No, more like a syringe. Her heart sank. Surely Isabel was not into heroin? She bagged it as evidence. On the other hand, she might have been diabetic, which would be a much more plausible explanation. She made a mental note to examine the body for needle marks during the autopsy.

"She looked like a real schmoozer to me," Tucker was saying from the doorway. "Always drinkin' it up all over town. Hobnobbin' with the who's who. You know?"

Riggs ignored him and progressed to the kitchen, where she found a bottle of vodka, half empty, a half-full glass of vodka beside it on the kitchen counter. Another empty bottle of vodka on the floor in the corner. A broken glass, smelling of vodka, in the trash. The doors to a liquor cabinet in the dining room were open, revealing a wide array of quality liquor. The story was pretty clear.

Sick at heart, Riggs asked, "Tucker, can you make sure the fingerprint guys do it right? Something is off here to me. I know her, or at least I think I do. This just doesn't seem right."

"Methinks you're barking up the wrong tree on this one. It's pretty obvious what happened here."

She shook her head and inhaled a deep breath. "If I didn't know her, I'd probably agree with you. Just humor me. Okay? I mean, I could be wrong, but sometimes things aren't necessarily what they seem. Everything is so neat. These bottles left out. That bottle on the floor, not even in the trash. It just feels staged. I've known a few alcoholics in my life, and their homes were generally not perfectly spotless except for their bottle or glass. No . . . they tend to lead messy lives, with DUIs, broken friendships, banged-up cars, perpetually late for work or no-shows—you get the picture? A trail is left in their wake. She had a thriving business, a weekly show, spotless home and vehicles. Unless someone comes forward with a story of her unraveling the past few months. No . . . I just don't see it." She shook her head.

"Geez, Riggs, it's all spelled out for you. She's a drama queen. The TV personality. It fits. The spoiled prima donna."

"Sometimes, Tuck, I want to punch you out like Panetta did. Keep it up!"

He bristled, puffing his chest out. "What? I'm callin' a spade a spade. You're just emotionally involved on this one, so I'm gonna let this pass."

Shaking off his irritating negativity, Riggs walked down the hall to get away from him and continue her investigation. She entered the master bedroom and found a red dress tossed into a chair. On closer examination, the dress was crusted with a dark substance all over the bodice, with a few drops on the skirt. Blood? She didn't see any cuts on the body. Perhaps the blood was someone else's?

Next to the bed, on the floor, lay the missing pearl earring. Had Isabel just had a terrible day and gotten drunk? Maybe come home and hit the liquor cabinet? Decided to undress and drink herself into a happy state, only the happy state turned into a pity fest? Or worse, an argument with someone that grew violent?

The king-size four-poster bed didn't appear to have been slept in. It was neatly made with a black-and-white-striped silk duvet cover and matching pillows. A black leather bench with iron scrollwork sat at the foot of the bed. A pair of heeled white sandals sat on the bench, with one shoe hanging off, the strap caught in the ironwork. Riggs examined both shoes. One had red smear marks. Possibly blood, like the dress? Riggs studied the pale carpeting for any signs of blood drops, but found nothing.

Discouraged, she sighed. What a sad end. She dreaded telling Richard about her. He admired her spunk and ingenuity. Her first responsibility, of course, would be to tell Isabel's parents. The weight of that hung heavy.

After a search of Isabel's bathroom cabinet, Riggs concluded that none of the pieces of the puzzle fit. No drugs, nothing out of the ordinary. No needles or insulin. No bloody tissues in the trash. She decided the blood must have happened somewhere else.

Tucker stuck his head in the door. "The forensic team is finally here. Oh, and the vic is loaded in the ambulance."

"Thanks." She pointed to the red dress. "Can you make sure this dress gets bagged and tagged properly? Looks like blood on the front of the dress."

"Will do. Anything else?"

"The shoes too." She frowned, then added, "Tucker you said she showed up for work last night at the TV station. Find out if anything unusual happened there. An argument with someone. Anything."

"Yeah. Sure. I already got the producer to meet me in about half an hour at the news station."

"Good."

With a heavy heart, Riggs walked to her car, ready to follow the ambulance to the autopsy bay. She was bone-tired. Not the best way to start her day. As soon as Rodriguez was safely tucked into the morgue freezer, she would inform the parents, then head to the Niki Francis press conference. A shit show for sure. At times like this, she had to rethink what she was doing with her life. Wasn't life precious? Was all this focus on death really worth it?

She sat in her car, the sun now up in the sky and promising another hot day, and pondered the question, finally deciding that Isabel's friends and family would want answers. Deserved closure. An opportunity to move on with their lives. That made everything worth it. Her job really wasn't about the dead; it was about the living.

13

Somewhat refreshed after a quick shower, Whit walked into the newsroom wearing a conservative navy-blue sleeveless A-line dress and matching two-inch pumps. Simple power clothes for whatever the day might hold.

"Nice story, McKenna." Irene Bradshaw's head popped up from behind her cubicle, her dark, unruly hair a mass of curls. She slung an arm over the divider. In her midthirties, on the full-figured side, and partial to polyester with bright prints, Irene covered the business section. Astute and hypersocial, she kept her nose to the ground. "Haven't sold so many papers or received so many hits on our internet rag since . . . I don't know when. Management has a group of temps coming in to handle the expected wave of advertising. Money, honey. Too bad about Niki, though."

"Yes, it is." A chorus of phones were ringing. Whit glanced around. The newsroom was already a beehive of activity at nearly every desk. Reporters generally worked the streets and came and went at odd hours. Almost no one showed up before nine. Like Stu said, it was like herding cats. It was true, at least until the witching hour around five PM when everyone got serious about filing their stories before the seven PM deadline. "Is Stu in his office?"

"I think he's been there all night. He's with Mr. Arenburg."

"The owner?" Her anxiety shot up a notch.

"The one and only." Irene pulled a piece of licorice from a jar on her desk and nibbled on the end of it. "Stu said to hustle in there. They're trying to decide which stringers to assign you. I volunteered, but they said they needed me to cover business. Huh, like opening a new super Walmart is as exciting as your bombshell. I'm *oozing* jealousy right now. Let me know if you need any help. We'll keep it under wraps. I'll trade. You can help me cover the RoxyAnn Winery tour next week. We'll make it a playday."

Irene was one of the few people in the newsroom who hadn't eyeballed her when she was first hired as if she were an alien from another world. Back then, Whit had felt like she was wearing a sign that read *Tragedy. Beware.* People were generally uncomfortable around someone in mourning, but in her case she also came from the snooty *Los Angeles Times*.

Not Irene Bradshaw, though; there was no shifty slinking away for her. She had looped her arm through Whit's and paraded her around the newsroom, introducing her to one and all as if she were a new trophy. Irene had even crossed into the bowels of the newspaper, the advertising and public relations department, to introduce her to a few friends of hers. She was the only reporter who could cross that bridge, because she was a business writer, but the rest of the reporters had to remain pure, untainted by the stench of sales and the stigma of the for-hire crowd. The creed of the Society of Professional Journalists must be adhered to by shunning even the *perceived* notion that advertising dollars might in any way influence their stories. True that advertising paid for everyone's salaries, but that was beside the point. Keeping an expectable distance was mandatory.

Once the news staff realized Whit was not cut from snooty LA cloth, they were perfectly happy to embrace her as a comrade-in-arms. A major contributing factor in her acceptance was her parents, who had retired in Medford and developed social roots over the past fifteen years, as well as the Rotary, the Women's League, and numerous fund-raising organizations. She had also visited her parents many times over the years and become familiar with the community, so the transition was not a difficult one. Thanks to Irene, her somewhat terrifying reentry into the world of journalism had been achieved with minor setbacks.

"Okay, Irene, it's a deal," Whit laughed. "I'll cave to your demands and suffer through a day of wine and food. A play-day it is."

Goal achieved, Irene took an earnest bite of her licorice. "You're on, dollface."

Whit ventured down the hall, semi-listening to the scanner crackle with police chatter. Stu's office consisted of half windows that faced the newsroom, all the better to keep an eye on the reporters, whom he referred to as "defiant toddlers." She tried to dampen a flicker of apprehension as she approached his office and fixed a half smile on her face. She had a niggling fear that Stu might abscond with her story. Pitch it to someone else. Taking a quick breath, she knocked on his open door.

"About time." Engulfed behind a large steel desk piled with books and stacks of papers, Stu's small frame appeared almost childlike. He stood up, thin and wiry in a green-and-white plaid button-down dress shirt tucked into corduroy pants. The satisfied smirk on his thin, moustached mouth pre-empted his introduction. "Robert, this is Whitney McKenna, the new star of the *Chronicle*."

Whit stepped forward and clasped hands with Mr. Aren-burg, who had been leaning over the desk reading the *Wall Street Journal*. He was a couple of inches taller than Whit; slender, well-groomed, late sixties, he sported classic features.

She caught a whiff of expensive cologne. An attractive man, exuding a refined grace she hadn't expected. He wore understated solids in gray and black business attire, a notable fact that she appreciated because she also adhered to solid colors on principle. She thought it garnered more respect without ever even opening her mouth, and more importantly it saved a lot of time deciding what to wear. She had a thing about efficiency. Especially the time required to shut off her alarm, roll out of bed, wash her hair, dress, drink coffee while watching the news, and slap on minimal makeup. She had it down to twenty minutes. She knew because she often timed it just to be sure. The obsessive-compulsive behavior probably had something to do with growing up as an Air Force brat, with a father who thought his house should operate like the base barracks.

Mr. Arenburg smiled pleasantly and said, "Congratulations on a well-written story. Your headline is making world news right now."

"Thank you. My phone's been going crazy with media calls. I'm not sure how you want me to handle them."

"Sit down, McKenna." Stu slurped from his coffee cup, which had *The Boss* printed on it in Times Extra Bold font. An open planner sat in front of him next to a plate of glazed doughnuts. He was still old school about his planner; he didn't trust computers for something so vital. He motioned to an empty chair across from his desk. "Coffee, doughnuts?"

She sat stiffly. "No thanks, I just had breakfast."

The confined air in the room smelled of a bakery, coffee, and men's cologne. But what she sensed was an anxious excitement and an underlying tension that fanned her fears into paranoia.

Stu cleared his throat, glancing briefly at Mr. Arenburg. "Here's the deal, McKenna. We're gonna help you manage the media. This story is *hot*. It's really hot. Phone's been ringin' off the hook. We've got you lined up with interviews with major networks. You'll need to appear on local channels, of course—we have to support our community. You're pretty much booked all day." He grinned, revealing coffee-stained teeth, obviously pleased with himself.

Stu hadn't come out and asked her, but he knew if she didn't cooperate, all that business would be down the drain. They were walking a thin line. Her interviews had more to do with the *Chronicle* taking advantage of breaking the story and less to do with her as a reporter.

Still standing beside the desk, Mr. Arenburg hastened to explain. "You must realize we need to leverage our lead on this story. The revenue it will provide is significant. Also, the national and international implications are astounding. This story will, in fact, put Medford on the map."

Whit nodded. "I understand."

A message was silently transferred between the two men with a quick glance; then Mr. Arenburg spoke softly. "I'm aware of your recent recovery from a personal tragedy."

Here we go.

Woven between the lines was an unspoken reference to her emotional breakdown at the *Los Angeles Times*. Not a breakdown, exactly, but a heated and tearful argument with her editor regarding her "lack of concentration" on the job and the subsequent forced leave of absence, which had ended with Whit's resignation. It was all spelled out in black and white in her personnel file, including the kidnapping events in Afghanistan.

After yesterday's disturbing flashbacks, she was more than a little apprehensive about her own emotional stability, but she would never let them see that. Whit said defensively, "I can handle the story."

"Yes, you're a very accomplished journalist." Arenburg paused, as if searching for the right words. "I'm simply concerned about the level of stress this story will generate. You're a recent widow and you're recovering from a head injury. We just want to be considerate of that fact."

Flushing to the roots of her hair, she said, "With all due respect, Mr. Arenburg. This is not my first rodeo. I'm a seasoned professional. I can handle it."

"Don't misunderstand. We have confidence in your abilities and we want you to continue to cover the story, but feel it best to bring in support." His gaze swiveled to Stu, who appeared uncomfortable. "What I'm trying to say is that, in light of your situation, we wouldn't want to burden you with undue stress. This story will attract some highly contentious media. The competition for information will be fierce. So we've assigned an assistant, George Cook, to help you."

Stu chomped into a glazed doughnut and swallowed without chewing. "I know. I know. George is still a rookie, but he writes sharp copy. And he's only one semester from his BA."

She'd seen George in the newsroom and during some of the morning meetings. He was one of the few interns Stu had assigned real stories to cover on his own. She'd been too busy learning her new crime beat and juggling investigative stories to pay him much attention. All she knew was that he was a preppy kid from Pepperdine University.

Mr. Arenburg crossed his arms in a fluid motion that suggested the matter was settled. "It will be a great opportunity for George to work with a journalist from a larger market. You'll have your hands full with these network interviews, so you'll need someone to do legwork. He's also very good with social media. And we'll have a couple of freelancers in the office to assist both of you."

She'd covered big stories with partners in the past. As annoying as it was to have George, a junior reporter, assigned to her, she could see the wisdom in it. If yesterday was a foreshadowing, she was in for a rough ride ahead, personally and professionally. And as much as she hated to admit it, she could use the help. "All right, it's a deal, but I take the lead."

Stu chomped another bite and swallowed, shaking his head. "Always have to get the last word."

Whit smiled. "Well, I have to have a little pride."

Both men laughed, the situation defused.

"Listen, McKenna." Stu briskly rubbed his hands together, dislodging doughnut debris onto a paper plate. "We have another reason for assigning George to your story. You start digging deep into this killer's turf and things could get dangerous. Bad things don't just happen to journalists in war zones. We want you to keep in close contact with George."

"Yes, Stu, I'm fully aware."

"All right then. Watch your back and keep me posted."

"Don't worry. Since my 'tragedy,' I carry a gun in the glove box of my car. I have a license to carry, so if I get nervous, I'll keep it close."

Stu's brows shot up. "You realize we have a no-gun policy at the paper."

Arenburg said, "Do what you need to do, McKenna; just check it at the door before entering the building. The security guard has a lockbox."

She nodded, grateful for the support.

"Oh," Stu said. "I almost forgot. I've arranged with the district attorney for you to sit front and center at the conference this morning *and* dibs on the first question."

Unless the cops made an arrest, nothing of any real interest would be shared with the press. It was a facade, merely damage control and grandstanding for city officials. Her front-row seat was just a power grab by the *Chronicle*. Still, better than the back row, and it would elevate her among her peers.

"Sounds great." Whit stood to leave and was halfway out the door when she remembered the Delano story. She pivoted around. "Oh, I met with the fire victim's wife this morning." She quickly relayed the interview. "*She's* convinced he was murdered."

Leaning back in his chair at a cocky angle, Stu said, "Oh yeah? What's *your* gut tell you?"

"That he was into something secretive. And that secretive thing killed him, either directly or indirectly."

"Another homicide." He bounced out of his chair, getting worked up. "We gotta nail it then. We're rockin' and rollin'." He turned to Arenburg. "So who do ya think? Breckenridge?"

Whit stepped up to the desk. "I'm meeting with Mrs. Delano tomorrow."

"Why don't we give that one to Breckenridge? You need to focus on Niki Francis. And I'll need follow-up copy by ten tonight. Anything. Whatever you got. We'll be flippin' stories on that one for weeks."

"Mrs. Delano specifically asked for me," Whit protested. "And as a new widow, she relates to me. Why don't I meet with her and get back to you?"

His bushy gray brows came together in a frown, the deep circles of a sleepless night evident.

Whit pressed her advantage. "If it looks like an in-depth investigative piece that would draw me away from Niki Francis, then you can toss it to Breckenridge."

"Sounds like an in-depth investigative story already."

"I'll check it out and let you know."

She hurried away before he had time to refute her. She'd already developed something of a bond with Mrs. Delano, and she'd written the lead story. Common sense prevailing, she should have lightened her load, but like any good newshound, when she smelled the scent of blood she had to follow the trail.

14

C ITY HALL HOUSED the mayor's office, the police department, and various other municipal agencies in a boxy, three-story concrete building with expansive tinted windows.

The media circus had begun. Roadblocks barricaded the streets nearest the building, which were jammed with traffic. Whit cranked the wheel toward a side street and backed into a parking spot two blocks away in front of an old Victorian house, the remnant of a bygone neighborhood.

She'd left her new partner, George Cook, at the office to coordinate her afternoon schedule and dig up any leads on Delano. He seemed eager to chase whatever bones she threw him. Now she could focus on Niki Francis.

Whit gathered her bag and marched across sun-drenched asphalt into the shade of the municipal building, which was clogged like a backed-up parade with media. She pushed her way through. The air was heavy and disturbingly still. The sky to the east swelled over the Siskiyou Mountains with eerily greenish storm clouds, as if laden with algae. She hoped it wasn't an ominous sign for the day ahead. It would be a nasty storm for sure and another hellishly hot day. A uniformed officer stopped her at the barricade. She flashed her credentials and hurried inside.

It felt like old times, excusing and pardoning her way through the clogged aisle to the front-row seats. After eight months of barren desert, as far as high-profile media assignments, this was glory land. Already the big hitters were in play. The networks, CNN, FOX, ABC, and NBC, were all there, along with the local pack. She sat down and took note of every detail of the posse of officials up front.

On the platform, Detective Riggs's blonde pixie under the lights caught Whit's eye. The only female on the podium, her petite frame was dwarfed by the five men around her. She wore cream slacks and a matching sleeveless top. As the spokesperson for the medical examiner's office, she attended every press conference of relevance.

After checking microphones and television feeds, the city manager introduced the mayor, who in short order introduced the district attorney.

Edward Littrell began with the official announcement of the death and ongoing murder investigation of Niki Francis. He then gave a long-winded statement regarding the unfortunate circumstances that had summoned the press to such an event. His sharp features, pale even in summer, held a snide contempt, as if he was above it all. He wore a tailored suit and tie. As expected, he shared nothing of any real interest.

Secretly, Whit was somewhat pleased, because that would force the rest of the media to seek out the *Chronicle* for information until they could dig up their own sources. Eventually Littrell opened the floor for questions. Ignoring the raised hands, he pointed to Whit, reminding the assembled, one and all, his tone not especially flattering, of her scoop in this morning's paper.

Without hesitation, she said, "My question is for Sergeant Blackwell. Do you have any suspects or persons of interest in this investigation?"

Blackwell lumbered up to the microphone, massaging his black moustache, thick stomach bulging under his belted uniform, his dark eyes roaming the crowd. He introduced himself and identified his position on the investigation team, his Texas twang elongating his words. Sloow and steeady.

"We're an interagency team. A network of detectives from city police, county, and state. Our clear rate is ninety-four percent. Much higher than other counties. We're confident that everything that can be done is bein' done. We have over thirty officers conductin' field investigations on this case. The FBI has been briefed and special agents are assisting. Now, Mrs. McKenna, I can answer your question.

"It's still early in the investigation. We're followin' up on any leads as they arise and cannot make any further comments at this time regarding persons of interest."

Another fifteen minutes of questions and noncommittal answers from various officials added nothing of any interest, at which time the DA called an end to the meeting. Deflated, everyone stood to leave.

Whit packed up her gear, ready to beeline it back to the *Chronicle* for her scheduled interviews, then paused when a woman from the back of the room shouted her name.

"Whitney McKenna."

She stood, searching out who had called her.

A woman stepped forward. "McKenna!"

All movement in the room froze. In the sudden silence, Whit faced a vaguely familiar woman, probably from one of the network channels. She was tall, long dark hair, dark eyes, and clothed in a red dress. "Tami Dunn with NBC. Aren't you the same Whitney McKenna who worked for the *L.A. Times* and was attacked in Afghanistan last year because you insisted on following the story into a dangerous area? Wasn't your husband killed? Photojournalist John McKenna shot and killed by al-Qaeda insurgents?"

Every head spun back to gawk at Whit. She heard sharply indrawn breaths. Papers rustled, chair legs creaked. Her gaze darted around the room like a trapped animal. The faces stared back, stark, blatantly curious, some with unveiled pity.

Cameras flashed.

The air, which had previously been pleasantly cool, was now cloying with prickling heat along her spine.

Blindsided by one of her own. No, another species altogether, a broadcast journalist. Not that there was much difference anymore.

Apparently the grace period was over, the gloves were off, and she was fair game.

Cameras spanned toward Whit.

All the guilt and media-led accusations that had swamped her on the return from Afghanistan flashed through her mind. The emails and letters accusing her of warmongering and grandstanding even over her husband's grave. As if her blood-thirsty desire to cover news in hot spots had led to her husband's death. John had a history of photographing war regions and dangerous locations, but none of that seemed to matter. The fact that Kabul had not really been on the danger list for years didn't matter either. She had been branded as callous and self-seeking. An egomaniac who would chase a story at everyone else's expense. It was true that over the years she'd amassed a great many news articles from dangerous places and situations, but that hardly classified her as a warmonger. Her own guilt at having asked John to accompany her was certainly enough of a head trip.

Heat flushed her face. Yesterday's anxiety came surging back, buzzing in her head like a thousand bees. Her knees nearly buckled, and heart pounding in her ears, she stared back at Tami Dunn, speechless.

The weeks of unrelenting negative public scrutiny had precipitated her breakdown at the *Times*.

She couldn't handle that kind of public betrayal right now. Her recovery was too fragile.

She sensed Riggs at her side, heard her whisper, "You don't need to respond to that."

If she didn't, they would hound her. She swallowed hard.

"Yes." She cleared her throat. "Yes. I'm Whitney McKenna. I don't think my personal history has any relevance here. I will not discuss it. I'm a reporter with the *Medford Daily Chronicle* now, and as you heard the district attorney say, I broke the Niki Francis story. She was the victim of homicide, her body buried in a shallow grave. Why don't we focus on that? She has millions of fans eager to hear any news. In light of that, does anyone have any questions for me regarding *Niki Francis*?"

They pushed forward, asking questions all at once.

The horde descended . . .

Did you personally know or have you ever met Niki Francis?

Can you give us the names of the eyewitnesses?

Who reported her missing?

Have you interviewed the family?

Did you see the body?

"That's it. That's all I have right now. If you want a more detailed account, you can contact my editor, Stu Davenport."

She caught Riggs's nod toward the back exit and hurried out the door. Whit blew out a breath. "Shit. That was . . . I wasn't ready for that."

Riggs grabbed her arm. "Come on. Walk with me."

They moved along at an easy pace for a couple of blocks in amiable silence, which Whit was grateful for while she collected her chaotic thoughts. She paid little attention to where they were going. Before she knew it they were blocks away from all the hubbub. Even at midmorning the heat was unbearable. She was grateful for the building's shadows along the walkway.

"Let's have a few shots and a smoothie." Riggs suddenly paused at the door of Wamba Juice, a small Mediterranean deli.

"I could use a drink, but it's early yet. Now that you mention it, I might have a mini-bar bottle in my bag."

"No, you lush. Not that kind of shot."

They entered the small restaurant, which had only one patron sitting at a side table, as it was only half past eleven. Riggs greeted the tattooed and pierced young man behind the counter. "Hey, Monte. Good morning. We'll take two double wheatgrass shots. One Green Goddess, and I think my friend would like the . . . Wamba Wizard."

Laughing, Whit rolled her eyes. "Of course. I should have known. I've had all kinds of shots in my life, but never a wheatgrass shot."

"You'll love it. Lots of energy. Good for the soul."

"Shoot me now. I was hoping for something stronger."

"My treat," Riggs said, and paid the bill. "You can have that bottle in your purse later. I'm not even going to ask how it got in there or why you carry it around." She motioned to a two-seater table. "Let's sit by the window."

Whit admired a painted mural on the wall of a ship in harbor and rolling green hills. It reminded her of a long-ago train ride through Italy that she and John had enjoyed. She sat with a sigh at the plastic-covered table, grateful to be away from the eyes of the media.

The shot glasses with foaming lime-green juice were delivered to the table. Riggs raised a toast. "Here's to being a survivor."

"To being a survivor." All for being a good sport, she choked down the bitter brew, but couldn't hold back her disgust. "God, Riggs, why don't you just go out and pluck some grass and chew it. I'm sure it would have the same benefits and sure as hell the same taste."

Unfazed, Riggs grinned. "Lots of antioxidants. Helps fight cancer and lower cholesterol."

Sucking air through her teeth, Whit looked around for some water.

"For all your hard-core journalistic fearlessness, you can be a real pansy."

"What! I can suck it up with the best of them, but for God sakes, get me some water."

Laughing, Riggs went to the counter for their smoothies. "Here, prima donna, the smoothie will make it all better."

Whit suspiciously sniffed the pinkish smoothie. "What's in it?"

"Berries, other fruit. Just drink it and stop your sniveling."

"Sniveling? I take offense at that. I never snivel." She sipped, pleasantly surprised by the sweet frothy cream. "Okay, I can officially let you back in my good graces."

"Great. Now . . . let's talk about that fiasco. I hope you're not going to let that 'one-shot wonder' derail all your progress."

"No. Of course not. I should have seen that coming. For some reason it just never occurred to me. I've never been a fan of ambush reporting. Not my style, and it lacks intelligence. She won't get far with it, and I don't think she accomplished anything of value today."

"Well, I'm proud of you. You handled it very well."

"Thanks. I've had my doubts the last couple of days. Wondering if I came back to work too soon."

"I don't think so." Riggs shook her head emphatically. "You were going stir-crazy, remember? Too much time on your hands. You're a strong person, McKenna. Don't let any of those jackals out there tear you down."

"I'll be okay. It's just going to take time."

"I'm here, sister," Riggs reassured her.

"Thank you. This damn story. It's huge. And there is more to come. I've been in the business long enough to get a feel for things. Instincts. They almost never let me down." She stirred her smoothie thoughtfully for a moment, then asked, "Do you have the autopsy report finished for Mr. Delano? The fire victim?"

Riggs raised her brows at the sudden change of subject. "The preliminary, pending tox. You said you're talking with his wife?"

"Yeah. Had a long chat with her this morning, and I'm meeting with her tomorrow. She's adamant that someone killed her husband. Anything substantiate that?"

Riggs shifted in her seat. "Nothing I can share right now, but I wouldn't rule it out either."

"So my Spidey senses are getting the right signals? There's something, isn't there?"

She frowned, brushing aside blonde bangs, and opened her mouth to say something, then thought better of it.

"What?"

"Just that you need to be careful out there. As you know, it's a dangerous world."

"That's funny. Stu just gave me the same advice."

"It's good advice."

Suddenly uneasy, Whit leaned forward. "Is there something I should know about?"

Riggs looked thoughtful, sipping her smoothie and taking her time. "You're investigating the story of a woman who was murdered. You need to respect the fact that the killer is still out there, and he may not appreciate you poking around in his business. There are lots of reporters in town now, but he's reading *your* name this morning." Riggs's phone buzzed. She read the text. "Dr. Weldon is expecting me at the morgue. We'd better head back."

Whit thanked her for the drinks and they hurried to their cars, both absorbed in their coming day.

Back in her car, Whit sat replaying their conversation. Something important had gone unsaid. Frowning, she cracked her fingers, replaying the dialogue in her head. Riggs's warning came after she asked about Mr. Delano. She hadn't seemed the least bit shocked to hear that Mrs. Delano thought her husband had been murdered. In fact, Katie had advised her not to rule it out. Could Niki Francis's murder be connected somehow with Delano? Maybe he wasn't the drug addict she suspected. Perhaps Mrs. Delano was right and something else was going on. But what? What could tie Delano to Francis? If only she could get her hands on those autopsy reports. She couldn't . . . but maybe someone else could.

15

RAIN AND HAIL pounded the roof, and frequent claps of thunder sent tremors through the single-level building as Riggs and Dr. Weldon worked wordlessly together on Isabel's autopsy. Riggs had tried but failed to think of her as a "vic." An anonymous victim that she could remain detached from, with no regard for the physical remains. This woman had been part of their social circle. She flinched at another resounding bang above them. The continuous pounding rain and booming thunder unraveled her nerves even further.

"Hell of a storm," Weldon commented as he biopsied the right lung, his loud voice strident in the small room. "I don't think I recall such an unrelenting heat wave in the valley."

For want of sanity, Riggs decided that casual conversation was better than her thoughts. "I've lived here for eight years, and this has to be a record," she agreed.

"Did a stint once with Doctors Without Borders back in the eighties in Haiti. Port-au-Prince. Treating cholera. Pretty, but full of death. Satan's playground if there ever was one. Boy, I'll tell you what. Those storms down there will put some hair on your chest! Scared the livin' daylights out of me."

"Oh? I didn't know you were affiliated with Doctors Without Borders."

"Thought I had to do penance. I have a dark and twisted past."

A sudden thunderous boom shook the building, followed by what sounded like an explosion, and the lights flickered and died, enveloping the room in pitch-black.

Riggs jumped, her hand clutching her throat.

"Holy Mother!" Weldon bellowed right next to her. "Bloody thing was close!"

The storm continued to rage outside, but in the sudden stillness, Riggs could hear her own heart banging against her chest. The dark was a childhood fear that she'd never outgrown. After her mother died when she was nine, she had pictured her trapped in a casket, lowered into the ground, dirt piled on, lost in an inescapable darkness. She had obsessed about the image, developing a habit of reading under the covers with a flashlight to escape her tortured thoughts, as she shared a room with her younger brother. Over time the worrisome images faded, but not her dislike of the dark. Richard had grown accustomed to having a nightlight in the bedroom.

She'd had only a few hours' sleep last night, so she was jumpy. Striving for normalcy, she said, "I bet lightning struck one of the power poles in the alley."

"I daresay. Our generator will kick on soon."

Even as he spoke, they heard the whir of a distant engine, and the lights flickered back on. Not every light. The far recesses of the room were shadowed now, the hallway to the locker rooms dark, but the surgical lights overhead were bright again. In the eerie light Dr. Weldon's hulking frame was still poised over the corpse, scalpel puncturing the flesh. She glanced up and caught him studying her.

He grinned. "If it would help, I could do a maniacal laugh right about now."

Riggs let out a breath and laughed. "Thank you. I appreciate your natural gift for drama, but I don't think that's necessary."

He wiped a big, bloody gloved hand on the front of his surgical gown. "We're safe enough in here." He turned back to the biopsy table. "Well, both lungs are free of fluid. She probably had a laryngospasm. Happens in about ten percent of drowning victims. We'll order the diatom test."

Riggs worked with enough drowning victims to be familiar with the diatom test. Water contained tiny silica-covered plant bodies called diatoms that adhered to tissues like the lungs, liver, and kidneys. They tested the lungs for traces of diatoms.

Weldon tapped the corpse on the shoulder. "You, young lady, should not have been swimming alone."

"Drowning seems like such an unnecessary death," Riggs said. "Apparently she went for a late-night swim. I'm not so sure this was an accident."

"What did you see during your inspection this morning to make you say that?"

"It's more of a hunch. I didn't know her well, but she was so driven."

Weldon nodded. "The few times I saw her out and about at events, she struck me as a very strong-minded woman. So I agree with you."

"I just can't picture her drinking to excess like that. Sure, occasionally she may have had a night out or something, but the evidence was more of a habitual heavy drinker. I just don't buy it."

"We'll be thorough here; no worries."

"I also find it odd that for some reason the DA put a rush on it. Maybe they suspect foul play."

"Speaking of foul play, you know Ruth and I have season tickets to the Shakespeare Festival in Ashland. You should come with us sometime."

Weldon peeled off his gloves and tossed them into a trash bin. "Saw *Othello* last week. Fabulous young actress by the name of Rita Fredinburg, played Desdemona. However, the bloke that played Othello didn't strike me as talented enough to robustly play the part. A bit weak for a soldier."

"You're quite the Shakespeare fan."

"Indeed. Those gloves felt too tight." Weldon wiggled his fingers into another set of gloves. "Anyway, I played Hamlet once in college. Probably would have become a stage actor, but my friend and I got drunk one night after the final show and wrecked my car into a tree. I spent months recovering and lost a year of college. Turned my attention to medicine after that. Fascinating business, as you know."

After applying a few drops of the fluid from the vic's eye on an analysis strip to test for the presence of alcohol, dehydration, and glucose levels, Riggs turned to face Weldon. "Sounds like the accident was very serious."

"I'm afraid so. It changed my life forever. Both of our lives. I lost my driver's license and the hearing in my left ear, but my friend was paralyzed from the waist down. Ronald Brady. Ronnie became an English teacher. The stage had lost its appeal for both of us."

"It must have been devastating at the time." That kind of guilt could last a lifetime. He had in fact just mentioned doing penance.

"It could have been much worse. We were lucky to be alive. And I've managed to stay involved with theatre in my own way." He sighed heavily. "Strange how in a moment life takes a hairpin turn."

She nodded. "We know that firsthand. We see it here every day. One minute you're alive and well, and the next . . ."

"On the slab, like this young lady." Weldon leaned over and studied the vic's face. "We may have an error."

"What is it?"

"Her stats say she's sixty-one years old, but that's not what my eyes are saying."

"I thought she was younger as well. Facelift? She's certainly had everything else."

Weldon scrutinized her through his bifocals. "I'd say she doesn't look a day over forty. I expected to see signs of a facelift, but low and behold, nothing. Maybe she's just loaded up on Botox. What is your secret, Ms. Isabel Rodriguez?"

Peering at the corpse, Riggs carefully studied the bloated face. Last summer, she and Richard had visited with her at the Britt Festival in Jacksonville while listening to Kenny G perform. At the time, Riggs had looked up into Isabel's face and thought she looked much older in person than on her television show. But here, now, she appeared so much younger. The bloat in her face smoothed out some of the wrinkles, but there was something more to this. Definitely no scars from a facelift. Nothing about this case was right. Isabel was a perfectly healthy, career-driven woman.

Riggs shook her head. Her sleep-deprived brain was not functioning at its best. "The DA's rush on this seems strange."

"They also put a gag order on the report until further notice. Makes me wonder what sinister plot is afoot."

Yes, Riggs thought. *What is that about?*

Ready to stitch the Y-incision, Weldon worked quickly, using wide stitches, and finished a few minutes later. He then traded places with Riggs and inserted the scalpel behind the left ear of the victim's head, pausing as hail beat with great velocity on the door a few feet away. They braced as if expecting the door to fly off its hinges.

Weldon mumbled, "Hell of a storm."

More focused now, Riggs shut out the darkened hall and disquieting thunder. For her, the autopsy was an opportunity to write the last chapter in Isabel's life. She'd always appeared bold and confident, a woman in command of her fate. Richard had called her a "live wire." She had a reputation as an advocate for the underprivileged. She certainly deserved to have her death explained to her family and friends and to the community as well. Life didn't end with death for the loved ones; it was simply the last chapter.

Weldon sliced through the skin on the back of the vic's head, then went on around to the other ear. With expert efficiency, he pulled the skin from the skull, like deboning a chicken, and peeled it over the top of the head, laying it inside out just above the brows. The woman's shoulder-length brown hair fanned out across the sagging skin on her face.

Riggs picked up the Stryker saw from the counter and handed it to Dr. Weldon. When she'd first transferred to the department, the saw had given her nightmares. That was when Richard insisted she had developed a morbid interest in death, and though she had argued with him, she wasn't altogether sure he was wrong.

The high-pitched whine of the saw pierced the air like a shrill dentist's drill, bringing her back to the moment. Weldon cut a circular hole in the victim's head. The unpleasant odor of burning bone permeated the room. He paused to form a triangular notch at the back of the skull, for proper future replacement after the brain examination.

He returned the saw to Riggs, who wordlessly replaced it with a hammer and chisel. Poor Isabel had never imagined when she arose from her bed yesterday that she'd be a corpse by midnight. Riggs studied the tattoo on her own arm, the cross and rosary, a symbol of hope. She believed there was a heaven and she hoped Isabel Rodriguez had found it.

Weldon tapped on the chisel and lifted the top of the skull, which pried loose with a sucking sound. He laid it aside on a nearby table. She handed him a pair of dura strippers—a type of forceps, so called because they helped peel away the thick membrane layer of dura that covered the brain. Weldon first used a scalpel to puncture the dura mater, then cut through it with a pair of scissors, following the edge of the skull opening. With a firm grip on the dura strippers, he tore it loose, tugging gently.

He slashed the spinal cord, cutting through the arteries that surrounded it. Next, he cut the cranial nerves to free the brain.

"Hmmm . . . a bit soft," he mumbled. "Ms. Rodriguez, we need to toughen you up."

Since the brain, as sometimes happened, was too fragile for immediate dissection, he set it gently into a brain bucket filled with formalin to soak for a day or two. The formalin would help stiffen the tissue for proper slicing. The DA would not be happy about the wait, but it couldn't be helped.

As Riggs picked up the bucket to set it on the scale, the brain rotated to its side.

Goose bumps chilled her spine, and she shuddered.

"Dr. Weldon?"

"Yes?" He replaced the top of the skull, aligning the triangular notch.

"You need to see this."

"What is it?" Intent on his task, he pulled the skin back over the top of the head, and the corpse once again had a face.

Holding the bucket as level as possible, she crossed the short space until she stood directly under the surgical lights.

Weldon adjusted his glasses and peered in. "I'll be damned."

Protruding from the brain was a mass with bits of hair and bone.

"Three teratoma victims in less than twenty-four hours?" Riggs asked. "What are the odds of that?"

"Impossible."

She stared down at the tumor, her thoughts crisscrossing with all the information she knew of each victim. All three had been in apparent good health. Better than good, actually— exceptional. And they all had money. Did they know each other? Medford had about eighty thousand people, and probably only a tenth of them were affluent. Presumably they all belonged to the same social circles.

Under the glaring light, they stared at the nude body of Isabel Rodriguez. She lay on the table where her skin had been sliced open, bones crunched apart, organs biopsied, fluids taken, just like the others. Yet the cause of death for all three victims remained a mystery.

She turned to Weldon. "What could cause these teratomas?"

"Hmmm." He pondered the question, drumming his gloved fingers together. "That's a question for the pathologist, Dr. Kessler. I sent the other two teratomas over this morning. We'll incise this one, and you can hand-deliver it as soon as we're finished here."

"Okay. And Blackwell needs to be informed immediately."

Weldon leaned over the body. "My question to you, Ms. Rodriguez . . . what is the source?"

"That's the million-dollar question, isn't it? Now none of them can answer." Riggs stripped off her gloves and tossed them in the trash. "These vics were murdered, Dr. Weldon."

"If that's true, wouldn't the killer know that autopsies would be performed and the teratomas exposed?"

She shook her head. "Not necessarily. The body of Niki Francis was never intended to be found. The fire victim was no doubt expected to burn up, leaving no evidence. Isabel came in as a drowning. So we find a teratoma. It happens. But the killer never planned on us finding the bodies of the other two and discovering *three* teratomas."

Weldon nodded in agreement. "With the possibility of murder and the lack of fluid in Ms. Rodriguez's lungs, I'd say she was dead before she hit the water. We'll see what the diatom test says."

"Maybe there's something in the tox report that links all three victims."

"Possibly, but that will take a good four weeks, even on a rush."

Reaching for her cell phone, she said, "Detective Panetta needs to witness the rest of the autopsy. Now that it's a criminal investigation. This is not a serial killer in the traditional sense of the word, but a serial killer nonetheless."

"Indeed." Ever dramatic, Weldon tapped the brain bucket with his scalpel. "With a teratoma for a calling card."

16

W HIT HUNG UP the phone on her desk and grabbed her
leather bag. "George, come on. You're getting a massage."

His brows lifted curiously. "A massage?"

Thankfully, she'd finished her last media interview for the
day before Bradshaw called. A call well worth a new tub of
licorice.

"Yes, Bradshaw, the business writer, just shared a solid
lead. She was at a chamber of commerce foray at Eden Retreat
and, eagle eye that she is, spotted our target."

George ran a comb through his short dark hair. Frowning,
Whit watched him flick imaginary dust off his pale-blue dress
shirt, sleeves rolled up to his forearms. He was a far cry from a
typical print journalist. Most were a rugged lot with more guts
and determination than etiquette. Georgie could have stepped
directly off the pages of *GQ* magazine. She'd done a bit of
probing and discovered he'd interned last summer at the *Seat-
tle Times*. He'd probably never made it past writing the obitu-
aries. No doubt he'd chosen the *Chronicle* for a chance at
decent bylines.

Hopefully he had some grit. "Come on, Ralph Lauren.
We'll talk in the car."

They were merging with traffic on I-5 headed south when lightning split a dark, menacing sky overhead. Rain pounded the roof, windshield wipers slapping back and forth. The storm she'd seen approaching this morning had finally hit with a vengeance. It was nearly dark as night, and traffic slowed as hail and wind assaulted the freeway.

She raised her voice over the storm. "Just got a hot tip that Mark Sorenson, Niki's son, checked into Eden Retreat. I thought if you went in for a massage, I could wander around, maybe get a chance to talk with Mark. That would give me a legitimate reason for being on the property."

"C'est la vie. I'll suffer for the cause."

She smirked. "You're sacrifice is duly noted."

A blinding burst of light struck so near the car that Whit thought they might have been hit.

George grabbed the dash and braced himself as Whit hit the brakes.

In a panic, he asked, "Do you think maybe we should pull off and take shelter?"

"Take shelter where? The next exit is six miles up the road, and now all these cars are driving like grannies."

"Excellent point." He leaned forward, anxious gaze focused on the tumultuous black sky. "But I'm relatively certain that last bolt nearly obliterated our lives."

"Believe me, if I had my choice, I wouldn't be out here. Freak storm. I saw it coming in this morning from the south."

"Maybe it's an omen."

Ignoring that, Whit focused on driving as hail the size of quarters pummeled the car and thunder reverberated from the ground. The road was a mirage of red taillights and gushing water.

"Care for a mint?" George asked.

She threw him a caustic glare. "I'm trying to drive."

"I thought it might take our minds off of our imminent death." He paused, popping one into his mouth, before continuing. "They're from an ancient abbey in Flavigny, Burgundy. They've used the same recipe since 1591."

George held the tin in front of her. The lid had a picture of a shepherd and a young girl, *Les Anis de Flavigny*.

"Sure. Why not?" The mint, a small white candy, round and smooth, had a brilliant flavor. It might be her last meal. She said, "Thanks. How did you find these?"

"I discovered the delectable little candies when I was on a four-week internship in France. They come in other flavors as well. Now I order them on the internet."

French candies, French slang. Whit asked, *"Parlez-vous français?"*

"Oui. Four years at Pepperdine and four in high school. *Et toi?"*

"A couple of years in college. Not well, but it got me around most of Europe."

"You were a war correspondent, right?"

"In the beginning and intermittently since then. Among other things." She braked as another semi flew by, dumping water across her windshield. "Bastard! Those things are a menace on the road!" She white-knuckled the steering wheel and prayed because she literally could not see two feet ahead.

George angled toward her in the seat. "What was it like? Covering war zones? Daunting, I presume?"

Daunting . . . really. What planet is this guy from?

"Why? Are you interested in becoming a war correspondent?"

"I've considered it." He pulled a nail file from his pocket and groomed while he spoke. "Seriously. I read the book *Embedded*."

"Uh-huh."

"So why did you do it?" he asked.

"Cover wars?"

"Yes."

"Because I was drawn to it. Like a moth to a flame. Especially after nine/eleven. I was young and outraged and in college at the time. So, I took a semester off and at my own expense, tagged along with a reporter from the *L.A. Times* who was covering the Iraq war. I met my husband in Baghdad. Ironic, really, because it's the remnants of that war that killed him."

"I'm sorry."

"Thanks. Let's stick with your question." Better to focus on that. "After traveling around with the *Times* reporter for three months, I was hooked on the adrenaline, the firsthand experiences. Like I had a front-row seat to history. Really, if you think about it, journalists are the first historians. And since we're writing about current events, our stories have the power to change the future."

"That's interesting. I'd never really contemplated journalism in that way, as historians."

"Sure. We also have an opportunity to expose injustice and provide a voice for victims of abuse or corruption. Especially for war victims, many of whom are women and children. Everyone can post stories now with cell phones, but it's still difficult to get any serious attention unless legitimate media backs a story."

She saw the exit sign and flicked on the blinker, steering for the off ramp.

"But what was it like? In the action?"

At the stop sign, she turned left and followed Dead Indian Road, twisting through foothills spotted with manzanita trees and shrub brush.

Images of war zones played out in her mind, most of them with John. She said, "It's . . . dangerous." During her career she'd personally known four journalists besides John who'd lost their lives. They were all dedicated reporters who believed in the cause.

"Care to expand on that?"

She thought about it for a moment. Remembering. Finally she said, "Reporters and photographers plant themselves in dangerous situations with a false sense of security. Like our press pass is a get-out-of-jail-free card. All we have to do is wave it and the horrors of war will pass us by. As if we're invisible ghosts, we wander through battlefields, and sniper zones, and land mines, taking notes and snapping pictures. All the blood splatters and broken bodies become part of the landscape. It's surreal."

"But you're justified. It's a noble cause."

"I believe in it, yes. But . . ." She shook her head sadly. "But that's naïve, George. It doesn't work that way. There's no protection in being noble. We're shot. We bleed. We're raped. We die. The press pass only gets you *into* the nightmare. After that . . . there's no guarantee you'll ever get out."

He studied her face, dark eyes searching. "Do you regret it?"

She thought of John and their adventurous lives together. The stories they'd covered, certain that it made a difference to someone somewhere. They'd lived more in their eighteen years of marriage than some couples did in fifty. Maybe that terrible day in Korangal Valley was the price they'd had to pay.

"No," she said, emphatically. "We loved being war correspondents. But after our children were born, I spent most of my time in the States, except for special assignments. John often traveled overseas on freelance jobs. We were happy with the arrangement. It was a good life for us. What happened to my husband and I while we were in Afghanistan is no different than what might happen to a firefighter or a cop. They're exciting jobs with high rewards that come with a high price. The common denominator is that, while we know the risks, we never think it will happen to us. Does that make sense?"

"Insanely, yes."

Whit's phone rang, automatically routed through her car speakers. She pushed a button on the steering wheel. "Whit McKenna."

"This is Gale Delano. I have some important news. I did as you asked and called my friend, Dr. Weldon, the medical examiner. Can you stop by? I think you'll want to hear this."

"I'm following up a lead right now. Would five o'clock be okay?"

"That's fine. I'll text you the address."

"Thanks." Whit hung up, hoping for the best.

George asked, "Isn't that the fire victim's wife?"

"Yes. I found out this morning that she's good friends with the medical examiner. They worked together on the Shakespeare Festival Board for years. I texted her and asked her to call him. Just see if she could get an off–the-record comment. If my hunch is correct, her husband's death may be connected in some way to Niki Francis."

On her right, they approached the sign for Eden Retreat. It promised "a renewing of mind, body and spirit." She could certainly use some of that. No doubt it cost a pretty penny. She made a right turn onto a narrow road that curved and dipped into a valley of rolling hills, with small thatched huts surrounded by a profusion of colorful flower beds. Walking paths crisscrossed on well-groomed lawns and wound their way to a huge central garden, and on a clear day would provide an unobstructed view of the valley below.

Two main buildings sprawled out beneath tall pines at the base of the hills. Serenity Hall was a two-story structure with dark wooden balconies and a long covered porch decorated with rattan tables and chairs spaced along its polished boards. Whit parked in the guest parking and turned off the engine.

"Okay, George. It's your birthday and Auntie Whit is buying you a massage."

"My first undercover assignment. *Fantastique!*"

They made a mad dash inside, wiping rain from their faces.

Gauzy white curtains draped either side of a picture window behind a large granite reception desk. Tinkling Tibetan music filled the gracious hall from speakers hidden above in the open-beamed ceiling. Whit thought the music begged for a mat and yoga pose. She scanned the massive reception room for her prey. But they were alone. Where was everyone?

A brass gong the size of a dinner plate, suspended in a wooden frame, sat on one corner of the desk. The sign beneath it read: *Ring me for service.*

"Excellent." George grabbed the mallet and hit the gong, making Whit flinch.

Taking a deep breath, she picked up a brochure from a gold rack on the desk. "Looks like it's either 'A Touch of Paradise Full Body Massage' or 'Must Be Heaven Deep Tissue Massage.' They both last an hour and are . . . *a hundred and sixty dollars each!*"

"May I help you?" A slender woman approached, wearing a white-and-gold robelike dress. Her straight, black hair flowed behind her, almost to her hips.

Whit wrapped her arm around George. "It's my nephew's birthday, and I've promised him a massage."

"Do you have an appointment?" The woman smiled pleasantly, though she cast a skeptical glance their way.

"No. Do we need one?"

"Usually, yes." She sat in front of a computer at the marble desk; her long red nails, *more like talons*, pecked on the keys. "Let me see if we have a massage therapist available."

Just then, a fine-boned man with dark features and curly dark hair, worn long over his ears and brushing his shoulders, emerged from the hall. He walked with a fluid stroll and approached the desk. He wore a pale-blue Tommy Bahama shirt and white cotton dress pants with leather sandals. He smiled, revealing straight white teeth. "Oh, what luck to come out of my office just when a pretty woman needs assistance. I see my beautiful wife, Charlene, is helping you. I'm Dr. Leon Heinemann, owner of Eden Retreat. Welcome!"

First impression: sleek, charming, a tad pompous.

Whit shook hands and introduced herself, wishing she could have avoided meeting the owner. Harder to fly under the radar. Just her luck. At least he seemed pleasant. A practiced charm to schmooze the wealthy? Little did he know he was barking up the wrong tree. She'd be lucky if the bank covered George's massage after all the back-to-school clothes and supplies she'd bought for her daughters this week.

Dr. Heinemann looked about twice the age of his "beautiful wife." Could this be wife number three or four? He cocked his head to the side, studying Whit. "I feel like I know you from somewhere. Have you been here before?"

"No." Uh-oh. She'd been on too many news stations today. "People say that all the time. I just have one of those faces, I suppose."

His dark gaze slowly perused her features, taking his time. "I can't say that you do. Actually, you have a very striking face, and that red hair is . . . memorable. You're beautiful." Was it her imagination, or did his voice thicken in a lusty sort of way? *Creepy.* "I'm sure I've met you somewhere before. I'm usually quite good with faces. Give me just a moment and I'll figure it out."

Whit glanced sidelong at Charlene, who didn't seem to mind her husband's mild flirtation. She smiled pleasantly and said, "It looks like Aleena had a last-minute cancellation. She'll be free in about twenty minutes, if you're willing to wait?"

"Perfect. Did you decide which massage you want, George?"

He lifted his gaze from the brochure. "The Touch of Paradise sounds fabulous!"

Dr. Heinemann smiled approvingly. "You'll love Aleena. She's from Bermuda and applies neuromuscular therapy along with Swedish massage techniques. We have traveled far and wide for only the very best products and services—and people, of course. Hippocrates, as you know, was the father of medicine, and prescribed a daily massage for the maintenance of good health."

"Fascinating," Whit said, as she was paying for the massage, praying that her debit card wouldn't be denied. She hadn't bothered to check her balance in weeks. It wouldn't matter in the long run when she turned it in to the *Chronicle* as an expense, but for now she was milking a turnip. "Lucky break for us you had an opening."

Charlene nodded. "Although we try to be accommodating, we're often booked weeks in advance." She handed Whit her debit card. "While you wait, can I offer you some iced tea or champagne?"

George jumped on it. "Champagne would be splendid. Thank you."

Whit threw him a discouraging look.

The astute Dr. Heinemann graciously offered to comp the drinks. "Enjoy the refreshments on the house. And feel free to wait here until the storm passes." His gaze rested on Whit. "And perhaps you'll come back another time and take advantage of our facilities."

Said the spider to the fly. Something about him creeped her intuition.

"When you have a moment, dear," Dr. Heinemann addressed his wife. "We have a special guest who needs our attention."

Charlene glanced toward the hall where Dr. Heinemann had emerged. They exchanged a look, and she gave a slight nod. "Certainly."

Noticing Whit's avid attention, the lovely Charlene explained, "My husband is a psychiatrist, and as you can imagine, he sometimes has patients who require privacy, so they come and go through a private entrance in the back."

"Yes. Of course."

Dr. Heinemann excused himself. "A pleasure meeting you. Enjoy your visit."

"Please." Charlene came around the counter and waved them forward. "Follow me. We have a lovely atrium sushi bar."

They followed Charlene to a set of elaborately etched double doors with swirling fish in a gold finish. Whit turned and glanced back over her shoulder. Heinemann had not retreated to his office; instead he stood behind the reception desk staring at her, the boyish charm gone, his gaze narrowed as if he'd somehow seen through their ruse and pondered throwing them out. She quickly stepped through the door.

Special lighting overhead illuminated the grand room in a sea of shimmering light. Red hibiscus and red ginger bloomed in various planters, and tinkling waterfalls cascaded from the back of the room to a small stream under a bamboo bridge. Every wall was clear glass.

No wonder the rich hung out here.

Charlene led them to a table overlooking the hills and a panoramic view of the storm. Here the music was the same soothing Tibetan sounds as in the lobby, but was nearly drowned out by the driving rain and thunder. The padded chairs were pale lime green to complement the garden effect.

"Thank you." Whit sat and scanned the grounds. Certainly no one was out in the storm. This might have been a bad idea. She could always resort to asking for Mark's bungalow. Fat chance they'd give it to her, but they might ring her through. Short of going door-to-door, she was probably screwed.

"I'll return when we're ready for you, George." Charlene signaled the waiter as she walked over the bridge, her long black hair swaying like a pendulum.

George sat with a satisfied grin. All he needed was a silk paisley smoking jacket to perfectly fit the ambience. Good thing she'd worn her pearls and navy dress; at least they looked the part.

A pale-yellow glass of sparkling champagne arrived for each of them. Her glass was adorned with a bright-pink hibiscus flower.

Whit frowned as George sipped his drink, pinkie raised. "Are you even old enough to drink?"

He feigned offense. "Madam, I'll have you know I'm twenty-two, going on twenty-three."

He did have the shadow of a beard and baby laugh lines around his eyes when he smiled with those orthodontically perfect teeth.

Whit dropped the flower on the table and sipped the champagne, wishing she could toss it back like a shot. Lovely little bubbles danced in her stressed-out stomach. She also wished like hell she had even three inches of story to fill tonight's thirty-inch hole. Blank space on a page was conveniently called a "hole" in the newspaper business. It felt like a screw twisting a hole right through her stomach.

So far her follow-up story consisted of Niki's fund raisers in Medford and personal history, which was okay for backstory, but certainly no lead. She *could* link it to other known contributions she'd made to charities around the world and create a "soft story" about her philanthropist philosophy on life. Getting the details of Niki's last days alive had been more difficult than she'd thought. Annie, the housekeeper, had been advised by police not to speak to journalists. George had reported that the only road to Casa Blanca Ranch had been blocked off. Niki's manager was simply refusing all calls.

In other words, *bullshit*. Stu would hang her out to dry. This was no fluff piece; this was one of the most notorious murders in history. Above the fold wasn't even half of it. This story better mesmerize readers for the full front page. The little *Medford Daily Chronicle* was now competing with the world's most powerful media. She had to outperform them in order to hold the readers. Her stringers were busy gathering details of Niki's day-to-day life since moving to Medford and collecting dates and names for further investigation.

"This place reminds me of my dad's country club," George suddenly blurted.

Whit shook her head and blinked. "What? Your dad owns a country club?"

"Yes. There's a lot of money in Bend, you know."

"That explains the whole Ralph Lauren thing. So how did you end up in the news business? There's certainly no money in it."

George leaned back, arms crossed. "A kid from my school, whom I hung out with sometimes, was kidnapped when I was eight years old. Mason Fleming. Everyone thought it was a ransom kidnapping, because his family had money, of course, but no one ever heard from the kidnappers. He just simply disappeared. I was interviewed by the cops and later by a journalist. Everyone had kind of melted away, the story died off, but this one journalist came back months later and interviewed me. He was sure he had found a new thread in the story, but I never heard from him again. I followed the story on the news for weeks and then months. I was obsessed with every scrap of information, every lead. I dreamt about Mason, and thought I saw him sometimes."

"I'm sorry. It sounds like a frightening time for you. I remember that story."

"Yes. What you'd call a watershed event in my life. Cataclysmic. I learned an appreciation for news. I watched the newscasters deliver the news every morning and read all the different print stories; gradually more and more of the other headlines caught my attention." He shrugged, "And that was it. I've been fascinated with the news since then."

"I can understand why."

As if making a confession, he looked sheepish, and added, "I've kept this under wraps . . . and I know it's tantamount to being a traitor, but my major is broadcast journalism, not print."

"That explains a lot too!" she teased, and they both laughed. "I won't hold it against you."

The ego that most broadcast "talent" brought to the table was a total turnoff for the humbler print journalist. Two-bit sound bites didn't qualify as real journalism. At least that had been true twenty years ago when she'd entered the field.

Things had changed. Not wanting to discourage him, she said, "Since print journalism is going the way of the dinosaur, broadcast is probably a smart move. Not much separates the two mediums anymore. They're both online and use video. Can't say that I'm liking all the changes, but I do appreciate the immediacy of the news and all its formats."

Out of the corner of her eye, she saw, to her utter amazement, Mark Sorenson enter the restaurant and head for the sushi bar. A tall, muscular man, he wore tan dress shorts, a short-sleeved black dress shirt, and Italian sandals. Casually, as if admiring the decor, she watched him take a barstool and greet the chef.

Observant, George said, "How fortuitous is that?"

"A gift from God, George."

At that moment, Charlene beckoned from the doorway.

"My massage awaits." He stood. "Good luck!"

He sauntered toward the bridge.

Now she could focus on Mark. They were virtually alone in the restaurant; aside from a young couple in the corner, everyone else had probably taken shelter from the storm in their bungalows. She decided to sit two seats away from him, close enough to overhear Mark's conversation with the chef but not so close as to appear predatory. She slipped onto the padded stool and set her purse on the counter in front of her.

The chef handed Mark a wineglass of sake. "You're early for dinner, Mr. Sorenson."

Mark gulped a healthy swig of the wine. "Actually, I'm late for lunch. I haven't slept or eaten in two days." He had a deep voice that articulated well, like a broadcaster's. Maybe his mother's stage and film DNA had something to do with it. "I thought I'd eat an early dinner and go to bed."

"Yes. Good idea, Mr. Sorenson." The chef leaned in and placed a set of chopsticks wrapped in white linen in front of him. "So sorry. We'll miss Ms. Francis. She always made me laugh."

"My mother was larger than life, that's for sure." He leaned his elbows on the counter, his head in his hands. "I couldn't stay at her house. Everywhere I look, I see memories of her. I can't say that it's much better here."

"I'm sorry, sir. I'll have your usual ready for you shortly. More sake?"

"Thanks, but that's not gonna cut it tonight. You got something stronger back there? Some Nikka? On ice?"

The chef nodded and placed in front of Mark a tumbler with ice, pouring an amber liquid into it.

"Thanks, Sam." He sipped and nodded his approval. "You might as well leave the bottle."

The chef set a small white tray with assorted sashimi before him, with smaller trays for sauces. He paused in front of Whit. "Welcome to Eden. Would you like a full meal? Or we do have a fine appetizer tray. All the fish is delivered fresh daily."

Without looking at the menu, Whit replied, "The appetizer would be great."

"And sake as well?"

"Ahh . . ."

Mark glanced her way as he wiped his mouth with a napkin. His tone was bitter. "You only live once. Might as well *drink* up."

"True. Life is short. Sake it is!" She'd have to crack out a credit card for this one, but it might be worth it.

His dark-brown eyes ran a quick appraisal as he seemed to analyze her. He exuded confidence. Someone used to getting his way, a stockbroker on Wall Street. As if coming to some kind of conclusion, he leaned over and offered his hand. "I'm Mark Sorenson."

"Whitney Robinson." She used her maiden name.

"You ever had Japanese whiskey?"

She shook her head. "Can't say that I have."

He turned to the chef. "This one's on me. Just give Miss Robinson a glass. I'll share from my bottle." Turning blood-shot eyes on her, he said, "I don't like to drink alone."

"I see." He had a John Wayne, take-charge gruffness about him, with a hint of refinement that she found charming and disconcerting at the same time.

He asked, "Are you staying at Eden?"

"No. I'm waiting for my nephew to finish his massage." It was just a tiny white lie. Friend, colleague; they were inter-changeable, weren't they?

The chef placed an appetizer tray and glass in front of her, then discreetly bowed his head and walked away.

"Had a massage today myself." He poured whiskey into her glass and handed it to her.

"Thanks." She swirled the amber fluid, listening to the ice clink against the glass. Suddenly she remembered John holding up a glass of Scotch, a cigar in his mouth, saying, "Here's to the good life!" They had settled down for the night in a bombed-out shelter of a house in Baghdad. She blinked the image away and the sharp ache that went with it. "I apologize, but I couldn't help overhearing just now. Was Niki Francis your mother?"

"Yes. Yes, she is . . . was." He raised his glass. "Here's to my mother."

Whit gently tapped his glass. "Here's to Niki." She gin-gerly sipped, and found the amber fluid surprisingly smooth, with a soft burn finish.

Mark downed his glass in one swallow. He turned squarely at her, a small smile on his lips. "I didn't come in here to tee-total. Are you with me?"

How did this happen?

Whit nodded, knowing she would regret it. "Cheers." She polished off her glass and came up sputtering and choking. *Holy mother!* It had been a while since she'd taken a shot like that.

After patting her squarely on the back with a hand like a club, he said, "It'll be better the second time."

He was about a hundred pounds heavier than her. There was no way she could match him drink for drink. She'd better get her questions in now. "What was your mother like?"

"She was beautiful. So passionate about life and so giving. She'd never hurt a fly. A more decent person you'll never know." He suddenly punched a fist into his hand, his neck blotching purple above the collar of his black dress shirt. "I want blood."

The bass voice sent a chill up Whit's spine. Suddenly very glad she'd kept her identity hidden, she confided, "I don't blame you. I lost my husband last year in Afghanistan." Was it manipulation if she was simply sharing the truth? No. As long as she was honest, she was in the clear. Her whiskey-addled brain was loosening her tongue. "It's terrible. I tried to suppress it, but I guess I can't."

He glanced up in surprise. "I'm sorry. I'm so caught up in my own pain, I never thought about how someone else might be feeling." Grabbing her glass, he poured more whiskey. "Here's to the ones we loved."

Whit raised her glass, and pretended to sip. She had a story to put out, and her thoughts were already swimming. Lack of sleep, an empty stomach . . . she was toast.

He patted the seat next to her. "I'm coming over."

The bird is in the cage.

Mark slid his glass over and sat beside her. She felt dwarfed next to his broad shoulders and barrel chest, his elbow and muscular forearm nearly brushing hers. It had been a while since she was so close to a man.

She sat up straight, forcing distance between them. Now that she had lured him in, all bets were off. Even if the police had not indicated that he was a person of interest in the case, he was an only child, and she assumed he would inherit his mother's fortune. She also reminded herself that, to an investigative reporter, everyone was guilty until proven innocent.

She reached into her purse and turned on the recorder. If she needed to use anything he said, she'd come clean and ask his permission.

She thought about Dr. Heinemann and wondered if Niki had been a patient. "I'm not trying to pry into your mother's private life, but when I came in just now, I met Dr. Heinemann, and I thought, well . . . maybe he could help me with my grief." Again, just a white lie; it never hurt to have a therapist.

He bottomed his glass again, and poured another. "She was a regular; swore he was magical. But I'm not so sure now. I spent two hours with the guy this afternoon. He suggested I focus on saying goodbye to my mother. Forget about the circumstances of her death. Let that go. It would prolong my grief. *Let it go?*" His neck was turning purple again. "To think that she was murdered makes me sick to my stomach!"

"Have the police said how she died?"

"They won't say. I'm not sure they know yet."

"Hey, Sammy!" a voice bellowed from behind them. They both turned to see a hulking kind of guy, wearing a white martial- arts robe with loose-fitting black pants. The robe had the Eden Retreat logo embroidered in black ink on the right breast. He had the whole Arnold Schwarzenegger thing going on: square jaw, muscles, and accent, with each word spoken like it was its own sentence.

"Can you toss together a tray of sashimi? I'm starving."

The chef nodded and quickly went to work. The hulk reached out a muttonlike arm and patted Mark on the shoulder. "Tough break about your mother. You know, I loved her like family. We all did."

Mark nodded. "She was easy to love."

"I've got a break in about thirty minutes. I can fit you in. Work out some of the tension."

"Thanks. I appreciate it, but I had a massage earlier with Adele." Mark lifted his glass. "I'm about to drink away my troubles and go get some much-needed sleep."

The hulk glanced her way, his hazel eyes sharp. "Sleep, huh?" He lifted his square chin toward Whit. "Who's this lovely lady?"

Mark twisted toward Whit. "Oh, sorry. I'm piss-poor company today. Whitney Robinson, this is Wilhelm. He's a physical therapist and a masseur here at Eden."

He stepped around Mark and offered his hand, which was surprisingly soft; it should be, with all the lotions and oils the massage therapists used every day. She could imagine him in a boxing ring more easily than she could see him doing yoga. Still clasping her hand, he said, "Any friend of Mark's is a friend of mine. My offer to Mark is an offer to you. I have a doctorate in nutrition and wellness. I offer an amazing massage, but overall wellness is my specialty. Mind, body, and soul. Niki was a regular for several years. I actually have clients that come up from California, Washington, and the Midwest. So you see, you would be in good hands."

Whit smiled. "Thank you. I can't right now, but I'll come back another time."

With a disappointed sigh, he leaned in close. "Consider it an open invitation."

Sam, the chef, called to him, gesturing toward a takeout box, and Wilhelm turned abruptly, collecting his dinner. Before leaving, he paused next to Mark. "Again, buddy. My condolences."

Whit turned to Mark and asked, "So, did your mother recommend him?"

Mark chuckled. "Oh yeah. Her and half the ladies in Medford. Why not? Good-looking guy like that?" He popped a piece of sushi into his mouth and chewed. "Why? Are you thinking about taking him up on his offer?"

She shrugged, feeling warm all over from the whiskey, the tinkling music soothing in the background.

"My mom loved the guy. You probably would too."

Whit quickly covered her glass when he offered her whiskey. "I have to drive."

He swung his arm toward the wall of windows, where lightning lit up the sky and illuminated the valley floor. "Not in that storm?"

"Afraid so."

"Well, I'm staying here tonight." He glanced at her plate. "You haven't eaten your sashimi."

She would have been much happier with a bowl of chicken lo mein noodles. But after munching a mouthful of sashimi, she reeled him back on point. "I'm sure the police are doing all they can."

He rolled his eyes, his expression suddenly thunderous again.

She waited patiently, as he seemed to disappear into his own thoughts, the dark circles under his eyes a testament to his troubled mind. "I'm going to find the bastard who did this to her if it's the last thing I do. I've hired a PI; he's flying in tonight."

"Do the police have any suspects?"

He snorted. "Not that I know of. I don't trust these local yokels." He put his head in his hands, rubbing his temples. "I don't understand what happened. She was going to New York this week to shoot a new movie. We had reservations at Nobu's."

"I'm sorry."

"You sure you don't want more?" He lifted his head and grabbed the half-empty bottle. "I haven't eaten much lately and I've got a nice buzz goin'."

"No thanks."

He topped off his glass. "The weirdest thing is . . . I just talked with my mother a few days ago. She never told me she was sick. I feel like she betrayed me. Why keep it a secret?"

"She was sick?" This was the first she'd heard of this. If Riggs had known, she'd not mentioned it.

"That's what the medical examiner said."

"What kind of sickness?"

"I don't know. She was such a health nut, it's kind of hard to believe. It hurts that she never told me." He nursed from his glass. He was clearly hell-bent on getting drunk. In fact, he was well on his way. His words were starting to slur.

"Was it cancer?"

"Something like that. A tumor. At the base of her skull." He touched the back of his neck and weaved on the stool, then caught himself with a steadying hand on the counter. "Whoa. Easy does it. Guess I better slow down. Anyway, yeah . . . the doc called it some kind of *monster* tumor. I asked the medical examiner if she suffered. He said she probably had headaches. And Annie, that's her housekeeper, said that Mother complained about not feeling well and refused to eat." He rubbed bloodshot eyes, clearly intoxicated. "Why did she shut me out? I would have been here for her, and none of this . . . I . . . I wouldn't have let it happen."

Whit wished he hadn't drunk so much so fast.

Blurry-eyed now, he smiled sadly. "She used to take me on pony rides. Down in California. On the beach. You know, I never missed my dad. They divorced when I was just a kid; didn't see him much. She always told me I was the man of the house. It was a ranch, really. We always lived on big property. Usually had some family or other living there with us. Kind of a commune. My uncle . . . Uncle William helped raise me. He's coming up tomorrow. Gonna be a hell of a day. Man, oh man . . ." His deep voice cracked. "I don't want to bury her!"

Whit felt the sting of tears. "I'm so sorry." Embarrassed, she blinked rapidly.

"Yeah. So *why* didn't she tell me?"

"Maybe she just didn't want you to worry."

"I don't know. Damn. It's too late now!" He suddenly stood up, staggering a little, and caught the counter. "How in the hell am I supposed to live in a world where . . . where the one woman on earth who loved me, no matter what, is *gone*?" He dug in his pocket and tossed a tip of rolled-up bills on the counter and waved to the chef; then, as an afterthought, he spun around and grabbed the half-empty bottle. "Hey. Thanks for . . . being my drinking buddy. And, Whitney Robinson, sorry about your husband."

"Thanks."

Disappointed, Whit watched him cross the bamboo bridge. He'd never said how the police believed Niki had actually died. In conclusion, she decided he seemed like a decent guy, probably not the killer. She reached in her purse and shut off her recorder.

Beyond the windows, dark storm clouds slowly boiled in the hot wind. The tension in the sky matched her mood. Time pressed in on her from all sides. The hordes of reporters from other media outlets had descended on Medford like locusts, devouring her leads faster than she could gather them. It was the nature of the beast, but she was in crisis, trying to navigate through a storm of her own. Maybe the stringers had gathered some good intel since she'd been away. The stress had begun to feel like an anvil slowly compressing her slightly sloshed brain. With any luck, Mrs. Delano might have something worthwhile.

CHAPTER

17

THE OLIVE GREEN–AND–WHITE two-story Queen Anne home sat well back on an expansive lawn. Oak trees lined the long driveway, the branches weaving in the blistering wind. The earlier torrential storm had dissipated, leaving behind scattered thundershowers.

Whit pulled into the driveway and parked. She stepped up on the wide porch and rang the doorbell. As she waited, she thought about her conversation with Stu. He'd called her as she was on the way over to Mrs. Delano's house, asking why she'd left George at the office. Not a happy camper, he didn't give a rip about Mrs. Delano's sensitivities, and he demanded to get a "visual" on her Niki Francis follow-up by nine o'clock.

She convinced him that George was researching vital information and she'd be back in the office in an hour, which was basically the truth.

Her little sojourn down whiskey lane had left her heavy limbed. She'd downed a Diet Pepsi at the *Chronicle*, but as yet it hadn't helped. What she needed was a good night's sleep.

Mrs. Delano opened the door wearing tailored, pale-blue slacks and a cream tank top. Her face was drawn and tired. "Do come in. We'll be on the back patio, because I still have a number of boxes to unpack. As you can imagine, I've been busy making funeral arrangements. We have relatives flying in from across the state. They're complaining that the hotels are all booked with journalists because of the Niki Francis murder."

Whit followed her through a living room still stacked with boxes to a screened-in patio. A clear pitcher of lemonade with two iced glasses sat on a dining table alongside a stack of papers. Pots of colorful yellow, red, and purple impatiens lined the windowsill. They sat beneath a fan clicking rhythmically overhead, stirring the sultry air.

Mrs. Delano motioned toward a stack of papers on the table. "I compiled most of the information you wanted, just in case. But now that I've spoken to Dr. Weldon, I'm not sure we need it."

"What did he say?"

"Here. I wrote it down so I would remember properly." She handed Whit a piece of yellow monogrammed stationery with the initials *GD*.

"'Teratoma,'" Whit read aloud. "What is that?"

She shrugged. "I'm not certain. Some kind of brain tumor. Dr. Weldon was quite hesitant to share information. So, I specifically asked if he had discovered anything that could explain Bo's odd behavior. I explained how important it was for me and my sons to understand what had happened to Bo."

"A brain tumor?"

"Dr. Weldon said it was in an area of the brain that would have caused personality changes. Aggression and mood swings, even delusional behavior. Just as I described to you." She smiled sadly. "Let me tell you. It was a great relief to hear him say that. At least my boys will know their father had a medical problem, not a moral one."

The last thing she'd expected was a brain tumor. What kind of tumor had Niki Francis been diagnosed with? She'd check her notes. She'd been half crocked at the time. Very odd that they'd both had tumors. "Will the medical examiner con-firm this?"

"I'm not sure. He said to keep it to myself, so I don't think so."

Why would Dr. Weldon ask Mrs. Delano to keep quiet?

Whit absent-mindedly gathered the paperwork Mrs. Del-ano had put together. Glancing through the list, she said, "I see your husband was a patient of Dr. Heinemann."

"Yes. It was part of his health kick. Once a week he went to Eden Retreat for massages and mental therapy. Why?"

"You'd think the doctor would have noticed dramatic changes in his personality."

"I should have insisted he see his physician. He certainly couldn't make sound decisions for himself. Aside from his behavior, his headaches should have been a clue."

Whit nodded absently. "Headaches can sometimes be caused by tumors . . ." She sucked in her breath. "That's it! Headaches *are* the clue. Niki Francis and your husband com-plained of headaches. And they *both* had brain tumors."

"What?"

"I interviewed Niki's son this afternoon at Eden Retreat."

Mrs. Delano shook her head. "I don't understand."

Whit stood up and paced the confines of the screened porch. Was she grasping at straws? Mrs. Delano had just found some semblance of peace. Was she justified in shattering that?

"I'm sorry," Whit apologized. "I don't want to jump to conclusions. Let's see what type of tumor your husband had." She picked up her phone and googled *teratoma*. She began to read the description aloud, with growing revulsion. "Not a pretty picture."

"It's detestable." Mrs. Delano grimaced.

"Yes," Whit tried to suppress her excitement as she contin-ued reading. "Teratoma is Greek for 'monster tumor.'" She grabbed her leather bag and dug through it. "Just a minute." Upon finding the recorder, she listened for a few minutes until she found what she wanted to hear, then played the tape for Mrs. Delano at the spot where Mark said his mother was sick.

"You see," Whit said. "Dr. Weldon told Mark that his mother had a tumor. A monster tumor."

Mrs. Delano's lips thinned in irritation. "I still don't understand what this is about."

"When Mark said monster tumor, I thought he was talking about the *size*. A *large* tumor. But he was actually describing the *name* of it. Do you see now? They both had these . . . teratomas! They both died within days of each other. Mark was confused about his mother's illness because she was such a health nut, just like your husband."

Very slowly, Mrs. Delano leaned back in her chair, her face pale.

"This cannot be a coincidence. It's too rare. Bo *was* murdered?"

"I don't know for sure. I need to do some more research. Do you mind if I go ahead and take the information you gathered for me? There may be something useful in it." Mrs. Delano nodded absently.

Whit reached across the table and gathered the papers, spotting Dr. Heinemann's name again. Both victims had been his patients. Could he be the killer? Psychiatrists had medical training. He also possessed a nice little handbag of psychological tricks. He would know all their weaknesses and precisely how to manipulate them. She felt like she was about to dive into murky water with something evil lurking beneath the surface.

18

R IGGS AND PANETTA practically sprinted through the long, green corridor at the pathologists'. The Diagnostics Clinic, located near Rogue Community Hospital, was housed in a newer two-story brick building. They were required to sign in, and given plastic clearance tags. Their escort, a thin woman with a harried expression, buzzed them through an electronic door. On a mission of her own, probably because she was working late on a Saturday night, she cut a quick path to Dr. Kessler.

"Detective Riggs." Kessler pushed away from his desk, shaking hands with them. He had a direct, no-nonsense manner that she appreciated. He often acted as an expert witness in court cases. Of medium build, early sixties, bald with piercing blue eyes, he wore a white lab coat over black slacks.

She introduced Panetta. "He's one of the detectives working the Niki Francis case."

Panetta shook hands, then gazed over Kessler's shoulder.

Taking notice, Kessler said, "My specimen collection."

A shelf on the divider that separated the lab rooms held glass specimen jars containing blobs of various shapes floating in cloudy, yellowish liquid. The "trophy" shelf ran the length of the room.

"This is a display of the tumors we've dissected over the years. Just a few," Kessler explained. "We keep these as a reminder of just how fragile our existence really is."

Panetta frowned. "How do you mean?"

"For instance, there are two hundred twenty cell types in the human body, any of which could go haywire while they divide into the approximately hundred trillion cells that make up our bodies. Only, maybe, one in ten of those cells is actually human. The rest are from bacteria, viruses, and other microorganisms."

"Fascinating."

Pressed for time, Riggs interrupted, "Dr. Kessler, what can you tell us specifically about teratomas?"

"Usually they're congenital or present at birth. Infants are sometimes born with large teratomas in the testicles."

From the corner of her eye, Riggs saw Panetta flinch. She teased, "What's the matter, Panetta?"

"Just got a visual that literally hurt." He reached up and adjusted his tie.

"Yes, I couldn't agree more." Kessler grimaced, but his blue eyes were alight with amusement. "This tumor, the teratoma, is made up of all three germ cell layers. It can present itself with hair, teeth, and bone. Rarely, it can form eyes, a torso, hands, feet, and tissue from the lungs, brain, and liver. A really exciting bit of tissue. I have a few on the end over there. That last one weighs two point three pounds and has a jaw with actual teeth."

Panetta walked over to inspect it.

Riggs retrieved a plastic container from her shoulder bag. "This is the third teratoma that Dr. Weldon told you about. Do you have time to look at it now?"

"Yes. Yes, of course. I'll freeze it in dextrin solution so we can get a clean slice for the microscope."

"Thank you."

Kessler went through a side door and returned in less than a minute, waving them over. "Let's take a look."

They followed him to the back of the lab, where he placed the slide into a microscope and peered through the lens. "Yes. I can see all three germ layers clearly. This is a mature teratoma." He stepped back. "You can see for yourself."

Eagerly, Riggs stepped forward. Fascinated by the purple paisley design, she stared at it a long while, but could make no sense of it. She backed away so Panetta could view it. "So you're saying that this is the same type of tumor as the others?"

"Yes."

"Okay. Then, in theory, say they weren't born with them. What could have caused them?"

"The most obvious explanation would be stem cells."

Panetta pulled out a notepad. "Stem cells?"

"Yes. Stem cells have a history of creating teratomas. That's pretty common knowledge."

Riggs and Panetta made eye contact.

"Not common for us," Riggs said.

"No. I suppose not." Kessler explained, "Under restricted circumstances, the FDA has approved embryonic stem cell therapy for spinal cord injuries. It's the first of its kind."

"Embryonic?" Panetta asked. "You mean from fetal tissue?"

"Yes. Americans have become tourists of the stem cell trade."

"What do you mean, tourists?"

"In order to get stem cell injections, Americans travel overseas or to Mexico. Usually planning a vacation at the same time. Thus the name *tourists*."

"Why hasn't the FDA approved the procedures here?" Riggs asked.

Kessler shrugged. "The vast majority of these procedures have not been approved by the FDA. And some of them are quite controversial."

"Why is it controversial?"

"Because the embryo is destroyed during the process of creating the stem cell line."

"I see." Riggs wasn't sure how she felt about that, but it wasn't something she could contemplate right now. She and Richard had conceived twice and miscarried both times. They were so busy with their careers, they just let it go. Then her cancer hit and any thoughts of children were abandoned for the sake of survival.

Panetta asked, "So you think stem cell injections caused these tumors. Where would they have gone for treatment?"

Kessler rubbed his chin thoughtfully. "Europe. The Ukraine. Mexico has a few clinics and they're just over the California border, so that's always been a popular choice. These clinics have elaborate websites that promise all sorts of cures. Anything from cancer to rebuilding your heart after a heart attack, curing Parkinson's . . . you name it. Even beauty treatments." He shook his head sadly. "People can be so gullible if they're ill. You can't blame them. But these clinics offer therapies that have not been tested for safety. They can cause adverse side effects, such as tumors. They lure people in with false promises, then charge a pretty penny. Only wealthy Americans can afford these types of treatments. They range from thirty thousand to sixty thousand dollars or more. It's quite a racket."

"That fits our three," Panetta said. "But aren't labs here in America producing the same stem cell lines?"

"Yes, of course. But not for human trials. No, I'd take a close look at any travel plans the victims made during the past six months or so."

They thanked Dr. Kessler and hurried back through the winding corridors.

Panetta's phone buzzed. He read the text and grinned. "Game on."

"What?"

"Crime analysis researched a thirty-minute call Niki Francis made just hours before her death. The call was to a company called Human Resources, Inc., near San Francisco. Guess what they do?"

Riggs stopped abruptly, her hand on Panetta's arm, pulling him back. "Stem cell research?"

"You got it."

19

THE MAUDI TEAM sat in stunned silence, Riggs and Panetta having shared the information learned from Dr. Kessler. Discovering they had a third vic who had suffered from a teratoma placed a momentary pall over the team. They were meeting in a room on the second level of the sheriff's department building on Highway 62 near White City. The five-person team was joined by chief of police Tom Holbrooks and lead FBI investigator Robert Rasmussen. The agent stood alone in the back of the room by the coffee pot, sipping from a Styrofoam cup. He was of average height and broad shouldered, with a droopy-eyed expression that seemed set in stone.

Blackwell massaged his moustache thoughtfully. He moved to the front of the board, where a picture of Niki Francis stared back at them in all her glory. Probably a promo shot from one of her movies, Riggs thought. He pointed to the picture. "She has to be our primary focus. The media will hang us out to dry if we so much as trip on the Francis case. They're circling around out there like vultures, but let's not let up on the others either. Tucker, you had time to get any info on Isabel Rodriguez?"

Chomping the last bit of an egg-salad sandwich retrieved from the vending machine downstairs, red-eyed and obviously sleepless, Tucker swallowed. "I paid a visit to the TV station. The producer said she'd been nervous last night. Complained of a headache. He also said that during her three years at the DA's office, Rodriguez developed a *personal* relationship with Edward Littrell. You get it? Personal?"

Blackwell scowled.

Tucker continued, "They kept it private. According to the producer, Littrell repeatedly promised to divorce his wife and marry Isabel, but he never followed through. Dirtbag. She got fed up and opened up her own practice. Then started her TV show. Somewhere in there, they had regular sex. So good old Littrell was banging the vic the whole time."

Blackwell appeared ready to chew the cigar whole. "That's an intriguing story. Full of angst and all that. What's the flippin' point? That our DA is an ass? We already know that."

"The point . . . they were doing the deed usually at Eden Retreat. The staff arranged for complete privacy."

"Yeah. So?"

"So . . . got it right here in my notes. Same damn thing with Delano. Burns and I spent the night at the offices of Olsen and Delano. Seems Delano represented Niki Francis's son, Mark Sorenson, in a DUI a few years ago. So they knew each other. The day before Delano bit the dust, he asked his secretary to make four phone calls. One of them was to Niki and one was for a counseling appointment with a Dr. Heinemann at Eden Retreat. According to the secretary, he was a regular out there."

"Hot damn!" Blackwell turned and wrote the name on the board. "Panetta, you said Niki Francis was a happy visitor at Eden Retreat. Sounds like they all liked to hobnob there. And maybe the good psychiatrist can enlighten us on his relationship with the vics."

The mood in the room became charged. Riggs felt it too. They had their second real break in the case.

Special Agent Rasmussen spoke from the back of the room. "We'll run Heinemann through the system. See if anything comes up."

Blackwell nodded. "Fair enough." He turned to the newest member of the team. "Burns, any luck on the truck lead?"

"Still working it," Burns answered in a calm, simple demeanor. "Nothing with a Ducks sticker on the back yet. There's a lab tech at Providence Hospital. He's the only medical person so far, and has no priors. He gave permission for the crime lab to test the back of his truck for residue from a sticker he might have removed. I don't think he's our guy, though. At last count we still have seventeen trucks to run through."

"Focus on Dr. Heinemann. See if he owns a truck." He pointed at Riggs. "Got anything else?"

Leaning forward, elbows on the table, Riggs said, "It seems apparent that these vics were involved in an experimental treatment. Our conversation with Dr. Kessler pretty much confirms this."

Tucker asked, "What nutjob would do that? Volunteer to be a freakin' guinea pig?"

"No. Not volunteer. I think they paid for it. And Tucker, people will do just about anything if they think they're dying." Her gaze bored into his bloodshot eyes, daring him to make one of his wisecracks. She'd have thought he would be more sensitive, knowing she was a cancer survivor. At that moment she was glad Panetta had punched him for making comments about his wife's drinking problem.

"Yeah." He slowly nodded, with a swift darting glance around the room. "Delano's wife went on record saying he snatched fifty grand from their savings account. Swiped it right out from under her. She busted him later, but he wouldn't break. Never told her what he did with it. She thought he was banging that Czech chick with it."

"When was that?" Blackwell asked. "We need to start a timeline."

"About eight weeks ago."

Riggs added, "We checked their travel history even further back than that, as Dr. Kessler suggested. Unless they used cash and drove, possibly to Mexico, nothing links their travels. So that puts them all within the U.S. and probably somewhat local. Which also indicates, according to Dr. Kessler, that the experiment would have to be illegal, since embryonic stem cell research has not been approved in the U.S."

Panetta interjected, "There's that thirty-minute call Francis made to Human Resources in Livermore, California, as well. Another thought: we have to assume, if three people were willing to participate, then there may be others. We also have to assume, if there were others, they're being hunted down and eliminated to prevent any of them from exposing whomever is responsible for the experiment."

"Catch the bastard." Blackwell pulled the cigar from his mouth, spitting tobacco into a nearby trash can. "Panetta, you and Riggs head out to Livermore. I want to know what Human Resources has to do with Niki Francis. I want to know every detail of that thirty-minute phone call she had with them. Tucker, head out to Eden Retreat. Chat with Dr. Heinemann. Burns, go with him. A little intimidation never hurts." He glanced at his watch. "It's almost five o'clock. It's been twenty-four hours since we found the Francis body. Let's move out. Keep in mind, the media is out there on a feedin' frenzy, so make no mistakes. They'd just as soon eat us alive."

20

"POOR RAVAGED SOUL." George rolled a chair up next to Whit and set her recorder in front of her. "I listened all the way through."

She polished off the last of her second Diet Pepsi and tossed the can into the recycle bin. Turning toward George, she was suddenly assaulted by his breath, which reeked of garlic. Blinking rapidly, she waved a hand in the air. "What *have* you been eating?"

He grinned. "I ate a sandwich from a deli down the street while you were gone. It was magnificent. Let's see . . . it had tomato, onion, basil, fresh mozzarella, and arugula with a lemon-garlic vinaigrette. Oh, on a French baguette. Delish!"

"Well, it smells like something crawled up in your mouth and died." Yanking her desk drawer open, Whit pulled out a pack of spearmint gum and offered him a piece.

"No thanks. I have my mints." He patted his pocket, reminding her of the French tin. "Oh no. I must have left it in my car."

Whit stared at him until he took the gum. "Good boy. Now I'll fill you in on my interview with Mrs. Delano." Whit shared what she'd learned, watching George's eyes grow round.

"So, by some fantastical event, Delano and Francis have this monster tumor?"

"That's what I think. Now, let's see what the hell this tera-toma really is."

"Definitely beyond strange and too bizarre to be a coincidence."

"Well, if there is a link, I *will* find it."

Whit ran a search on the internet for teratomas and started jotting down notes.

"Wikipedia?" George asked. "We need peer-reviewed medical journals."

"Yes. I know. I'm just making a list of technical words that are associated with teratomas so we can look them up." She tapped into one of the newspaper's many databases looking for peer-reviewed science articles. She typed in *teratoma* and read with disappointment. "Oh. This article says they're usually present at birth. It says teratomas are most common in the tailbone, ovaries, and testicles. I guess that's possible. It just doesn't seem likely for our victims, given the circumstances." She blew up the image of a teratoma on her computer monitor. The thing had an eyeball and part of a leg with hair.

"My God!" George pulled back, looking pale.

Whit grinned over her shoulder at him. "This is some gruesome stuff! What great copy it would make. I've just got to find the link, damn it."

Growing frustrated, she typed in *germ cells*. Again . . . nothing. *Pluripotent cells and teratomas.* She read with growing excitement.

George moved back to his desk and sat waiting with a look of dread. Sifting through peer-reviewed articles was slow read-ing. Trying to decipher medical terms was above her pay grade. After an hour of searching, she was able to find enough to at least make a decent guess.

"Here we go, George. I cut and pasted these articles to my file, but so far, this is what I've got." She motioned him over. "Slide your chair back. This one is talking about mice used in an experiment back in 2011. It says that injections with pluripotent cells caused brain tumors in five mice. Whatever pluripotent is. That's old data anyway. This one here is from June of 2010: a story about a boy in Russia injected with embryonic stem cells that caused a brain tumor. Here's another article from 2019, but it's more scientifically technical. I'd need an expert to decipher it. Still, if I understand this correctly, we may have our answer."

"What is it? What causes that ghastly thing? Please tell me it's not contagious."

"Embryonic stem cell injections, George. They cause teratomas."

"Who in their right mind would chance that? And for what?"

Whit shrugged, stumped for an answer. "Niki Francis and Bo Delano were both in good health. *Exceptional* health, in fact. It really doesn't make any sense."

"Certainly not. Not if *that's* a possible outcome. I think I'm traumatized for life!"

She ignored him, trying to think. "Just because we don't understand it doesn't mean it didn't happen. People can do some pretty stupid things. That 2010 article said the treatment was for a brain tumor. I find it hard to believe that both of our victims had brain tumors before the injections, but I guess it's possible. Whatever Delano was into, health nut that he was—anyone who would spend a bloody fortune for water two thousand feet below the ocean's surface is willing to go to any length, I'd say. Like try some kind of fringe treatment for even better health."

"Like superhero health."

"Yes, something like that. Only the teratomas were not supposed to be part of the treatment plan. My guess is whoever botched it didn't want to be exposed."

"So, what now?"

Whit shook her head. "I don't know. I need to think. At the very least, this is some kind of medical malpractice, or worse, a madman is using an illegal medical trial on unwitting participants, like lab rats."

"That's hard to imagine."

"Yes, it is, George, but it's the only viable answer to our questions."

Whit glanced over her shoulder at Stu's office. He was still conferencing with Breckenridge. She half-suspected Stu was tossing the veteran reporter her Delano story. She needed to get in there and convince Stu that Francis and Delano were connected; hence, they belonged to her. It was nearly seven on a Saturday night. Tracking down decent sources would be tough. Unfortunately, Stu would never believe her without more proof. Luckily the majority of the newspaper staff were still laboring over last-minute stories, as the next day was Sunday, their biggest publication day and most profitable ad day, which would buy her more time.

"George, can you do me a favor? Get into the system and bring up all the photos you can of Niki Francis that were taken in or around Medford. Especially if you find any pictures with Niki and Mr. Delano. We need to lay out a case for Stu that those two knew each other. Knew each other well enough to be involved in something off the books together. And I want to know everyone else Francis was friends with. Make a list."

"I'm no slacker." George looked offended. "I mastered that plan this morning."

"Oh. I was so busy with those stupid media interviews, I haven't had time to dig through the notes. Where are they?" Her desk was a nightmare of sticky notes and copies from various interns delivered over the past twenty-four hours.

"I sent it to you in an email."

Her inbox was swamped with emails. Hundreds of them, mostly from other media; wading through that would be a nightmare. Glancing at George's computer screen, she asked, "Can you just pull it up on your screen?"

"That's definitely an easier challenge."

She watched as he flicked through an array of photos of Niki Francis at various events around town. A tennis club. Fund raisers. The park. The Britt Festival. Then a photo of

Isabel Rodriguez popped up. "Stop there. That's Isabel with Niki. I know her; she's one of my contacts. I didn't know they knew each other."

"It's a small town." George chomped his gum, popping it every little while. "The socialites have few pickin's."

Whit shook her head. "Eighty thousand people live here."

George sat straighter, adjusting the collar of his crisp blue shirt. "The cream is always at the top. That elite group is a small one. Trust me, they know each other."

"All right, smarty-pants. Who's the other woman they're with?"

"That's easy. She's in half a dozen of these pictures. Her name is Celeste Cordero. She's a hotshot realtor. She owns Cordero Realty." He flipped through a few more photos of her. "Here she is with Bo Delano *and* Isabel Rodriguez. See? Small world."

"Yes, I've heard of Cordero Realty. Her signs are everywhere." She reached over to still George's hand, her heart starting to race. "Can you make that picture larger?"

George frowned. "I think so." He clicked on it and transferred it into their photo program. In seconds it filled the computer screen.

"Look." She pointed. "Where have we seen that porch?"

"Eden Retreat!"

Whit stood up and stretched. "Well, it's clear that Delano and Francis knew each other and were possibly close friends."

She glanced across the aisle to the health writer's desk, but Yolanda Diaz wasn't there. The woman was territorial about her sources and confrontational, but if Whit needed a medical or science source, Yolanda was her best bet. There wasn't a health care enterprise in a single nook or cranny of the Southern Oregon valley that she didn't know about.

George rolled his chair back to his desk. "I'm going to put together a file of all the pictures with Niki Francis and friends."

"Works for me. Print that out and a list of names too. We can follow up tomorrow. Set up some interviews, if they'll speak to us. Now, at my own peril, I'm going to go hunt down Yolanda to see if she can provide a source to decipher some of that medical data. I saw her earlier, so hopefully she's still here and in a decent mood."

Whit hurried through the maze of desks and down the corridor to the lunchroom, where a couple of copy guys were picking off yesterday's birthday cake. No, they hadn't seen Yolanda. She pivoted back down the hall and entered the ladies' bathroom. There, at the mirrored counter, stood Ms. Diaz, liberally applying makeup. A slender woman with dark windswept hair that fell just below her shoulders, Yolanda stood about five foot five and wore a silver sequined tank and a short black skirt accompanied by four-inch heels. To accent her ensemble, she wore large silver hoop earrings and several silver bracelets.

"You look nice." Whit paused next to her. "Got a hot date?"

Yolanda slanted a quick glance her way but continued applying a dark liner to her upper eyelid. "Maybe."

Whit cringed inwardly. Not exactly friendly banter. You never knew with Yolanda; sometimes she was animated and gregarious, while at other times she was sullen and withdrawn. Not for the first time, Whit wondered if she was bipolar. Since Whit was not particularly patient or fond of tiptoeing around people, she suppressed the urge to ditch her and go find her own sources. She was up against a hard deadline, and this was not a good day to test her negotiating skills. Groveling went against her moral code. Walking a fine line, she tried again, using a more direct route.

"Since you're busy, I'll make this quick. I need a source that might know something about embryonic stem cell research."

Again the slanted glance.

Whit waited impatiently, then asked, "Can you help me?"

"I'm thinking!" Yolanda leaned back from the mirror and faced Whit. "Does this have anything to do with the Niki Francis story?"

"Yes. And Delano, the fire victim. With the right source, I think I can link the two deaths."

Yolanda put her hand on her hip. "A double murder?"

Her big, brown eyes blinked at Whit, one eye still wearing the daytime version of her makeup. It was a stare-down. Clearly, no information was going to be forthcoming without Whit divulging her hypothesis. Talking quickly, Whit outlined her theory about an illegal stem cell experiment.

"No shit?" Yolanda nodded, eyes narrowed. "*That* would make great copy. Sure, I'll help. Just let me finish here. Meet you at your desk in five."

Relieved, Whit blew out a breath. "Thanks, Yolanda. I appreciate it!"

Racing back down the hall, Whit noticed that Breckenridge was still in Stu's office. She grit her teeth and changed course. If he brought in Breckenridge to cover the Delano story, it would be problematic to wrestle it back, even if she found the right sources to prove her theory. She approached Stu's office, determined to do battle, and perhaps knocked too sharply, making both men jump.

"Sorry to interrupt, but are you guys talking about the Delano story?"

They stared at her blankly for a moment, which confused her. She expected guilt for taking the story from her. And something else was wrong. They looked stricken. Not much shocked seasoned journalists. By the time you'd covered ten to fifteen years of humanity's triumphs and tragedies, you'd seen it all two or three times, and both of these men had been in the business for several decades. Little alarm bells sounded in her head. "Is . . . is something wrong? Has something happened I should know about?"

Stu motioned her in with quick little hand movements, which was also telling. She quizzically glanced at Breckenridge.

Nearing sixty, he was thick all over, and mostly bald, with wire-rimmed glasses. A history and government buff, he generally covered municipalities, city hall and so on, and any other in-depth story they tossed his way. He was a fixture at the paper, having started his career with them back in the early seventies. He was also mild-mannered, slow to speak and a thinking man. When she watched him walk around the office, he reminded her of a turtle, head down, slow-moving, methodical and determined, but he was anything but slow intellectually. His mind worked like a computer; whatever went in there stuck. Everyone assumed his slow response time was because he had a lot of stored files to process. If staffers couldn't find something on the internet, they just asked Breckenridge.

At the moment, he simply raised his hand, like the Pope, to usher her into the room.

Stu snapped, "Come in, come in. We don't have all day." His hands started jabbing the air like a little marionette. "Tomorrow's Sunday. This is going to be a big spread. I just called in a couple more stringers. When it rains, it pours."

"What is going on?" Whit asked, stepping into the room and taking the second chair across from Stu's desk, next to Breckenridge.

"I'll tell you what," Stu answered. "Another high-profile death. The implication is homicide."

She asked, "Who is it?"

"A lawyer named Isabel Rodriguez."

"I know Isabel." Whit felt her heart quicken at the shock. "What happened to her?"

"Breckenridge, you tell her."

He nodded slowly and pursed his lips as he gathered his thoughts. They waited in silence until he finally explained, "Late this afternoon, a contact at the district attorney's office called me. He told me Isabel Rodriguez was found dead in her pool this morning. Not many people know this, but she was the lover of Edward Littrell, the DA. I have known this for some time. Apparently the DA did not want any doubt cast on him. Especially when there are swarms of media in town already covering the Niki Francis murder. His goal was to prove that there had been no lover's quarrel that resulted in her death. An autopsy was ordered stat. Littrell expected the autopsy report to come back as death by drowning, which would exonerate him, of course, at least technically. I'm sure some people would still have their doubts. However, that's not what happened."

Out of the corner of her eye, Whit saw, through the glass window, Yolanda standing by her desk with her arms crossed, looking pissed. Whit waved, caught her eye, and held up one finger, pleading to have just a minute. Yolanda heaved a sigh but remained still. Turning to Breckenridge, Whit asked, "What did the report say?"

He shook his head. "No one knows. It's under wraps. Even the DA has been shut out, which is causing quite a stir, but the police won't budge. That's why this contact called me. The DA is sitting on pins and needles because he is fully aware that enough people know about the affair to point a finger at him if someone wanted to. 'Someone' being a person he has slighted in the past and might want to wield this bit of info into significant leverage, if you know what I mean. Basically, blackmail. Since Littrell is known for his heavy hand and smart mouth, I can imagine there may be a few who would be too happy to use negative press against him, including his opponents running for office. So, this contact wanted to know if any of *my* contacts might be able to sniff out any autopsy information, but it's shut down tighter than a drum."

Whit's immediate suspicion was that Isabel's death was linked to Francis and Delano. She and George had just seen a half dozen pictures of Isabel with the other two. The association was too freakishly coincidental. Same age, same pocketbook. But, before she could approach Stu with her theory, she needed more than just a hunch.

"I may have more to add to this story, but first I need to speak with Yolanda; she's waiting for me at my desk. I'll be back later."

Yolanda was in fact scowling. "I don't have all night. I'm doing you a favor, and you keep me waiting?"

She quickly changed her tune when Whit filled her in on the latest developments. She looked horrified.

"Isabel was a shining light for *all* Hispanic women—a role model. Only the devil would do something like that."

"I couldn't agree more."

"So now we have *three* murders?" Yolanda held up three fingers. "Three?"

"Maybe. We have to continue the investigation."

"Holy shit, it's gonna be a busy night!" Yolanda exclaimed. "Oh, and I got something." Yolanda opened her clutch purse and pulled out her phone. "It came to me when I was busting out the eyeliner. A couple of months ago we ran a story about researchers at Oregon State University. Some of the scientists there are working on stem cells. I got a name and number in my phone."

"Great!" Whit grabbed her phone.

"Here it is: Stenosky. Dr. Bredevo Stenosky. He's a scientist at the Oregon National Primate Research Center. There. I sent it to your phone."

"Got it. But . . . primate?" Whit frowned, looking doubtful.

Yolanda rolled her eyes. "Girl! You're making this difficult. They research embryonic stem cells to solve things like Parkinson's disease and MS. Serious shit. Just give them a call."

"Thanks."

"You need anything else, call me. I'll help you track down the asshole who killed Isabel. Wish I could stay and watch the drama play out, but you were right. I *do* have a hot date." With that, she marched away on her stilettos.

Sitting down at her desk, Whit called the number Yolanda had given her, surprised when a real person answered instead of a recording. "This is Whitney McKenna with the *Medford Daily Chronicle*. Can I speak with Dr. Bredevo Stenosky?"

"He's not in right now, but I can have him return the call. If it's urgent he will contact you this evening."

Whit assured her that it was more than urgent, left her cell number, and hung up.

She and George gathered their collective information and presented it to Stu.

"What the fuck is that?" Stu came around the desk and grabbed the eight-by-ten glossy. Whit had insisted they print the pictures of teratomas on photo paper just for the effect.

"That, Stu, is the reason we have three dead bodies."

"I feel sick."

He did, in fact, look green around the gills. Whit very carefully filled him in on all the facts, while George handed him photo after photo. She described her phone conversation with the scientist, explaining the reason that experiments with embryonic stem cells were illegal in the United States.

"Holy shit!"

"I know. It's an insane story. But, if I can collect written statements from Mrs. Delano, Mark Sorenson, and Isabel's family, that they all three had this teratoma thing, would you be willing to run the story?"

Stu stood up and paced back and forth in a three-foot square. "If you bring me names. Not sources, names. People willing to go on record. *With* signatures. Right now, because of Niki Francis, we have the whole world as our audience. If this thing blows up in our faces, it could be catastrophic. You got it? And the more signed documents, the better. Nothing gets written until you run it past me."

Whit gave him a curt nod. "I got it."

"Go!" He sighed, rubbing his eye brows. "It's gonna be a hell of a night."

Back at their desks, Whit turned to George. "I need Mark Sorenson, and he's probably three sheets to the wind by now."

Recalling his rather violent fist-slapping moment and that deathly deep voice proclaiming, "I want blood," she shuddered to think how he might react to her waking him up and finding out she was a reporter. Unfortunately, he was too big a piece of the puzzle to leave out; she had no choice. She needed his signature. "We have to find him tonight and convince him to sign a statement about what the medical examiner said about Niki." She sat down in her chair, drumming her fingers on the desk. "If only we knew what bungalow he's staying in."

George feigned outrage. "Did you ask *moi*?"

Her head snapped up. "Are you kidding me? You have that information and didn't tell me?"

He spread his hands wide. "Might I remind you that after you tossed me the car keys and told me to drive, you fell into a drunken slumber for the entire trip back to the *Chronicle*?"

"Hey, keep it down." She nodded toward a few reporters within earshot. "And that wasn't a drunken slumber—that was an exhausted slumber. There's a difference."

"Right . . ."

She stood up, collected her pad, pen and recorder, and tossed them into her purse. "Now cough up that bungalow number before I have you fired."

"Oh, that hurts!" George laughed.

"By the way, how did you discover what bungalow he was in?"

"After my fabulous massage, a decadent bouquet of flowers—red orchids, by the way—were delivered to Eden Retreat . . . from the owners, I believe."

"And?"

"I overheard Dr. Heinemann's wife telling one of her staff members to deliver said flowers to Mark Sorenson." He flashed a perfect smile. "Bungalow eight."

"SHIT!" WHIT WIPED perspiration from her brow. "Are you sure it was number eight? Could you have misheard?"

"Au contraire . . . I heard right," George scuffed. "Eight is eight."

"Well, we're batting a big fat zero." Whit was losing patience with the whole thing. Between the sickening heat and the fast-approaching deadline, her temper was starting to flare.

Dusk had surrendered swiftly to night as ominous clouds blocked any ray of light from the setting sun. Beneath the inversion layer, the day's searing heat smothered any chance of a cool breeze. The air, heavy with moisture, clung to their skin, and seemed to afford lower levels of oxygen as they trudged up a softly lit path at Eden Retreat.

They'd identified eleven bungalows, which were spaced about fifty feet apart, with tall shrubs and trees planted between them for privacy. Unfortunately, motion sensor lights clicked on as they tried to see the number on the front door of each unit. Illuminated like actors on a stage, they scurried away into the darkness across uneven ground. Twice Whit stubbed her toe on rocks and bit back a few choice curses.

"As obvious as we've been, I'm surprised someone hasn't reported us." She flexed a painfully throbbing and bloody toe, hoping the nail was still intact. "The occupant of bungalow number four peeked through their mini-blinds. I've been waiting for the police to show up and escort us off the property."

"I don't look good in shackles."

"Stu is going to roast us alive if we go back empty-handed. I'd rather be arrested."

George stopped dead in his tracks. "We've traversed every crevice of this retreat."

"Well, we can't give up. We need that signed statement from Mark, and I'm pretty sure he might shed some light on Niki's involvement here at Eden." They'd been traipsing up and down the paths for over an hour, losing precious time. "Think! We've zigzagged back and forth pretty much laterally, but there was one path we didn't pursue. It traveled *up* the hill, away from the main walkways. I thought it led to a shed or to an employee residence, but let's try it anyway."

Without waiting for an answer, she pressed ahead, past the pond and three bungalows, pausing at the base of an uphill path that curved off to the left through a row of shrubs. This path was also softly lit with solar lights, but away from the overhead lights of the main path, darkness encroached on either side. The peaceful theme of the retreat vanished. It looked like a place to tuck a storage shed. Not especially inviting.

George voiced his misgivings. "I feel the jungle calling. Anything could be lurking out there in the dark."

She had to agree, but said, "No worries, George," and launched up the hill at a fast clip, praying they were on the right track.

George huffed along behind her. "*Oh, merde*! It's like Africa hot! I wouldn't have taken this internship if I'd known what the weather was like."

"It's usually hot here at the end of August, with the recorded high of a hundred and fourteen degrees back in the early eighties. Our weather guy said that storm this afternoon set a record for lightning strikes. A lot of downed power lines and trees. He's writing up the story as we speak."

"Our high of one oh eight doesn't seem so bad, then . . . obviously I'm joking."

They crossed over a wooden bridge with a shallow stream, and sure enough found a bungalow hidden in a clearing. A few steps closer to the porch and the light sensor flashed on. There in all its glory was the number eight. "Yes!"

"What . . . do you think?" George swatted at a swarm of gnats. "Is he in there? It's awfully dark."

"He's probably asleep."

"Or passed out."

Years of "bothering" people at all hours of the day and night, and in almost any conceivable situation, should have prepared her, but Whit's heart began pounding in her chest. Facing a six-foot-three grieving drunk whom she'd earlier deceived required just about every ounce of courage she had to confront him.

Taking a deep breath, she climbed the stairs and knocked. It seemed loud in the quiet of the night, with only a few crickets marring the tranquil evening.

No response from within. Whit leaned her ear to the door. Rustling in the bushes near the creek startled them.

George sucked in his breath. "What was that?"

"An animal of some kind."

"What if it's a mountain lion?"

Whit peered into the darkness. "Then it's probably stalking prey."

"Hilarious!"

She cocked her head, listening. George panted beside her. "Shush."

"I have to *breathe*."

Something crunched in the bush; then something else darted, rustling through the grass into the water, as if frightened by a predator. The only predator she feared was human.

She'd learned a long time ago that asking too many questions was like a direct threat to any criminal element. Usually it put her right in the cross hairs. If she was right, then they were after a murderer who had already killed at least three people, which made him a lethal adversary.

Whit knocked on the door again, this time using the side of her fist, while keeping one eye on the bushes.

From inside the bungalow came a thump and a muffled curse.

Relieved, she said, "He's awake now."

"Thank God." George inched closer to the door.

From the dark a twig snapped; more scraping and shuffling followed. This time Whit sensed a presence, like the direct gaze of a person. The hair on the back of her neck stood on end.

The door opened a crack. Mark's voice, thick with sleep, greeted them. "Who is it?"

"My name is Whitney McKenna. We met today at the sushi bar."

Confused, he opened the door wider and rubbed sleep from his eyes. "What do you want?"

The reek of his whiskey-sloshed evening left little doubt that he'd polished off the bottle. "I need to speak with you about your mother."

"My mother?" His tone sharpened. "How did you find me? Go away before I call security."

He started to shut the door, but Whit thrust her foot against it. "Wait! You don't understand. I'm a reporter with the *Medford Daily Chronicle*. I think I know what happened to your mother."

Silence stretched into the quiet as his muddled brain processed her words. "You're with the *Chronicle*?"

"Yes. Sorry I didn't mention it earlier. We need to talk. There may be other lives at stake."

He released the door and stepped forward into the porch light. Disheveled, he wore the same clothes from earlier in the evening, as he'd obviously slept in them. His dark hair was tousled; he towered over her, squinting with bloodshot eyes. "Look, I feel like shit. Drank too much. Can't this wait till morning? *I'm raw*, man."

"No, it can't." Whit held her ground. "We may have evidence that your mother's killer is out there stalking other victims."

Mark smacked a dry mouth and swallowed hard. "I don't feel well. I'll be back."

He shut the door and locked it, leaving them on the doorstep.

Like bait on a line.

She pivoted in place, her back to the door facing the porch steps, eyes keen, ears straining. In the still, moisture-laden air came not a sound, not even a cricket's chirp. The unnatural quiet spoke volumes. Her pulse quickened in her ears.

The whites of George's eyes widened as he glanced from her into the darkness and shivered. He whispered, "Something evil?"

Yes. Evil. She sensed it too, a malevolent presence that meant them harm. The isolation of this bungalow probably suited the rich and famous just fine, but right now it felt like a trap. Despairing of Mark ever coming back, she leaned over a porch rocker and peeked into the window between the drapes. "Come on . . . come on," she said under her breath.

George wiped perspiration from his brow with a monogrammed handkerchief, his gaze darting about. He whispered, "I'm sufficiently petrified."

In the silence, the night shadows loomed. This inkling of danger was not a figment of her imagination. She'd experienced too many threatening circumstances in the course of her journalism career not to take heed. Instincts had kept her alive and intact.

Her ears pricked with the faintest shuffle, like steps bending and sweeping slowly over blades of grass. "I don't like it."

The lighted path curved down the hill to the bridge, the trees and bushes illuminated. But the blank canvas beyond represented a void . . . no moon, no stars, just blind night.

The locks on the door clicked sharply, flooding her with relief. The door swung open. She and George exchanged glances and scurried over the doorstep.

Mark stood wiping his mouth, a hand towel over his shoulder, oblivious to their fright. "Shit, this better be good. If I let you in here and it's some kind of bullshit, I'm suing that pathetic rag." He stood in the entry, blocking their entrance to the living room. "I want to see some ID first."

They produced their picture identification cards issued by the newspaper.

She flicked a glance over her shoulder. Lurking beyond the porch light, something or someone was watching them. She was sure of it.

"Come in." Mark handed the cards back to them. "I'm going to put on some tea."

George shut and locked the door behind him. They passed through a comfortable living room with floral rattan furniture into a smallish kitchen with a round dining table under a palm leaf fan. On the counter sat the red orchids George had mentioned earlier, next to them a nearly empty bottle of Japanese whiskey.

"Have a seat," Mark offered. He moved haltingly about the kitchen, putting on hot water to boil, sifting through an array of tea bags, and then placing several into the pan. "Despite my dishevelment, i.e. drunken state, I'm very concerned with my mother's case or you wouldn't be sitting in my bungalow." He glared at them through hooded eyes. "I'll take information from anyone. Including journalists. My PI stopped by earlier. He's already working the night. This better be good. What is it?"

Whit introduced him to George, then shared Mrs. Delano's story. "Can you confirm that your mother had the same type of tumor? A teratoma?"

He poured boiling tea into a cup and carefully carried it to the table. "Would you like tea?"

"No thank you."

He sat down with a groan. "Man, I am toast." After taking a few sips, he leaned back in his chair. "Blessed tea." He looked haggard. "This is by far the worst time in my life. I don't usually carry on like this."

"It's understandable," Whit said.

Mark sipped his tea, eyeing her, his expression guarded. "Okay. Here's the deal. The medical examiner stopped by my mother's house to talk to me this morning. He told me she had a tumor, but that wasn't what killed her. He basically said they have no clue yet. We're waiting for lab work. And, yes, he called it a teratoma. I don't know much beyond that."

Whit described what she'd researched about teratomas and their genetic makeup.

Mark rubbed his eyes with the back of his hand. "That sounds like absolute lunacy. You're not convincing me of anything. You sure you don't work for the *National Enquirer*?"

"I'm very serious." Whit's voice was strong, but she sympathized, "I'm sorry. I know you're going through hell right now. But if your mom's killer is stalking other victims, this story needs to go to print. I suspect a new homicide, Isabel Rodriguez, may be a third victim. She was a defense attorney with a local TV show. Did you know her?"

He blinked and swallowed, nodding his head. "I know Isabel. She and my mother were friends. I hadn't heard. We have no television or internet in the bungalows here."

"The police haven't released any information anyway." Whit shared all she knew about it. "The police are focused on catching the killer, but I'm more interested in saving the victims."

"How did they get these teratomas?"

"I believe from stem cell injections."

"Why did they have stem cell injections?"

"I don't know. I'm still investigating." Whit could see he was doubtful, and she didn't have anything more to offer. "It sounds crazy, but I think your mother and the others developed these tumors after the injections. I think they were then killed to silence them."

"I'm a very practical man. I deal in stocks and bonds. Hard facts." He sighed heavily. "It still seems farfetched. You don't even know if Isabel had a tumor. How did Mrs. Delano find out about her husband?"

"She's close friends with the ME. He was just trying to appease some of her confusion and frustration over her husband's crazy behavior before he died." She shrugged. "I seriously doubt he thought she'd share that information with a journalist. And if I hadn't talked to you this afternoon, I would never have put the pieces together."

He sat back and closed his eyes, a little gray around the mouth. She hoped he wasn't getting sick again. "George, show him the file."

With a flourish, George produced the file they'd shown Stu. He sat it in front of Mark and began flipping through the photos. He stopped when he came to the teratoma.

"That's the tumor? You didn't photoshop this thing?"

"No." Whit shook her head. "Of course not. You can look it up yourself."

With a dark frown, he said, "As preposterous as all this sounds, it also makes sense. So, where would they get these injections if it's illegal?"

"I have a theory about that." Whit pushed for a close. "Your mother and Delano were both obsessed with health and looking youthful. And they all frequented Eden Retreat."

His head snapped up at that. "Eden Retreat?"

"Yes. Dr. Heinemann was their therapist. And I saw a picture tonight with Isabel and Niki right here, at Eden Retreat. Dr. Heinemann is a psychiatrist. He understands pharmaceuticals.

He *could* persuade vulnerable people to participate in a stem cell study."

Mark's eyes narrowed, his face flushed beneath the stubble along his chin.

Alarmed, George shot a panicked look at Whit.

"Dr. *Heinemann*." His jaw clenched. "Now that I think about it, he did encourage me to forget how my mother died. Maybe he *is* the killer." Mark stood and paced, teacup in hand, rattling delicately. "I don't trust the police. I'm calling my PI as soon as you leave. I want that bastard checked out top to bottom."

"We think our story will flush him out," Whit pressed. "If there are other victims, they might come forward and identify the killer. For self-protection, if nothing else. This is serious business. That's why your statement is so important. And when we leave here, we'll be talking to Isabel's family."

He set his cup on the table and leaned over, brown eyes fraught with suppressed rage. His voice fell, becoming dangerously subdued. "My mother was murdered and thrown into a ditch. I want the son of a bitch who did it. You publish your story. If we can flush the bastard out, then I'm all for it. Where do I sign?"

Whit and George wasted no time hustling back to the car. Still leery of whatever had been watching them outside Mark's bungalow, they jogged down the hill, signed statement in hand.

Suddenly, emerging from behind a palm tree, Dr. Heinemann stepped in front of them. Startled, Whit let out a cry, coming to an abrupt halt. George nearly ran into Heinemann, who grabbed him by the shoulder.

"Didn't I see the two of you here this afternoon?" Heinemann demanded. His tone tonight was not so charming. "Why are you in such a hurry? And why, exactly, are you here at such a late hour?"

Breathless, Whit replied, "We were visiting a friend."

He glanced over their shoulder and waved to what at first glance Whit thought was a security guard, a hulking outline beneath the lights. But as the figure stepped forward, she recognized him as the masseur, Wilhelm.

"We received a call from bungalow four that we had prowlers on the property."

Shadowed by an overhead light from the pond area, Whit stared into his dark eyes and thought they looked hollow and lifeless. When he wasn't smiling, his features were angular and sharp, cunning. Or maybe she'd changed her perspective since she now thought he might be a maniacal killer.

She steadied her voice. "We came to visit a guest, but forgot which bungalow he was in. But it's fine now. We found him and we're just headed back to our car."

She tried to step around him, but once again he blocked her path.

"Which guest did you come to see?"

She had no alternative. "Mark Sorenson."

Wilhelm stepped in front of her on the path, blocking her exit to the car. "Aren't you that reporter from the newspaper? I saw you on television tonight."

Before she could answer, Heinemann instructed, "Call bungalow eight. Ask Mr. Sorenson if he's had visitors tonight." He asked Whit, "Do you have some ID?"

George had pulled free of Heinemann's grasp and stood beside her. As Wilhelm verified with Mark that they were in fact *invited* visitors, they dug out their identification.

It occurred to Whit that Heinemann meant to intimidate. That he was playing out a charade for his own benefit. She thought it likely that *he* had been the noise in the bushes earlier and he knew very well that they had come from Sorenson's place . . . and why they were there.

"Any guest of Mr. Sorenson is a guest of ours." The gracious host was suddenly back. He smiled and stepped to the side, waving them forward. "I'll walk you to your car." He chatted amicably about the responsibilities of caring for all his guests while Wilhelm dogged their heels.

As they approached the parking lot, Heinemann asked, "So, are there any new developments in your story?"

Whit hesitated, then decided to needle him with the truth, wanting to gauge his response. "Yes. I think we may have linked Niki Francis to two other murders. I'm about to go write the story now. You can read about it in tomorrow's paper."

He visibly stiffened as his dark eyes narrowed to slits. "That's outrageous. Surely you're mistaken."

George stepped forward. "We better get going. Thanks so much for the escort to our car, Dr. Heinemann. Sorry to have disturbed you."

"Best of luck with your story." Heinemann waved and smiled, but he did not look pleased.

22

THEY WERE SEVERAL miles outside Livermore, California. Night had fallen, obscuring the barren foothills in a starless veil of black onyx that seemed to suck the illumination even from the rental car's headlights.

Riggs squinted through the steady raindrops on the windshield. "We should be getting close now. What do you think?"

Panetta eyeballed her without answering, as if the question didn't warrant the effort. He was in a foul mood. Just before they'd caught the flight from Medford, his ex-wife had called. Riggs had not overheard the conversation because he retreated outside the sliding glass doors of the terminal. When he returned, his expression was dangerous. He had said very little since then. The tension radiating from him had driven Riggs into silence as well, so she'd used the opportunity for some much-needed sleep on the short plane ride.

In the car, his grunted responses to her questions had produced an uncomfortable silence. Twice she'd thought about asking what the phone call had been about, but thought better of it.

Suddenly, from a crossroad, a white van spun past them, kicking up gravel as it narrowly cut the corner. Panetta braked hard.

"I ought to write him up!" Panetta glared after the van, then watched it turn left up ahead. He slowed the car as they reached the turn. The headlights shimmered against the glass as he read the simple black letters on a white sign: *Research Facility*.

"According to the GPS, this is it," Riggs said. "Looks like that guy is headed to Human Resources as well. Odd that they don't have their name on the sign."

"Maybe they don't want to be found." He turned the car onto the side road, following the arrow on the sign as directed.

Within minutes they came upon a spotlight from a guard shack and a security gate flanked on either side by a chain-link fence; barbed wire stretched off into the encroaching darkness, presumably to surround the complex. The place was more like a high-security prison than a business. A place of carefully guarded secrets?

"Security level is over-the-top," she said.

"Maybe because stem cell research is worth big money." Panetta stopped the car at the gate, under the shelter of a covered driveway next to the guard station, and rolled the window down. The night air, damp and musty, invaded the small confines of the car.

The guard, a young man with a military buzz haircut, spoke through an intercom. "May I help you?"

Panetta told the guard they had an appointment.

A metal arm extended, like the drawer of an old drive-through bank. "Please provide identification. A driver's license and police badges."

The guard used a handheld device and scanned their IDs, typed something into a computer, then returned everything. "Have a nice evening, Detectives."

The gate slid to the side, metal wheels screeching against metal brackets, and they proceeded along a narrow road toward a six-story building that sat alone on the hill, as if it were a fortress, its windows alight and oddly welcoming. Riggs, however, felt an intuitive warning to be on guard. They parked in an almost vacant parking lot. The white van that had cut them off on the road sat in a loading zone near the front door.

"There's our lunatic driver," Panetta commented.

"I wonder what he was delivering in such a hurry, and so late at night."

"We can always ask."

As they walked toward the glass entrance, Panetta remarked, "Reminds me of a military compound."

"Strange, isn't it?" The rain had stopped; the air was warm and pungent with damp earth.

Panetta opened the double glass door for Riggs, and she stepped through, her gaze immediately taking in the amazing sculpture above them. Suspended in the six-story foyer hung a massive red-and-purple glass orb. Within it dangled hundreds of shining balls, like a giant mobile.

"Wanna bet that's a stem cell?" Panetta asked.

"I'm not taking that bet. Just how gullible do you think I am?" Riggs asked, glad that he was at least trying to be more cordial. She craned her neck, admiring the work of art above them. It must have taken someone months to assemble the structure. Light reflected from each of the hundreds of balls, creating a kaleidoscope of color.

They proceeded through the lobby, designed with well-placed cream leather couches, and plants. Soft elevator music filled the open space. A guard stood behind a long desk that divided the lobby from the passageway into the interior of the building. They stopped at a walk-through metal detector, which was the only entrance.

"Wow." Riggs nudged Panetta. "It's like airport security."

"Yeah. I'm not feelin' the love here."

The click of heels on tile shifted their attention to the hallway. From it emerged a tall, slender brunette, well dressed in a professional pale-cream dress suit.

"Welcome to Human Resources. I'm Lillian Gray, communications director." The woman smiled a megawatt smile; her large green eyes lingered on Panetta, a fact that Riggs guessed he appreciated, since his shoulders squared a little. "Hal will take your weapons, if you have any."

Hal provided a plastic bucket on the counter. "All metal objects in here, please."

Panetta grumbled as he reached beneath his suit jacket and unclipped his Glock, carefully placing it in the bin provided. Riggs complied as well.

Lillian stepped forward. "I feel your pain, I really do, but it is company policy."

"If you don't mind," Riggs said, "I like to record my interviews."

She nodded. "Well, of course!"

After leaving their phones, watches, and key chains, they followed Lillian to an elevator. Her office was on the sixth floor. The office was spacious, decidedly feminine, with a large bouquet of wildflowers on her desk.

Lillian directed them to a seating area near tall glass windows. Their reflections moved against the night sky as they sat on gold fabric couches with a coffee table between them.

Riggs said, "We apologize for the late hour. Time is critical."

"No problem. I often work late. This is my home away from home. I'm not exactly sure of the nature of your visit. Elliot, the president of HR, indicated that you had questions regarding a phone call from the now sadly deceased actress."

"Yes." Riggs turned on her recorder, holding it in her lap while Panetta pulled out a pen and pad. Lillian was vivacious despite the late hour, offering them coffee or tea, then pouring ice water from a pitcher on the table. She set a chilled glass in front of each of them. "I'll try to get to the point," Riggs said.

"We know that Niki Francis made a thirty-minute phone call to you the afternoon she died. We asked your staff to trace it."

Lillian nodded and picked up a folder from the table. "I have printed out the date in question. Our telephone system is computerized and records the day's events. Ms. Francis called at two seventeen PM and spoke briefly with our receptionist, who then transferred her to our stem cell development department. I checked to see who was working that afternoon and came up with a list of twenty-nine employees. We made inquiries and traced her call to Dr. Elizabeth Brum, a stem cell biologist and our department chief."

Panetta took the folder from her and read through the report. "It doesn't say what they talked about."

"No. We like to maintain privacy. But I can tell you a summary of the conversation. Apparently, Ms. Francis simply wanted information. She wanted to know the risks of stem cell injections. The kinds of complications that might arise from such a procedure."

Riggs asked, "Did she say why she wanted to know?"

"Why yes, she did. But I think first you need to understand what we do here. You see, stem cell research is really just regenerative medicine. Research in this field holds great promise for biomedical science and our ability to treat debilitating diseases. Already science has created a device, a type of envelope filled with embryonic stem cells, which, planted under the skin, become pancreatic cells and cure diabetes. So far it's cured hundreds of mice, and eventually it might cure humans. That's about two hundred thousand deaths a year that will be prevented."

"That's an amazing achievement," Riggs said. "But isn't it true that embryonic stem cell treatment is controversial and that's why the FDA hasn't approved it?" She was thinking that might be the reason their killer was disposing of his subjects.

Lillian sighed and confessed, "Unfortunately, that is true. Frankly, I don't contemplate that aspect of the research very often. I feel like we have entered into a new outer space, only this time it's inner space that we're exploring, and we have a responsibility to investigate it. Like the astronauts of the 1960s. They didn't question too deeply the moral aspects of exploring and conquering new territories. And perhaps it's best if we don't either."

"But," Riggs said, "we'd like to understand the process. Can you explain where these stem cells come from?"

"Usually in vitro clinics."

Panetta scribbled on his pad. "Can you explain the process at the clinic?"

Lillian smiled. "Of course. It's a relatively simple procedure. Women are given medication to help create two dozen or so ova, or eggs. These are extracted, then fertilized in the lab using her partner's sperm. Three days later, surviving embryos develop into what's called a blastocyst. One or more of these blastocysts are implanted into the woman's womb. The rest are deep frozen in liquid nitrogen for future use."

"That's where we get stem cells from?"

"Yes. Some of them don't survive the freezing and thawing process. Sometimes there's equipment malfunction. Some parents ask that the embryos be destroyed to save the cost of storage. And some donate them to science. Those are the ones that are used to make some of our stem cells."

Pondering this, Riggs continued, "So they're either destroyed for science or thrown out?"

"Usually. Sometimes the parents put them up for adoption to other couples who can't conceive."

Panetta lifted his pen. "For how long? How long can they be frozen?"

"Theoretically . . . indefinitely." She leaned forward, as if sharing secrets in a conspiratorial tone. "In fact, a woman recently gave birth from an adopted embryo that had been frozen for twenty years. Interestingly, the baby now has a *twin* that was born twenty years ago to his biological mother. Fascinating, isn't it?"

Panetta shook his head. "Confusing, more like."

Lillian added, "It's estimated that there are currently over eight hundred thousand frozen embryos in various clinics or banks throughout the United States."

Riggs was amazed. "An entire population on ice."

"In a sense, yes. But they're simply cells at that stage." She shrugged. "Besides, we have advanced past that. We use cloned cells now for much of our research."

"Cloned cells?" Panetta asked. "So they don't come from clinics?"

"Just the ones we already had. We can clone cells from human skin. Just like Dolly the sheep. Remember her?"

Panetta frowned. "I remember hearing about it, but that was a long time ago."

"Well, the cell that created the first cloned animal was taken from the mammary gland of a sheep." She laughed gaily. "The scientists couldn't think of a more impressive pair of glands than Dolly Parton's, so they named her Dolly!"

"Sounds about right," Riggs said, rolling her eyes. "So how is this done? What's the procedure?"

"It's less complicated than you think. Take an egg from one sheep, then transfer the cell from another sheep into it, electronically charge the egg to activate it, then implant it into a surrogate sheep. Ta-da! You have Dolly."

Riggs leaned forward, frowning. "Now let me see if I understand this. Are you telling us that you're using that same procedure to clone *humans*?"

Lillian nodded. "Yes. It's called somatic cell nuclear transfer. I have a media packet put together for you when you leave."

Alarmed, Riggs repeated the question. "You're cloning humans? Is that legal?"

Waving her hands, Lillian chuckled. "Oh, no, no . . . I see what you're thinking. No. We're not *growing* actual humans. We only use the cells to create stem cell lines. We take skin cells and fuse them with a donated human egg, which is essentially creating an identical human from the skin cell."

The fine hair on the back of Riggs's arms stood up. "So, if I give you my skin cells, you can clone an identical me? A whole other me?"

Lillian smiled broadly. "Now you get it."

Riggs rolled her gaze at Panetta, who looked as if he'd just seen a ghost.

"But like I said," Lillian continued, "we don't actually implant the fertilized egg in a donor and grow a human."

"Could you?"

"Theoretically. The procedure has not been approved by the FDA, but I believe it may already be taking place in other countries, such as China and the Ukraine."

Riggs shook her head. "Cloned people. Why am I surprised?"

"It's very exciting." Lillian leaned forward eagerly. "We are breaching the boundaries of human science. We believe that from these stem cell lines will come the cure for nearly every disease known to man."

Riggs pulse quickened as she comprehended the ultimate power of a single stem cell. This science was far more advanced than she'd thought. Now it was time to get the information they'd come for. "I think we understand the basic process. Can you tell us what this has to do with the call from Niki Francis?"

Lillian nodded, her expression oddly teasing. "What do you think is the ultimate scientific quest for humans?"

Panetta responded, "Good health."

"Yes, but think deeper."

Riggs asked, "A long life?"

"You're both right, but it's more than that. Plastic surgeons are the highest-paid group of physicians in America. And Americans pour millions and millions of dollars into plastic surgery. Why? Our aging baby boomers want to recapture their youth with facelifts, tummy tucks, and liposuction. Who can blame them?"

Panetta asked, "What do facelifts have to do with stem cells?"

"Why, eternal youth, Detective Panetta. Niki Francis was not seeking treatment because she was sick. She wanted eternal *youth*. She wanted to look and feel young again."

Riggs shifted forward in her chair, her back stiff from long hours of sitting in the plane, car, and now at Human Resources. "Stem cells can do that?"

"Not exactly. Not yet. But clinics overseas are promising to take twenty years off your life with embryonic stem cell injections. You see, once injected into the human body, these cells travel to any area that is weakened or not working properly and begin to rejuvenate the organs. The younger cells multiply, replacing the exhausted older ones. Over several weeks, in theory, the body literally rebuilds itself into a fresher, younger, more energetic you!"

"Twenty years?" Riggs blinked hard at that. If Niki was sixty years old, the process could basically rebuild her into a forty-year-old woman. She recalled Dr. Weldon thinking Rodriguez was the wrong cadaver because she looked so young.

"Yes. It's being hailed as the fountain of youth; time travel, if you will. It's called rejuvenative embryonic stem cell treatment, otherwise known as REST."

Something tweaked Riggs's memory, but it was fleeting. Then she remembered taking a picture of the items in Niki Francis's bedside drawer. The actress had written *REST* at the top of the brochure from Eden Retreat.

"So," Panetta said, "this is all in theory?"

"More than theory. It's been around for ten, some places twenty years overseas for wealthy people who incorporate a vacation with a clinic visit. It's called medical tourism. Very popular. And here in the U.S., bioartificial organs grown from the patient's own cells in a petri dish are already being cultivated. Cells from the patient's own organs don't cause tumors. The body has no reason to see it as a foreign object and reject it. But sadly, those types of cells don't work on things like cancer or rejuvenative medicine, which is why we need the embryonic cells."

Riggs thought of her mother and wondered if these injections might have saved her life. How different her childhood would have been. That sense of security that was stolen from her. The fear of knowing her mother would die and the anguish of not being able to do anything to stop it. And afterward, the terrible loneliness that gripped her in the dark, night after night. All of that need never have happened. But would her mother have consented to the procedure, wondering if she had taken a life to save her own? She thought of her own battle with cancer a year ago. Would she have taken the treatment?

Panetta was saying, "So the FDA has not approved this youth procedure, REST, here in America?"

"That's right. Unfortunately, there are complications that the FDA is aware of. The embryonic stem cell injections can cause tumors; specifically, teratomas, or monster tumors. Until that complication is rectified, no studies can be done on humans in the United States. That's why we have such hope in cloned stem cells."

Riggs caught Panetta's eye. "That explains our killer."

Lillian nodded. "I can see how a doctor might end up going down that path. The restrictions we have in the U.S. are very frustrating to scientists. America is falling behind the rest of the world in the application of science because of it."

"One more thing," Panetta said. "Does Human Resources have satellite offices anywhere else?"

"No. This is our only location."

"Do you ship any stem cells to Medford?"

"No."

"What about any staff who might own or operate an office in Medford? Do you know of anyone who travels there regularly?"

"Our doctors all work here. I seriously doubt that anyone on our staff is involved with this. Our researchers are highly credentialed."

"That may be true, but we'll need a list of employees. Doctors especially. Ask around and find out if anyone on that list spends time in Oregon. We can subpoena the information, but it would be easier if you'd cooperate."

"Well . . . that might take some time, but I can look into it."

Riggs stood to leave. "We'll need that list right away. Can you fax it to us in the morning? We don't have any time to waste." She added, "Our killer is still out there. He may have more victims."

"I understand the urgency. I'll do my best."

When Lillian walked them to the elevator, a tall, gangly, shaggy-headed guy raced passed them.

"What's up?" He waved to Lillian, then disappeared into the second elevator, headed down to the first floor.

Riggs asked, "Who was that?" thinking he might be the driver of the van. "Does he work for you?"

"Yes. As a matter of fact, he is one of the few people that travels to Medford regularly, but he's not a doctor. His name is Peter Figoni."

"What does he do?"

She hesitated. "Well. He's a harvester."

"What's that?"

"It's difficult to explain. Like most research institutions, we work with human body parts. He harvests body parts for us from hospitals. He travels to five or six cities a week. But he's not a biologist or even a stem cell technician."

Panetta asked, "You mean he cuts out body parts and delivers them to Human Resources? From cadavers?"

"Yes. We use some of them and sell the rest to universities and other research centers."

Riggs glanced after Figoni, wondering if it was too late to question him. She turned and stepped over to a window overlooking the parking lot. She watched as the floppy-haired guy climbed into the van and, with just as much speed as before, spun the van toward the guard post, headlights beaming a clear getaway path.

Panetta said, "Where does he live? We'll need to speak to him before we return to Medford."

Lillian stiffened. "I really should check with personnel before I give out that information."

Determined now, Riggs raised her voice. "We'll just be back in an hour with a subpoena. Save us all some trouble."

Lillian contemplated the best course of action. "Actually, I know his schedule. He's headed over to the hospital in Walnut Creek to collect samples. You can interview him there. In the morgue."

23

"SHOOT. LET'S HEAR it. I'm not gettin' any younger."

Whit wanted to say, *That's for sure.* The past twenty-four hours had ravaged Stu's appearance. He sat on the side of his desk holding a mug of steaming coffee, one foot skimming the floor. He appeared shrunken, thin wisps of hair separated by hours of stress-sweat clinging to the top of his head in a comb-over. She thought he should go home and get some rest but refrained from suggesting it.

Concerned, she asked, "Are you feeling all right?"

"Sure. Why wouldn't I be?"

"Just wondered."

"I'm stellar." He slurped coffee and swung his foot rapidly. "I've been keepin' an eye on the competition. So far no one is even close. Even TV news is sputtering out of fuel. That windbag Geraldo Rivera is in town. Heard he's working the police hard. Can't let that blowhard get a leg up. So what do ya have?"

Whit sat and recounted the visit to Eden, including her sense that they were being stalked the entire time, and the threat she felt from Heinemann. She handed over the two signed statements from Mrs. Delano and Niki's son. She flipped through her notepad. "I also have a statement from the

Oregon National Primate Research Center. They just faxed over some information on the subject."

"Primate?"

Whit held up her hand. "Just listen. I'll read it to you. Dr. Bredevo Stenosky explained how embryonic stem cells cause teratoma tumors. Here. Listen. 'The body's natural reaction to anything foreign is to reject it. When we used embryonic stem cells, the subjects grew teratoma tumors among other problems. This is why the FDA has not approved many of the stem cell experiments being performed in other countries.'" She beamed what she hoped was a winning smile. "You see, this explains how these teratomas were formed. It's the quote we needed to support our theory." She glanced down, semi-reading from her notes. "I thought George could write a sidebar on stem cells. Dr. Stenosky said now they use cloned cells that don't cause transplant rejection. They take DNA from the individual and transplant it into an egg that's been stripped of genetic material. It's called a . . . somatic cell nuclear transfer."

"I like it. What about Isabel Rodriguez? Anything?"

"On the drive back, George hunted down her parents' phone number. According to her father, she didn't have any health problems. But George and I stopped off at the TV station where she did her show, and two of the staff said she'd complained of headaches. They saw her taking aspirin a couple of times. And the weather guy saw her stumble and nearly fall down in the hallway the last night she worked. He called out to her, but she hurried into her dressing room. The producer said she complained of a headache during the show on Friday night. It sure fits the pattern."

Stu hopped down from the desk and paced, taking sharp turns every three feet, like a caged animal. He stopped in front of her. "You've got a lot of bases covered, but I want an official police source."

She blanched at that. "Are you *kidding*? You know they're not talking. Even Breckenridge couldn't get his sources to open up."

"Yeah, but you managed to get your source to spill details on Niki Francis."

"I had a great trade. Since then I've been trailing the police. They already know about the teratomas. That's why they hushed up Isabel Rodriguez's death."

He shook his head stubbornly, pacing again, stabbing his little hands in the air. "Nope. Gotta have it. What if Rodriguez has nothing to do with this case? What if these teratomas just happen to be a coincidence? We're not even sure Delano is a homicide yet. You're jumping to a lot of conclusions. Here's what we've got so far. One buried body, most certainly a homicide. Two dead attorneys, cause unknown, and neither has been declared a homicide by police. Two people we *think* have teratomas. No *official* documents to support it. And a lot of science about stem cells that may or may not have anything to do with our teratoma theory. Basically, nothing. Until we get a solid source to confirm, I'm killin' it."

Whit blushed to the roots of her red hair, then felt the color drain away. It was like getting the wind knocked out of her. She'd worked so hard to pull the pieces together. She'd spit nails before she'd let that pack of out-of-town news junkies steal her story, especially after the way she'd been treated at the news conference. "Stu, be reasonable. All of that coincidence in the space of two days?"

"Maybe. Maybe not." He paused at his desk and slurped some more coffee. "That's just it. We don't know. Go turn all of those assumptions into hard facts."

"But you said if I got the documents from Delano and Sorenson and my quote from the science people, you'd run with it."

"Well, I rethought it. The whole world is watching our little enterprise. Because of that, Arenburg is not printing it with anything less than a police source. Now go get my source."

It was not the first time an editor had gone back on his word. She tried to think of a way around it and came up with nothing.

Finally, she pressed for one tiny advantage. "Okay. You printed my first Niki Francis story from my police source, off the record. If I get her to confirm, off the record, will you take it?"

He pursed his little moustached mouth. "Same solid source?"

"Yes."

"Okay. You got a deal."

Deflated but still determined, Whit stood and meandered down the hallway toward the break room, trying to think of any tidbit of information worth a trade with Katie. Possibly the Heinemann theory, but they were probably already onto that too. After all, most of the police force and half the country were working the case.

Everyone had cleared out of the break room, so she was alone with the buzzing hum of candy and soda machines. She opened a drawer by the sink, looking for the money bowl. People threw extra change into it for anyone that might not have funds for a soda. She dug out a dollar and a quarter and pumped the money into the machine. She needed caffeine. After what sounded like a pinball machine, the Pepsi can clanged to the bottom. She grabbed it and popped the lid. Leaning back on the counter, she guzzled half the soda and belched softy.

Just then, Irene Bradshaw, the business writer, popped into the room carrying half a tray of croissant sandwiches, apparently back from some business event. She was wearing a royal-blue polyester dress with a bright floral jacket, and several imitation sapphires in her ears and around her neck. She set the tray on the lunch table. "Hey, Whit. Are you hungry? Just came from the grand opening of O'Mar's Art Supply store in Ashland. They had several leftover trays of food."

"Sure." Whit picked a turkey–and–Swiss cheese sandwich and bit into it. "So how did it go? Get any good quotes?"

Irene laughed and tossed her dark curls over her shoulder. "Dollface, you are talkin' to a quote-collectin' fool here.

Anybody who is *any*body was at this shindig." She started dropping names, and that's when Whit tuned her out and focused on the sandwich. She hadn't realized how hungry she was. She ate fast, drank some more Pepsi, and reached for another sandwich, wondering if she might be able to chase down Isabel's alleged lover, Edward Littrell. Fat chance the DA would talk to her, though. Maybe she and George could locate Isabel's law partners. They'd know more about her actions last week than anyone else. ". . . caused quite a commotion. But you know how head wounds bleed."

"What's that?" Whit asked, taking a bite from a roast beef and cheese. Her brain was starting to fire back to life.

"Come along." Irene stuffed the sandwich tray in the refrigerator and flounced out of the room, heading down the hall. "I'll fill you in on the rest of it at my desk. I've gotta write this little piece in the next thirty minutes."

Whit followed her, thinking about snagging a few pieces of red licorice for dessert. She decided Isabel's law partners were the best bet. If she could get a hold of them in the next ten minutes by phone, she might still get the story written in time for the Sunday edition. The big *if* remained: would they be able to support her story with concrete evidence? She needed a nice solid quote, like, "Yes, the medical examiner told us she had a teratoma." The odds of that were slim to none. Even then it wasn't exactly a law enforcement source.

They arrived at Irene's desk, and Whit pointed to the licorice. Irene nodded agreeably, holding the lid while she selected two pieces. "As I was sayin'," Irene continued. "She looked peaked and kept rubbing the back of her neck. I asked if she was okay. She said, yes, just a little headache. Then . . . boom! She keeled over and hit her head on the edge of a table. Sliced it right open. Blood everywhere!"

Whit bit off a chunk of licorice and stopped midchew, the word *headache* jolting her back to the conversation. "Who is this?"

"I told you." Irene grabbed a handful of licorice for herself and replaced the lid. "The real estate tycoon. Celeste Cordero."

"Oh . . . my . . . God." Cordero had been in several photos with Niki Francis. She was one of the "cream" that George had preened about.

"What?"

Whit shook her head, heart pounding. "What happened to Cordero?"

"Well, she bled like a stuck pig, but came to right away. She said she was fine except for a headache, but her husband—you may know him. Judge Cordero?" She sat down, kicking her shoes off and slipping her feet into a pair of leopard-print slippers she kept under her desk. "He's running for state representative. Anyway, Judge Cordero whisked her off to the emergency room to get stitches. I hope she'll be okay. She sure scared everyone spitless."

The synapses in Whit's brain started firing all at once. Pure adrenaline surged through her, and she grabbed Irene and kissed her on the cheek. "Thank you, thank you, *thank* you! You have no idea how grateful I am!"

With a laugh, Bradshaw shrugged. "Don't mention it, dollface."

Whit raced back through the maze of cubicles and found George half asleep at his desk, still researching his sidebar science story.

Covering a yawn, he said, "You were gone long enough. What did Stu say?"

"He killed the story," Whit said, plopping down in her chair. "But you're about to witness a resurrection. A true miracle, George. Get me everything you can find on Celeste Cordero. Fund raisers, friends, business associates."

"The real estate woman?"

"Yes. I'll do some digging too. I'd like to know what her financial situation is like." What, she wondered, was Cordero Realty worth?

Within a few minutes she was scrolling though property taxes. The Cordero holdings were impressive. It seemed Cordero owned twenty-three homes in the area and some prime residential property, as yet undeveloped, worth millions, and some commercial property under development that was worth even more. Researching her business licenses, Whit discovered that Cordero was listed on a number of non–real estate business ventures, probably as an investor or silent partner. Too bad it was a weekend. If city hall had been open, Whit was pretty sure she could have interviewed her source there and gotten a behind-the-scenes story.

Whit cracked her fingers. This scenario was of a very powerful woman, at least in this community. That kind of wealth didn't happen because Cordero was a sweetheart. Behind that tanned grin was a hard-core business woman with a great deal of influence and social persuasion. No doubt she possessed political sway as well.

Whit shared her information with George and asked, "Anything on your end, besides what I just told you about?"

"From her website, it looks like she's sold homes to all the victims in the past five years. She's also into some charity work. Habitat for Humanity, and she's donated some land for a sports park."

"That fits."

George turned in his chair. "So who's the savior?"

"A friend. A source that I can use only off the record. You understand? Never mention her name."

George nodded solemnly.

Whit grabbed her phone and dialed Katie's number. Riggs picked up on the second ring. "Hey, McKenna."

"Hi, Riggs. You still on the Niki Francis case?"

"Yes."

"Probably working the fire victim, Bo Delano, too?"

This time there was a small pause. "Yes."

Whit could hear the smile in Katie's voice. She was no dummy.

"So you're working them together?"

"Okay, McKenna. What's this about?"

"I need confirmation. I know Niki Francis and Bo Delano both had a nasty little tumor called a teratoma. Can you verify?"

"On the record?"

"Yes."

"No. And I can't imagine where you got that information."

"I'm also suspicious of Isabel Rodriguez. She was complaining of the same symptoms before she 'allegedly' drowned in her pool. Did she also have a teratoma? And were they the result of a botched medical trial? And did that trial take place under Dr. Heinemann's care at Eden Retreat?"

"You've been busy." She sighed into the phone. "This is an ongoing investigation; you know I can't talk about it. Unless, of course, you have something vital that could help the department?"

Whit smiled and waved George closer to the phone. He leaned in to listen next to her ear, which she allowed so he could back her up with Stu. "I not only have a trade, but you may even be able to catch the killer in the act."

Silence greeted her statement for several seconds. "That's a lot of information to confirm."

"What if you just confirm that all three victims had teratomas? I can take care of the rest."

"What kind of trade do you have exactly?"

"I think I know who the next victim is going to be." She heard Riggs cover the phone with her hand and speak to someone else. The voices were muffled, so she couldn't hear what was being said.

"Detective Panetta and I are out of town right now. But I can call Blackwell and get immediate protection. How certain are you?"

"Based on all the evidence, I'd say ninety percent."

"All right. Who is it?"

"So you're confirming that Francis, Delano, and Rodriguez all had teratomas?"

"Off the record?"

"No direct attribution. A police source."

"Then . . . I confirm."

Whit grinned at George, holding up her hand for a high-five. "Okay. I think Celeste Cordero is next on the killer's list. Do you know who she is?"

"Yes. Are you sure about this?"

"Like I said, based on the evidence." She filled Riggs in on the details of Irene's story and her own research. "Cordero is a high roller. The kind that I'd say could maybe get themselves into trouble and no doubt buy or bully their way out of it. But this time, I think the stakes are very high for someone."

"That does make sense." Another long pause. "I think you might be right. Thanks. I'm calling Blackwell right now. I hope you're right, McKenna, because this feels like a free fall for me. My career could take a big hit if you're wrong."

"I'd bet all my money I'm right, Riggs. Besides, I value our friendship more than any breaking story."

"Okay. Let's do it."

Whit hung up and grabbed George by the arm. "Come with me, but whatever you do, don't mention my source's name. Not ever, to anyone." The clock on the wall said it was almost ten thirty. She'd have to write fast. Dragging George into Stu's office, she entered without knocking.

Stu was hunched in front of his computer pouring over stories submitted for the Sunday edition, shaking his head. "These stringers are going to be the death of me. Sloppy. Sloppy." He straightened and slurped some coffee from the now-cold mug.

"I have it. Confirmation."

He looked dubious and glanced at his watch. "You've only been gone thirty minutes."

"My police source confirmed that all three victims have teratomas. Off the record, of course." She nudged George in front of her. "Tell him, George."

George raised his hand. "I swear to tell the truth, the whole truth, and nothing but the truth."

Stu snapped. "Keep it pithy."

George sniffed. "Yes, sir. Mrs. McKenna's source said the words: 'I confirm.'"

Suspicious as always, Stu asked Whit, "A minute ago you had nothin'. What'd you trade? No way you pried that out of them without something hot."

Smiling like a Cheshire cat, she leaned on his desk and whispered, "I told them who the next victim is likely to be."

Stu bounced out of his chair, spilling his cold coffee. "Who is it? We gotta get people over there while you write."

24

Fluorescent lights buzzed overhead, the room chilly as Riggs and Panetta stepped through the door. Every surface gleamed white except for the steel tables in the center of the room. The metallic coppery scent of blood, stringent formaldehyde, and other chemicals were familiar smells to Riggs.

Pete Figoni stood hunched over one of the dissection tables. A tall, lanky man in his early thirties, he reminded Riggs of Abraham Lincoln, with the exception of the scraggly goatee. He was in the process of incising the brain of a cadaver, seemingly unaware of the detectives, the faint sounds of AC/DC's "Highway to Hell" droned from an iPod tucked into his white surgical jacket.

His scalpel sliced and separated the cerebral hemispheres of a cadaver, watery blood oozing between Figoni's gloved fingers. He fixed the left half in buffered formaldehyde, then drained and set the bisected brain in a petri dish with sterile cell culture. His movements were precise. Riggs thought he might have made a good surgeon and wondered why he hadn't finished his education. According to Lillian at HR, he had been a promising medical student at NYU.

"Mr. Figoni?" Riggs stepped forward, mindful of the blood splatters on the floor, and waved her badge in front of his vision.

Figoni glanced up, his scalpel poised over the cadaver brain. His gaze darted back and forth nervously from Panetta to Riggs. He slowly removed his lime-green earbuds.

Panetta leaned against the counter. "I'm Detective Panetta; this is ME Detective Riggs. We'd like to ask you a few questions."

Figoni nodded and flexed back and forth on his heels, stretching his legs. "What's this about?"

"We saw you at Human Resources an hour ago," Panetta continued. "Actually, your van cut us off at the road to Human Resources. You might want to slow down."

Riggs, sensing a pissing match, spoke up. "We are investigating a murder in Medford. We were told you travel to Medford in the course of your job, is that true?"

With a nod, Figoni said, "Yeah, man. Once a week or so, depending, I go to the hospitals. Got a girl there I hang with, so sometimes I spend the night."

Panetta raised his brows at this. "Who is this girl?"

"Izzie." Figoni flashed a lascivious grin. "She's got all the curves in the right places, you know." He used his hands like an hourglass, the scalpel dropping a splash of blood on the floor. "Double Ds, you know."

Riggs suppressed her distaste. "What is Izzie's last name and phone number?"

"Her last name's Thompson. She works at the movie theater. Tinseltown. That's where I met her. So, I still don't understand the whole intel probe thing. I'm just a grunt."

"Just covering our bases." Riggs had had enough. She hated subterfuge, and this guy was obviously feigning stupidity. "Her number?"

He rattled it off while Riggs wrote it down.

"What would I have to do with your investigation anyway?"

Panetta folded his arms and leaned back as if he had all night. "You've heard of the Niki Francis murder? We're investigating that. We know that Human Resources works with embryonic stem cells. Do you have any knowledge of that?"

"Yeah. Sure. I know what HR does." He massaged his goatee. "But hey, I'm just the slice-and-dice guy. I'm not, like, privy to the stem cell work. I just deliver the body parts."

"So you don't have access to stem cells?" Riggs pressed.

"No! I mean, no. I travel all over, well, in a two-hundred-mile radius. I work at night mostly, 'cause it's more convenient to access the morgues. My job is just to collect body parts. I have no idea what goes on in the whole science gismo world at HR."

Riggs shared a glance with Panetta. Neither of them was buying the *I'm a dummy* routine. Riggs said, "I spoke with Lillian Gray. She read your personnel file. You were on the dean's list at NYU. Why did you quit with only a year left to finish?"

With careful deliberation, Figoni removed his gloves and walked to the counter, pulling out a small paper cup and filling it with water from the faucet. He took a drink. "Not sure what this has to do with the whole Niki Francis thing, but when I was a third-year, my parents were in a really nasty car accident. A pileup on I-5. My dad died at the scene, but my mom, she . . ." He sighed, clearly struggling with the story. "Look, I'm an only child. Late-in-life kind of thing. So when my mom was hospitalized, I left college to be with her, and she was on life support for five weeks. I lost all that time at school. Then, when she finally got better, she needed long-term care. Brain damage. So I ended up at HR. It pays the bills, man. You know?"

For all his scruffy looks, Riggs decided he understood more than he let on; his demeanor was more facade than reality. She could see this was not going to get any better, so she handed him her card, in the process picking up the distinctive scent of pot, which made her think that maybe she was wrong and he might simply have lost his ambition after his parents' accident and become a pothead. "If you think of anything that might tie in to our investigation of embryonic stem cell use, call us?"

"Yeah, sure. Right on." He pocketed the card and reached into a box on the counter for more gloves.

They turned to leave, but Riggs looked back as the door closed and watched as Figoni popped the earbuds back into place.

"All right, the Beatles!" He sang cheerfully, "All you need is love, love is all you need." He sprayed the table as the remains swirled to the end and were sucked into the disposal, which hissed and gulped as Riggs left the room.

25

REGGIE SNORTED IN Whit's ear, dragging her from a deep sleep. For the first time in months she awakened with no anxiety. She yawned and stretched lazily. Sunlight streamed through the window blinds into her bedroom. Reggie slept against her, upside down, his jowls hanging open, paws peeking out of the covers. This was weirdly comforting. Her eyes drooped closed again, and then the door flew open.

"Mother . . . you have to see this!" It was Emma, in her Hello Kitty nightgown; at fifteen, her figure was anything but childlike now. Where had her baby gone?

Emma spread out the *Medford Daily Chronicle* on the bed. "Check it out!"

Niki Francis and Two Local Attorneys Victims of Serial Killer Dubbed 'Dr. Frankenstein'
Police search frantically for more victims who have deadly 'monster' tumor

Emma perched on the bed beside Reggie, who was wide awake now and trying to turn over. "Priceless headline, Mother!"

Whit cringed at seeing the headline in print once again. "I begged Stu not to write that. It sounds like tabloid trash."

"I especially *love* the monster tumor part. It's gruesome!"

"You sound like George."

"*Love* the teratoma pic, too! Where's Jordan? She's not in her room."

"I let her take your dad's camera equipment to the coast. She left early this morning, picking up some girlfriends on the way. She was hell-bent on taking some sunrise photos for a photography competition. I hope she's all right."

Whit half regretted that decision, but if all went well, Jordan would be back later this evening. Photos were an avenue of escape for Jordan. They gave her a sense of companionship with her father even though he wasn't here. It was certainly a better way to channel her grief than pot.

Emma grunted. "I'm sure she's just fine. She's like a goat. Who wants to traverse cliffs and cling to dirt on the sides of mountains anyway? It's not even slightly sanitary or progressive. *Ugh!*"

Whit yawned and stretched, trying to remember whether everything in her teen years was *so* dramatic. "What time is it?"

"Almost eight."

Streaks of sunlight shimmered on Emma's long blonde hair as she teased Reggie, tickling him under the chin. Whit reached out and tucked Emma's hair behind an ear. She loved her so much. John had called her Princess because she was so much more prissy than Jordan. How could she have given birth to two complete opposite personalities? And she loved them equally. With all the stories she'd written in her career . . . what felt like a lifetime of sorrow and sin, war and famine, accidents and heartaches . . . could she ever think of her girls as safe?

She sighed. Sitting up, Whit asked, "What do you say to breakfast burritos?"

"Sure! Put extra cheese on mine."

Reggie had escaped the covers and now licked and chewed on Emma's fingers, his tail wagging happily, while his paws held her hand down.

"Do me a favor and give Reggie a quick walk while I make breakfast."

Emma grimaced. "Do I have to?"

"Yes. He gets so tired of being cooped up in here. If you don't take him now, it will be too hot. The temperature today is supposed to be a hundred and eight again. This heat wave has been unrelenting."

Emma rolled over onto her stomach and pretended to sleep. Whit smacked her bottom. "Now get going."

She howled in mock pain and rolled off the bed. "Violence is never the answer."

"Ha-ha."

Whit grabbed her robe and headed to the bathroom. Twenty minutes later she was in the kitchen after a quick shower and dressed in a tailored soft-yellow skirt and white sleeveless blouse. She had yet to put on her makeup, but she could do that after breakfast.

Her phone rang. "McKenna."

"Mrs. McKenna, my name is Celeste Cordero. I have to talk to you about the story you wrote in this morning's paper. In private."

"Wait. I thought you spoke to the police last night. Why do you want to speak to me?"

"No. I didn't talk to them. I had a minor accident last night and had to get some stitches. The police somehow found me at the hospital, but I refused to talk with them."

Whit's heart sank. If Cordero had not cooperated with the police, then Katie would have been left high and dry. No proof that her lead was legitimate. She could possibly be in serious trouble for misdirecting the investigation. She'd have to call her as soon as she hung up.

"Did you have anything to do with the stem cell injections?"

"All I can tell you is that I have some very important information to share with you. I need to meet in person."

Given what she knew of this woman, there was no way she was some kind of innocent bystander. She was a social manipulator who held all the strings, with enough power to enforce her will on everyone around her while pretending a generous benevolence.

Whit decided she had to warn her anyway. "If you were involved, you do realize you could be in danger?"

"Yes, of course. That's why I'm calling you."

"What do you mean?"

"This is strictly off the record. Our name cannot be anywhere near this story. The election is in just a few weeks. I have a business reputation to maintain. You understand?"

Thank God for politicians.

"Yes. I understand."

"Good. Can you meet me at my cabin at Lake of the Woods? About two PM today? Alone. I can text you the address."

Whit hesitated. She had no idea how involved Cordero was with the medical trial or how desperate she might be.

Cordero continued with a veiled threat. "I hope I can count on you to keep my name out of it. Mr. Arenburg, who I'm sure you know, owns the *Medford Chronicle*, and I are old friends. He would not be happy with a reporter who exposed someone off the record. *You* understand?"

"Text me the address. I'll see you this afternoon."

Whit hung up. Cordero was just as she'd imagined. All that primping and preening in those photos was just a facade for a duplicitous heart. It was hard to imagine Cordero as a victim. She'd soon find out what her part in all of this was about, though she didn't expect the truth. No, that would come later after some more digging. But for now, this interview was a good start. Maybe she could give her lead to Riggs and make up for the debacle last night.

Another front-page story *and* an exclusive. Three known deaths could be attributed to this madman, and she suspected there might be others.

26

Blurry-eyed, Riggs and Panetta arrived back in Medford by eight fifteen in the morning. They pulled into the sheriff's headquarters and headed straight for the conference room, where Blackwell and the MADIU team were waiting.

After taking a seat at one of the tables, she stole a quick glance at Blackwell's scowling face and saw a copy of the *Medford Daily Chronicle* on the table. Her jaw dropped at the title. Seeing it in print was like a splash of cold water.

"Dr. Frankenstein?"

It was sobering, to say the least. No wonder Blackwell was unhappy. She read the first paragraph, admiring Whit's writing, yet hating everything it exposed in their investigation. Especially because the tip that Cordero could be the killer's next target hadn't panned out. She glanced around and realized everyone in the room was trying to avoid eye contact. Her name would be dirt for a long while.

Blackwell turned and waved a hand at the board. "All of this could be for nothin'. Our unsub is probably on the run. What do ya make of it, Panetta? You've got some FBI profiling in your background. What do you think of our guy?"

Panetta had gone to the coffee machine at the back of the room and poured a cup. "I don't think he'll run if he has live victims out there." He sipped his coffee thoughtfully. "Right now we have no real leads to take us directly to our suspect; if we did, we would have arrested him. He knows that. Why expose himself by panicking? No. This guy is too methodical. He's a man of science and high intellect. He's going to assume he can outsmart us, which makes me think he will take the time to kill anyone who can expose him."

Blackwell nodded, chewing on the end of a cigar. "Makes sense. Riggs, did you learn anything from Figoni, the body-parts guy?"

Riggs shook her head. "No, sadly. We talked to him in the hospital morgue. He swears he's basically just a delivery driver for body parts and doesn't know anything about the science behind Human Resources. But I think he's lying. He has nearly enough credits to be a doctor. He's smarter than he lets on. I don't know. He's the only employee from Human Resources who works in Medford, but who knows," She shrugged. "Our killer may have gotten his stem cells from another company or even a university. We can start looking into other sources."

Shaking his head, Blackwell spread his hands. "Wake up, folks. If any of you have anything to contribute, speak up now!"

A muffled cough from the back of the room broke the awkward silence. A stalemate between agencies, each vying for supremacy. Silence. Too much testosterone in the room, as far as Riggs was concerned.

Her phone buzzed. She glanced at the text from Whit.
Meet me for a run?
Sure. I could use a good workout. See you in 30
She set her phone down and twisted in her chair to have a look at the back of the room. The MADIU team had naturally gathered around the conference room tables, while the FBI boys, a new group from headquarters in Quantico, graced the

back row. The two factions had taken a hard stand, with neither team willing to divulge crucial information to the other.

"This impasse is *not* going to move this case forward."
Blackwell clamped his teeth around his cigar. "We need to
throw all our hats into the ring to catch this sucker. Not one
more life should perish on our watch." He paused to massage
his moustache. "This unsub thinks he's outsmartin' us. Goin'
about his murderous business as if he ain't got a care in the
world. Right under our noses! Nothin' fires me up more than
a cocky son of a bitch. We are all, every one of us, accountable
to the victims' loved ones. We need to use every resource in
our power to find and arrest this monster. If we don't collaborate our efforts and another victim winds up dead, we are all
gonna stink like shit on a shingle. Now speak up! My team
first. You"—he pointed—"Tucker! What do ya have?"

He'd been leaning back, his hands linked behind his head,
but he straightened up immediately. "I met with Dr. Heinemann yesterday afternoon. Real charming guy. Real chatty.
He was acting all cut up about Niki Francis. When I asked
about Delano, he admitted to being his psychiatrist. What's he
gonna say? We already know that. Then he rambled on about
doctor-client privilege. That's it."

"My guys, anything else?"

"Yes," Panetta said. "Lillian Gray faxed a copy of Human
Resources board members early this morning. Guess who's on it?"

"Our pretty boy, Dr. Heinemann?"

"He invested some start-up money and holds shares in the
company."

"I like it! Connecting the dots."

"What we don't have," Panetta added, "is any direct connection between Figoni and Dr. Heinemann."

"We'll find it." Blackwell pulled the cigar from his teeth,
smoothed his moustache, and jerked his chin at the back of
the room. "What about it, boys? We're hot on his tail. You got
anything on Heinemann that we don't have?"

For whatever reason, maybe deciding Blackwell was a decent detective, Special Agent Robert Rasmussen finally spoke up. "We ran him through the database this morning and found some interesting information. He was charged with negligence in treating four patients with injections of growth hormones and some other ingredients he'd picked up from a Ukraine clinic. That was in 2012. He failed to issue warnings of possible side effects, so his license was revoked, and later reinstated after several mandatory classes on medical malpractice."

Riggs's heart skipped a beat. "What were the injections for?"

"Diseases of aging."

"Ya don't say?" Blackwell stood, hands on hips. Riggs realized he was fuming because they were just now sharing vital information. "Plan on making an arrest without us?"

Rasmussen had the decency to look uncomfortable as he explained, "We're not finished with the investigation. We had a team evaluating records from other countries: Bolivia, Costa Rica, and others. We wanted to nail down any loose ends before we shared. Those countries don't have our database, so it takes some time."

Not buying it, Blackwell chewed the tip of his cigar, his dark eyes intent.

Rasmussen continued quickly, perhaps to make amends, "There's more. Dr. Heinemann ran a clinic down in Mexico for underprivileged children back in 2004. He left the country in a hurry when local police started sniffing around because several children had been reported missing."

"That's good enough for me." Blackwell turned to the whiteboard and circled Heinemann's name. "Hog-tie the bastard and bring him in, but do it as a team. We got enough to arrest him as a suspect now, but I'm not ready for that yet. Each of our vics were patients of his. He's directly tied to Human Resources as an investor, and he has a history of illegal experimentation with 'diseases of aging.'"

He eyeballed the room, his gaze evaluating each team member. "Panetta, you bring in Heinemann. Burns, you get a search warrant for Eden Retreat. I want every man available searching that property." He moved to a blueprint on the wall behind him. "Eden Retreat has sixty-something acres. Twelve bungalows all in this area, a large building with unknown usage sits here, the main building here, the restaurant, and several outbuildings we assume are maintenance. I want no mistakes on this one. Take cadaver dogs. You better call your families, 'cause you won't be home for dinner." He glanced at the clock. "We got us a press conference in three hours. Riggs, make sure Dr. Kessler, that pathologist, is at the conference to explain those teratomas."

"Excuse me." The unit secretary, Louise, paused in the doorway. "I think you better turn on the television. Fox News has a special report."

Blackwell turned on the flat-screen mounted on the far wall. A banner ran across the bottom of the screen that read *Breaking News*, while Geraldo Rivera, a reporter with Fox News, held a microphone to an older Hispanic woman's face. "You can verify the staggering report in the *Medford Daily Chronicle* this morning?"

Riggs said, "That's Isabel Rodriguez's mother."

The woman was saying. "My daughter did *not* drown. The autopsy report said there was very little water in her lungs. And she was a good girl. No drugs. She . . . she . . . was a good swimmer."

Geraldo asked, "What about the tumor? The teratoma tumor?"

"Yes. Just like that. It's just like the other two murders. She had the same tumor." The woman's face crumpled with her plea. "Please, please, if you know anything that can help us find my Isabel's killer, call the police."

Blackwell barked at Riggs, "How the hell did *that* happen?"

Riggs shook her head. The day was going from bad to worse. She wondered who else could have gotten their hands on those autopsy reports. Surely Dr. Weldon hadn't handed them over, but she had a suspicion he was the leak. He was a softy at heart, and when heartbroken people came calling on the coroner, he couldn't stop himself. She sighed; at least this new leak would take the pressure off of her. Whit's story had been released before Geraldo's, but hers leaned very closely on speculation because she lacked official documents and names of official sources.

The camera panned, offering a close-up of Geraldo. "You see this." He held up a white piece of paper. "This, my friends, is a copy of the autopsy report for Isabel Rodriguez. It does indeed report a teratoma tumor. We have *no* doubt that this poor woman's daughter is a third victim of the serial killer known as Dr. Frankenstein."

Blackwell turned purple and pointed an accusing finger at Riggs. "Find that damn leak!"

She simply nodded, afraid to say anything. This was not the first time Dr. Weldon had "comforted" the bereaved. It was the most sensationalized, though, and she didn't see how she could protect him from the fallout.

Geraldo continued, "That's right, folks. We have an official document verifying that Dr. Frankenstein is no myth. He exists, and may kill yet again. I *urge* anyone with any information to contact the local police department."

Blackwell cursed and spat in a nearby trash can. "That man nauseates me."

27

"I CAN'T TELL YOU how sorry I am," Whit apologized between breaths. They were running on the last quarter mile of the popular Roxy Ann Peak Trail to Prescott Park. The trail was a 4.9-mile loop that offered great valley views with a thousand-foot elevation above Medford. Both Whit and Riggs had dressed down to running shorts and tank tops. Even at nine thirty in the morning, the temperature had scaled past the ninety-degree mark. The best part about the trail for Whit was no pine trees, so it had become a regular route for them. The dirt path was sparsely populated with madrone trees, an abundance of wildflowers, and scrub—no forests to trigger her phobia. It was also just a three- or four-minute drive uphill from her townhome.

Riggs gave her a friendly punch. "Apology accepted. We knew when we started our quid pro quo that things could go wrong. I'm not holding you responsible. You gave me a great lead, and I think it may yet pan out. Besides, blowhard Geraldo took the edge off of me, at least for the time being."

"What a shit show. You can't turn around in this town right now without running into story-hungry media. I had to take side streets to get here because my car has been tagged, and I'm now as much of a target as anyone."

"Your notoriety is right up there with the best of them."

Whit wondered if there might come a time when they would face a dividing line because of their jobs. She decided that in the end, none of it would be worth it. "Well, I just want you to know that none of this . . . this masterpiece theater, is worth losing your friendship."

Riggs shook her head. "*That's* not going to happen. We both enjoy the challenge of our professions, and there's nothing wrong with a little healthy competition. We'll see which one of us finds Dr. Frankenstein first."

Whit laughed. "Not fair . . . You have the advantage!"

"How so?"

"You have a police badge that opens doors I can only dream of."

"Don't forget that sometimes a cop is the last person people will speak with. You have an official journalist badge. That parts waters too."

"Not the same."

"Almost."

"No. Own it. You have an advantage."

"No way. You get leads from people because they don't want to talk on the record. It's much harder for me to make those kinds of promises."

"That's debatable. You have authority, while I just have what . . . publicity? It's not the same at all."

Riggs teased, "So weak! No excuses. That was my dad's motto for me and my three brothers. He retired thirty-two years in the Fresno Police Department. That was no cakewalk. Fresno was fifth in the nation per capita for murder back when he started. So his mantra . . . no excuses. Period."

"I totally get it. My dad, Air Force sergeant, took no pris-oners. By the book, baby!"

With a breathy laugh, Riggs said, "Seems like we had some interesting similarities growing up."

"Yeah. You know, it's funny. He's become almost a softy in his old age. He's a total pushover with my girls. They can do no wrong in his eyes. My mother just shakes her head in amazement."

"Well, grandparents are allowed to spoil their grandkids. But yes. My brother's kids, all boys so far, love to go fishing and hunting with my dad. He's put on a bit of a beer belly, but he's still active."

Whit glanced ahead and saw they were close enough to the trailhead for a sprint. "Let's knock this out of the park."

Not to be outdone, Riggs charged ahead, and they reached a bench overlooking the city in a breathless sweat.

An inch ahead, Whit bragged, "See, that boot camp has put me in the best shape of my life."

Riggs bent over, catching her breath. "No doubt. God, I needed this run! Had to burn off all the travel kinks and stress."

"I know." Whit plopped down on the bench, wiping sweat off her face with the bottom of her tank top. A haze hung over the Rogue Valley, its rolling hills, now at the end of summer, a dull dry yellow. Whit loved to come up here in the spring when it was fabulously picturesque, with white pear and red cherry blossoms in all the orchards, and in fall when it was ablaze with colorful leaves. Today the mountain ranges were a pale-blue landscape behind distant storm clouds.

Riggs joined her on the bench. "Looks like we may have more storms today."

"Freakish storms lately," Whit said.

"You should have seen me yesterday. I had to do an autopsy in the dark—well, sort of. The power went out and the generator only lights some of the building. And you know Dr. Weldon can be such a drama queen. It was creepy."

"He is amusing, that's for sure." Whit inhaled a deep breath and let it out. "I had some not-so-amusing issues with my girls the last few days."

"Is everything all right?"

She briefly shared Jordan's defiance and Emma's clingy manipulation. "You know, when John was alive, we were partners in raising the girls. Now I feel like I'm split in two, always trying to be everywhere at once. My parents have certainly helped. Thank God for them. But I know my girls are hurting. I also know there's nothing I can do. I can't protect them from all of life's hurts. Their dad died. They're going to hurt. I just have to accept it."

"You'll figure out what's best for them. You're a good mom. I confess I envy you. I always wanted children, or at least thought I'd have one or two by now, but I guess that's not meant to be. With all this talk about embryonic stem cells and embryo banks, it makes me wonder."

"About what?"

"Well, it's like there's these natural checks and balances. Science messes with a developing embryo, and what do we get? Monsters."

Whit nodded. "It does kind of make you think."

"We've had the pro-life groups dropping off all kinds of information down at the police station. Some of the more extreme ones demand we arrest people in the embryonic stem cell business because they're murderers. Raising weird questions like, from a homicide perspective, when is it murder? I don't know what to think, especially when I'm beginning to want to try for a child again."

"I think in the end it's an individual's personal understanding of life. God only knows, Riggs, and that's the truth. Are you sure about wanting a child? You know the strain it can put on your body. Is that a good idea after the cancer?"

Riggs shrugged. "I don't know. I've been much more con-templative since I went through chemo and started evaluating my life. Life and death in general."

"You're a Socrates at heart, Riggs. Always looking for answers. Sometimes there just aren't any. We can philosophize the subject for hours and never really answer the questions. Every person has to follow their own heart."

"That just about sums it up, doesn't it?"

"With ambiguous subjects like this, yes. Now, look." Whit leaned forward. "I need to talk shop. I got a call from Cordero this morning. She's never going to talk to the police, but she wants to talk to me, off the record."

Riggs brows shot up. "You're right about that. At the hos-pital last night Blackwell explained to her that she could be in danger. She denied any involvement in the stem cell trial and refused to talk without an attorney. Did she admit anything to you?"

"No, but she is involved, and obviously she's scared or she wouldn't be talking to me."

"I agree, which makes me think you need backup." She sat forward, appealing to Whit. "She's a powerful force in this community. What her involvement could be in the stem cell trial, I'm not sure, but I don't think I'd trust her at all. You're not meeting her alone?"

"Yes, and I plan on keeping it that way. As soon as I have the information, I'm going to call you. You'll be the star detective on this one. Whatever else has happened will be forgotten."

"You're not putting yourself in danger because of what happened with the Cordero lead last night, are you?"

"Hell no!" Whit stood and stretched. "I'm doing what I always do. I'm hunting down my story. I just plan on making sure you benefit from it too."

"I appreciate that."

Whit added, "You can trade some vital piece of the puzzle that I don't have."

"That's only fair," Riggs nodded.

They began their jog back down the mountain, the air laden with heat. They paced themselves during their descent on the Ponderosa Trail, careful of loose gravel, each lost in their own thoughts.

As they neared their cars parked at the base of the road, Riggs said, "Just be careful, Whit."

"I know what I'm doing," Whit reassured her.

Riggs persisted. "Keep in mind, desperate people do desperate things."

Whit leaned against her car, catching her breath, and nodded. "You're not the only one with a license to carry."

28

"IT'S A PROVERBIAL madhouse down in the lobby!" George pulled up a chair at Whit's desk.

She asked, "How did the morning interviews go?"

Whit had arranged for George to take her place in the media spotlight while she met with Riggs. Today she had dressed casually in pale-blue capri pants and a white blouse. No fancy interviews today if she could help it.

"Excellent, if I do say so myself. I'm still somewhat alarmed that Stu is going to be enraged, spitting and snarling like a bad-tempered Chihuahua."

Whit laughed. "Perfect image. Don't worry. He'll be fine after I file my interview with Celeste Cordero."

"Do write lean and sharp prose. Your finesse might appease him."

"What'd you find out so far this morning?"

"Well, the receptionist at Cordero Realty was quite chatty. She said Cordero always carries this elaborate thank-you basket to the close of her high-end sales. Did I hear referral, referral, referral? I didn't grow up in the midst of elite entrepreneurs without learning that basic tidbit."

"Of course," Whit said dryly.

"Anyway, these baskets are like the Cordero signature dish, if you will. She makes a personal trip to Harry and David Country Store, where she has a clerk design a shrink-wrapped basket full of her client's favorite things. Like wine and cheese, crystal glasses, fruits, little delectables. Sometimes she throws in one of those famous spiral hams."

Whit gave him the evil eye, and he hurried to a close. "Okay. Here's the coup de grace. My dear esteemed colleague, I bet you can't guess what items of import are in these elaborate baskets?"

"*What?*"

"An Eden Retreat spa package and a meet-and-greet with the big cheese . . . Dr. Heinemann."

Whit's brows rose at that. "Oh, what a tangled web we weave . . ."

"When first we practice to deceive."

"Sir Walter Scott."

"I'm impressed," he teased, as he popped one of his French mints into his mouth. "I presumed you were the hard-boiled news type."

Whit chugged the last of her Pepsi and tossed the can in the recycle bin. "Actually, I have a master's in English, my dear boy; that's how I write such captivating prose."

"Who knew?"

"I try not to let on that I'm the literary sort. I also have the mind of a crime writer, so it occurred to me that Cordero could be avoiding the law because she's duplicit in this whole murderous scheme. Dr. Frankenstein's partner, perhaps. She could be enticing me into the wilderness so she can murder me. Bury my body in the middle of nowhere."

"Do you have to be so graphic?"

Whit laughed, somewhat enjoying ruffling his newbie feathers. "That's what good storytellers do."

George looked horrified. "I think you should take me with you."

"I can't. She won't talk if you're there. I shouldn't have even told you about her, but since you were so good at keeping my police source to yourself and you're my writing partner, I figured you should know." She leaned back, pondering the situation. "I'll text you as soon as I get there. Then you text me every fifteen minutes. If I don't respond right away, then you have my permission to call the police."

George shook his head. "It won't do any good to call the police if you're already dead. I'm going with."

"No. George, you can't. Celeste specifically asked me to keep this private. Besides, you're the only person that knows I'm meeting with her and where. I need you here as backup. Just in case."

"You're frightening me."

"Don't worry. I've got my gun."

Stu barked out her name from the doorway of his office. Glancing at the clock, she decided this might be a good exit strategy. She grabbed her purse. The door was open, so she walked right in.

"Come in. Come in." Stu waved her to a chair in front of his desk. "Shut the door."

Whit closed the door and sat down.

"Got some buzz on the scanner. Something's going down at Eden Retreat. Not sure what. Instead of taking Highway 140 to the interview, take Dead Indian Memorial and stop in at Eden. Find out what's going on."

"Sure. I'll leave now, then."

He didn't know that George wasn't going to the interview or who she was interviewing. She planned to keep it that way. He'd probably insist and might ruin her chances of getting Celeste to talk. She nodded, but kept her mouth shut.

"On a side note. Since you and George scheduled this interview, I sent Renee Perkins to cover the press conference over at South Gym. We won't learn anything new there, most likely, but we need to cover our bases. Listen." He stood and started to pace, slurping from his coffee cup. He had at least gotten some rest and showered, because his clothes were new and his wispy hair had that flyaway thing going on instead of being plastered to his head. "You've done a great job on the Frankenstein story. Star reporting. But now we've got every wacko out there hounding us. And the police too, for that matter. It's kinda at a point where I feel responsible for your safety."

"What do you mean?"

"Your stories have created a frenzy in the public. They . . . the public, want blood. Dr. Frankenstein's blood. There's more than a few doctors out there afraid for their lives. They're getting threats. The police are afraid some nutjob might lynch an innocent doctor." He set his cup down on the desk and picked up his pacing. "Dr. Frankenstein didn't just kill three people. He killed three very prominent people. One of which was a Hollywood darling. The media is eating it up. The world's biased that way. My point." He paused at his desk, facing Whit. "I mean, that you're the point man on this one. You're out there gathering the facts, workin' the story. Possibly closing in on him. The thing is, he knows that too. Journalists have been killed for less. You know that firsthand."

His reference to Afghanistan was not helpful. Of course she understood the risks. Hadn't she lived it? "What exactly are you saying?"

"I'm saying Dr. Frankenstein could feel cornered. Watch your back."

She recalled the threatening presence at Eden Retreat the night before and Dr. Heinemann's strange behavior. "Don't worry. I'll take precautions."

Stu glanced down, uncomfortable. "That's all I'm sayin'. Keep a sharp eye."

Touched by his concern, she decided to put an end to his suffering and stood up to leave.

"Thanks, Stu. Don't worry. I'm armed and dangerous."

"Good. Keep me informed. You and George use the buddy system."

Sure thing, Stu.

29

KIDS WAILED AND grown men shouted abuse at each other while Mayor Ostrander tested the microphone; its shrill whine momentarily quieted the place down. A disheveled, sweaty stream of vagabond citizens continued to file into the air-conditioned South Medford High School gym. With the heat at a dangerous 104 degrees outside, Riggs was surprised by the turnout. The two-thousand-capacity seating was challenged. This was a community up in arms with unreasonable fears of monster tumors and killers on the loose.

Riggs had overheard numerous conspiracy theories. She and Blackwell had gotten a kick out of the ridiculous imaginings: Terrorists had poured chemicals in the drinking water. The government was secretly using Medford as a test site for cancer cures. The growths were the result of radioactive fallout from a hushed-up nuclear accident. Her favorite had her laughing out loud: aliens had invaded and implanted their fetuses, and the government had assigned a secret assassin team. She couldn't wait to share that one with Whit.

Her gaze swept the crowd at the door. The cacophony of voices and speaker checks drowned out her yell to Dr. Kessler, who stood in the doorway. She hustled toward him. It was strange to see him without his requisite lab coat. She'd called earlier and made sure he was available to speak to the crowd, as Blackwell insisted. At least his appearance was professional: light-gray slacks, crisp white dress shirt, and dark-gray tie. She hoped the presence of a bona fide pathologist to explain the teratomas might calm some of the irrational fears.

"Thanks for coming, Dr. Kessler. We're sitting over here."

His sharp blue gaze traveled the stadium seating. "Quite the turnout!"

"Yes. It is."

She led him around a group of television and print reporters gathered together on the polished gymnasium floor to a row of chairs in the center of the gym, where a microphone and podium had been set up. Above, on the mezzanine level, bystanders crowded near the new banner, consisting of large block letters in royal blue: *HOME OF THE PANTHERS*. The school gym had recently been painted, so instead of the pungent scent of teenage sweat, it smelled of fresh paint.

Blackwell motioned to Mayor Ostrander, and he nodded and approached the microphone.

"Quiet down. Quiet down." Ostrander repeated himself several more times before the crowd responded. "We are here to help the citizens of Medford understand this very complex case. We believe if you know the proper chronology of the investigation, we can put your fears to rest. Now, of course, we cannot share every detail of the case, but enough to alleviate any undue fears. Lieutenant Sergeant Blackwell and Special Agent Rasmussen with the FBI are going to run through the case with you, and then medical examiner detective Katie Riggs and Dr. Kessler, a pathologist, will help enlighten all of us regarding the complicated science involved in this case. At the end, police chief Tom Holbrooks will take questions. If you'll all remain quiet and calm, we can proceed."

All things considered, Riggs thought the proceedings went fairly well, with only an occasional interruption. Sleep deprived, she felt fatigue settle in as she waited her turn to speak. Evelyn Zagorski from the crime lab in Central Point had sent a text saying she had some potential DNA evidence from the Niki Francis burial site that she'd run through CODIS, but with no match. Riggs wanted to take a look at it anyway. On the way to the crime lab, she'd stop at All's Natural and get a green smoothie with a blueberry kicker.

When Blackwell informed the crowd that MADIU was in the process of interrogating a person of interest, a collective sigh came from the bleachers. They would not release his name to the public until they had enough evidence to arrest him. The circumstantial evidence against Dr. Heinemann was certainly overwhelming, but they were following policy to the letter and shared none of that with the public. Blackwell cautioned that the investigation was still ongoing.

Using a whiteboard, which was projected onto a giant screen, Detective Blackwell detailed all the steps that the combined task force was taking. He methodically, in his slow drawl, explained the procedures set in place for the protection of the community.

Eventually, Riggs was introduced.

She planned to keep her presentation short and sweet. After sharing some of the details of the autopsy and the discovery of the teratomas, she went through the chronology of each event before finally passing off the mic to Dr. Kessler.

With a quick wave to Blackwell, Riggs ditched the gym and headed back to the sheriff's office so she could see how Panetta's interrogation was going with Dr. Heinemann. When she arrived at the sheriff's station, she found Tucker standing in the hall, watching a monitor outside the interrogation room. On the screen she could see Panetta sitting across a small table from Dr. Heinemann, who wore white linen and a loose-fitting black-and-white short-sleeved shirt. He'd make a great poster boy for the Caribbean. His curly dark hair had that windswept, casually cool look as he half lounged in his chair. Not a good sign.

"How's it going?" Riggs asked.

"Blackwell is on his way over, but he's probably wasting his time." Tucker made a sour face. "We ain't got shit."

"So he's not talking?"

"Oh, no. The guy jabbers like a parakeet on crack. Just none of his squawking is worth anything." He spread his feet apart and crossed his arms, biceps bulging. "I told Panetta to cut the feed to the monitor and let me have at him."

Riggs chose to ignore that. "How long has Panetta been in there with him?"

"About thirty minutes. Burns just left with a dozen squad cars and the cadaver dogs to search Eden Retreat."

"Why did it take so long?"

"Couldn't find a judge for the warrant. Everyone's out playing. It's a holiday weekend, remember?"

She had forgotten. She hit the button on the monitor to turn up the sound. Heinemann was saying something about the joy of living with a clean conscience, free from guilt and fear of the law. His past was a lesson learned . . . blah, blah, blah. Tucker was right. He was a windbag. And worse, a psychiatrist. Panetta's training with the FBI might trip him up. But they were probably looking at hours and hours of interrogation.

"Well," she sighed. "Maybe our search at Eden will turn up something."

"Yeah. I can't watch this bullshit anymore." He ran a harassed hand through his crew cut. "I'm gonna go help Burns pilfer this scumbag's property."

She watched Tucker stride down the hall, not exactly sorry to see him go. If the team didn't come up with something concrete, they would have to release Heinemann and put a tail on him, which of course he would be fully aware of. She had hoped Whit's story might unearth a victim who could identify

Heinemann. They would need it if Cordero didn't pan out. The story had generated an avalanche of calls, more than they could handle, and created an impossible mess to sort out. Now they had more "victims" than they could count. Most were loonies that jammed the system, because precious time had to be wasted checking out each lead.

Heinemann might respond differently to a woman. She opened the door to the interrogation room and popped her head in. "Hey, Panetta. Need a break?"

"Actually, I'm feeling parched." He stood up and indicated that she should take his chair. "Dr. Heinemann, this is Detective Riggs. She assisted with the autopsies of our three victims."

The good doctor's demeanor changed dramatically; he straightened and smiled, holding out his hand politely. She shook it, and found it warm and soft with just the right amount of pressure.

"My pleasure," he said. "I'm trying to explain to Detective Panetta that he has the wrong man. We are all aware of my past mishaps with the law, but I'm a reformed man. I'm cooperating in every way. However, in my own interests, I did call my attorney. But in the meantime, ask any question you like."

Riggs glanced at Panetta, who shrugged. They both knew that unless they found something damning at Eden, or unless a legitimate witness or victim stepped forward, they were just fishing.

Panetta quietly left the room, allowing Riggs to gain authority over the space.

Her technique during interrogations had always been to find common ground. It was amazing what people confided when they felt a shared empathy.

"I'm sorry about all this," she said. "You've managed to quite successfully redesign your image at Eden. That's not an easy thing to do with a criminal history."

"I'll probably sue the *Chronicle* for linking my retreat to these heinous murders." He smiled pleasantly. "I'm a respected member of this community."

Riggs nodded. "It's a shame that your reputation is being tarnished by the public nature of this case. Is there anything you can tell us that might help? You know, get the spotlight off of you?"

He flashed an appreciative smile. "Nice empathetic approach to gain my confidence. Detective Panetta worked the angle of my interest in science and my legitimate desire to help humanity. It appears the law enforcement community has evolved since my last encounter. Oh, except for Detective Tucker. He's a classic Neanderthal, brute force type." He glanced at the door. "I'd appreciate it if you kept him at bay until my attorney arrives."

Riggs changed tactics. "All right. You see through us. What if we ask you for help? With your background in medicine and psychiatry and your previous interest in diseases of aging, you could be a real asset to this case."

"As a consultant?" Heinemann found this idea intriguing. "I'll play. At least until my attorney arrives. I think she'd counsel against it."

"*If.*" Riggs leaned forward and pulled out her notepad from her back pocket, hoping to convey an air of respect for his psychiatric skills. The corners of his eyes crinkled, amused. "If you were putting together a profile on this killer, how would you describe him? What motivates him?"

"I've read the newspapers, watched the news, like everyone else. But there are things I don't know." He folded his hands primly together on the table. "What have you learned about the manner of death?"

Heinemann was no fool. If she wasn't careful, he'd know every detail of the investigation, making it impossible to outwit him. "We don't actually know. As you've heard in the news, we're waiting for toxicology."

"You must have *some* suspicions?" he pressed.

"Not really." She thought it best to redirect the conversation. "So can you help us with motivation?"

With an air of deep thought, he leaned back, drumming his fingers together slowly, his gaze never leaving her face. "This is a deeply psychotic man, but he is not delusional. He is displaying the typical pattern of a sociopath: a pervasive disregard for others, willing to violate them without remorse. He is aware of his lack of empathy. He is cunning and can be ruthless, clearly, but may have adapted a charming personality to conceal his true character. Each victim was no doubt lured into his trap with his charisma, a tool he uses to manipulate, to seduce."

His description of a sociopath was like a mirror image of himself. She wondered if he was aware of that. His unblinking stare bore into her with seemingly malicious intent. Riggs felt goose bumps on her arms. Was he manipulating her? She sensed he was playing with her, not in the least concerned. Most people were intimidated the minute they stepped into the interrogation room, unless they were high on drugs or alcohol. His absolute calm was unnerving.

At the sound of a tap at the door, he smiled and broke his stare. A woman Riggs recognized as a defense attorney walked into the room and asked her to leave while she consulted with her client. Her name was Laura Frye; a no-nonsense schoolmarm type, she could wipe the floor with you with one piercing glare over her bifocals.

Riggs stood up to leave and felt Heinemann's hand rest on her arm. He held out a business card. "In case you need more assistance, public or private."

She suppressed a shudder and took the card.

CHAPTER

30

WITH THE HOPE that she might be able to decipher something useful from Panetta's half of the Heinemann
interview, Riggs sat reviewing the recording at her desk in the
sheriff's office when her phone rang. The only thing she could
note for sure was Heinemann's colossal arrogance.

With a disgusted shake of her head, she answered. "Riggs."

"We got bodies." Blackwell huffed, as if he was walking
over rough terrain. "The dogs sniffed out two cadavers jammed
into a narrow mine shaft about an hour ago. Can't haul 'em
out till you get here. We're out in the back forty, so I'll send
Panetta back down to the parking lot to guide you in. Hurry
up, it's hotter 'n' hell!"

When she drove into the Eden Retreat parking lot, which
was overrun with police, FBI, state, and sheriff's officials,
enough to cover a hundred murders, she squeezed her truck
onto the grass divider by the road. A wall of hot air buffeted
her when she opened the door. The day's humidity had boiled
into a seething mass of dark clouds and scalding wind. At least
the clouds blocked some of the sun's intensity. She grabbed her
cadaver kit and her camera.

Panetta, still in his white dress shirt, though his tie was loosened, waved from under the shade of a tree.

"This place is hardly Eden today, more like Hades." Panetta relieved Riggs of the heavy cadaver kit. "It's this way, up the hill."

"Thanks. Yeah, heaven and hell, just like Milton's Paradise Lost. Am I going to find Satan and all the fallen angels up there?"

"You're gonna find some dead angels. Both women. Possibly early sixties, maybe older. I'm looking into any missing persons reports in the past twenty-four hours."

Panetta led her up the paved path, but where it curved off to the right, he kept going. For the next hundred feet they walked across neatly mowed green grass, then stepped over a two-foot rock wall and began the ascent up the hill across tall, wheat-colored dry grass and loose rocks. South of them, down in a shallow valley, rested the city of Ashland, famous for its Shakespeare Festival that Dr. Weldon loved so much. To the north stretched rolling hills of vineyards and pear orchards, a picturesque view if not for the grizzly task at hand.

She steeled herself against the inevitable shock and revulsion that accompanied the detailed investigation of murder victims, reminding herself that she was here for the living. For the loved ones who would inevitably want answers. This place was aptly named after all; like the Garden of Eden, evil had snaked its way in.

Hot wind whistled up from the valley, swirling bits of sand into the air around them.

Panetta leaned into it. "Breathe through your nose, or you'll be picking sand out of your teeth."

"I'm more concerned about my eyes." Riggs squinted against the wind, blinking rapidly.

They proceeded over more rolling hills, the blistering wind stealing her breath the higher they climbed. The retreat was far behind them with nothing but wilderness up ahead, dotted with scrub brush and red-barked manzanita trees. Three vultures, their wings black against the stormy sky, were circling high above them. They crossed a road of sorts strewn with loose gravel, where, directly ahead, stood Blackwell and a clan of police and FBI.

Panetta pointed down the gravel road. "We tracked the road to an abandoned logging camp off Dead Indian Memorial Road. This area here is still technically Eden Retreat. There's a metal gate that we're working on getting the keys to so you can drive your truck up here to retrieve the bodies. If all else fails, we'll cut the gate open."

Blackwell stepped over a downed tree, the requisite cigar clamped firmly in his teeth. "I figure we got maybe an hour or two before this storm comes over the mountains and spits fire down on us. On top of that I'm having to rotate the officers, all of us, FBI too, because we're concerned about heatstroke. Two of the guys are already passed out and had to be carted off to the hospital. So I had a bunch of bottled water brought up. Pour it on your head if you have to."

Riggs nodded and approached the cadavers. The mine shaft had been cleared of the initial layer of dirt, just enough to make out two bodies, their limbs intertwined. From the length of hair and color of clothing, she could guess that they were women. Her face flushed with anger to see life treated with such callous disregard. With renewed energy, she retrieved her bag from Panetta, thanking him, and placed it on the ground. She pulled out latex gloves and put them on. Before touching anything, she snapped pictures, then Tucker and Burns helped her batten down two tarps with metal stakes so the wind didn't blow them away.

Blackwell cursed, "It's like the fucking Mojave Desert up here."

Riggs couldn't agree more, but as much as she'd loved to hurry up and get finished, she worked carefully, sifting the sand and dirt onto a third tarp behind the shelter of a makeshift plastic windbreaker stretched between two metal poles. The bodies didn't appear to have been in the ground very long; she estimated twenty-four hours, maybe less. The vics were wedged so tightly into the space they had to shovel around the hole before they could pull the bodies out. It was slow work, as they tried not to disturb the crime scene any more than they had to. Gusts of wind whistled eerily through the twisted branches of a manzanita tree, and the sky turned ominously dark.

Riggs eyed the stormy sky. "Bizarre weather this weekend. It's as if somebody up there doesn't like what's going on down here. Like this place is cursed."

"The Gods are angry, for sure," Panetta said. "From the storm yesterday, we can plainly see tire tracks on the logging road. Recent tracks. My guess is late last night after the rain stopped and the road was muddy. There are a couple of good muddy boot prints as well. So whoever dumped the bodies had access with a key for the gate. Since this is technically Eden property, that narrows our suspects."

"Dr. Heinemann?"

"That would be a pretty good guess. He certainly has the right history, but that doesn't necessarily mean he's guilty. But yeah, he'd be my first bet, even though I didn't get that good a read on him."

"I know. He could be a pathological liar and a remorseless serial killer, but we need more evidence than just proximity."

Tucker chimed in, "I got a read on him. He's a murderin' egomaniac windbag. I say we haul his ass back in right now and charge him with murder."

A state trooper came jogging up the gravel road. They had cut the chains free on the gate blocking the road, and it was clear for her truck to enter now. Panetta offered to go get it for her, so she gratefully tossed him the keys.

Riggs glanced down at the two bodies now spread out on tarps, hot wind wiping sand over them as if the earth was fighting to reclaim them. "Evil. It's a place of evil."

She knelt down and blinked sand from her eyes. The first vic was tanned and wearing a pink bathrobe over a floral nightgown, no slippers or jewelry. No makeup on her face. The second vic had shoulder-length brown hair and was wearing a T-shirt and shorts, no shoes. Both were slender and probably about the same age.

"What do ya think?" Blackwell asked, covering his nose as the wind whipped his way. "A day, maybe two?"

She nodded. "I think so. The first vic doesn't appear to have been in the hole as long as the other one. Her bowels have disengaged, which is some of what you're smelling."

Tucker swallowed hard and backed away. "Is that what that is?"

Burns said blandly, "That would be my guess."

Blackwell scowled. "Don't puke on the scene, Tucker."

"You don't see me hurling up my lunch at crime scenes, do you?" He planted his feet apart and crossed his arms, bulging the muscles. With his face bright red and streaked with sweat, Riggs was concerned.

With a snicker, Burns said, "You've always been my role model, Tucker."

Riggs suppressed a laugh, and hastened to take the scowl off Tucker's face. "Thanks, guys, for helping pull the vics out."

"Okay, we're all singin' kumbaya now. Let's focus," Blackwell warned. "I've got every kind of law enforcement in the country aiming their sites on me, and I ain't gonna do nothin' to screw this case up. You got it? Now, Riggs, am I right in thinkin' they weren't killed at the same time?"

"That's my best guess at the moment. The first vic was probably killed sometime in the middle of the night, given what she's wearing. The second one, maybe Friday? I would also suggest they were drugged. I don't see any defensive wounds. Won't know about teratomas until the autopsy, of course, but I wouldn't be surprised."

A few large drops of rain splattered the ground around them.

"Damn." Blackwell glared at the stormy sky. "Crime techs are almost here, but it's gonna be a muddy mess soon, and puttin' up a tent is out of the question in this godforsaken wind."

"We need to work as fast as we can," Riggs confirmed.

"Agreed. Can you do the autopsies tonight? I'd like to confirm the teratoma link and get some IDs."

"Yes, I'll set it up as soon as I can."

Blackwell's phone rang, he answered, and a moment later he broke into a string of curses. Everyone paused, waiting for an explanation.

"What the fuck, Blackwell?" Tucker asked.

"It's Heinemann. Somehow he managed to ditch his tail. No one knows where he is."

Tucker's jaw dropped. "That maggot got away?"

"Hell and damnation! I was just gonna arrest that piece o' shit." Blackwell stomped off in a huff down the hill, punching numbers into his phone.

Just then, gravel crunched under tires, and everyone cast their eyes toward the road. There came a row of vehicles, the crime crew among them to set up a grid. Little good it would do them in the wind and rain.

31

WITH STU'S WARNING still pinging around in her head, Whit joined the traffic on I-5 headed north toward Ashland and the Siskiyou Summit. Perhaps she should have listened to Stu and taken George with her. Maybe stowed him under a blanket in the back of the car. Cordero wouldn't have known he was hiding; then at least if she texted him, she'd have immediate backup. Well, it was a moot point now.

A bit paranoid, Whit kept an eye on her rearview mirror to see if anyone was following her, which was basically an impossible task. Traffic was congested as usual. Storm clouds loomed ahead. The temperature gauge on her car read 103 degrees. After she turned off I-5 and neared Eden Retreat, the traffic backed up. A congestion of law enforcement overwhelmed the entire parking lot and clogged the side road that led up to Lake of the Woods and Celeste's cabin.

Whit inched along with the traffic, trying to see what the commotion was about. A slew of media were clumped down in the parking lot with a few stand-up cameras rolling. She caught sight of Panetta walking across the parking lot and pulled off the road, wedging her car into a spot on the opposite side of the street and facing the wrong direction. Ticket time if any of those cops took notice. Grabbing her pad and pen, she raced across the street.

"Panetta!"

He didn't appear to hear her as she ran between two cars approaching in opposite directions, one of which honked at her. The driver flipped her off. She smiled and waved. *Jerk.* Closer now, she called again as he was climbing into Riggs's F-150 truck. "Panetta!"

Thankfully, he heard her this time and stepped back, leaving the truck door open. "McKenna. Great reporting on your article this morning."

"Thank you." She was pleasantly surprised by the compliment.

"Dr. Frankenstein?" He raised a brow, clearly amused, his brown eyes teasing.

Even though she found the title rather ridiculous, she suddenly felt defensive. "Can you think of a better name for a doctor turning human flesh into monster tumors?"

"You make an interesting argument."

"I'm on my way to an interview and I've only got a few minutes, but can you tell me what's going on here?"

Panetta's gaze searched her face for a moment, analyzing. She wondered briefly what he was thinking, but soon found out. "I know Riggs trusts you, but she knows you a lot better than I do. I cannot share information with the media during an ongoing investigation even if I wanted to."

"Oh." She glanced over at the group of media swarming the wide porch. Her chances of getting through the throng were not great in the small amount of time before her interview.

Panetta shook his head. "No, those journalists are not getting any information either. They're being told that we have a search warrant for the property and that is all."

Whit looked him in the eye. "That's it? That's the best you can do?"

Panetta merely laughed.

"Come on, Panetta. Give me something."

With a mischievous grin, he said, "Riggs is at the scene. You understand?"

"Yes. I do. Thanks, Panetta."

With a salute, he climbed into the truck. Whit happily crossed the road, using a bit more caution this time. She'd make sure to use her interview as collateral for whatever was going down at Eden. If Riggs was on scene, then they had discovered at least one body. However, that didn't necessarily mean the body was related to her story, but she'd bet money it was.

For the next thirty minutes, she drove through rolling hills and gradually climbed in altitude until the road was flanked by tall pines. It would have been a pleasant trip, except the nearer she drove to the Cascade Mountains, the more anxiety she felt. Would she always have this creeping fear of the woods? It was a sobering thought. A phobia wasn't something she could rationalize. Riggs had suggested a technique called desensitization—repeatedly subjecting Whit to a walk in the woods until the fear gradually disappeared. It was an entirely unpleasant prospect, but she could see that it was probably necessary in order to overcome the paralyzing panic.

Conscious of gripping the wheel with tense hands, she flexed her fingers, not surprised to find her palms sweaty. Fixing her eyes on the road, she sighed with relief when she saw the sign for Lake of the Woods, but soon the road got bogged down in holiday traffic headed for Aspen and Sunset campgrounds, which were no doubt jammed with trailers, tents, and kids on bikes enjoying the Labor Day weekend.

She turned left onto Mt. McLoughlin Lane, named after the nearly 9,500-foot dormant volcano that overlooked the lake. During the winter months its huge angled peak gleamed like a white beacon from almost any viewpoint in the valley. Now it was a dry, brown, rocky specter that cast a dark shadow

onto the lake, which was twenty-six square miles of water surrounded by thick pines.

Tension mounted, along with real regret that she hadn't
brought George along to at least keep her company and, frankly,
keep her from coming unhinged. As Cordero had instructed in
her text, Whit made a left at a fork in the road where pavement
turned into packed dirt and a small sign nailed to a tree read
Private Road. The sun-dappled narrow lane twisted around a
bend beneath dense towering pines. She could feel the adrenaline seep into her system, ready to mount an attack. It washed
over her in white-hot waves, creating a mindless need to escape,
as if she were suffocating underwater.

"Damn it!" Whit abruptly jammed on the brake and
inhaled a deep breath, counting, then slowly releasing. She
gripped the steering wheel and leaned her head against her
hands. She couldn't catch her breath. The breathing wasn't
helping; she had to get out. She shoved the car into park and
stepped out, gasping for air. Abandoning the car in idle, she
paced back and forth on shaky legs, willing the fear away.

Talking as if to a child, she said to herself, "It's not Afghanistan. It's over. You're safe." She paced and talked, repeating
the refrain, fighting the image of John's horrified expression
when the bullet ripped through his head and her terribly inef-
fectual efforts to stop the bleeding. The utter helplessness.

Changing direction, she circled around the car a half dozen
times. "It's over. There's nothing you can do. You're safe. The
girls need you." She walked, talked, and gradually absorbed the
sounds around her. The crunch of leaves under her feet, the
whine of a distant motor boat, the bees swirling in the trees.

Thank God no one was around. No doubt she looked like
a lunatic.

"Fucking Afghanistan!"

She grabbed the door handle and got back in the car. After
a few minutes, she felt in control again. She put the car in gear
and pressed on.

As soon as she turned the next bend, the road opened into a quaint, sunny clearing. Thank God for small mercies. Sky and sunlight. She could breathe. A two-story cedar log cabin with a lovely wraparound porch and an exposed stone fireplace was perched near the base of the lake, with a few Douglas firs providing shade. A footpath sloped down to the water, where a jet boat and a canoe were tied to a dock. The expansive lake sparkled like diamonds in the sun, with Mount McLoughlin looming in the distance. The gravel road dipped around the front of the cabin. She parked next to a truck and sent a quick text to George.

I'm at the cabin. Contact me in fifteen minutes or so.

She pushed send, then gathered her purse and opened the car door. As her foot hit the ground, she remembered her revolver. Should she take it? It seemed a little overly paranoid. Her phone dinged, and she glanced down at George's text.

Take your gun.

Maybe she should. In preparation for such an event, she'd gone into the downstairs bathroom at the newspaper and clipped her Flashbang bra holster onto the front of her bra. Now she opened the glove box, removed the Ruger LC380, and made sure the safety was on; then, ducking down in the seat, she discreetly lifted her blouse and slid the gun into the holster. No doubt it was overkill for a completely harmless interview.

Her hands were still sweaty, so she wiped them on a napkin from the glove box and grabbed her phone, tucking it into her back pocket. A quick glance in her purse reassured her that she had her steno pad, pen, and recorder. By five o'clock she'd be back in the newsroom writing the final chapter in this bizarre string of murders. She'd ask for next weekend off to spend some time with her girls. Maybe go to Brookings at the coast. She wondered how Jordan's photo shoot was going. On the way back to the paper, she'd call her.

Gravel crunched under her feet as she approached the front steps. The porch had a couple of rocking chairs, a wooden two-person table in the corner, and a variety of potted plants with colorful petunias. Someone must come around pretty often to keep them watered. She doubted if the Corderos were up here that frequently. She rang a doorbell and waited. Engraved on a rock next to a flowering stump were the words *Martha Stewart does not live here.*

After a decent amount of time, she rapped her knuckles on the screen door. It had certainly taken her longer than expected to get through the traffic at the lake, and her mini-breakdown in the woods made her even later, so Cordero might be waiting around back, but surely she'd heard Whit drive up. She walked along the creaking boards and found the back porch empty except for a couple of redwood lounge chairs. The only sounds were birds high up in the trees, the water gently lapping at the dock. She tried the back door and found it unlocked. Hesitating for only a moment, she pushed the door open. It wasn't like she was breaking and entering. She was there by invitation.

"Hello?" Whit called, blinking her eyes to adjust to the sudden gloom. The kitchen and living room were combined into a great room with a vaulted ceiling and soaring river-rock stone fireplace. A large black-and-brown chiseled-edge granite island in the kitchen divided the room. Tan leather sofas surrounded the fireplace, and a long, rustic, wooden dining table sat before a two-story picture window facing the lake. The soft ticktock of a grandfather clock near the front door filled the silence. The place smelled of old wood fires from the previous winter, and coffee, probably from the morning.

Cordero might have taken a nap and overslept. She did hit her head the night before and had to get stitches at the hospital. An afternoon nap would make sense. This thought was dashed as Whit noticed two glasses on the counter with melting ice, rivulets of condensation on them, next to a pitcher of iced tea, most likely in preparation for her visit. She had to be here somewhere. Perhaps the bathroom?

Whit set her purse on the kitchen counter and approached the bottom of the stairs near the front door. She mounted the first step, her hand resting on the polished mahogany banister.

"Mrs. Cordero? Hello?"

She contemplated just waiting on the porch for a while. Remembering her panic attack, she decided the sooner she finished this interview and drove back to town, the better.

With a bit more gusto, she called again, eyeing the landing at the top of the stairs.

Silence, except for the grandfather clock ticking rhythmically.

She wondered if she should search upstairs, and the longer she stood there indecisive, the deeper her misgivings became.

Tick . . . tock . . . tick . . . tock . . . The gold pendulum's rhythmic swing back and forth in the grandfather clock beneath the stairs was somehow unsettling in the absolute quiet.

The hair on the back of her neck began to rise.

Something was wrong. A sense of peril accelerated her heart rate.

Whit progressed up three more steps, her gaze fixed on the upper landing that stretched across and to the left in an L shape. Two closed doors on her left and two open doors at the top of the stairs. Nestled in the corner sat a cozy wide-windowed nook with bookshelves and a small desk. Through the nook window she could see dark clouds gathering, the silver lining dimming the sunlight to a soft haze and creating shadows upon the stairs and in the hall above. Swallowing her unease, she took a determined step upward. Her hand was slick on the banister, so she wiped the sweat onto her blouse, silently cursing her phobia of the woods. She slowly proceeded to the top of the landing.

"Celeste? It's Whit McKenna from the *Chronicle*. Hello?"

In the answering silence, she let out a long pent-up breath. She was debating which door to try first when she glanced down. A red smear streaked along the left side of her white blouse. She frowned, wondering how that had happened, then looked at her hand. It was sticky, but not with her phobic sweat.

Blood?

A darting glance at the bottom railing revealed a smear of blood, feathered in a red streak by her hand. And midway down the stairs, she'd stepped in a pool of blood, overlooked because it lay in shadow on the dark mahogany. Her heart catapulted to a fast gallop in seconds. She reached under her blouse and yanked her gun out, ears straining. She unlocked the safety and began slowly backing down the stairs, trying to see everywhere at once.

Her breathing rapid and shallow, she gripped the gun in both hands, pointing at the ground as her instructor had shown her. With each descending step she sensed that she was not alone. Mouth dry, Whit edged to the next step, holding her breath as the pulse of her heart swished through her ears.

The floor creaked above her and she jerked around, nearly losing her balance.

"Celeste?"

Dust motes swirled in a sunbeam from the nook window, but all else was still and quiet. A flitting shadow bounced across the wall as a large bird flew beyond the panes of glass. Though the cabin was warm, a sudden chill shuddered through her. No longer questioning her instincts, she sensed imminent danger. Avoiding the puddle of blood on the stairs, she retraced her steps to the bottom, paused, and cocked her head to listen.

She stood frozen . . .

Whit jerked her gun toward a thump on the front porch. Another *clump, clump,* and her finger was on the trigger. Someone was on the porch. Just as she tightened her finger to pull the trigger, the head of a deer appeared in the window. It nibbled at the potted plants and pulled the blooms off the petunias. Sick with relief, she lowered her arms, and let out the breath she'd been holding.

She had certainly let herself jump to conclusions. The blood on the stairs had unnerved her. Cordero had prepared tea for her visit, so she was around somewhere. Perhaps she'd fallen on the stairs and opened up her head wound. She was probably upstairs even now, dressing her injury.

Determined to stop being so afraid of everything, she resolutely climbed the stairs. "Mrs. Cordero, are you all right?"

The first bedroom to her right appeared to be a guest room with a brass queen bed draped in a country quilt. A dresser and a chair finished the simple room. Everything looked in order. She tried the next door; it opened to reveal a small office with a window overlooking the lake. Distant boaters glided across the lake, creating white wakes behind them, and at the water's edge the dock stretched its wooden planks out over the lake with the boat and canoe tied to it. Her gaze followed the lakeshore, and in the distance were two similar cabins.

Turning from the window, she examined the desk with its stacks of papers. Most of them looked like real estate contracts, and a half dozen scrolled house plans scattered the floor behind the desk. One wall had a large bulletin board with development plans for East Medford.

No rest for the wicked.

Back in the balconied hall, the next door was partially open. Droplets of blood dripped down the white wood siding inside the doorframe. Whit checked the safety on her gun. It was still off. She knocked and gently pushed the door wider. "Mrs. Cordero?"

She cautiously stepped into the room, her gun ready. Heavy drapes were pulled closed in the bay window, blocking much of the sunlight and casting shadows over two leather reading chairs. Directly in front of her was a huge log bed with a green floral bedspread. One side of the bed was turned back, the pillow dented as if Cordero had been resting. Above the bed hung a large gold-framed painting of mallard ducks in flight. Light from the adjoining bathroom fell upon a white bearskin run at the foot of the bed. A few drops of blood trailed the rug to the bathroom.

She glanced nervously over her shoulder through the open door and down the stairs. Deciding she had no choice but to check on Cordero, she slowly crossed the room and pushed the bathroom door all the way open. The counter, littered with perfume bottles, lotions, and assorted makeup, was splattered with blood. More frightening than that, bloody handprints smeared the sink and mirror. A brightly colored glass bottle of some sort lay shattered at her feet.

Clearly this was the scene of some sort of struggle. Alarmed for good reason now, Whit stepped carefully over the broken glass and saw a claw-foot bathtub with a white shower curtain. A bloodied hand, glittering with diamonds, protruded from the curtain at the back of the tub. Cordero. Her heart skipped a beat.

The chime on her phone dinged. *George!*

In the same instant she saw movement in the mirror behind her and found herself staring into the hazel eyes of Wilhelm, the masseur from Eden Retreat.

"All you had to do was walk away, but you just had to snoop."

Whit flipped around, gun ready, only to have Wilhelm's vicelike grip catch her wrist and twist. When she tried to wrench away, he slammed her wrist against the counter. She cried out in pain as the gun dropped onto the sink. In seconds she was disarmed. Wilhelm tucked the gun into his belt, then pulled her roughly into the bedroom and shoved her into a leather chair.

"I was just about to clean up my little mess when you arrived." Wilhelm shook his head. "Ah, well, two birds with one stone."

"The newspaper knows where I am." Whit told him, rubbing her wrist.

"They don't know *I'm* here."

"You can't clean up all the blood. Forensics will find it."

"That doesn't matter. She fell down the stairs, busted open her stitches, you arrived and helped her clean up, and then you both went for a boat ride. All that matters is that they don't find her body. The teratoma in her spine. They will have no way to connect her to the other deaths. Hers will be a tragic boating accident."

"So you admit to killing the others."

"They killed themselves with their greed for more. All I had to do was appeal to their egos." Wilhelm opened the closet door and dug around looking for something.

"Why?" With his back to her, Whit edged to the side of the chair, waiting for an opportunity. Unfortunately, the closet was between her and the exit. "What was in it for you?"

"Here." He pulled out a couple of cloth belts from the closet, stretching them between his hands. "For me? Fifty grand each. All cash."

Whit stood, defiantly taking a step toward him. "This is not going to end well for you. You'll be caught and spend the rest of your life in prison. If you left now, you could disappear with all that money."

He cocked his head to the side as if considering her suggestion. "Too many loose ends. Give me your hands."

She faced him, considering her options. If she tried to scramble over the bed, he would just catch her. There was no time to open the window and leap out, landing on who knows what.

With a jerk on the belt, he warned, "If you don't, I'll do it for you. Make it easy on yourself."

He could easily overpower her. Pretending to give in, Whit held out her hands close enough to bring him nearer. When he seized her wrist to pull her to him, she bent over and clamped her teeth into his hand and bit down hard.

He yanked his hand free with a scream of pain.

She tried to run past him, but he was surprisingly quick for such a big guy and grabbed hold of her arm and swung her around to face him. He backhanded her across the face, knocking her into the dresser, then grabbed her by the shoulders to haul her up. Furious, her cheekbone throbbing painfully, Whit kicked her knee up as hard as she could between his legs. Wilhelm bent double, groaning, and let go of her.

With a burst of adrenaline, she rushed past him, shoving his hand aside, and raced down the stairs. She could hear his panting breath right behind her, his stumbling steps. He caught hold of her hair, yanking her head back. She twisted and landed hard on the stairs, punching her fist into his eye. She half stumbled away from him, missing a step, and slammed into the wall, using it to keep herself upright.

She'd reached the bottom of the stairs when Wilhelm's brute weight landed on her, knocking her to the floor. Gasping for air, the wind knocked out of her, she turned her head to the side and shoved away from him, but he was too heavy. He flipped her over, his face purple with rage. His beefy hands wrapped around her throat. She tried to pry his hands away, but they were like steel and she felt herself fading, her lungs burning for air.

In a blind rage, he squeezed her neck until she thought it would snap like a twig.

In that half-conscious moment, she remembered her gun tucked into his pants. Letting go of his wrists, she fumbled around his belt, frantically searching. The tips of her fingers felt hard metal, but the gun was jammed into his pants. She clawed and pinched until she had the butt of the handle. With a last surge of lucid energy, she yanked hard. So intent on choking her to death, he realized too late what she was about to do and released her throat. She gasped, fighting for oxygen, while he wrestled with her arm; fortunately, she managed to get a strong grip on the gun before he could stop her. She squeezed the trigger, aiming at his stomach. With a howl of pain, he rolled to the side.

Whit scrambled backward, coughing and choking for air, grasping at the front door handle, and pulled herself up. Before she could open the door, Wilhelm lunged at her again, trying to wrestle the gun from her hand, but she squeezed the trigger twice. One bullet shattering the front window, glass splintering, and the other bullet blew through Wilhelm's jaw. Horrified, eyes bulging, he fell backward, holding his profusely bleeding bits of jaw together and moaning.

The back door flew open and two police officers rushed into the room, guns drawn, shouting for them to raise their hands.

Sick with relief, Whit raised both hands. Wilhelm fell backward on the stairs, blood oozing between his fingers holding on to his jaw.

One of the cops moved forward and removed the gun from her grasp, while the other officer radioed for an ambulance.

The officer who had taken her gun asked, "Are you all right?"

Coughing and wheezing, she nodded.

"Anyone else in the house?"

Remembering Cordero, not knowing if she was dead or alive, she managed a raspy whisper. "Upstairs. She's hurt." Eyes tearing with the effort to talk, she wiped her face with the back of her hands as the cop cautiously climbed the stairs, his gun still drawn.

"McKenna!"

To Whit's amazement, George stood in the open doorway. She almost burst into tears, she was so happy to see him.

He hurried over. "Are you injured?"

She shook her head no. Still wheezing, she began to tremble.

"Here." He offered his arm and led her to the couch.

She leaned back with her eyes closed, rubbing her bruised throat, still consciously forcing air into her lungs. She was lucky to be alive. She heard George rummaging in the kitchen.

George shoved a glass in her hand. "Drink this."

She sniffed it. "Whiskey?"

"Nature's remedy for catastrophic events."

She tossed it back, felt the burn, and breathed a sigh of relief. She darted a glance at Wilhelm, who was whimpering in pain and bleeding profusely. As one of the officers administered aid to him, he went limp, and appeared to have passed out on the floor.

Coughing, trying to clear her throat, she asked, "How did you get here so fast?"

"I arrived not long after you and parked in the woods. When you didn't answer my text, I was sure something was wrong, so I called state park police."

"Thank God you had the sense to follow your own judgment."

"I couldn't stop thinking about what you said. Cordero being the bad guy, so I looked up Cordero's property taxes, found the cabin's address, and drove on up."

Whit shook her head. "You might make a damn good reporter after all."

32

RIGGS PUSHED THE elevator button for the fourth floor of Rogue Community Hospital and stepped back as the doors closed. Not long after collecting the cadavers at Eden Retreat, Whit had called to tell her about the frightening experience at Cordero's cabin. Although Riggs was sorry Whit had experienced such a close call, it was a huge relief to catch the killer. And it didn't hurt that her quid pro quo with Whit about Cordero had actually panned out as a legitimate lead. Maybe now she'd be back in the department's good graces.

A few minutes earlier she'd stopped by the intensive care unit on the third floor to see Cordero. The doctor said she'd been injected with sodium barbital, which had induced a heart attack, but she might pull through. She was still in a coma. They had also done a scan and found a tumor on her spine that would need surgery when she was stronger, if she survived.

Judge Cordero sat next to his wife's bed, looking lost and suddenly old. He had answered all her questions, and it appeared he had not known about his wife's involvement in the clinical trials. He confided that he planned to drop out of the state representative race so he could focus on helping Celeste recover. If she survived.

Riggs thought of all the lives destroyed by one man's ruthless grab at . . . money. For the others, a fleeting second chance at youth? All of it shallow in the face of the broken, destroyed relationships and all the innocent deaths. Even poor Dr. Weldon, the medical examiner, had had his license suspended for his loose tongue. There were still a lot of unanswered questions. Like where did Wilhelm get the stem cells? How did he create the serum?

The elevator doors opened and she stepped out across from the nurses' station, suddenly feeling very tired. The smell of coffee guided her feet to the waiting room, where she poured a syrupy dark liquid that sort of resembled coffee into a short Styrofoam cup. It would have to do. It was after six thirty and she'd missed dinner. She glanced down the hall to her right and saw a uniformed police officer standing outside a door talking with Detective Tucker. That would be Wilhelm's room. She sipped the bitter brew and waited a minute for it to hit her system, then closed the space toward Tucker. Panetta and Blackwell were still combing over evidence at Eden Retreat.

Tucker nodded to her. "I still think that slick-talkin' Heinemann is involved. I'd like to shake this perp awake and ask a few questions, but the doctor won't let me. Imagine that?"

The officer standing next to him laughed. "I'd let you, but there's too many security cameras everywhere."

Riggs glanced into the room, but a curtain was drawn. "What has the doctor said about Wilhelm's condition?"

"A bullet sliced right through his jaw." Tucker found this amusing. "They had to wire it shut. The other bullet ripped through his intestines. He had extensive internal bleeding. Now they gotta watch him for somethin' called sepsis. They loaded him up on antibiotics and pain meds. He's pretty much worthless right now."

"When will he be able to communicate?"

"The doctor said he could wake at any time." He glanced over the top of her head at the nurse's station. "They pop in here every few minutes. I'm gonna go sit by his bed. That way, if he wakes up . . . I get first dibs on the scumbag."

"Well, I'm going to go down to the cafeteria and grab a bite to eat, then head over to the morgue with my two Jane Does."

"Try the meatball sandwich. It's hearty. You could use some meat on your bones."

"Thanks, Tucker."

Riggs rode the elevator down to the basement and found some vegetable soup and a wheat role in the cafeteria. She ate at a table by herself, wondering if Blackwell caught up with Heinemann. It seemed likely he had partnered with Wilhelm in the stem cell trial, but Whit said Wilhelm never mentioned having a partner. The idea that Heinemann could be innocent didn't sit well either. She had to ask herself whether she just wanted him to be guilty because she found him repugnant. However, she didn't think Wilhelm had enough of a science background to devise the stem cell therapy. As yet, they didn't have much information on him. Heinemann certainly had the medical background. Most likely, once Heinemann knew the game was over, he'd slipped away into some crack, letting Wilhelm take the fall. With the level of law enforcement in town, it was very unlikely that Heinemann would get away. One way or another, they would find out if Wilhelm worked alone.

She could understand why the stem cell trial was so alluring. Finding a youth elixir that could extend life—more than that, create a younger, healthy life—now that would be worth all the money in the world. If such a thing existed, she could imagine all the ailing people out there healed by a simple injection. In theory, if it hadn't created teratomas, the only reason not to do it might be the embryos that had to die to create the stem cell line. She wondered, if her cancer came back and she was terminal, would she have submitted to a trial like that? Regardless of the embryo? That was not a question she felt she could answer with any certainty. She had her faith now, but it was still all very confusing, and it was getting late. The sooner they got through the autopsies, the better.

The soup helped replenish her flagging energy. She decided it was time to get the night started. She gave Panetta a call.

"You ready to meet me at the morgue?"

"Stop talking dirty to me. Your husband's gonna get jealous."

"Richard doesn't mind," Riggs laughed. "You must be getting loopy."

"Jesus, Riggs. This is one crazy case. I was sleepless to start with, and now I'm not sure what I am. Heatstroke from today on the hill, maybe? Got some news. The FBI gave us a rundown on Wilhelm. He was not just a massage therapist; he had a doctorate in physical therapy and had worked for seven years at a clinic in New York. Like Heinemann, he'd lost his license for questionable practices."

"Wow. That would make them perfect partners in crime." Riggs picked up her tray and carried it to the trash, dumping her plate and stacking the tray. She headed up the stairs to the first floor.

"Exactly. Apparently, Wilhelm failed to refer his clients to doctors when their injuries required more than physical therapy. He preferred to treat them using his own methods of natural and herbal remedies. The penalties for this malpractice were fines and suspension. Even after he'd served his time regaining his license, he continued the same procedures until his license was finally revoked."

"So at Eden he was just practicing as a masseur? Aside from the illegal trial?"

"That's right. Any news on your end?"

"Nothing yet. I'm going to stop back by Wilhelm's room before I head to the morgue."

"All right. Let's go burn the midnight oil. See you soon."

Riggs found Tucker pacing in front of Wilhelm's room.

"Is he talking yet?"

"Nothin' sensible. He's high on morphine." Tucker snickered. "This guy's a real perv. Keeps talking about dickin' some girl. All that time lathering oil over rich hard bodies. 'Dick her. Kiss her.' His mind is in the gutter. Gotta wonder what all goes on at that fancy retreat."

If she didn't have the autopsies tonight, she'd try to question Wilhelm herself. Tucker's version of life was different from the average bear's. "Do what you can to get information out of him."

"Kinda hard when his jaw is wired. I kept after him to talk, but the nurse complained and the doctor ordered me from the room . . . like *I'm* the criminal."

"That explains why you're out here. He probably won't be coherent for several more hours. Try not to get yourself kicked out of the hospital. And keep a sharp eye out for Heinemann. If they were working together, he might decide Wilhelm needs to be silenced and find a way to get to him."

"Not on my watch, sister."

33

"WHAT POSSESSED YOU to go off half-cocked?" Whit had been summoned to Stu's office upon her arrival back to the *Chronicle*. He paced in front of her, pausing long enough to dig some Tums out of his corduroy pants pockets. He chomped a few, slurped them down with hot coffee, and resumed pacing, punctuating the beginning of each sentence with a quick jab of his hands. "What happened to the buddy system we talked about? Don't you listen? I'm having a heart attack here. Is that what you want? You want to see me keel over and *die*?"

Whit suppressed a smile behind the cold-pack she was holding to the right side of her cheek. He would certainly not appreciate it at the moment. "No, of course not."

"And you're not off the hook on those media interviews from this morning. Mr. Arenburg called wanting to know who George Cook is, and where were you?"

"I'm sorry. I just thought, since you assigned George to help me, it would be all right. He's a broadcast major, you know, so it makes perfect sense."

Stu came to an abrupt halt, his expression pained, his gray-ing moustache bunched around thin lips. He pointed to the door. "Just get out of here and go write that story. And I want a personal account on the sidebar. You know: 'My near-death experience at the hands of Dr. Frankenstein.'"

"We're still not sure what role, if any, Dr. Heinemann played in this story. Wilhelm never mentioned him, so I'm assuming he worked alone. He certainly had the trust of those people."

"He's our guy. He admitted it. That's good enough for me." Stu waved her from the room. "I'm following my gut. Go write the story."

Escaping relatively unscathed, Whit hurried toward her desk. Just then, the stringers and interns who were helping her with the story, including George and even Breckenridge, stood up and clapped, cheering enthusiastically. She felt her face flush all the way up to her hairline. Unable to think of what to do, she performed a quick curtsy.

As she passed Breckenridge's desk, he held out his hand. She stopped to shake it and waited as he gathered his thoughts. His bespeckled gaze drifted to the bloodstain on her white blouse and back to her eyes. "We are delighted that you are safe, and that you successfully brought home another spectacular exclusive."

"Thank you. I appreciate it." The hero's welcome was unexpected and endearing. Somewhat embarrassed, she addressed the crew of five assigned to help her, six counting George. "Okay, back to business. Whatever information you have gathered over the past twenty-four hours, transfer it into one file each, titled 'Frankenstein,' and send it to me. George and I will read through each of the files and compile the story from everyone's notes. Since this has been a collaborative effort, we will all share the byline. Let's get to it!"

Galvanized into action, the staff got busy with the task at hand. George rolled his chair next to hers. "After we put the story to bed, we all want to take you to Four Daughters Irish Pub. What do you say?"

"That sounds great, George. Thanks." It was nearly seven; they'd be lucky to get out of there before nine or ten. She needed caffeine. She grabbed some change and headed to the break room.

After the ambulances arrived for Celeste and Wilhelm, the police had questioned her at length. On the way back to the *Chronicle*, she'd called Riggs to give her a firsthand account. Because of the remote location, Medford police weren't aware of the shooting, and the great part about that was that neither were local media. A story like that wasn't contained for long, so she needed to write fast and post it online.

After guzzling a Diet Pepsi, Whit threw her energy into the details of the story, and she and George wrote what she thought was one of her best. All the while, Stu paced back and forth behind them, leering over her shoulder, making suggestions. Irene had heard about what happened through the employee grapevine and stopped by to see if Whit was all right. She promised to meet them later at Four Daughters.

When Whit finally pushed the send button on her computer, Stu practically danced in the aisle and offered to buy their drinks at the pub if she agreed to be available for media interviews first thing in the morning. He, of course, stayed behind to make sure the copy people didn't slash and trash his prized edition. Everyone else bailed.

Four Daughters, located in the Historic District downtown only a few blocks from the newspaper, had a traditional Irish pub feel, with dark wood and deep leather couches around brick fireplaces, pool tables, and a continuous stream of lively music. It would have been a decent walk on a good night, but the storm had let loose, and warm rain poured down in horizontal streams with dangerous gusty winds. Everyone disbursed in a hurry, racing toward their cars. The parking lot behind the newspaper was fenced, gated, and well lit. She hurried to her car, jumped in, and sent a text to Jordan and Emma that she'd be home in a few hours.

During the short drive to the restaurant, thoughts of a chilled glass of wine and a steak sandwich made her mouth water. She had sufficiently recovered from her ordeal. Her jaw was sore and her throat felt strained, but all things considered, not bad. After her television and radio interviews in the morning, she planned on taking the afternoon off to spend it lounging at her parents' pool and enjoying the Labor Day barbecue with her family. As far as she was concerned, the lion's share of the Dr. Frankenstein story had been written up by her and her team, and any tidbits that had to be wrapped up could be left for the media vultures to consume.

Time to celebrate.

All the parking along the street was taken, so she turned down the back alley and pulled into a small space behind a closed shoe store. When she turned off the engine, she thought the only thing missing from her victory party was John. The deep ache that came with that thought brought instant tears. Suddenly, celebrating lost some of its appeal. She longed for his touch, even the smell of him. Certainly tonight he would have held her in his arms, whispering words of love and encouragement. He would have nursed her bruises with soft kisses. Though he was a man of the world, hardened in some respects by his lifestyle on the front lines of the world's most desperate struggles, he had a tender heart, often quiet and introspective. Twelve years her senior, he had initially been reluctant to venture into a romantic relationship with a junior reporter. But he had come to admire her work in Baghdad, and their love, despite the horror of that war, found lasting hope in each other.

Damn it! She wasn't ready to let him go, but it was time.

She leaned her forehead on the steering wheel, willing herself to shake off the grief.

The thrill of putting to bed one of the hottest stories on the globe was now marred by this unending ache. Perhaps that would be her life for a long while. Acceptance was the first step. For now, she couldn't let the others down, not after they'd worked so hard to help put the story together. She wiped tears away. Like it or not, she faced the rest of her life without John. The empty void he'd left behind had been replaced with anxiety, anger, and fear that twisted through her like a destructive tornado, leaving behind broken bits of who she used to be.

She understood now that getting better was going to take a lot of work. Her phobia of the woods was not going to go away on its own. She'd try desensitizing, as Riggs had suggested, with walks in the woods until she could be free of the horror associated with it. Maybe Jordan and Emma would walk with her. It was at least a place to start.

That decided, she dug through her purse for a tissue, but found only an old McDonald's napkin. She never had tissues when she needed them. She blew her nose on the napkin and gathered her umbrella from under the seat. A gust of wind caught her car door as she opened it and nearly slammed it into a black Mercedes rolling past. Rain pelted her in the face as she jerked the door back and awkwardly opened the umbrella. Head down, she hurried along the sidewalk, past the occasional homeless person huddled in the shadows of darkened storefronts. Lightning illuminated the clouds in quick successive flashes, making her wonder if her umbrella was a bad idea.

Nothing like carrying a lightning rod.

She quickened her pace and crossed an alley where a stray cat huddled beneath a stairwell. Amid the low rumble of thunder came blaring music, a lively tune from up ahead, accompanied by clapping and joyous howls.

Rounding the corner, Whit spied George waiting outside Four Daughters under a canopied cover. He wore a pale-pink polo shirt and light-blue dress slacks with tan leather Sperry's. So very Ralph Lauren. She smiled. Since she couldn't go out wearing bloodstained clothes, he had kindly lent her one of his pastel-pink dress shirts, which happened to be a near perfect fit because he was so slender.

As she dove under cover of the awning, he smiled. "Come on, twinsie." He guided her through the throng at the door. "Irene, bless her well-connected heart, saved a table for us upstairs."

They paid their cover charge at the door and received a red stamp of a unicorn on the back of their hands. Music pumped, inebriated people sang an Irish ditty along with the band, dancers cavorted, and laughter filled the space as they weaved around the dance floor to the staircase. Upstairs was just as crowded, but not as noisy. Their table sat next to a long bar and beside a lounge area where a group of twenty-somethings were celebrating someone's birthday with laughter. Whit envied all that happiness for a moment, then reminded herself that she had two beautiful daughters, loving parents, and an adorable pug waiting at home for her. She was not alone. With a sigh, Whit sat down with the other reporters and smiled. Someone shoved a beer into her hand, so she raised her glass to Irene's toast.

"Here's to gutsy reporters!"

34

"WILHELM BIT THE dust," Tucker announced through her truck's speakerphone.

"What? I just talked to you ten minutes ago! What happened?" Riggs flipped the blinker on to turn right onto Barnett Avenue, headed in a procession to the morgue. The cadavers had been x-rayed at the hospital and were now in transit. No surprise that the x-rays showed signs of teratoma tumors. They wouldn't know for sure until the autopsy, but probability was high. "I thought the surgery went well."

"The guy's a bleeder. Who would think it? A big guy like that."

Tucker would associate a man's size with health. "Didn't they figure out he was a bleeder during the surgery?"

"I don't know. His gut filled up with blood and he croaked; that's all I know."

She flipped the windshield wipers on high as rain beat on the truck. "Did he ever say anything else besides what you told me earlier?"

"Naw. Just dickin' some girl. Kept saying he wanted to kiss her. Horny bastard."

Another call came in; she glanced at the phone number but didn't recognize it. "Gotta run, Tucker. Thanks for letting me know." She answered the new call.

"Hey, Detective Riggs. It's Figoni from Human Resources. You interviewed me at the morgue."

Riggs tensed and sat up straighter. "Yes, of course. Mr. Figoni. How can I help you?"

"I need to talk. I read about Dr. Frankenstein this morning."

"Do you know something about that?"

"Yeah, man."

Riggs thought he sounded like he'd been drinking. His words were slurred, and she knew he smoked pot. Still, she flashed back to Figoni's history. He'd left med school to help care for his parents. His mother remained in critical care from a brain injury. He'd paid her expenses at the Rose Garden Nursing Home in Pleasanton, California, since the accident five years ago. It was a tragic twist to his academic accomplishments and a heavy burden for a young man to carry. If he was somehow mixed up in the stem cell treatments, he was not exactly the criminal sort. If he was involved, he might well want out now that murders plagued the treatments.

"Why are you suddenly willing to talk?" Riggs asked. "Has something happened? Are you being threatened? We can bring you in for protection."

"Nah, it's not about me. It's about my mom. I need protection for her."

For a moment, Riggs wondered if he was lucid. "You want to talk about Dr. Wilhelm so you can protect your mother?"

"No. I don't know who that is. I want to talk about Dr. Frankenstein."

"Figoni, are you high?"

"Maybe."

"Listen, why don't you call back in the morning, and we can set a time so you can come in and tell us what you know." With Wilhelm dead and Heinemann on the run, she didn't see the point. At least not tonight.

"I kinda need to talk tonight. Can you come to my hotel? My mom needs help, so like, it's important tonight."

"What does your mother have to do with it?"

"She has one of those teratomas too. At least I think she does." He suddenly broke into tearful laughter. "It's sick, man. Dr. Frankenstein collects those teratomas. His trophies."

Riggs sighed. Could the day get any weirder? After all the years of being a detective, she knew better than to discount a lead, no matter how crazy it sounded. "Okay, Figoni. I'm going to send some officers over to bring you in for questioning." She had to follow the cadavers for chain of custody, so she couldn't go herself. "Where are you at?"

Figoni gave her the name of his hotel and room number.

Riggs hung up and called Blackwell. "Figoni wants to talk."

"That's about the prettiest thing I've ever heard you say. Almost as good as my dream of Shania Twain singing sweet nothin's in my ear. I might even actually light my cigar."

"You still have a thing for her?"

He snorted. "What man in his right mind wouldn't?"

She made a turn onto Highway 99, following the rain-drizzled red taillights of the caravan toward the morgue. "He's at the Hilton Garden. Room two twelve."

"Hell, we need this. So far we've got a dead suspect, a confession to a journalist of all things, and a fourth vic in a coma. Basically zip . . . like a dog chasin' his tail."

"This is weird, but Figoni said he didn't know who Wilhelm is, so I'm not sure what he might contribute. He sounds high. Interestingly, he also said his mother has a teratoma."

"Hell, I'll listen to anything right now."

"Well, we can't overlook Figoni's employment with Human Resources. It makes sense that he's somehow mixed up in this."

"We'll find out soon enough. The chief will be shittin' bricks when I tell him we're a step ahead of the FBI."

"Any sign of Heinemann?"

"No. The little bastard has gone to ground like the rodent he is. I'll let you know about Figoni."

She hung up just as she was pulling into the state police parking lot, then waited as they were cleared through the electric gates and drove around back. She was tired. Bone weary, like after her third round of chemo. The stress and lack of sleep were catching up to her. Richard was practically a stranger lately, had chastised her for working so many hours. As a state prosecutor, he could tally hours away from home too, but his concern was always for her health. She wondered if perhaps he was right. Was she risking the reaper's return by pushing herself so hard? She faced at least three hours of autopsy with two cadavers in a high-profile investigation. Going home and going to sleep was not an option, but she promised herself to spend time evaluating her job over the next few weeks.

Panetta was waiting at the morgue already in scrubs, leaning against the counter scrolling on his phone.

"What are you reading?"

He showed her the latest *Chronicle* story. "Have you read it?"

She shook her head. "No, but Whit debriefed me before she wrote it. I hope there's nothing in it that we don't already have on the books. That would send Blackwell into another tizzy."

"The article confirmed your intel on Celeste Cordero. Quite the little investigator, your friend McKenna. Beat us to the punch a few times."

"Yes, she's very good at her job."

"I contacted a friend in my old FBI office. He ran a profile on her. War zone junky until she had kids. She's reported from some pretty nasty places. Accumulated a nice batch of headlines over the years. Then there's the tragedy in Afghanistan. She would be dead now but for a special ops recon mission in the Korangal Valley. It was pure luck that they were there at that moment. I'd say somebody's looking out for her."

"It sure sounds like it." She stared at him a moment. "Why did you check up on her?"

He shrugged. "Thought we should know who we're trading info with. Every time you work a trade, you're putting your career on the line. And since I'm working with you, mine too."

"That's it? Protecting your interests?"

He had the grace to blush a little, a lopsided grin on his face. "I kind of like her style, I guess."

Her brows rose at that. "It doesn't hurt that she's drop-dead gorgeous either."

"Yeah, well. Can't help but notice that. I'm also fully aware that she is grieving her husband's death, so let's just call it curiosity."

Riggs sighed. "She's working through it the best she can. Covering this story has been difficult for her, but I think it's helped her process some things." The scent of fresh soap drifted from Panetta. "You smell pretty good for a guy who spent the better part of the day out in a-hundred-and-eight-degree weather."

He smiled sheepishly. "I availed myself of your locker room showers. Got here early and couldn't stand my own stench. I keep a change of clothes in the car. I almost feel human now."

The shower had refreshed him, but Riggs noted the blood-shot eyes. "I know. I dozed in my car this evening while I waited for the x-ray tech to get back from dinner."

"Lucky you."

She filled him in on the Figoni lead.

"Damn, I'd like to be there," he said as he followed her into the locker room and sat on a bench by the door.

She proceeded around a dividing wall to the privacy of her locker. While she stripped down to bra and panties, she asked, "What's on your mind?"

"How did you know something was on my mind?"

"Because you have never followed me into the locker room before. I assume it's because you want to talk." She shrugged into a long-sleeved T-shirt and sweat pants. Although the night was still a balmy ninety-eight degrees, the autopsy bay was always cold.

"Actually, I've been thinking. Now that my divorce is final and my son is in Eugene at University of Oregon on a football scholarship, I might get back with the FBI."

"Really?" He was one of the few detectives she truly respected. "Where to? Back to Langley?"

"No. I'd like to stay closer to my son. We haven't had the best relationship the past few years. He blamed me for his mother's . . . condition. If it's not too late, I want to build a new relationship with him, as adults. When I left the Bureau, they gave me an open-door option. I talked with them last week when Tucker and I got into it. They'd like me to be Bureau chief in the Portland office."

Dressed now, Riggs bent and slipped on her tennis shoes. "I'd hate to see you go, but it sounds like a good opportunity. It isn't that thing with Tucker, is it?"

"No. Just another reason among many."

"So you're not happy here, as a detective?"

"I don't really fit in with the guys. They resent me, I think. Now that Ellen is no longer in the picture, I thought it'd be good for me to move on, literally and figuratively."

Riggs stepped around to stand in front of him. Those deep brown eyes were soul searching. As fatigued as she was, she empathized. Hadn't *she* just been contemplating a change?

"As much as I'd like you to stay, I think it's a wise choice. It would be a big loss for the department, but God knows, with Portland's crime rate, they could use you more. And it's only an hour from Eugene, so you could see your son more often. Opportunities don't come along like that every day. But before you go for it, you might consider the FBI office here."

He nodded slowly, as if coming to a final decision, and rose to his feet. "I'll check it out, and I'll notify the chief after this investigation is over."

They heard the outer door open and headed to the autopsy bay. Riggs said, "That must be the new ME." Tonight they would work with a medical examiner from Josephine County, since Dr. Weldon was on forced leave. She wondered if he wasn't the lucky one, probably sitting on the porch of his winery eating gourmet cheese and drinking a fine Merlot.

CHAPTER

35

WHIT FELT A heavy fatigue as she stepped out onto Main Street from Four Daughters, the music still rowdy but muted as the doors closed behind her. George and the others had ordered another round of drinks, but she'd insisted on going home to see her girls. Jordan had texted earlier to say she was home safe from the coast. She wanted to embrace them and feel their warmth. After today's brutal experience, she could think of nothing more comforting than being with her children.

It was still raining heavily, so she broke out the umbrella and headed toward her car. Her shoulder and stomach muscles had begun to stiffen from her fall at the cabin. No doubt she'd be seriously bruised in the morning, especially around her throat. All things considered, that was not so bad.

The puddles along the sidewalk were deeper now. She rounded the corner down the side street. Quieter here, the rain drummed on her umbrella, and her feet and ankles were getting soaked. Stepping off the curb into the alleyway, she landed in a deep rut and nearly slipped out of her sandals. Two glasses of wine was probably a glass more than she should have had. Noticing a dark shadow in the doorway of an abandoned pawnshop, the windows boarded up with plywood decorated with a liberal amount of graffiti, she sidestepped onto the street. She hurried past a wino sitting in the doorway leaning against the wall, head lulling to the side.

Poor bastard.

Nearly to her car, she dug about in her purse for her keys; finding them, she clicked to open the doors. Her headlights flashed briefly and the dome light came on. She opened the door, tossed her purse in, and then fumbled with the umbrella, cursing as it pinched her finger.

The sudden stabbing pain in her neck shocked her. She responded with a sharply indrawn breath. Before she could turn to see what had happened, her legs collapsed.

*   *   *

She lay still, listening.

Soft scratching sounds.

A constant hum to her right that was almost soothing.

Sleep beckoned. Sooo drowsy . . .

Something awakened her.

Eyelids heavy, she fought to open them as a growing unease filled her soul.

Her head ached . . . dull, throbbing.

She opened her eyes, expecting to see the pale-yellow walls in her bedroom, but nothing was familiar.

Murky shadows were relieved only by a dull light from a computer screen.

Rain pelted against a row of transom windows high on the wall.

Was she in a hospital?

What could have happened?

An accident?

Yes. She had left the pub. Made it to her car.

So thirsty.

She licked dry lips with a dry tongue.

No relief.

Her head felt heavy. She tried to lift her hands but felt resistance.

Through a glass sliding door to her left, in the dreary haze, were pale-green walls and black counters littered with tubes, glass jars, buzzing machinery, and stacks of clear plastic containers imprisoning white furry mice; a pair of red eyes stared out at her.

Sudden panic shot through her, careening her heart into a wild thing in her chest.

Twisting her head awkwardly, she saw a beehive of computers humming along the farthest wall.

Lightning blanched the room white, staining her retinas. In the seconds that followed, thunder growled in the sullen gloom.

She had a terrible conviction that something horrible was about to happen.

She tried to recall her last memory. She saw the wino in the doorway . . .

"You're awake. That's very good." Glaring lights flicked on overhead. "I've been waiting. Afraid I'd given you too much sodium barbital. You had, after all, two glasses of wine."

She blinked at the sudden blaze of lights and turned her head toward the voice, encountering a bald man with dark brows and vivid blue eyes set in a pale face. He was slender and wore a white lab coat. "Who are you?"

"You of all people should know." His lips stretched into a mirthless smile and his eyes burned pure hatred. "As your article stated, I'm Dr. Frankenstein."

"I . . . I thought that was . . . Wilhelm."

He seemed pleased. "Yes. Because that's what I wanted you to think." With slow, steady steps, Kessler approached the bed. "You have destroyed my chances of conducting my research undetected. If you hadn't blasted the front pages of the newspaper with blow-by-blow accounts, I could have simply disposed of a few bodies and continued my research."

"The police would have found a connection."

He shrugged. "Maybe. Wilhelm was sloppy. Still, I studied your history. You don't quit. You would have kept digging and digging until you found me. The police would have been satisfied with Wilhelm. Not you. So you see, you've left me no choice." He leaned over her and smiled wickedly. "A mistake you'll have to pay for with your *life*."

Of all the ways she'd imagined she'd die, this had never been among them. She realized her hands were strapped down and tried to free them, but the grips were too tight.

"You can't escape. Don't try." He pushed a chair next to the single bed and sat down, pulling a scalpel from his lab coat pocket. "I've used this room to sleep during long nights spent in the lab. I never envisioned using it like this, but as fate would have it . . . You're lying on plastic to protect my bedding and to wrap you up in when I've finished. While you bleed to death, I'll give you your last exclusive. The irony is that you won't be around to write it." He chuckled at that.

Desperate for an edge, she appealed to his obvious ego. "But wouldn't you want me to write it? Even just as a keepsake?"

He reached for her wrist. "I'm going to slice through the radial artery so that you bleed slowly. I want you to have time to hear my story."

With quick flicks of the scalpel, he sliced first her right wrist, then her left.

Whit squeezed her eyes shut against the piercing pain, refusing to give him the satisfaction of crying out.

Sick bastard!

"You're behaving exactly as I imagined you would. The tough journalist finally meets her end."

She opened her eyes, lifted her head, and watched blood, warm and slick, stream from the wounds, her heart hammering a rapid rhythm against her chest. Resting her head, eyes closed against the seeming inevitability of death, she pictured Emma and Jordan. They would be parentless. The rest of their lives, they would have only each other and her parents. They hadn't really had the chance to mourn their father's death. How would they cope with *this* nightmare?

God, please . . . they still need me.

Whit felt rage. It swept through her, bringing a flush to her face. He wasn't just taking her life; he was forever marring her children. If she'd had a weapon, she would have gladly killed him.

"Let's begin, shall we?" From his pocket he set out a small recorder. "You see, I don't need you to write the story, because I'm recording it. Feel free to ask whatever burning questions you have."

He wanted to play. He was enjoying it. If she refused to participate, he would probably just kill her and get it over with. The longer she could keep him talking, the more likely she would be to survive. She desperately hoped someone had seen the abduction. Her kids were expecting her. They'd call the newspaper. She had to buy some time.

"What about Wilhelm?" she asked. "What exactly was his role in this? Just the money?"

"It starts with Heinemann. He had all those weak-minded people as clients that Wilhelm and his lover Celeste were able to manipulate into the trial. It was really quite easy. All the women liked Wilhelm." He shrugged. "So he used his power of persuasion. And Celeste, with her introductions—well, she also knew how to pull a few strings to get her way."

"How did you know Wilhelm?"

He laughed. "I actually met him a few years ago after I injured my back in a skiing accident on Mount Ashland. He became my masseur. With regular visits, we got to know each other. I discovered he was short on cash because of a lawsuit from some escapade of his in New York. A few clients were suing him. That's when I came up with the idea of setting up a human trial for my Regeneration Elixir. My formula was working very well with the mice, so I thought it was time. By then Wilhelm was having an affair with Celeste, so he could quite easily manipulate her as well."

"So, Wilhelm and Celeste brought you the clients. What about Heinemann?"

"Heinemann unwittingly provided the facilities for our secret trial. He is so conceited that we worked right under his nose, completely unaware. All the participants were sworn to silence or faced jail time."

A little light-headed now, Whit pressed to keep him talking. "But how did you get the stem cells?"

"Oh. Yes. I used to work in government-sanctioned facilities at multiple universities, the last of which was NYU. We conducted biological experiments using stem cells. I'd been searching for the Holy Grail, the serum that would extend life indefinitely. Government restrictions forced me to go underground with my work. My off-the-books experiments were discovered, and I was called before the ethics board and stripped of my license. After my exile from academia, I tried to find employment in the private sector. And although I had a long list of prestigious accomplishments, I was forced to open my own business. Alas, now I have this lab."

"So you got the cells from a university?"

"No. While I was at NYU, I happened to know a student there. His name was Figoni. He tragically had to leave school about the same time as I got fired. Since I work closely with the Rogue Community Hospital across the street from my lab, I happened to come upon Figoni one night working in the morgue. Pure chance, really. I discovered his mother was still in nursing care. So I made him a proposal. If he could provide embryonic stem cells from Human Resources, I could offer his mother a cure."

"But how can you work if you don't have a license?"

"I employ two licensed pathologists. No one knows about my basement experiments. When I was searching for a location, I found this building directly across from the hospital with a finished basement and a private entrance from the office upstairs, and a well-placed exit door to the parking lot. I could hardly ask for more. For all intents and purposes, I'm merely a businessman. I still call myself a pathologist, and no one around here is the wiser. The hospitals are woefully understaffed and their pathology takes too long, so I started a twenty-four-hour service, and before long I picked up more work than I could handle. Ironically, I process most of the law enforcement pathology."

Ignoring his attempt to be clever, she asked, "Do you really think it's possible to live indefinitely?"

"Yes, and I'm not the only scientist working on it. I have, in fact, succeeded with mice. Some of my furry subjects over there have been around for four years. That's twice to three times their normal life expectancy, and they show no signs of aging. Here, I'll give you a demonstration."

He walked out of the glassed-in room and crossed to the plastic containers of mice. He paused and pulled on rubber gloves. While his back was to her, she strained against the tie wraps, but only succeeded in cutting the flesh on the palms of her hands. The cuts on her wrists stung, but the pain kept her alert.

A moment later he returned with a white mouse. "This one is from the container of four-year-old mice. Doesn't look old, does he? Muscles are still strong, no signs of aging." Without warning, he retrieved his scalpel and split the belly of the mouse wide open. Whit cringed in horror as its little legs kicked. Unfazed, he squeezed and spilled out the bleeding insides. "You'll notice how pink and perfect the organs are. Not a trace of deterioration." He smiled, enjoying her shock, then pivoted around and tossed the mouse into a hazardous-waste bin, peeled off the gloves and threw those in too.

This man would have no remorse at all for killing her. Her situation was hopeless. No one knew where she was. Even if her daughters reported her missing, the police probably wouldn't search for her until morning. By then it would be too late. She had to keep him engaged in conversation as long as possible.

After inhaling a deep, steadying breath, she asked, "What went wrong in the human experiments?"

He sat down and crossed his legs. "Alas, the human body has all kinds of check systems in place. I mixed stem cells with steroids and growth hormones, and a glucocorticoid—that's an immunosuppressive drug. It suppresses the immune system so the body won't combat the stem cells as a foreign object. Organ transplant recipients are required to take immunosuppressive drugs so their body doesn't reject the new organ. My experiments worked beautifully on the mice, but humans have a more advanced immune system. The longevity trials I've conducted on humans inevitably result in teratomas."

The puddles of blood alongside Whit's bed on the pale-green linoleum floor were alarming, yet the bleeding had slowed. That would buy her some time.

"How did you convince those wealthy people to participate in your trial?" She licked dry lips. "I mean, they were intelligent, accomplished people, taking such a risk."

"Oh, it wasn't difficult. Wilhelm is a . . . *was* a great schmoozer. His job at Eden Retreat allowed him to massage his way into vulnerable people's confidence. He found their Achilles' heel. Vanity. It was surprisingly easy in the end. Everyone wants to be young again, no one more so than the very, very vain."

"So he appealed to their biggest weakness?"

"Yes, and Wilhelm convinced them that these trials were already being conducted overseas with great success. They had only to go on the internet and read the hype publicized on various websites to believe him."

"Sad that these people were so blinded by their vanity."

"Yes. It didn't hurt that Dr. Heinemann is a psychiatrist who recommends massage therapy. Needy people with lots of money. Wilhelm had only to tap into that ready-made delivery system." His face suddenly flushed. Those striking blue eyes bore into her. "I was so *close*! All I had to do was increase the immunosuppressant."

His sudden surge of fury spun her heart into a frightened gallop. Redirecting him, she asked, "Why are you so intent on this mission?"

His eyes narrowed. He leaned back, lips pursed in thought. "My grandmother raised me until I was eight years old, when she died of a heart attack. After that I became an unwanted burden, shuffled from home to home. The last home I was transferred to was the worst. Without going into details, let me just say I learned despair and ultimately fury. I killed the foster parents and ran. I changed my name and learned how to take care of myself."

"No one ever found you?"

"No. I lived hand to mouth. Soup kitchens, handouts, and whatever I could steal. A few years later I took the identity of another runaway after I killed him." Something of the revulsion she felt must have been reflected in her face. "Don't look so shocked. He had it coming."

"So that's what you do? Kill anyone you think might get in the way of your plans?"

He shrugged and nodded. "Only when necessary. I'm not a monster."

"I'm a human being, just like you. I have hopes and dreams too." Maybe if she could force him to visualize her as something other than a target, he might have doubts.

"Are you all out of questions so soon?"

Her breathing felt shallow; she didn't know how much longer she could stay lucid. "You . . . you still haven't told me your motive for wanting to find the perfect elixir."

He sighed. "During the years that I was on the run, I kept thinking, 'If only Grandma hadn't died. If only . . . if only!' It was an incessant reel that played over and over in my head. I used to dream about it. About Grandma living forever. An obsession, really."

Whit found it difficult to relate him with a loving caregiver, like a grandmother. He had apparently loved her. Those early years had not prevented him from growing into an evil man. Whether it was genetic or environmental, she didn't know, but either way, he was clearly insane.

Kessler rambled on. "While in college, I studied the myths of Thoth and Hermes Trismegistus, both of whom drank a mythical potion—a 'liquid gold' that gave them immortality. It's also referenced in the Nag Hammadi texts: twelve leather-bound papyrus codices found in a sealed jar in 1945 in the Egyptian town of Nag Hammadi. The texts were perhaps written in 367 AD. I'm telling you this to give you context to the quest for immortality or, more importantly, eternal youth. Many alchemists in various cultures and through the ages sought this elixir. Ironically, numerous Chinese emperors are suspected of dying from drinking elixirs contrived with precious metals, even mercury. So you see, I'm certainly not the first to acquire casualties in the pursuit of immortality. You'll be among a very long and prestigious list of subjects."

Chilled now, trembling, close to tears, Whit felt her voice growing weaker. "You know a lot about it."

"I read everything I could find on the subject. So naturally it became my passion as a scientist." He stood, glaring down at her. "I believe I was only mere weeks away from achieving what mankind has sought for centuries. I've decided to take my research to the Ukraine, where they have none of these moral obstacles. I've already made arrangements. I'll just hire a business manager for the lab. No one will be the wiser."

She had to prolong his conversation, praying that by some miracle she'd be found. "How did you go from a runaway to becoming a doctor?"

"I took my GED, passed, and applied for college. During my placement testing I scored high in math and science. I'd always been a good student, even in the abysmal places I lived. With government funding, I succeeded."

The room dipped and swayed sickeningly. She shook her head to stay focused. "That's quite a story."

"Yes. One you'll never write."

CHAPTER

36

T HE AUTOPSY FOR Elaine Boccioni concluded, Riggs
stripped off her gloves and washed her hands. The
teratoma had been found on the fifth vertebra, leaving little doubt that these vics were also members of Wilhelm's
experiment.

Dr. Brennan, the Josephine County medical examiner,
paused on his way out. "Nice working with you folks. Can't
say I've ever worked on such a high-profile case before." Short
and lean, he had a hawkish profile and a thatch of thick brown
hair. He was in his late thirties but seemed even younger.
"Shame about Dr. Weldon, though."

Riggs nodded. "Once this is all over, I think he'll be
allowed back."

"Well." Brennan headed toward the door. "We have an
early morning, and I never sleep well when I'm staying away
from home. I'll see ya'll tomorrow."

Panetta joined her at the sink. "Blackwell just called.
Figoni was not in his room. They found his body behind the
hotel in a ditch. Shot in the head."

"Damn it!" Riggs tossed the towel she was using to dry her
hands into the sink. "When are we going to get a break?"

Panetta said, "Hey, you tried. We were just minutes too late."

"I guess so. I'm really just exhausted." She pulled off her paper booties and tossed them in the trash. "Now . . . of course we have to answer the question of who shot Figoni. We know it has to be Heinemann, unless there's something we don't know."

"I think you need to call it a night and get some rest. You can deliver that teratoma to Dr. Kessler in the morning."

"True. I'll wait until morning, after we finish the other autopsy. But I'll leave a message for Kessler so he has a heads-up." She yawned loudly.

Panetta suddenly grinned. "He'll probably be thrilled. After this case is over, he'll be able to add several more teratomas to his collection."

"His collection?"

"Yeah. That grotesque row lined up on the shelf in his lab."

Warmth spread through her stomach, and she reached out and grabbed Panetta's arm.

"What?" He frowned.

"Oh my God!" Her mind raced back to Tucker's voice. "He said, 'Dick her. Kiss her.'"

"What the hell is wrong with you?"

"Tucker. He said, 'Dick her, kiss her.' Doctor Kessler! Dr. Kessler has a collection of teratomas. When Wilhelm was dying, his jaw wired, he kept telling Tucker, 'Dick her, kiss her.' He meant Dr. Kessler! Figoni said Dr. Frankenstein has a collection of teratomas. Who else do you know with a collection of those things? Come with me." She yanked his arm and grabbed her truck keys. "While I drive, you call Blackwell; get some patrol cars to Kessler's home. You and I will stop by his lab; it's on the way."

Racing behind her into the rainy parking lot, Panetta said, "Dr. Kessler is *Dr. Frankenstein*? Weirdly, that makes perfect sense."

· "Yes. Looks like we were wrong about Dr. Heinemann after all. And Kessler was right under our noses all this time." She unlocked the doors and started the truck, peeling out on wet pavement as Panetta buckled up. "He must have been laughing at us. Even teaching the community about teratomas at the gym."

Panetta called Blackwell, who belted out obscenities perverse and loud enough to make her blush.

Over the years she'd worked with Dr. Kessler, she'd always thought he was odd, but he was a lab geek, so she'd written it off as normal. But now, she realized he had an aloofness that was sometimes disconcerting. And those intense blue eyes that seemed to stare right through her . . .

Traffic was light, as it was nearly midnight. She drove through several red lights.

She shook her head, frustrated with herself. "I let Tucker's crude mind affect my own judgment. I mean, Wilhelm's jaw was wired. Of *course* he couldn't articulate clearly. And he was high on morphine besides. *Damn it!* Tucker relates everything to muscle power and sex. I should have known better."

"I wouldn't have picked up on it either. Besides, this is day three with almost no sleep. It's taken its toll on all of us."

"Yeah, but when Figoni called, I still didn't think of Kessler. Who else collects tumors?"

"True, but you told me he's worked with the department for five years or so. That's a long time to trust someone."

"And didn't he play on that?"

They were nearing the intersection of Barnett and Black Oak, half a block from Kessler's lab.

Panetta said, "Circle through the parking lot first."

Riggs turned onto the main road and entered the parking lot from the rear of the building, then jammed the brake while her stomach did a sick flip. She stared at the white SUV.

Panetta asked, "Whose car is that?"

"That's Whit McKenna's car."

"Park. I'm calling for backup."

They bolted into the rain and tried the back door. Locked. Staying close to the building, guns drawn, they proceeded to the front door. Also locked. Riggs shot the glass and watched it shatter. Panetta reached through and opened the door, immediately setting off an alarm that sent the ceiling lights flashing.

Moving forward in single file, staying close to the wall, the lights strobing, Panetta led the way to Kessler's main lab door; Riggs raced past him and jerked the door open. A few lab techs were huddled in the far corner. A heavyset woman with jet-black hair was on the phone, presumably talking to police because of the alarm.

Panetta showed the woman on the phone his badge.

"We're police," Riggs said. "Have you seen Dr. Kessler tonight?"

They all shook their heads no.

Panetta approached the group. "What about a reporter named Whitney McKenna?"

Again, no.

Stumped, Riggs glanced up and saw the glass jars of teratoma tumors so proudly displayed on Kessler's shelf. With a shiver, she wondered if some of those had been from previous victims. Turning, she spotted a door near the back of the room that read PRIVATE. Panetta had seen it too. He tried the knob, but it was locked.

Pointing, she asked, "Where does that door lead?"

The woman who'd been on the phone responded, "That's Dr. Kessler's office, but he's not in there."

"Can you open the door?"

"No. I'm Dr. Hartwick, the night pathologist, and even I don't have access. He's the only one with a key."

Panetta wasted no time and sent two rounds into the door, splintering the wood. He nodded for Riggs to be ready and shoved his shoulder into it, cracking open the frame, the door burst open.

The room was empty. It was a typical office with a large oak desk, filing cabinets, and bookshelves.

"Damn!" Riggs marched out into the hall and spotted two patrolmen. "Guys, take the second floor." She and Panetta searched two back closets attached to the office but found no one, just shelves of supplies and outdated or broken lab equipment.

They returned to Kessler's office. Riggs searched his desk and was flipping through his papers when Panetta said, "Hey, there's another door."

They'd overlooked it because it was behind a decorative divider, and with the flashing lights it had blended into the wall. He stepped forward and slipped behind the divider, kicking it in. "We have stairs to the basement. Come on!"

Riggs followed, racing down the concrete stairs with Panetta, and found a large laboratory. Turning to her right, she bit back a cry. In the strobing lights was a macabre scene from a horror movie that instantly chilled her to the bone. Even from where she stood, she could smell the unmistakable, metallic scent of blood.

Whit lay bleeding, her red hair spilling over the side of the bed, the floor beneath her flooded with an alarming amount of blood. Her forearms had been slit wide, and blood pumped in small arcs. Trails of red streaked across the walls and dripped in streams to the floor.

No sign of Kessler.

Panetta grabbed her arm. "Go to her. I'll find Kessler."

He raced to an exit door on the other side of the room and scrambled up the stairs. Riggs rushed forward, slipping on the bloody floor, down on one knee, and caught herself on the side of the bed.

So much blood . . .

She grabbed both arms and applied pressure, but had to let go and unclip her phone to call 911 for an ambulance. At least they were right across from the hospital. After giving the operator the vital information, she yelled, "Hurry up!"

Even in the few seconds she'd used the phone, blood had pumped out of the exposed wounds. She clamped her hands around the cuts, pressing down with all her weight on both arms.

"Whit? Can you hear me? It's Riggs."

Whit opened heavy-lidded sunken eyes, her face pasty white. She whispered, "He wanted to watch me bleed to death . . . When the alarm went off, he . . . cut deeper."

"You'll be all right now." She looked around but didn't see anything to cut the straps loose. "He's not getting away. I promise you that."

Whit's body had begun to shake violently.

"Hang on. Don't you dare pass out on me!" Riggs felt her throat tighten and blinked back tears. There was too much blood on the floor, the walls, everywhere. Out of pure fear, she could hear her own heart pounding in her ears. She saw the cross and rosary imprinted on her wrist and started to pray.

Damn. The ambulance was taking too long.

"You have two beautiful daughters at home who need you. Just remember that."

Whit slowly nodded, a half smile on her face; her teeth chattering, slowly her eyes drifted closed, her body still . . . and the smile faded away.

EPILOGUE

TWO MONTHS LATER

S EAGULLS CRIED OVERHEAD in a bright blue sky; the beating of their wings was briefly heard over the ocean's waves cresting on the sandy shore. The beach stretched as far as the eye could see, with fawn-colored grass waving in the wind on low-rolling dunes. Not a building or person in sight, just the never-ending blue ocean sparkling under an October sun. The air was pleasantly warm, about seventy-five degrees. Brookings was known as the Banana Belt of the Oregon coast. Inland, autumn had come, the leaves turning sienna and burnt umber, with a crisp bite to the air, but here, on the sandy beach, a warm, gentle breeze caressed their skin.

Riggs watched Emma clutch a handful of sand and slowly release it at arm's length into the wind, carefully watching which way it blew. Jordan was weighed down with photography equipment—a shoulder bag with lenses and film—though she used a digital camera as she snapped pictures of her sister. Waiting patiently, honored to be there, Riggs held the polished pewter urn. Her heart heavy, she breathed in the ocean air. Only yesterday she'd attended Dr. Kessler's preliminary hearing, packed with a never-ending media circus. The public couldn't get enough coverage of the murders, or of the twisted scientist's sick exploration of stem cells. The trial was scheduled for November. It would be lengthy and highly publicized. The night he was arrested, Kessler hadn't even made it out of the parking lot at the lab before police cars blocked his exit. Panetta had the privilege of arresting him. He would rot in prison. That, at least, gave her some satisfaction.

"We're ready," Emma said soberly, her pretty face set in hard lines. Just sixteen, and she already bore signs of long-term grief. Her distant gaze sheltered a deep sorrow.

Fighting back tears of compassion for these brave young women, Riggs turned at the sound of footsteps crunching on the sand.

Whit waved a handful of tissues. "I had to run to the car. I never have tissues when I need them."

"I might need one of those," Riggs confessed, wiping a tear away. It had been such a long journey of recovery for this family that she'd grown to love. As Whit handed her a tissue, Jordan captured the moment with her camera. She was a natural and would follow in her father's footsteps, her photography credits already well beyond her years.

With a deep sigh, Whit embraced her daughters. "Are you ready?"

They nodded, their gaze turning to the urn.

Riggs passed the urn to Whit, noting the scars on her forearms. She'd undergone blood transfusions, surgery to reconnect the tendons, and months of physical therapy. She brushed a hand across one scar. "Does it still hurt?"

"Sometimes I get jabs of pain. The doctor said it would take a few more months, but eventually the pain would stop."

"How is the physical therapy going?"

"Fine. The worst part is I've lost my ninety-words-per-minute typing speed. I'm lucky to get forty-five now. You know I'm not the most patient person."

Riggs laughed. "That's true enough." In reality, Whit had had a miracle recovery. She'd stubbornly refused to die, largely for the love of her daughters.

"Well, I guess it's time."

"Are you all right?" Riggs asked.

"Yes. We need to do this, not just for me, but for my girls. They need closure as much as I do. Not that John will ever truly be absent from our hearts and minds, but we can learn to live without him in a physical sense."

"I understand."

"I know you do. You lost your mother at a tender age. That's part of why I wanted you to be with us. To help me with Emma and Jordan."

"It's my pleasure to be here. I'll help all I can."

Whit took a deep breath and let it go. "It's been over a year since John's death. It's time to let go . . . and he loved the ocean. Years ago, just after nine/eleven when we first met while reporting in Baghdad, we reconnected in the States and decided to spend a week at the coast to sort of decompress after the terrible images of war, and somehow ended up in a small town on the Northern Oregon Coast. We watched the most amazing sunset on the beach that night. John said to me: 'The sea revives a person's spirit, his soul. Just the sight and sound of the waves and the vast expanse of the ocean makes me forget the horrors of war. Like all of my pictures are just from a bad dream, that nothing but beauty exists in the world. Every ugly thing is washed away.'"

"That's beautiful, Whit."

She nodded, tears on her cheeks. "Because of that, after we married, we spent every Christmas here on the Oregon Coast. We both like the rocky shores and the hiking trails through the woods. No crystal-blue waters and palm trees for us. This place, with its stormy winter months, the waves crashing into the cliffs and the rocky shores, was both thrilling and cleansing. I know it's where John would want to be. I was reminded of that when Jordan showed me her sunrise pictures of the coast. He loved his freedom more than anyone I know. Keeping him in a box was wrong."

"I think it's best for all of you, since you've found such peace here."

Whit nodded, wiping away the tears. "Would you say a prayer?"

Emma and Jordan gathered with them as they all held hands, the wind from the sea flapping their dresses against their legs as the sand shifted under their feet.

With a quiet voice, Riggs prayed for John's soul to find a final resting place free from pain and sorrow, and for Whit and the girls to feel his love with them always.

The girls each held the urn, saying a private farewell before passing it back to their mother.

Whit walked into the surf, the water lapping at her ankles, and removed the lid from the urn. With her red hair swirling in the breeze, she raised her arm and slowly emptied the ashes into the wind, while Jordan tried to focus the camera through her tears, and Emma stood stiffly watching.

Riggs circled an arm around Emma's shoulders. The gesture of comfort was Emma's undoing, and she buried her face in Riggs's shoulder to cry.

"I didn't want to cry for Mother's sake," Emma sniffed. "I tried . . . I tried so hard to be strong for her."

"It's natural to cry. You don't need to be strong for your mother. She's strong enough for all of us."

Standing in the waves, facing the sun, Whit said her final farewell.

ACKNOWLEDGMENTS

First of all, thank you to my agent, Mark Gottlieb at Trident Media Group, for finding a home for my manuscript.

Thanks to my publisher, Crooked Lane Books, for taking a chance on a new author. And special thanks to Jenny Chen, my editor, for her enthusiasm and amazing editing advice.

Tim Pike, medical examiner detective in Medford, thank you for providing a rich foundation for my character Riggs.

A special thank-you to family: first to my children, Morgan and Whitney, for all the hours listening to my brainstorming, and to my father for his generous support in helping me raise my daughters while I wrote this book. To my sister Eddie, my stepsister Lisa, and my brother Chuck, thanks for reading and providing valuable feedback.

To my husband, Jeff Crosswhite, I give all my love and thanks for providing a beautiful work space and endless encouragement.